T0304913

THE
MAPMAKER'S
WIFE

Hannah is based in Gower, South Wales, and works in communications and as a staff writer for *Santes Dwynwen* magazine. She was a part of the Hachette Future Bookshelf prize. *The Mapmaker's Wife* is her debut novel.

THE
MAPMAKER'S
WIFE

HANNAH EVANS

ORION

First published in Great Britain in 2024 by Orion Fiction
an imprint of The Orion Publishing Group Ltd
Carmelite House, 50 Victoria Embankment
London EC4Y 0DZ

An Hachette UK Company

1 3 5 7 9 10 8 6 4 2

A CIP catalogue record for this book is
available from the British Library.

ISBN (Hardback) 978 13987 1620 9
ISBN (Paperback) 978 13987 1621 6
ISBN (eBook) 978 1 3987 1623 0
ISBN (Audio) 978 1 3987 1624 7

Typeset at The Spartan Press Ltd,
Lymington, Hants

Printed and bound in Great Britain by Clays Ltd,
Elcograf S.p.A.

www.orionbooks.co.uk

For my mum and dad, for everything.

No matter how fast moonlight runs, daylight catches up

– West Indian proverb

Prologue

Her hand hovering above the notepaper, she paused at how to sign the letter.

She couldn't write 'Mother', as that wasn't what she would be to this child. Writing her first name felt impersonal, overly formal. She frowned, panic rising in her chest.

Time was running out: the constant beeping of the machine beside her maternity ward bed marked precious seconds passing, each one drawing her closer to the moment her child would become someone else's.

Blankets scratched her back, the material providing no comfort. The baby shifted slightly in her cot beside the bed, raising a clenched fist above her head. Her hair curled in dark spirals, sticking to her scalp in patches. Her eyes were bright brown, her skin so soft. The baby wriggled again, lifting her other arm in a defiant gesture.

The love that had been lacking throughout the pregnancy came crashing down once more, just as it had the minute her daughter had been placed in her arms.

She looked back down at the letter, not wanting to waste another second. Its page was already crumpled from having been screwed up in her hand and smoothed back out, the pencilled words creasing. She hadn't known how to address it, and there was a slight smudge across its opening. In the end, she'd simply opted for:

My dearest,
How can I explain what I'm about to do?

After reading it once more, she decided how to end the letter, signing it and tucking the note into the baby's blankets. She lifted the child from the cot, the baby's solid weight anchoring her. They would only be mother and daughter for a few minutes longer. She dropped a tender kiss on the little girl's forehead as she held her close.

She knew the baby wouldn't remember this – wouldn't remember her – but as she rocked the child to and fro, she repeated a lifetime of good wishes and I love yous and I'm sorrys under her breath.

For a second, she wondered if she could make it out to the phone she'd seen at the nurses' station. Surely it wasn't too late to reverse the decision? To pick up the cool plastic of the phone and dial, say she'd made a mistake.

But promises had been made, and there was no going back.

A knock on the door startled her, her head snapping up and her arms instinctively tightening around the child. She willed the door to stay closed, to let her exist in this moment for a second longer.

'One minute,' she called, the words stumbling out faster and louder than she'd intended. The baby stirred, doe eyes snapping open and locking with her own. She felt a tear snake down her cheek, and swiped it away before it could drop onto the baby. Her gaze darted back to the letter; she suddenly regretted her decision even to write it. The knock on the door started up again, sending ripples through the room's still waters.

As the door handle slowly began to turn, she felt something within her fray and snap: she reached back into the baby's blankets and grabbed the letter, stuffing it into the pocket of her hospital gown.

'I'm sorry,' she whispered to the baby she hadn't known how to love until it was too late. 'It will be for the best.' A sob threatened to choke her.

The door finally opened and footsteps approached. She let her eyes fall closed, running her fingers up and down the baby's chubby little arm one last time.

She'd meant what she said: this was for the best. Her daughter would be loved, and maybe this time, love would be enough?

PART ONE
Grenada, 1954

Grenada, West Indies. Map sketch in pencil.
P. J. H. Anderson, July 1954.

TELEGRAM

28 June 1954

Father,

Left British Guiana last week – [stop] – Finished charting
map – [stop] – Staying with John Coleridge for fortnight in
Barbados – [stop] – Moving Sat 15.07 to Grenada – [stop] –
tiny rock middle of nowhere – [stop] – Hope all well with you
in Blighty – [stop] – Love to Moira – [stop]

Pat – [stop] –

P.S. Finished darning my socks: Hope Tiny Rock has more to
do than BG.

July 1954

Chapter 1

Beatrice

Glancing up at the office clock, its ticking hands confirmed Bea's suspicions: she wouldn't be making it home in time for dinner. It was Friday, which meant fish in the Bell household. Bea could practically taste the salty-sweet meat on her tongue at the thought of spiced clams, saltfish patties, or fresh catch of the day fried in a tangy tamarind sauce. Bea's stomach grumbled in protest at still being seated behind her desk, last month's balance sheet splayed beside the typewriter.

The office radio trilled its countdown to the seven o'clock news, a plummy-accented Empire World Service reporter stating the headlines. Announcements of '...rationing officially over in Britain...' and '...world's first Boeing 367-80 aircraft takes flight...' drifted over the click-clack of Bea's typewriter and the scratch of her manager Julien's pen. As she typed, Bea pictured the aeroplane casting great shadows over criss-crossed English streets, Brits decking terraces in Union Flags and taking gluttonous bites of sweet, buttery sponge cakes. The thought made her even hungrier, and she checked the clock once more.

Bea and Julien's other co-worker, Seb, had left the bank's book-keeping office at least an hour earlier despite his books remaining unbalanced. His absence eased the tension in Bea's shoulders by a notch – even if she knew, deep down, it would be her having to correct the faulty sums in his ledger.

Sitting back in her seat, she was about to turn to Julien to ask if he was joining the family for dinner that evening. Since he'd started courting her older sister, Millicent, he had barely been away from their hilltop house.

But before Bea could strike up a conversation, a noise caught her attention. Mr MacLean's staccato-stepping heels drowned out the radio reporter's drawl, and Bea rolled her eyes at Julien.

'First drink tomorrow night says he asks me to stay late, and sends you home,' she whispered as the footsteps got closer. She and Julien, along with her sisters and their shared circle of friends, were all heading to the carnival fund-raiser dance at the local high school that Saturday night. Bea's youngest sister, Bette, was in her final year at Our Lady R.C. High. This gave the rest of them the excuse to go along in support, despite being the wrong side of eighteen to set foot in a school gymnasium.

Julien laughed, straightening his tie and leaning back in his chair. 'You're on.' Bea was about to ask him what time they would meet at the dance, if he was joining them at the beach tomorrow afternoon and, if so, could she hitch a lift, but the shadow cast from the office doorway made her swallow the questions. Julien reached over and turned the radio down low.

Bea's eyes landed on MacLean's too-loud shoes before seeing anything else about him as he entered the room. She disliked look-ing directly at him; his face was constantly sunburned – despite his having arrived on the island at least two years previously – and he always seemed to be frowning at her.

As he strode into the room, Bea let her gaze drift towards the window. Even in dusk, the sea was just visible beyond the low harbour wall that wrapped its way around the Central Bank's edges.

Bea often liked to watch the boats, large and small, bob towards the skyline when she needed a brain-break from the intense arith-metic of bookkeeping, wondering who was in each boat, where they were headed for that day, and what they'd catch. Whether they were ever tempted to turn on their spluttery engines and see how far they could get with the wind behind their sails. In these heady summer days, the water was so clear it often looked as though the boats were flying.

'An excellent match yesterday, wouldn't you say, Julien?' Mr MacLean's clipped voice sailed straight over Bea, landing squarely on Julien's desk. Julien blinked, before nodding. Bea knew he had absolutely no idea what sport MacLean was referring to, despite the cricket match against Saint Kitts having drawn record crowds. She and Bette had attended to cheer on the local boys, while Millicent and Julien had probably been at a political meeting or campaigning for an obscure seafood to have greater representation on dinner plates. Bea could never keep up with their latest causes, although she did try to be as supportive as she could without actually having to do anything. She'd exhausted her efforts with the rallies and talks back in 1951, and since women had won the vote, she'd struggled to maintain interest in the more obscure campaigns.

'I thought it was a lucky win, myself,' Bea responded, saving a grateful-looking Julien. 'Saint Kitts were the stronger team, after all.' MacLean's eyes tracked the full length of the room before landing on her, and for a second she saw herself through his eyes: the lady of the office, this woman bookkeeper he'd inherited when he'd taken the job at the Central Bank in 1952. How it must irk him that she always outshone Seb with her rows of neat, precise sums, getting on far better with their shared manager Julien. MacLean liked Julien because he had to, but it seemed he liked lazy, loud-mouthed Seb purely because Seb wasn't Bea.

'I didn't think the cricket would be of interest to you, Miss Bell,' MacLean replied, arching his eyebrow.

Bea threw a smile back at him, tapping out the sign-off on her letter to Westinghall Enterprises about their account balance. 'My sisters and I go from time to time. It's nice to support the local boys,' she added, shrugging, as she began to pack up her desk for the day.

MacLean laughed, although it sounded more as though he was being momentarily strangled. 'Of course – a good place to find eligible suitors.' Bea wanted to throw back a rebuttal, but a wide-eyed look from Julien made her hold her tongue. 'Now, I didn't come in here to gossip,' MacLean continued. 'See what the influence of a lady in the office does!' Bea's cheeks grew hot with the effort not to hurl her typewriter at him. 'Anyway, I will need you to stay a little later this evening, Beatrice, just to finish up a few errors that were made earlier this afternoon.'

'Oh dear. What errors?' Bea replied as innocently as she could manage. 'Julien checked through my account summaries earlier, and all were in order.'

MacLean sighed. 'We're all a team here, Beatrice. Sebastien had a challenging account to finalise, but I'm sure you will be able to solve it if you work hard enough.'

Bea closed her eyes for a moment. 'Fine,' she said at last. *He's paid double my wage for half the work.* 'That's fine.' She pulled herself up a little straighter in her chair before adding, 'And what time is the taxi collecting me?'

MacLean took a step back. 'Taxi?'

'I shan't be expected to walk home by myself, after dark, shall I?' Bea raised a hand to her chest, lifting her chin in what she hoped gave her a look of earnest concern. *You want to treat me like some feeble little creature? Two can play at that game.* 'As the lady of the office, I'm sure I don't have to remind you that my personal safety is paramount. We wouldn't want customers to think we allow our female staff to wander around in the dead of night, would we?' She turned to Julien, who nodded hastily in support.

Silence fell around them, and Bea had to avoid Julien's eye so she wouldn't break character. MacLean looked in physical pain when he eventually replied. 'You're quite right, Miss Bell. We couldn't have you walking home on your own, like you say.' He nodded curtly to Julien, signalling for Julien to join him. 'I shall arrange the car for eight o'clock, and you tell your father I personally insisted we call you a taxi.' With that, he turned on his heel. 'Julien, walk with me,' he called over his shoulder.

Julien stood up too quickly, sending a spray of papers onto the floor. 'I'll sort it out,' Bea promised, and Julien gave her a grateful smile.

'Thanks, Bea. I'm in your debt.'

She grinned back. 'A couple of rum punches at the dance to-morrow night will see you right.'

He laughed, and waved goodbye. Bea rose to her feet, winding her neck left and right. She let out a long breath and switched the radio over to the local calypso station, turning up the volume louder.

Chapter 2

Patrick

In truth, the islands were a touch too hot for Patrick Anderson's liking. He'd researched the Grenadines as best he could before stepping off the boat in Port Louis Marina that Saturday morning, but had found remarkably little information on what made the place tick.

All he could gather was Grenada's geographical location (southernmost island in the Lesser Antilles, Caribbean Sea); its main languages (English, some French – he also assumed some Creole); and the latitude and longitude of its principal city, St George's (12° 3′ N, 61° 45′ W).

He didn't think this information would be particularly useful for his three-month placement on the island, so thought it best to find out in person what sort of customs, music, sport and entertainment he could expect from his stay. Even he could acknowledge that cartography wasn't as interesting a topic to other people as it was to him, so he'd need some other conversational avenues.

He only hoped there were no hyper-local customs he should be aware of, like the time he'd met a Japanese ambassador and marched straight into his house still wearing clunky outdoor boots. The memory always made him shudder.

Lugging his holdall down the gangplank, Patrick's eyes struggled to adjust to the shapes and colours before him. He blinked, wondering if too long spent below deck was making his eyes sensitive.

No such thing had occurred; the island unfurled before him in a tapestry of bright hues and glorious colour. Windswept trees blanketed undulating mountains, their emerald green leaves beckoning him on to land. The lapping shore foamed like the candyfloss he'd eaten as a child at Rosslare or Brighton Pier, the water a shade of blue he'd say was unnaturally bright if he saw it reproduced in a painting.

He reached for his pocketbook, flipping far enough to find a page without a sketched city outline or distance calculations, and jotted down a reminder to write of what he saw to his father.

'You clearly aren't from around here if you're taking notes already.' A friendly face came into view as Patrick looked up from his page. In front of him stood a tall, broad man with a deep voice and a head of thick black hair. 'I'm just messing with you,' the man said, sticking out his hand for Patrick to shake. 'You're the new surveyor, right? Anderson?'

'That's right.' Patrick grinned, shaking the man's hand enthusiastically. 'Patrick Anderson. I've just come over from Barbados.'

The man cracked a smile. 'You don't sound Bajan. Don't look it much, either.'

'Ha!' Patrick returned the man's grin. 'I was just there for a short project between postings. I was staying with John Coleridge from the Commonwealth Office – do you know John? I was a boarder at Hartbridge with him, and we've worked pretty closely ever since. He was here in '52 or '53, I think. Good man, John.'

'Can't say that I do, but I'll take your word for it. I'm Ron, by the way – Ron Allen. You'll be lodging with me.' Ron smiled again and gestured towards Patrick's large holdall. 'Give me that bag, and I'll show you the way.'

After a hike that made Patrick curse his lack of workout regime, the house they eventually approached brought him great relief.

It stood on slightly rickety stilts, its white painted exterior bright in the late morning sun. Heavy shutters hung from their hinges, off duty until the next hurricane required them to be shut up tight. A towering fruit tree Patrick didn't recognise swayed above the steps that led to the door, its branches full and bending. The house was even trimmed with a hardwood veranda, which wrapped around the front and sides: two chairs and a low table placed to look out at the town below. Propped up beside the door was an old bicycle, and Patrick smiled at the overall impression: this would certainly do. Ron gestured for him to head inside, and the two men started up the steep, narrow steps to the porch.

'I think I'll go and get a little refreshed at the beach,' Patrick said, placing his last crumpled shirt on the rail and stepping into the kitchen. The house held two bedrooms, a kitchen-cum-lounge and a washroom, with Patrick's bedroom just off the kitchen. 'Would you like to join me?' he asked his new room-mate, who sat reading a paper at the table.

Ron shook his head, looking up from his paper. 'I'm good, thanks all the same. You can borrow the bike out on the veranda if you like. It's a little old but it goes just fine.' He paused for a moment, his pencil hovering over twelve down in the crossword. 'A few of the fellas are heading to a dance tonight, actually,' he added. 'Come along, and I'll introduce you around. If you aren't too tired from your travels?'

Patrick grinned, pulling himself up a little taller. He was tired, but he didn't like to admit it. 'A dance. Haven't been to one in years, probably since school.' His mind was momentarily cast back to his days as a boarder in his early years in England, forced to dance with the girls' school down the road for any Christmas or Easter occasion. They'd laughed at his faintly Irish accent, gained from his first five years in Dublin before his mother had passed away; their jeers had caused him to bury his accent over time until he'd drowned it out entirely. 'I imagine a dance will be a bit different, here.' He pulled himself back to the present, shaking his head a little to dislodge the memory.

'It sure will,' Ron said, with a short chuckle. 'And if you can solve this one,' he indicated his crossword puzzle, 'you're in. It took me ages! Seven letters, has to start with an S. "For having fun after, fly first to the stars."'

Frowning, Patrick leant back. 'For having fun after ... so a synonym for "fun" has to come last in the word? I'm out of practice with crosswords, to be honest.'

'You're close! A word for fun is the second part, it's something that can fly…'

Patrick hesitated. 'Skylark?'

Ron slapped the table, shaking his head. 'Good man. Be ready by six tonight. I've already promised some friends I'd give them a ride, but I can show you the way. The walk won't be far.'

Propping up the rickety borrowed bicycle, Patrick stood at the sand's edge and exhaled. This white-gold bay had so much more life about it compared with the cold, rain-soaked pebbles of England's coast.

Small groups peppered the shore, a colourful patchwork of sun hats and towels and umbrellas bathing in the afternoon sun. While Patrick had mostly known drizzly British and Irish summers, the sun saying, *All right, I'll come, but only for an hour*, this island sunshine called out, *Relax, put your feet up, I've got all the time in the world.*

Before he could muse too long at the international differences between shores, a scrap of laughter caught his attention. To his ears, it sounded like sheet music coming to life: the pitch and rhythm perfectly syncopated, its melody singing. He'd heard of jazz sounding blue and classical songs sounding green, but this was a shade he'd never heard before. It seemed to glow gold. He glanced round, suddenly overtaken by the need to find where it had come from.

It didn't take long to home in on the sound: standing just at the edge of the water, seemingly encouraging others to join her in taking a long run-up, was the most beautiful woman Patrick had ever seen. She was waving her arms, calling to two other women who sat upon towels a little further up the sand. One of them relented and unwrapped a silk scarf from her hair to join in. The two looked related to each other, with the same oval faces and bouncing curls.

Patrick could just about hear a countdown – followed by a 'ready, set, go!' – before the two women threw themselves right into the swell. White foamy waves pulled them in, and they stayed below the water for a second before shooting to the surface and throwing their heads back with a flourish. Patrick knew by this point that he was staring, but he couldn't drag his eyes away.

The girl he'd first noticed had a tight mass of black curls cut just below her chin, and huge brown eyes. As she swam, her skin sparkled with seawater droplets. Her long arms and legs brushed through the water as though she were painting the landscape with her body, a red bathing suit outlining her curves as she swam further and further out to sea.

Watching her dive beneath the water reminded Patrick of all the Romantic poems he had been forced to read, then accidentally enjoyed, throughout school. *The waves beside her danced; but she outdid the sparkling waves in glee.*

He was suddenly all too aware of himself. If only he'd stayed up at the house and rested before the dance that evening, or gone straight into the sea on his own. But then he wouldn't have seen this woman and wouldn't have felt the ground shift beneath his feet. *My heart leaps up when I behold.*

He knew he had to go over, make some kind of contact and introduce himself as she clambered out from the waves. Even just to say, 'Hello, I'm new here – fancy showing me around?' It had to be worth a shot.

Squaring his shoulders, Patrick could picture himself doing just that: standing up and striding over without a care in the world. The suave Englishman of storybooks, the luck of the Irish on his side. Arm outstretched, cracking a joke and throwing her a winning smile.

Of course, Patrick did no such thing. He was 27 years old, and still positively terrified of beautiful women.

Chapter 3

Stepping back from the hallway mirror, the three Bell sisters took one last look at themselves. Millie's sunny yellow skirt beside Bette's dark green and Bea's deep red complemented their line-up, and all three beamed at their reflections. Music oozed from the kitchen radio, smooth beats swaying through the hall.

'Just a second, Bea, come here,' Millie instructed, reaching to straighten the waist belt of Bea's dress. 'There. Perfect.'

'Thanks.' Bea gave a twirl to make her sisters smile. She grabbed Bette's hand and spun her under one arm in time to the music. 'Looking good!' she enthused. 'That dress suits you far better than it did me.'

As Bette spun around the room, catching Millie's hands and dragging her into step, Bea remembered, momentarily, the night she'd worn that green dress she'd given to Bette. She'd been waving off her oldest friend, Nella, who had headed to London. Nella had seen an ad for nurses in the new National Health Service after years of umming and aahing about whether or not to leave the island – and her golden ticket had turned out to be a smart starched uniform and cap. '*They're inviting us, they want us islanders over there to fix them up after the war. Can you imagine – me, neighbours with the new Queen?*'

Except Bea hadn't had much time to imagine, as it had become a reality when Nella's crossing was booked and she was away within a month of posting her application. Nella wrote regularly, but Bea had been feeling the lack of Nella's arm in hers each day that had passed.

Millie's voice brought her back into the present, and Bea realised she'd been involved in a conversation the entire time she'd spent daydreaming. 'So what do you think? You'll do it?' Millie asked earnestly, still tapping her feet to the beat.

Bea cursed herself. She hated admitting to Millie that she'd zoned out, but her big sister had a tendency to drone on about her work in the school, or the latest campaign or recent injustice that demanded her attention. Bea gulped, hoping she wasn't agreeing to attend another picket line. Her arms always ached after holding signs up for too long. 'Um … sure. Why not?'

Millie clapped her hands together. 'I knew you would. We always have way too many people doing the acting and no one to help with props or curtain or anything like that. You'll be great. Ron can show you the ropes, he did prompt book and curtain last year.' Millie nudged Bea, her smile widening. 'Get it – show you the ropes? For the curtain?' Bea's face stayed blank. 'Oh, never mind.'

As Millie marched into the kitchen to say goodbye to their mother, Bea turned to Bette. 'What have I just agreed to?'

Bette shrugged. 'I'd switched off, too. I think you're doing backstage for the next am dram show. Millie's directing again. She decided today.'

Bea frowned. 'Aren't we meant to vote on who directs?'

Bette shrugged again, adding a final flourish of kohl around her eyes. 'Yes, but no one else turned up to the meeting. So Millie chose herself and wrote it up on the noticeboard in the community centre. I saw it after class this afternoon.'

'Sounds about right,' Bea agreed. She smoothed down her skirt, wondering if the perfume-sized bottle of rum in her handbag would be enough for the evening. 'What play are we even doing?'

'It's *A Midsummer Night's Dream*, another Shakespeare. She already said I should be the Fairy Queen, Titania.' Bette rolled her eyes, although Bea knew she loved taking centre stage. Shakespeare might annoy some of the group – too many lines, too many outdated jokes – but Bea perked up at the thought of another classic. She'd always found Shakespeare plays strangely emotive, like listening to music in a foreign language.

16

The three sisters observed one another's hairdos when Millie returned, patting it down or bouncing it up as required. While all three of them took after their mother's paler complexion, their hair couldn't have been more different. Millie always wore her beautiful coils in a display, tied with a silk scarf atop her head, while Bette's hair was grown out long and worn dancing around her shoulders in tight spiral-curls. Bea's was bobbed short, much to her mother's disdain, with decadently layered curls creating a halo around her face.

'Right, enough preening,' Bea instructed, just as Millie fixed a final pin to Bette's updo. 'What time is Ron coming to get us?'

'Before you go, girls, your mother has asked me to have a quick word.' Their father's baritone sang out from his office as he emerged and leant against the door frame. Mr Bell was still holding some casework in his hands, his days spent presiding over the island's courtroom often bleeding into home life. 'All right.' He reached behind him to place the paperwork down. 'Girls, you behave yourselves now, and don't you let me see you in court for drunk and disorderly behaviour.' He raised his eyebrows, lingering a little too long on Bea.

'Pop, that was once, and you know they only dragged me in as a joke.' She rolled her eyes, feeling Bette nudge her in the ribs from behind.

'Well, don't go letting it happen again, child. You have a respons-ibility, all of you, not to embarrass your mother.' Mr Bell's eyes twinkled, as Bea and her sisters waited for the inevitable cry from the kitchen.

They were not disappointed. 'That wasn't what you were meant to say at all! Girls, ignore your father.' Mrs Bell appeared, flicking a tea towel at her husband. 'Don't embarrass yourselves, and for the love of God, do not let anyone accuse you of poor comportment. You represent more than just yourselves, you know.'

'Yes, Momma,' the three sisters chorused, saved from any further protestations by the car horn beeping outside.

★

Thanking Ron for the ride, Bea grabbed her sisters' arms and dragged them straight into the dimly lit hall.

The quartet – singer, sax, steel drum and guitar – were illuminated by a spotlight the school hadn't had when Bea had been a student, their rhythmic tunes giving no other option than to tap your feet and sway your hips. Heels clicked on the gym floor as arms encircled waists, multicoloured skirts spinning and catching the light from overhead lamps. The hall felt like midnight, spiced rum thick on its breath.

Evenings like this made Bea miss Nella, and she made a mental note to write and tell her all about it. Nella was in English dance halls now, going to jazz clubs playing imported American music. As Bea stepped in time to the music alongside her sisters, she wondered, not for the first time, what it would have been like to go to the Mother Country with Nella. Throw her favourite books and shoes and dresses into a packing case and sail off to see what lurked below the horizon. But there had been no ads for bookkeepers.

'You look miserable!' Bette shouted in Bea's ear, leaning over and grabbing both her hands. The two of them were standing near the dance floor. 'It's a party, you know.' She pulled Bea towards her in an elaborate spin, and Bea couldn't help but laugh. They wound to the beat, changing direction as the music sped up. Bette almost collided with Millie as she returned from the bar, balancing three colas, ready for Bea to spike them with rum she'd smuggled in her purse. 'The punch looked disgusting, so we'll have to go with Plan B,' Millie explained, passing a cup to each sister.

'You didn't get a drink for your chauffeur?' Ron appeared beside Bette, making her jump.

'Lord, Ron! You scared me.'

He laughed. 'Didn't mean to.' He slapped Bette on the back as though she were his kid sister, and she rolled her eyes at him. 'You got any of that rum left, Bea? I wouldn't say no to a dash.'

Bea smiled, as Bette saw a friend from school and floated back towards the dance floor. 'I suppose I can get you a cola, spare a drop of rum or two.' Millie waved to someone standing behind

Bea, throwing a 'back in a moment' behind her as she left their circle.

Ron nodded. 'Two sounds good. I gotta introduce you to my lodger.' He turned, but no one was standing behind him. 'Eh? I swear he was just here.'

Bea scanned the crowd, unfamiliar faces always easy to spot. 'What does he ...?'

But she knew exactly what he looked like, because her eyes had landed squarely on an incredibly tall, unreasonably handsome man she'd never seen before. *This has to be him.*

The stranger smiled at one of the blokes he was talking to, revealing a row of straight, white teeth. His smile crinkled his eyes, which, even through the shadows of the hall, Bea could tell were the kind of blue the sky turned just after sunrise.

Despite herself, Bea felt a wave of self-consciousness roll over her. She reached her free hand up to touch her hair before smoothing down her skirt. She ducked away, in case he saw her and she wasn't ready. This was odd: Bea usually felt ready for anything.

If Ron noticed her strange behaviour, he didn't react. 'I think he must've gone outside. Er ... how about you get us each a drink and I'll find him? You'll love his stories, he was telling me about England the other day.'

'I think he's ...' But when Bea turned to point towards the man, he'd gone. 'Never mind. I'll grab the drinks.' She marched over to the bar, wondering if she'd made up the handsome stranger after all. They didn't get handsome strangers appearing out of nowhere on this island.

'Two colas, please,' she ordered, for Ron and his lodger, sensing someone standing behind her. Her skin prickled. *Can it be ...?* She plastered on a winning smile, thanked the bar lady, and spun around.

Her shoulders dropped. It was Ron.

'Let me give you a hand with those.' He gestured to the drinks, relieving Bea of the paper cups. 'Anyway, as I was saying, I gotta introduce you to my new lodger, Patrick. The new surveyor for land and ordnance, working out of the government office next door to mine.'

'Surveyor, eh? The ones who make maps.' Bea nudged Ron playfully, despite the churn in her stomach. 'So we could say he's "putting us on the map"?'

An unfamiliar laugh caught Bea off guard, and she looked around to find the source.

'I like that one. I've heard it before, but it's always good.'

His accent sounded sharp, like a June plum sauce that hadn't had enough sugar added to it. Up close, the man – Patrick – was even more handsome than she'd first thought: sweeping brown hair just brushing above his eyes, light blue shirt revealing strong arms beneath, broad chest that she could already imagine leaning into.

Bea realised she was supposed to say something back. Ron might have been talking, but all she could focus on was the man standing before her. Her skin felt as though it would melt a little if his hand shook hers. Her mouth went dry as she shifted her weight to steady herself, a feeling too close to seasickness washing over her, her eyes locked on his, his face breaking into a smile.

Zoning back in at the sound of her name, she caught the end of Ron's words. '…is Bea. One of the Bell sisters who I drove down this evening. Bolted from the car the second we got here, had to chase her down for payment in rum.'

'If Patrick had been in the car with you, I might have stayed a while.' *Did I just say that out loud? Apparently.* 'What I mean to say is,' she added hastily, her cheeks growing hot, 'I'd have been far more polite had I known Ron was escorting a new visitor to the island. It's a pleasure to make your acquaintance, Patrick.' Her body was being pulled towards his almost of its own accord, as though she were caught in a trawler's net being hauled along the seabed. Without realising, she'd taken two steps forward and reached to shake his hand.

'A pleasure to meet you, too.' He glanced to the door, his hand clasping hers in a firm grip. 'Shall we catch our breath?'

Bea thought her breathing might stop altogether. 'We could step outside. But—'

Before Bea could ask if he'd care to dance, arms were encircling her from behind. 'Bea, it's our song!' Millicent shouted into her ear. 'Get over here!'

And before she could protest, Bea felt Patrick's hand fall from hers as she was dragged into the centre of the dance floor. A familiar tune twirled her under its arm as Millie, Bette and even Julien danced in the centre of the room, their arms outstretched to pull Bea into the fold. She turned back, hoping to gesture towards Patrick to join them. But he and Ron had gone.

Chapter 4

Patrick

Patrick couldn't believe it: the girl from the beach. He'd been just about to ask her to step outside and talk awhile when she'd been spirited away, and Ron had walked him out to meet some more of the guys.

'So,' Patrick began as the two men he'd been introduced to headed back inside, 'did you say that girl's name was Bea? Is that short for anything?'

Smooth, Patrick. Why not just ask to see a copy of her birth certificate while you're at it?

Ron smirked. 'Do I detect an interest in the middle Miss Bell?'

Patrick didn't know what to say, and Ron just clapped him on the back. 'I'm messing with you. Bea's great – sure she'd be happy to dance with you if you asked.'

'Is that ... Is that how it goes?'

'How else would it "go"?'

Patrick opened and closed his mouth. *What he meant was, Is it proper for me to ask her to dance, just like that? In front of all these people? What if she's spoken for, or she doesn't want to? Will she feel obliged?*

But instead, he said, 'I mean, she's not married?'

Ron raised his eyebrow. 'Did you see a ring?'

'And she's not ... you know – stepping out with anyone? I wouldn't want to make her uncomfortable.'

At that, Ron snorted. 'If Beatrice Bell is ever uncomfortable, she'll be sure to tell you.'

Patrick nodded. 'All right, then.'

'Is he going back in? He's going back in!' Ron slapped Patrick on the back, throwing back his head and laughing.

Patrick dismissed Ron with a wave, determined to find Bea again.

And across the hall, there she was. Yet again, he saw her from a distance and felt the breath leave his body, just for a second.

She was looking back at him – there was no mistaking it; her eyes tracked across the room before landing to meet his. *Is now the time to make my move?*

He started to walk towards her, ready to ask her to dance. *Did people say may I have this dance here? Or was that old-fashioned? Can I have the next one? No, that couldn't be it.* His palms started to sweat.

Just as he reached her side, ready to tap her on the shoulder and see what invitation tumbled from his lips, she slipped away again – pulled out of the side door by a friend. Or a sister – he couldn't tell.

Only one thing for it, he said to himself, and marched out after her.

She stood with her back to him, in conversation with a tall, striking woman with her hair tied up in a colourful scarf. He steeled himself, ready to go over.

Just as Patrick approached, he heard footsteps pounding behind him. 'I've got you, Pat,' Ron said, appearing beside him. He raised his eyebrows, gesturing for Patrick to join the two women before them.

'Millie, so glad I found you,' Ron began, addressing the tall woman Bea was speaking with. 'I hate to do this at a party, but I have some urgent questions about the staging for the play. Can I discuss it with you, now?' Ron threw Bea a look as Millie nodded and ushered him inside. 'Bea, you wouldn't mind keeping Patrick company for a moment?'

To Patrick's amazement, he and Bea were left standing alone. He owed Ron a drink.

'Hi,' Bea said, turning to face him.

'Hello.' *Why did his voice sound like that? Calm down, Patrick.* 'Nice to meet you, properly.'

23

Bea smiled up at him from under long lashes, and Patrick could feel in his bones that he was done for.

'Sorry Ron stole your friend.'

'Millie's my sister,' Bea said. 'She will love it, don't you worry. She could talk about the play for hours.'

'What's the play?'

'*A Midsummer Night's Dream*, with our amateur dramatics society. It's just a bunch of us young people, a good excuse to meet up of an evening.' Bea turned and faced him properly. 'You should join us, if you're going to stick around. I can lend you a copy of the play if it's something you're into.'

Patrick nodded enthusiastically. 'That would be great, thank you. I'm here for a few more months yet, and I like a Shakespeare comedy.'

'The tragedies a bit much for you?'

'Aren't they a bit much for anyone?'

Bea laughed, the sound hitting Patrick like a breaking wave. 'Not the way Millie stages them. You should've seen her version of *Romeo and Juliet* – the local paper called it "a captivating masterpiece".'

Patrick gave a wry smile. 'I went to an all-boys school, so I'm probably just a bit scarred. There's nothing less captivating than a teenage boy reciting iambic pentameter.'

To his delight, Bea laughed again. He could have spent all evening listening to that sound. 'Too right. They should have just let you do a farce, or something modern.'

'That's what I said, too.'

He wanted to keep her there, her eyes locked on his. They'd looked brown when they'd stood at the bar, but in the moonlight, he could see flecks of amber and honey and gold. Everything about her was gilded, as though just moments ago she'd escaped from the frame of an oil painting and found herself swept into the land of mortals. 'And how about you?' he asked. 'Did you go to school here? On the island?'

'Of course. My sisters and I went to the convent school,' she

24

leant a little closer, her tone conspiratorial, 'so if I never see a nun again, it will be too soon.'

'Ha! I know the feeling. I'm Catholic, too – Irish Catholic.'

Bea's eyebrows rose. 'You don't sound very Irish.'

'I get that a lot. I was born in Ireland, schooled in England after my mother died...'

'Oh goodness, I'm so sorry.'

He raised one hand in the practised manoeuvre of dismissal. 'Thank you. I was very young... It... um... you know.' He coughed lightly, wondering at what age he'd grow out of that tickling feeling in the back of his throat every time he mentioned his mother. 'Then it was boarding school until National Service in Palestine until '49, then straight into the Commonwealth Office and out across the Empire.'

Bea's eyes flashed with interest. 'Where in the Empire?'

He paused, in pretence of trying to remember all the fascinating places he'd visited with his map-making kit in hand. He could name the locations to the area code, and dates to the hour, but hoped the pause gave him some sort of gravitas. As though he were totally at ease being the sort of man who flitted across the world at a moment's notice. 'First to Kenya for a couple of years, then back in London, and some time in Belfast on desk duty. My aunt lives in Dublin, so I stayed with her most of the time. Almost sent to Korea, but then the fighting broke out so I went to British Guiana instead. A quick stint in Barbados for a month or so, and now I'm here. On placement for the next three months, until the end of September.' He shrugged, hoping he seemed more like an international man of mystery than a mathematics fanatic who'd simply asked his schoolmaster what job he could do to use maths and be outdoors as much as possible.

'And being a surveyor got you to all those places?'

'Yes. I calculate distances and angles between land points to create maps and—'

She laughed, cutting him off with a hand on his arm. 'Yes, I know what a surveyor does. Think I'd enjoy it myself, what with all the arithmetic needed.' She pulled her shoulders back, bringing her arm to her side and smoothing down the deep red folds of her skirt. 'I'm a bookkeeper, at the Central Bank. Have been for almost six years now, since I left school.'

'And what's that like?'

She shrugged. 'It's just fine. I like the work, don't mind the late nights or even the most complex accounts. Have to sit a couple more exams, too, but the studying isn't so bad.' Her eyes grew distant, her gaze leaving him and tracking out beyond the schoolyard. 'I just doubt I'll ever do much more than I'm already doing, you know? There's a promotion coming up, and I can already tell my boss won't even consider me.' She went quiet for a second, and Patrick's hand reached out to gently graze the bare skin of her upper arm. At his touch, her eyes darted back up at him. 'Sorry, I don't know why I'm telling you all this. You're barely off the boat and I'm here pouring my problems out to you.' She gave a short laugh, her eyes glancing down to where his hand had brushed below her shoulder.

'Hey, I asked a question and you answered. Some people might even say you were being polite.'

She scrunched up her face in an expression that made Patrick laugh. 'Polite. One of the most boring descriptions you can give to someone.'

'And here I was thinking I was paying you a compliment.' He took another step towards her, dropping his hand from her arm so their palms touched. 'What would you prefer I say?'

The way she threw her head back to look up at him, for a mad second Patrick thought she would close the gap between them entirely and place her lips on his.

But instead, she said, 'I'll think about that. Shall we go inside and dance?'

He nodded, taking Bea's hand as she led him onto the dance floor. Bolts sparked when their hands touched, and coursed from his fingertips to the hairs on the back of his neck. *So this is what it feels like.*

The next song began, a faster one than before, and she moved his hands to her waist and swayed her hips in time, stepping out and in and twisting so her red skirt flashed around her legs. He kept to the rhythm, catching her eye. He wanted the clock to stop as he felt the other dancers fade away, the world slowing outside their embrace as the music drew them closer, her cheek pressed to his.

And then the music paused; the hall came back to life around them. Patrick was instantly aware of the murmured conversations, footsteps, bottles opening and shouts of goodbye and goodnight.

'Can I walk you home?' he found himself saying.

Bea's eyes darted past him. 'Not tonight, I need to get back to my sisters.' Her gaze returned to him, making his stomach flip. 'But I'd like to see you again.'

She started to pull away, but he reached out to touch her hand. 'Tomorrow?'

She gave a small nod, keeping her voice low. 'Meet me at the end of my road, where Lower Lucas Street crosses Cox Alley. Around four p.m.?'

'Perfect.'

They held each other's gaze a second longer, the only two static bodies in a whirlpool of movement. She was the one to break the spell when someone called her name from the back of the room, turning on her heel and disappearing into the crowd.

Chapter 5

'Working, on a Sunday! This bank man, does he not understand that it's a day of rest?' Mrs Bell clucked, the concern in her voice pricking Bea's heart. She couldn't tell her mother the truth: that she was running off unescorted to meet a foreign man.

She wasn't even sure what had brought the invitation tumbling from her lips when she'd suggested meeting Patrick. Her logical brain told her they'd only danced, talked a little. *What am I so hung up on?*

But she'd danced with male friends and boys trying to court her at parties gone by, of course – she'd just never felt so aware of her own quickening breath and the tingle of sweat on her brow before. Something urgent told her she simply had to see this man again.

'I'll tell the bank you disapprove, Mom. It won't be for long, we just need to sort out the end of month reports.' She straightened up from slipping on her shoes, reaching to collect her hat from the peg in the hallway. Her sisters were both out – Bette was sailing with a friend, Millie had gone to some kind of political meeting – and her father's head was buried in his books. The afternoon was hers, and the whisper of guilt that brushed its lips to her ear for lying to her mother was quickly silenced by an excitement so palpable she could hear its heartbeat.

'You and your sister, both so hard-working.' Mrs Bell nodded, as though Bea had been waiting for her approval. 'Millicent is never out of the schoolhouse these days. You know she's back in her classroom today, preparing for their carnival pageant in class?'

Bea frowned, realising she wasn't the only one lying to their mother about where she was going that afternoon. Millie had definitely said something about a protest group when they'd been walking home from church that morning: some kind of political agitation. She'd spoken in hushed tones, which Bea had assumed was just to coat her words in drama. Now she understood.

'Yes, Millie and I spoke about both having to work on a Sunday. We're lucky to have such fine jobs, we shouldn't complain.' Her mother beamed at the line, nodding again and making her way back towards the kitchen.

'Don't be too late. I'm doing banana fritters for after supper.'

Bea smiled, placing her hat on her head and tightening the sash around the waist of her dress. It was a pale lavender and fairly worn, but it suited her beautifully. 'Sounds delicious. I'll see you later.'

Her stomach flipped as she slipped out of the house, pausing to take a breath beneath the shade of the guava tree. Theirs were modest by island terms, but the trees laden with guavas, mangos and breadfruit jostled for space along the length of their one-storey house. Bea and her sisters had grown up playing hide-and-seek among their branches and leaves, and she could tell just by looking which branches could take a girl's weight and which would snap. She could also tell, to the day, when the fruit would be most sweet for harvest. Her mother's guava stew was a favourite of Bea's, its syrupy sweetness the flavour of sunbeams.

She rested her back against the mango tree's trunk for a second, hoping to slow her pulse. It had started racing the second she'd stepped out of the house, its beat drumming a bassline which grew stronger with each step she took. All this, for a man she'd laid eyes on for just one night?

'It's all right if you've changed your mind, you don't have to hide from me.' A low voice with a funny accent weaved its way through the small crop of trees, and Bea emerged to see Patrick, hands in pockets, wearing a faded green shirt and slacks. In the full afternoon light, set against the single-track road that curved its way up and around the crest of the hill, he looked like a Hollywood movie poster. His dark hair was as floppy and soft as she'd remembered, his eyes kind. The way he looked at her made her chest swell.

'I haven't changed my mind,' she replied, readjusting her hat and stepping out from the trees' shade, 'but we'd better go. If my mom sees you hanging around the house, she'll have you.'

He looked puzzled, but didn't take his eyes off her. 'Right, best be off then. Where are we heading?'

'I thought we could go down to the cliffs, round the corner from Grande Anse beach.' Bea joined him on the road, looking left and right. 'Didn't you bring the truck?'

He shook his head, a twinkle in his eye. 'I thought we could cycle.' As he spoke, Bea's gaze landed on the rickety-looking bicycle propped against a breadfruit tree on the other side of the road. 'You didn't tell me where we were going,' Patrick continued, 'so I wasn't sure how far we'd have to walk.'

'Don't you walk around measuring hills for a living, basically?'

He laughed. 'I've never heard it described in that way, but pretty much.' He walked over to his bicycle, gesturing for her to join him. 'And since I'm now off the clock, I need a break from all that walking.'

She hesitated, enjoying the uncertainty she felt. It had been so long since something had surprised her.

'You'll be fine! I'm an excellent cyclist, I promise.' He mounted the bike, throwing her a lopsided grin. 'Come on, you sit up on the handlebars and I'll spin us down. I think I remember the way to the beach. Left at the bottom of the hill and along the track?'

Bea nodded, wondering how she'd describe this to Nella when she wrote to her next. Millie would scold her for running off with a stranger; Bette would congratulate her on taking a chance. Her mother would have a heart attack if she saw Bea resting her behind on handlebars. She silenced these voices in her head, and before she could really think about what she was doing, she found herself hurtling down the hill's winding streets and heading on towards the cliffs.

It was a hot but windy afternoon, and she pulled her hat from her head so her curls bounced above her shoulders. She kicked her legs out as they sped along, ducking and laughing as she narrowly avoided the overhanging branches laden with nutmeg and cashews. Patrick tried to say something, but the breeze snatched the words away before they could reach Bea's ears.

For that second she wasn't a bookkeeper, someone's sister, someone's daughter; she was simply soaring, skimming across the sky like a pebble thrown out to sea.

'This view ... it really is something,' Patrick said, his words slightly drowned out by waves crashing against the cliff below. They'd strolled along the cliff path discussing how he was settling into island life – Have you felt heat like this? *Yes, in Nairobi. Nice sea breeze here, though.* Eaten food this flavourful? *Almost – Guianese fruit tastes nearly as sweet.* Heard music so soulful? *Never, I wish I could fit a record in my packing case* – and headed out towards the horizon line. The cliff stuck out perpendicular to the road, with the sweeping gold of Grande Anse Beach to their right and tree-shaded Morne Rouge Beach to their left. The wind whipped Bea's curls around her neck, which was growing hotter each time Patrick's hand brushed hers.

'It's stunning, isn't it?' Bea agreed. 'We used to come up here all the time as children, to play hunting. We still do, from time to time.' She dared reach for his arm, trying not to smile too widely when her fingertips clasped his wrist. 'If you come out just to here,' she said, pulling him closer to the edge, 'you can sit. It's perfectly safe.' She gathered up her skirt and sat down so her legs dangled over the cliff edge, her hand lingering on his arm.

'If you say so,' he agreed, sitting down beside her so their thighs touched. He looked out at the view for a second, before turning to face her with a bemused smile on his face. 'Sorry ... did you say "hunting"? What would you hunt from a clifftop?'

'You might see now, if we're lucky.' Bea raised her eyebrows, enjoying the wondrous expression on Patrick's face. Her arm still rested on his, and she gave him a playful nudge. 'Prey might come swimming into view.'

They didn't have to wait long: a few moments later, a cry arose from the beach beside them. A red-and-white striped beach ball bobbed into view, and Bea reached out to point towards it. 'There, you see?' At the confusion in his eyes, Bea laughed. 'We'd come up here with Pop's old rifle, an ancient thing he used to shoot away pests from the fruit trees, and we'd aim for the beach balls.'

Patrick looked incredulous. He raised his hands, disbelieving, but his eyes crinkled as he spoke. 'You'd never shoot one from here, surely. Rifles are way too inaccurate.'

'We got a lot of practice over the years,' Bea replied, a memory of Nella shooting down a bright orange beach ball filling her with joy. How she'd clapped Nella on the back after she'd shot it, and they'd all gone to the beach bar for gin served inside coconuts by way of celebration.

Patrick leant back on his elbows, laughter making his whole body shake. 'I'd love to see that. You'd probably make an excellent sniper, with that sort of aim,' he added, gesturing to the beach ball now floating further and further out to sea. 'How do you do it?'

Bea scrambled to her feet, pulling Patrick up alongside her. The heat and weight of his hand in hers made her almost lose focus, and just before she let go, he gave her hand a light squeeze.

Her head snapped towards him, but he was looking out to sea. 'Almost sunset,' he remarked as though he hadn't just caused her heart to beat double time. He turned back to face her, gesturing to the view. 'So how would you do it, if you were here with the rifle?'

Bea exhaled, steadying herself. She hadn't noticed time ambling on. The sun had started its full descent behind the water. She squared her shoulders to turn in profile, her feet a hip's width apart. 'Well, I'd raise it up like this, hold the stock, elbows down.' She borrowed the words from her father, from the memory of him teaching her and her sisters. 'We got clever with it after a while, taking shots standing on one leg or something,' she said with a grin.

'Surely not!'

'On my honour.' She placed her hand on her heart, making Patrick laugh. 'But you just have to make sure the butt of the rifle

32

is in tight, snug, on the shoulder. Then it's just a case of taking position, aiming properly, staying patient, and then ... *bam.*'

She mocked a shot out at the beach ball, picturing it deflate and spiral along the water. 'Hey, I think you got it,' Patrick said, rubbing her shoulders and pointing out to sea. She laughed, not wanting to turn away from him. She angled her face up to kiss his cheek, sparks firing when he turned at the last moment so their lips met.

'What time do you call this?' Millicent hissed, catching Bea right as she slipped through the front door.

'Relax, I told Mom I was at work. Did she save me a plate, or shall I sort something out myself? Do you want anything?' Bea spoke over her shoulder as she untied her shoes and removed her hat, her skin still flushed hot. She'd only kissed Patrick for a second before pulling away, and they'd walked back down the cliff to make sure she got home before dark. Their hands had stayed intertwined the whole walk back as they'd talked about books they loved and books they hated (*Agatha Christie's my favourite, too – how could you not figure out the twist in* Murder on the Orient Express?), music (*I didn't realise you'd get Billie Holliday here.* Of course we do, what do you take us for?), schooling, jobs, her siblings and his lack thereof.

She'd told him about Nella leaving back in the March of that year – how everything felt jumbled since. He told her of his friend John, whom he'd known from his boarding days, both now in the same Surveying and Ordnance department, but often in opposite corners of the world.

She offered to lend him a copy of *A Midsummer Night's Dream* and conversation had lapsed into Shakespeare, poetry, their favourite classics. *Sorry, but Austen is far better than Dickens. How many stories about Victorian orphans do we need?*

She could have gone on talking with him until the moon made itself known. After he'd dropped her home, she felt so bright she'd turn bitter cocoa sweet just by drinking it.

'You want me to relax?' Millicent snapped, her stormy expression cutting through Bea's thoughts. 'Bea, I saw who just left here.

Mom would've seen, too, if I hadn't hurried her into the kitchen! What are you thinking?'

Bea frowned. 'Coming from the one who was out planning some kind of protest this afternoon. You want me to run and tell Mom about that?'

Millie scoffed, dragging Bea by the arm into the empty sitting room.

'Beatrice, is that you?' their mother's muffled voice called out from the kitchen. 'There's oil down on the stove for you, some dumplings need doing to go with it.'

'Thanks, Mom. I'll be there in a minute,' Bea called back, shooting a questioning look at Millie.

Millie sat down on the couch, pulling Bea beside her. 'You know why you can't see him again, don't you?'

Bea almost laughed. 'I've only met him twice, Millie, what's the big deal?'

But Bea knew what the big deal was. This wasn't like the handful of dates she'd been on with boys she'd known all her life: walks along the beach surrounded by others; trips to the picture house or picnics packed by mothers. She'd agonised on such afternoons, waiting for that spark to hit. She'd waited and waited to feel a shift, to experience what she'd previously only read about: Cathy describing feeling with Heathcliff that *whatever our souls are made of, his and mine are the same*; Elizabeth seeing Mr Darcy, realising *'til this moment, I never knew myself*. Until that afternoon, she'd wondered if it had all been exaggerated for fiction.

But then she'd drawn back from Patrick on the cliff, and she'd known that was it. *We are such stuff as dreams are made on.*

'He's just some foreigner come over for a month or two, right?' Millie said. 'One of the government boys staying in Ron's spare room?'

Bea disagreed with the exact description, but nodded. 'Yes, he's here a while yet.' She tried desperately to resist playing with her hands in her lap. 'He doesn't leave until the end of September.'

Millie shook her head. 'Bea, that will fly by. What do you think a man here for five minutes is really after? Especially,' she dropped her voice to a deep hush, 'a British man? Do you have any idea what they're like?'

Bea's stomach dropped. 'You don't even know him.'

'Neither do you! You met him less than twenty-four hours ago!'

'Just because you can't stand the thought of committing to someone,' Bea threw back. 'Julien's desperate to marry you, and all you can think about is your classroom or your oh-so-important causes! We've got the vote now, so things are bound to start changing without you needing to meddle.'

Millie flew to her feet, and Bea wasn't far behind. Their voices were rising, and Bea knew they'd be heard if they didn't calm down quickly. 'Don't bring Julien into this. He supports me, and you have no idea how much more work there is to do. The vote is just the start of it, Bea, come on.' Millie took a deep breath, raising her hand to silence Bea before she could give a rebuttal. 'You can't see Patrick again, and that's the end of it. The English have been coming over here for centuries and doing nothing but take, take, take.' Millie's eyes met Bea's, her gaze level and serious. 'We mustn't let this one take you.'

Bea rolled her eyes. 'Millie, you don't need to make everything political. You're being—'

'Stay away from him. I don't want to see you together in the street, at the beach, if he comes to the play – nothing. It's one thing to dance with a foreign white man of an evening, but to continue to see him after the fact? It can't happen. It stops now.'

As Millie turned on her heel to leave the room, Bea played her ace. 'And so where were you this afternoon? You think you can tell me who I can and can't spend time with, based on acts of their forefathers, but you won't tell our mother where you were on a Sunday afternoon?'

Millie froze. 'She wouldn't understand.'

'None of us will, if you don't tell us.' Bea softened her voice, trying to keep her breathing even. 'What have you gotten into?'

Millie turned to face her, her chin raised high. 'It's nothing to worry about, I haven't joined the circus or the Fascists.'

Despite their argument, Bea laughed. 'Glad to hear it.'

'I just know there's more we could be doing here, making our own rules on how things get done. Striking, even, if that's what it takes.' She shook her head, her eyes tracking across the room and out of the window. 'We have the right to make our own decisions.'

'Funny,' Bea said, 'since you seem hell-bent on making my decisions for me.'

Millie's jaw dropped open. 'Well, that's different.'

'Is it?' asked Bea coolly, sidling past Millie on her way to the kitchen. She hoped Millie couldn't see that her hands had started to shake.

August 1954

POSTCARD

14th August 1954

Dear Nella,

I thought you'd like this picture from home – isn't it a beautiful photograph of Grande Anse?

I have so much to tell you but no time to write, in case I get caught. Nella – I've met someone! An English-Irish surveyor, here to make a map of the island. It's been six weeks or so since we met, and it feels like not a day has passed where we haven't seen each other somehow.

His taste in books, music and films is wonderful, his cooking leaves much to be desired. He cooked me dinner a few nights ago over at Ron's place where he's staying, and all I'll say is, he's lucky he's so handsome.

We're having to sneak around so Millicent doesn't find out. He's helping out at the play so we hide in the wings and make excuses to see each other after work and on weekends. He's funny and he can dance, he thinks the world of me. I think I've fallen. Where do I go from here?

With love, B

Chapter 6

Patrick

'You're walking too fast!'

Bea rolled her eyes. 'You were the one who insisted on bringing such a big picnic basket. I said we should just bring snacks, keep our arms free.'

'We can't walk all this way and not make a proper meal of it,' Patrick replied, catching up to Bea and taking refuge from the morning's heat in the shade of a particularly tall maruba tree. They'd had to postpone their walk by a few days, as the rain had finally fallen and kept them apart for almost a week – the longest they'd gone without seeing each other since they'd first met. Halfway through the hike, as his shirt stuck to his back, Patrick almost wished they'd opted to come out while the rain fell.

The forest surrounding them loomed large, its greenery blanketing the side of Morne Fédon and stretching across the park all the way to the waterfalls: Concord, Au Coin and Fontainebleau. Mahogany, teak, gommier and maruba trees jostled for space, their branches winding together to create a shady canopy beneath which the weary travellers were able to rest a while. Patrick was glad for the shade, catching his breath while Bea tapped her foot impatiently, a one-woman path beater.

'We're pretty much here anyway, it's only a little further to get to the view. Come on, you're going to love it. After Grande Anse, it's my favourite spot. It's so peaceful. And there's never anyone else around...' Her voice trailed off, and Patrick thought back to the evening they'd spent at Sauteurs Rock the week before. They'd waited for night to fall, filling the evening with talk of how the play was going and where on the island she'd show him next. They'd practised some lines from *A Midsummer Night's Dream*, reading from the copy she'd lent him. He'd watched her face light up at the inscription he'd added, the notes he'd scrawled for her in the margins.

Their talk had turned quiet, tender, as the night enveloped them in its embrace. They'd fallen back upon the sand, the cooling air tickling their bare skin as he'd kissed her and pulled her towards him and wished time would melt into the moment their bodies intertwined for the first time.

Bea grabbed his hand, rooting him back into the present, and the grin on her face told him she'd been thinking of the same thing.

'Do you think we're running out of places we can go without being seen?' Patrick asked. 'It might be time to come clean, tell your family about us?' He tried not to sound too hopeful, given how firm she'd been about keeping what they were doing from her sisters and parents.

To his disappointment, she shook her head. 'They wouldn't understand. Mom thinks everything's a scandal, and she'd be mad about me running around with someone from so far away.' They emerged from the trees, finally arriving into the full heat of the lakeside. Bea wiped her brow, and glanced left and right to check they were alone. 'Bette probably wouldn't care much, neither would Pop. It's just Millie ... You know she has a problem with the English.'

Unease churned in Patrick's stomach. 'I know that feeling myself. I get why she'd have an issue with an English bloke coming into her world.'

Bea laughed. 'Being Grenadian's not quite the same as being Irish, but thank you for trying.' She paused, scanning the grassy bank to choose the best spot. 'Millie just doesn't think of you as a person ... you know – an individual? She's just seeing you and painting you with the same brush as all those greedy Englishmen who stole our land and our people. Where someone's from and what they represent seems to matter more to her than what that person wants or thinks for themself.' Bea shrugged it off, and the knot in Patrick's stomach loosened slightly when she grabbed his hand.

'Do you mind?' Patrick asked, stopping where they walked.

'That you're English?'

'Half-English.'

'Right.' Bea sighed, and Patrick wondered if he'd made a mistake by asking. 'I can't say I expected I'd ever date a foreigner. But I like unexpected.' She glanced along the bank of the lake again, the sunlight bouncing off her curls and framing her face. Patrick wished he'd packed a camera. 'And my family history is full of people from all over, so I don't know why Millie has such an issue. We know we're this light-skinned because a Portuguese sailor jumped ship and ended up here a couple of generations ago, so we're a little European, too.'

'Really?'

Bea nodded. 'He can't have been the only European in the family, obviously. But his name is one of the only ones we're certain of.'

Patrick considered this as they began walking again, Bea gesturing towards a sun-drenched spot on the bank of the lake. Water lapped lazily upon the bank, its ripples royal blue and sparkling in sunlight. 'It must be strange, not being able to trace back your family,' Patrick said after a beat. 'In Ireland, there were still records of Catholics. We hardly had any rights, but we could at least say, "This is where Grandpa Parnell was born before he was hauled away by the Black and Tans."'

Bea's head whipped towards him. 'The who?'

'Oh, no, it's an army. Black and tan was the colour of the British uniform.'

'I was going to say.' She motioned for Patrick to put down the picnic basket, and she spread out the red and white checkerboard blanket for them to recline upon.

'Not being certain who my ancestors are is more sad than strange, really,' she said, once settled on the blanket. 'Records are so full of lies or were often left incomplete, covering up whose baby was really whose during slavery and what have you. I do wonder about the stories we could know, if only birth records and handed-down stories told the truth.'

'It's a travesty, so it is,' Patrick said, clueless as to whether he was saying the right thing. 'And being with me, you really don't mind that I'm...'

'Would I be here if I minded?'

Patrick gave a short laugh. 'All right, fair point.'

'Do you mind?' Bea repeated back to him, her back straightening where she sat.

'That you're Grenadian?' Patrick almost repeated her word for word but thought the better of it. 'I like that we're different.'

Bea rolled her eyes. She'd started to reach into the picnic basket, but her hands stayed resting on the top of the wicker rim. 'I swear to God, if you refer to me as "exotic"...'

'That's not what I mean!' Patrick protested. 'I've just always found myself with other people exactly like me – private school, country house, everyone spouting the same opinions their parents held. Reading the same dull books or listening to the same dreary music because they think it makes them seem smarter, rather than actually for the joy of it.' He could tell Bea was trying not to laugh at that, so he continued. 'Spending time with you has given me some sort of spark, you know? It feels free, natural. I'm not just a ticket to a manor house and inheritance and afternoon teas so dull you'd want to poke your eyes out with your cake fork.'

'I'd been waiting to tell you this, but I'm actually just here for the inheritance. I guess the cake fork comes free with that, does it?'

Patrick laughed, reaching over the picnic basket to encircle Bea's waist. 'You can have all the cake forks you like, just please never ask me to go fox hunting.'

'There goes my plan for next week.'

Patrick dropped a kiss on her cheek, finally letting her go. 'What are you like?' he said. He had meant to say, *I've fallen in love with you,* but lost his nerve right at the last second.

They turned to face the water, allowing Patrick to properly survey the depth and breadth of Grand Etang Lake. It formed a small oasis that seemed to have appeared just for the two of them, sunlight making the water sparkle in flashes of silver and gold. He dragged his eyes away from the water to get their food ready, and began unpacking the modest picnic of prepared plantain, fresh roti, a small jar of pickled mango with ginger, and sugar apple for dessert. His hands couldn't help but brush hers as she helped to assemble the feast, stealing glances at one another.

'Bea? Bea!'

The two of them froze, their hands hovering over uneaten food.

'Did you hear that?'

Bea nodded, motioning for him to be quiet.

'Bea, I can see you.' Bette appeared before them, breathing heavily. Her face was glowing with sweat, her hair pulled back in a tight ponytail. 'Get away, quick.'

'I can explain—'

'There's no need,' Bette said, laughter in her voice. 'I've known about you two for weeks.'

'What?' cried Bea. 'How?'

Bette raised an eyebrow and fanned herself with one hand. 'I know you still think of me as a baby, but I wasn't born yesterday. You left to study a few nights ago, but your Advanced Accounting textbook was still in our bedroom.' Bette straightened up and started packing their picnic back into the basket for them. 'I also borrowed your copy of *Midsummer* to go over my lines and I saw the inscriptions. Very sweet. Hi, Patrick.'

Bea scrambled to her feet. 'But how did you know we were here?'

'Ran into Ron earlier. Millie and Julien are coming up here this afternoon, so I thought I'd better beat them to it.'

'Sorry, Bette,' Patrick said. 'We've wanted to tell you.'

'No need. It's kind of exciting, isn't it?' Bette said with a grin. Patrick's brow began to sweat as he accepted the refilled basket from Bette's hands. 'Now get out of here, before Millie catches you,' Bette continued. 'I'll see you both at opening night.' She ushered them through the trees, gesturing to an alternative route back.

Patrick waited until Bette was out of sight before turning to

Bea, whose expression looked more troubled than he'd like. 'At least Bette knows now,' he said, hoping he sounded reassuring. 'That's bound to make things easier when we tell everyone else.'

'Bette was never going to be the problem.' Bea shook her head, and took his hand. 'Come on, let's go. We can't risk Millie seeing us.'

September 1954

Chapter 7

Beatrice

Bea looked over at Bette to make sure she was really asleep. Watching the rise and fall of the sheet atop her sister's sleeping frame, Bea felt a pang of gratitude for her baby sister. Bette had been keeping her secret for weeks, and covering for Bea every time she needed to escape to meet Patrick.

That night, Bea was heading to meet Patrick at the hill fort, just at the end of her road, for a midnight feast 'Grenada-style'. He'd promised nutmeg marmalade sandwiches with slices of sweet, sticky grapefruit pound cake, and had even brewed up a flask of cocoa tea. Bea hoped his cooking skills had improved since he'd attempted to roast a chicken a few weeks previously; tonight's menu had her salivating at the mere thought of it. She couldn't wait to write to Nella again and tell her all about how they were getting on. She meant to write a full letter, rather than just a hastily scrawled postcard, but could hardly find the time.

Bea peeled back the sheet on her bed and slowly got to her feet, avoiding the creaking floorboards to pick her way out of the door and into the lounge.

'Bea? Sorry, I didn't mean to wake you.'

Bea froze, turning slowly towards the voice in the lounge. Millie sat on the sofa, curled up with her legs beneath her. A tower of school books was threatening to collapse beside her, a weary expression on her face.

Bea sank down beside her sister, subtly glancing at the clock illuminated by slivers of moonlight. It was 11.20 – she still had plenty of time to meet Patrick.

'What are you doing?'

Millie brought a hand to cover her face. 'I'm so behind on marking these books. I gave the kids a spelling test last week, and I haven't got around to making all the corrections. I've been so busy...'

She trailed off, and Bea winced at the look on her face. She'd been so wrapped up in her own life – seeing Patrick, doing Seb's job as well as her own, guarding so many secrets – she hadn't noticed her sister had become so withdrawn. 'With the play? Anything I can do to help?'

Millie shook her head. 'The play's fine. It's work, it's seeing Julien enough, it's helping Mom around the house, and the meetings I've been going to.' She avoided Bea's eyes. 'Political meetings, trade unions, all legal. Just...'

'A lot?'

Millie exhaled. 'A lot.'

Bea knew she was running out of time, but Patrick would understand. She took a deep breath and reached for the book on top of the teetering pile. 'Come on, then. Let's get these books marked, so you can get some rest.'

'I also have to finish blocking the finale for the play.'

'Not tonight, you don't. One thing at a time,' Bea said softly. This was new: Bea taking charge, comforting her big sister. She took the pencil from Millie's hand and opened the workbook on her lap. 'If we both mark these, you'll be done in half the time.'

Millie shook her head but didn't move to stop Bea. 'I suppose it wouldn't hurt.' She sat up straighter, winding her neck from side to side. 'How do you do it, Bea? Work all day, out at the play, and studying for your next exams?'

Bea felt a stab of guilt at that, wondering whether now was the moment to confess. *Surely in this state, Millie wouldn't be angry?* She might even understand what it's like to get swept up in something, like a tide you don't even notice has turned until you're halfway out to sea. 'Well—'

'I'm proud of you, Bea. I don't think I tell you that enough.'

Bea shifted in her seat, flipping open the next book and jotting down the corrections. *Large, Story, Another, Thank.* She moved on to the next one, a neat row of ticks filling the page.

'Thanks, Mill. I'm proud of you, too. You take on so much, you know? You know you don't have to do it all on your own.' Bea finished the last book in the pile, handing them back to Millie. She was definitely late to meet Patrick now, but she knew he'd wait. 'Just tell Julien you need more help at the play, ask me and Bette to do more around the house.' Bea flashed her a grin, leaning in closer. 'And give the children easier spelling tests, so you don't have to correct them.'

Millie laughed at that, clapping her hand over her mouth to silence the sound. 'Thank you.' She sighed again. 'I guess I needed to hear that.'

Bea gave her sister's shoulder a squeeze, and ushered her off the sofa and into her bedroom.

'Any time,' she whispered as Millie climbed under her covers. 'No one can help you if you don't say something, can they?'

As she crept out the door and into the fresh midnight air, Bea almost laughed at her own hypocrisy. If she didn't tell Patrick that she'd fallen in love with him, how could he know to say it back? If she didn't say let me come away with you, how would he know to ask?

Chapter 8

Beatrice

'Bette has real talent, don't you think?' Bea enthused as the opening night curtain closed for the interval.

So far, she and Patrick had managed to stay hidden from any wandering eyes, but their luck was surely going to run out during the break. Bea felt cheated, somehow; their time together hadn't been enough. 'We'd better go, though. I can congratulate her at home. People will be sure to see us and tell Millicent if we stay up here.'

Patrick nodded, getting to his feet. 'Meet me out the back?'

Bea agreed, counting to five before following him out of the side door. Millie would be inside, schmoozing with the other teachers and local councillors and potential donors in the audience.

She found him leaning against the back wall, his head tilted up towards the stars. Everyone else was smoking or gossiping out the front, drinking in the views of the beaches far below. On hearing Bea approach, Patrick's face broke into a smile and he reached out one arm, pulling her into his side. The night was still warm, yet they stood close together as though trying to keep out the cold.

Bea wondered whether now was the time to ask what had been on her mind. To ask whether he'd thought of what came next, where they'd go from here. If she could go with him.

She dared not think of what it would mean to leave her family, her work, the only home she'd ever known. She just couldn't shake the feeling of wanting to see what lay beyond the horizon, even if it meant falling off the edge of her world.

'Do you think anyone will need prompting in the second half?'

Patrick asked, his arm staying looped around her waist. 'We could just stay out here.'

Bea swatted at him. 'Don't tempt me. Don't you want to see how it ends, anyway?'

'I've seen enough Shakespeare to know how they all end. Either a wedding or a tragic fall from grace, right?'

'Most stories have one or the other,' Bea conceded.

'I must have read almost all his plays cover to cover, and those were pretty much his only finale options. A few deaths thrown in for good measure.' He paused. 'My mother left me a copy of every Shakespeare play, she had *The Complete Works*.'

Bea looked up at him, her curiosity written across her face. 'Your mother liked theatre, then?'

'She did.' Patrick went quiet for a minute, and Bea wondered where he'd gone. 'She'd loved literature in school, so used to read me all the classic stories from when I was a baby, my aunt tells me. She'd even make up her own tales on long winter evenings or when we were travelling somewhere. We did a fair bit of travelling when I was little, just me and my mother, leaving Dublin for the seaside for whole summers. Or, it felt like whole summers – it was probably just a fortnight or so, maybe only once, but you know how funny a child's memory can be.' He smiled. 'I think I got my travel spark from her side.'

'That sounds wonderful,' Bea replied warmly. 'What was her name?'

Patrick cleared his throat. 'Margaret. Margaret O'Shea, before she married my father.'

'A beautiful name.' Bea moved closer to him, hoping they couldn't be heard from inside the community centre. A palm tree towered above them, its rustling leaves punctuating their conversation. 'And your father didn't mind, the two of you going away without him?'

Patrick faltered. 'He wasn't exactly the family holiday type. He was away most of the time anyway, training other officers or on a tour.'

'How did your parents meet, then, with him being away with the army so much?'

Patrick cocked his head to the side, a half-smile on his lips. 'She was his nurse in Dublin. He had to go over there as part of the ceasefire. End of 1921, early '22, I think. He kept having to go back over the next few years as part of so-called peacekeeping, and they must have kept in touch. They didn't actually get married until the summer of 1926, though.'

Bea's brow furrowed as she did a quick calculation. 'And you were born in the January of 1927?'

'So I'm sure you can guess why they had to tie the knot,' Patrick said, laughing bitterly. 'I don't think my father ever forgave me.'

'For what?'

'For arriving, messing up his plans for a perfectly uneventful life.'

'He told you that?'

'He didn't have to.' Patrick's eyes grew misty and distant, barely skimming the tops of the trees in the distance.

Bea wrapped her arm tighter around his waist, resting her head lightly on his shoulder. 'And what actually happened … to your mother? Was she sick? You don't have to tell me, of course,' she added hastily, 'if you don't want to.'

Patrick was quiet for a moment. His face fell. 'Cancer,' he said softly. 'Nothing we could do.'

'And you had to go and live with your father?'

'Sort of. We'd … Mum and I had been summoned to Surrey so my father could keep a closer eye on her. Now I realise they were clearly on the brink of divorce, living completely separate lives, but at the time I just thought he was working away a lot.' Patrick ran his hand through his hair, clearing his throat. 'He hadn't even timed us going to Surrey to help with her end-of-life care. It was all about getting me to arrive in time for my place at this ridiculously fancy boarding school my mother had promised I didn't have to go to. My dad dropped me there the week she died and didn't even stay for an hour, told me to grow up, stop crying like a little girl, behave like a man. Said boys my age shouldn't still need their mothers.'

'How old were you?'

'Five.'

A gasp escaped Bea's throat. She felt crushed picturing the red-eyed little boy clutching a suitcase and a teddy bear, left all on his own. 'That must've been awful.'

Patrick made an 'Mmmm' sort of response, before pulling his shoulders back a touch. Bea knew the interval would be ending soon, but couldn't bring herself to part from him.

'It wasn't easy,' Patrick said eventually. 'My Aunt Nancy was brilliant, though – my mother's sister. She'd visit me as much as she could since my father was always busy, and I'd go back to hers in Dublin every summer, most Easters, too.'

'Well, she sounds lovely,' Bea replied, keeping her tone gentle. Calls and shouts were rising from the hall, and she knew their time was almost up.

'Nancy's great, she's so funny. And she'd love you.' Patrick seemed to relax, much to Bea's relief, turning to drop a kiss on her forehead. 'And, Bea, I've been meaning to say . . .' He kept holding her close, his chest rising as he took a deep breath. 'These last three months – they've been nothing short of wondrous. Every day we've been together, even the days we haven't, I just . . .' He cleared his throat; Bea's breathing quickened. *Say it.* 'What I'm trying to say is that I've fallen in love with you. I love you, Bea.'

'I . . .' Bea's heart swelled. 'I love you, too.'

As he kissed her, she allowed herself to picture what may come next: sitting down with a cup of tea and a spread of sweet treats to meet Patrick's aunt, the two of them laughing at a shared joke; a grandfather clock striking midday; a log fire burning in the corner to keep out a type of cold she'd only ever read about. She pictured the words *frost* and *snowflake* and *winter* morphing into ice-bright realities, visible through a pane of thick glass steamed up from the warmth of a terraced home. Patrick at her side, smiling.

A bell-ring from inside signalled their break was over, and Bea found herself beneath the towering palm tree, sweat clinging to her back. She drew away from Patrick, both of them grinning like

Cheshire cats. She forced herself to walk in ahead of him, picking her way over backstage debris.

As she narrowly avoided tripping over the piles of cardboard trees, she made up her mind: she'd talk to him once and for all, let him know he couldn't leave without her.

Chapter 9

Beatrice

12 Claverdale Road
Brixton
London

12th September 1954

Dear Bea,

    I am well, thank you for asking, and the London summer has been kind to me. Not too hot on the wards, since the English wouldn't know humidity even if it kissed them smack on the lips.

    And now, to your news – I can't believe you've met someone, a British fella, no less! Or sorry, an Irish-Englishman.

    I am so happy for you, I really am – but have you thought this through, Bea? When you say you've fallen for him, do you mean you'd consider leaving when he leaves? Coming to England, if that's where he's headed?

    Of course, I'd love nothing more than to see you strolling through Clapham Common, but I have to ask if you've considered this from all sides. It isn't an easy journey, uprooting yourself and leaving home. The people can be so nasty to girls who look like us, no matter how good our family name was back on the islands or how educated we are.

    For me, it wasn't as though I had much choice: it was either leave or stay on the island and become a fruit-seller like my Momma, scraping by and praying for good harvests. We never really talk about it, but you and I are different, Bea. You have options. You can drive a car, you work at the bank. Your parents might even set you up in a house of your own if you marry

51

someone local – just think of that. Is it worth throwing away
for a man you've just met? Just do your old friend a favour and
think about it.
　With love,
　Nella

Pulling out all her dresses onto the bed, Bea felt frustration prickle along her back. She had to look perfect tonight; she'd pluck up the courage to ask, once and for all, if Patrick felt the way she did. She needed an outfit that said *take a chance on this.*

'Why don't you wear this?' Bea hadn't noticed Bette walk into their shared bedroom, and in her hands was the emerald green dress Bette had worn to the carnival fund-raiser dance. It seemed so long ago, now. 'I have something else to give you, too.'

'Thank you, Bette, but I really have to go,' Bea whispered. 'I'm going to be late to meet him.'

'You can't go without this.' From beneath the folds of the dark green dress, Bette produced a large brown envelope. Bea reached for it, gingerly raising it to the light. 'B – Open Me' sloped along the front, the ink bleeding ever so slightly on her initial. Bette grinned, placing the dress on the bed and moving over to sit on her own.

'Well, put this dress on quick and then go. I'll cover for you. Say you're out shopping for me.'

Thanking her, Bea took the dress and stepped into it, yanking her faded smock over her head and stepping into the swathes of jewel-green materials. She thought she heard a seam tear in her haste, but pretended she hadn't.

'Do I look all right?'

'Perfect,' Bette enthused, darting behind Bea to button up the back. 'Now you gotta get going.'

Bea clutched the envelope close to her chest and slipped from the room. Seeing the empty corridor, she stuffed her feet into her slip-ons and raced for the front door. She would have liked slightly more elegant footwear to match the dress, but didn't want to waste any more time. Once around the corner from the house, she reached into the envelope and pulled out a single sheet of paper.

A sketch, revealing itself to be a hand-drawn map, looked back up at her. She turned the page around in her hands until she held it the right way up, cocking her head to the side as she began to decode. 'You are here' the map told her, its silvery outline dusting her fingertips. She traced the tiny, hand-drawn footsteps which sent her to the end of the road, instructing her to take a right and head towards the hill fort that overlooked St George's.

As she walked, frissons of excitement darted up and down her body: her footsteps moved quickly, and an unfamiliar combination of impatience and wanting to savour the moment fought for her attention. She thought they'd agreed to wait until after dark to meet that evening, but the idea of seeing him sooner made her footsteps pound the ground with more urgency.

The map outlined the south-west side of the island, leading her out to the hill fort along Grand Etang Road. She looped around, heading back down Melville Street along the coastline, past the cricket stadium, and up towards Grand Mal Bay.

Dusk thickened as she strolled, the sun setting behind her and elongating her shadow as though to guide her way.

'Find me here,' the map instructed, pinpointing a palm tree drawn far too large to be to scale.

As she passed Cherry Hill, she arrived at a small, sandy cove flanked by palm and coconut trees.

'Right on time,' Patrick said, standing up to greet her. 'I was worried it would be too dark before you managed to find me.'

She laughed, handing him the map. 'Luckily, I had some well-drawn instructions. You'd almost think the map had been created by a professional.'

He took it from her, folding it up and placing it carefully in a small picnic basket to his left. Bea ran over to it, peering inside to find two paper-wrapped sugar cakes and a bottle of cloudy lemonade. She clapped her hands in delight.

'They're still warm.' Patrick motioned for her to sit down as he unfurled a chequered picnic blanket, and pulled the sticky pink treats from the paper. He handed her the larger one, their fingertips brushing lightly.

Leaning back, Patrick pulled his shoulders back and began pointing to the sky, now a bright yet deep blue, dotted with stars. 'You see now, Lynx is so clear here. You can see it from Dublin, too, but there's so much smog and city lights there that it's never this bright.' He continued to gaze up at the emerging constellations as Bea stole a glance at him – this international man who made her feel that maybe she could take on the world, too. 'And Ursula Major is—'

'I'm sorry, did you just say "Ursula Major"?' She arched an eyebrow, licking the sugar coating from her fingers. She'd get around to speaking to him properly, getting serious, but she couldn't help lapsing into rolling conversation.

'Yes, see it just there? Beside the Lynx constellation?'

Bea nudged him playfully on the arm, unscrewing their bottle and taking a thirsty sip. 'You know it's Ursa Major, not Ursula? It's a constellation of stars, not a sea witch.'

Patrick nodded far too enthusiastically. 'Oh, yes, of course, I was just testing you.' He flashed a grin at her and reached for the lemonade.

'Liar,' Bea said, laughing.

They each moved a little closer, their knees touching, and looked out over the cove. It had a captivating beauty to it as twilight fell upon the water.

Patrick turned to face her, their eyes meeting. Bea's breath quickened. 'I know it isn't exactly champagne, but shall we toast?'

She was about to say yes, before she paused. She looked at him, knowing the time had come. 'Pat, I think I do need to speak to you properly, you know.' She took a deep breath. Bea had always been told that if you want an answer, you gotta ask the question. Or as Nella so beautifully put it in her favourite phrase: 'piss or get off the pot.' 'I don't want to watch you go.'

Patrick frowned. 'And you won't, will you?' He reached out to take her hand. 'You're coming with me.'

He said it as a statement, not a question, and Bea could swear she heard fireworks going off somewhere nearby. 'Yes, I'm coming with you.' She stated it, too, the words emboldening her. She ignored the warnings from Nella's letter, ignored the thoughts of what her family might say.

He smiled back at her, his relief written across his features. 'I suppose you'll be wanting your ring, then?'

She threw her head back, laughing. 'I think what you mean is, "Will you marry me, Beatrice?" Would you like to try your line again?'

'Well, clearly I had a bigger speech planned,' he countered, gesturing around at them. 'Do you think I make hand-drawn maps for just anybody?'

'So why didn't you say it?'

'You beat me to it!'

Bea shook her head, pulling him up so they stood eye to eye on the blanket. 'I want to hear it – your speech.'

She thought he'd laugh along, play the game, but he became serious all of a sudden. He took a deep breath, and shifted so he was down on one knee. She wished she could bottle the way he was looking up at her.

'Bea,' he began. 'Meeting you has been the greatest thing that's ever happened to me.' He paused, taking her hand. 'I've never really known how it's felt to belong to someone else before, but from the moment I saw you, it was as though I'd been waiting for you all my life. Like, "*Ah, it's you. Glad you could make it.*"' She laughed, and he squeezed her hand. 'I know it won't be an easy ride to choose someone like me and to leave your home here, but I promise I will do everything I can to give you the most wonderful life.'

'It will be an adventure!' Bea protested.

'That it will. Not everywhere we go will be easy, though.'

'Where will we go first?' Bea asked, hardly able to keep still with excitement. She let her mind overflow with visions of towering metropolises, evergreen and sprawling countryside, yellow brick roads to Emerald Cities. All theirs for the taking.

His face broke into a grin. 'Could be anywhere. Africa, the Americas, Australasia. What do you say?'

'That depends on what you're asking, exactly.'

'Come on, you know where this is going.'

'I still want to hear it.'

'I suppose that's fair.' He paused for one more second, and Bea wasn't sure she could bear it. Finally, he retrieved a small velvet box from his pocket. 'Beatrice Bell, will you do me the honour of being my wife?'

Chapter 10

The fragrant perfume of Bea's home hit her the second she stepped through the front door. Her mother must have been cooking something delicious for supper, and Bea couldn't help but fill herself up with the frying turmeric and breadfruit scent every time she inhaled. She'd miss how the house filled with island flavour at every meal, layering the air with spice and salt.

'Bea, honey? Is that you?' her mother called, coming through from the garden and into the front room.

'Yes, it's me,' Bea began, trying to stop her voice from wavering. Her knees weakened beneath her, as she realised she'd actually have to own up to what had been going on. 'And I have some news!'

Holding her head high, she pushed open the door and stepped into the lounge. Her father sat on the couch, squinting through his glasses at the newspaper. Her mother stood removing her gardening gloves, her shirt stained with earth.

Bea took a deep breath. 'I've met someone,' she said, looking from parent to parent. She faltered; she should have rehearsed her lines. 'And he's asked me to marry him.'

Her father said nothing, simply looked up from the newspaper in his hands. Ink stained his fingertips, the detail tugging at Bea's heartstrings.

'And what did you say to this man?' Bea's mother asked as her eyes grew wide.

Bea gulped. Hearing it out loud made it sound rushed, quick, unconsidered. 'Well, I said yes.' She twisted the ring round on her finger, instantly drawing her mother's attention to it.

Mrs Bell grabbed Bea's hand, raising it up to the light. 'Who is this man, who we haven't heard of? Swanning in and buying you gold and diamonds? Does he think you are for sale?'

Bea's hand trembled in her mother's, and she willed her father to say something. 'It's not like that, Mom, I love him. I've fallen in love with him, and we can't be together unless we marry.'

Mrs Bell scoffed. 'Times have changed, Beatrice. Look at Millicent and Julien – they've been courting for years and they're still being sensible. Waiting for the right time. You're only just sitting your advanced exams! Why do you have to be so damn impatient?'

Bea hadn't heard her mother curse out loud before. It threw her off. 'You're right, times have changed. That's the other thing.' She took a deep breath, lowering her hand from her mother's grip. She looked back at her father, who was beginning to get to his feet. 'He's been here for the last three months, on a work placement from England.'

'He's British?' her mother asked, her tone shifting to the clipped way she spoke to new ladies who came to church. 'Does he come from money?'

'He's English-Irish, Catholic faith. Had his First Communion and everything.' Bea faltered, but tried not to let it show. She wasn't actually sure whether he'd had his First Communion, but soldiered on. 'He works for the government, travelling through the Commonwealth as a land surveyor.'

Her father cocked his head to one side, his movement disrupting the tension that clung to the room. 'He sounds like a good match.'

'A good match?' Mrs Bell exploded. 'A good match, Gabriel?' She spat the words, raising a pointed finger towards her husband. 'Just because he shares our faith and has a decent income, you think it's a good idea for Beatrice to run off with someone we've never even met?' She turned back to Bea, the hurt in her eyes making Bea's chest ache. 'You were so ashamed of us, you didn't bother to bring him here to meet your parents before you decided to disappear halfway around the world with him? Is that it?'

'Not at all, Mom, it wasn't like that. I was afraid of what you'd say, how you'd react to someone so different. And we all know

Millicent would be furious if she knew I was even talking to an English bloke.'

'Don't blame this on your sister. You can't marry a man you barely know, it isn't proper and you know it.'

'But, Mom, I don't have any other choice.' Bea's explanations bubbled up inside her, cascading out in a waterfall. 'He's made me feel more excitement and wonder and joy than I have ever felt, and I'm sick of being talked down to at work and sitting in the wings in the theatre and waiting for something to happen.' Tears had started streaming down her cheeks, and she swiped at her face in jolting movements. 'He's interested in what I have to say, and he loves me and he wants us to see the world together. I don't want to get left behind, with no prospects beyond the job I'm already doing and no hope of ever meeting someone who makes me feel this way again. This sort of thing, it only comes around once.'

'How could you know that? You're young, Beatrice, you'll get over this infatuation.'

At her mother's sharp words, Bea's shoulders began to shake. She felt a firm hand come to rest on her back. 'You deserve all that, Beatrice,' her father said. 'I hate to say it, but it sounds like you need to take a chance on this. If it's truly what you want.'

'But, Gabriel, when will we see her?' snapped Mrs Bell. 'And how will they treat her, over in England? The hateful rumours I've heard about life over there – they're uncivilised. Mrs Jamieson's son is over there, and she said they treat their own people like second-class citizens all cooped up in factories and slums, let alone ...' Mrs Bell shook her head, her face hardening. 'We can't let her go.'

'Look at her, Mayra. We can't let her stay, if this is the state she's going to be in at the thought of it. Let the girl have an adventure, for once.' His voice softened, his hand leaving Bea's back and reaching over for her mother. 'And if it doesn't work out, she can always come on home again. No shame in that.'

Mrs Bell paused. 'No, there's no shame in coming back.' Her back straightened as she smoothed down her shirt. Bea fought the urge to protest their lack of faith, wiping away subsiding tears. 'We must meet this man,' her mother continued, 'before anything further can be discussed. Bring him round for supper, this evening. You've hidden him away long enough.' Mrs Bell marched from the room, glaring at her husband as she left. Bea sniffed, impressed with herself that she was still standing.

'Oh, Bea, it's beautiful!' Bette squealed, grabbing Bea's splayed fingers and bringing the ring closer for inspection. 'I knew it was something special when he gave you that map.' Bette stood up from the bed on which the two of them sat, opening their shared wardrobe and pulling the dusty packing case from the top shelf. 'What sort of thing will you need to pack? Where will you go?'

Bea knew telling Bette would lift her spirits. She'd write to Nella that night, too; tell her the whole story. 'I'll need everything warm for England,' she said. 'Nella says it's bitter cold in winter. I'll probably need to buy a new coat, a fur one maybe.' She pictured herself waltzing up a high street wrapped in glamorous animal print. She'd probably get stockings, too – real ones with the seam running down the back, as she'd seen in imported magazines from the United States.

'That will be wonderful! You'll look like Princess Margaret.' Bette's eyes lit up as she moved over to the bookshelf, reaching for a magazine and leafing through it to find the princess's birthday photographs. 'Look at this one – you should get a dress like this. You could even pin your hair like that. I bet she has to tease hers to get that sort of volume, but yours sticks up like that naturally.'

'Mine does not stick up, it grows out. Like a crown,' Bea couldn't help but retort, accustomed to having to explain this to her lank-haired little sister.

Bette threw a sideways glance at Bea. 'You know what I mean.' She leafed through the pages a little further, exclaiming over all the beautiful clothes Bea could buy when she was a British government wife.

'What's all this?' Millicent's tone was sharp as she entered the room, her expression questioning. The gap between Bea and Bette's beds was narrow, and Millie skirted between them. She came to stand with her back against the wall, beside the window, a defiant look in her eyes. Her gaze fell to the suitcase, and her expression darkened. 'You're going somewhere?'

Bette closed the magazine, her gaze dropping to the floor. Bea looked up at Millie, instantly feeling sick. 'I was going to tell you—'

'You never stopped seeing him, did you?' Millie's eyes narrowed, her hands coming to rest on her hips. 'You've been running around with that Patrick. And let me guess… He's promised to whisk you away and live happily ever after?' She practically spat the words, her tone mocking. Her eyes burned as she spoke, taking a step closer to Bea. Bea did her best not to shrink from her sister, trying to piece together a response. 'Well, what do you have to say for yourself?'

Bea squirmed. 'It's not like how you're making it sound. It's real, what he and I have, and I'm sorry I didn't tell you but I knew you'd react like this.' Her voice grew louder, as she reminded herself exactly what was at stake. She locked eyes with Millie, willing herself not to cry this time. *Get it together, Bea.* 'I know you don't agree with it – with us – but how can we move forward from the past if we don't let ourselves love who we fall for? What purpose does that serve?'

'Oh, come on, Bea. Don't give me that. You can't love someone after only knowing them for three months. This is nothing but lust, and you're choosing to ignore it.'

'Why can't you be happy for me, Millie? I didn't choose to fall for an Englishman, but it's happened now. There's nothing I can do about it.'

'Except you did choose this, didn't you? All those late nights "studying" for your advanced exams, you've been running off. I bet you've given him exactly what he wants, and he'll use you until he gets bored. That's what they're like, Bea. These Englishmen can't be trusted.' Millie shook her head, her upper lip lifting in a snarl. 'Don't you remember what happened to Sanjana from school? That English fella she met in Canada ran back to Britain the second he found out about their baby. She hasn't heard from him since, and she still hasn't come home from the shame of it all.' Millie's eyes darkened. 'After all they've taken from us, from here – and you'd run away with one of them? How can you do this?'

'Stop it, Millie!' Bette exclaimed. 'Bea has met someone she loves, and you're ruining it. Patrick's not like that awful street urchin Sanjana picked up. He's Catholic, like us.'

'But why do you think we're Catholic, Bette? They shove Colonial education down our throats here. I'm sick of teaching it to the children like what happened was acceptable.' Millie shook her head, adopting an exasperated tone. 'The British came over here and after slaughtering indigenous people, enslaved genera-tions. Told us we were savages, uncivilised, forced us to take their religion, ignored our culture and customs, forced us to live as second-class citizens. And now you want to marry one?' She turned back to face Bea, tears in her big brown eyes. 'How can you be all right with that?'

Bea twisted her hands in her lap. 'I don't see all that history when I look at him,' she eventually said. 'He's just a man, and I'm just me. We don't all have to represent more than ourselves.'

'But you will,' Millie said, her voice wobbling. She sank down to sit beside Bea on the bed, her lips twisting in what looked like genuine concern. 'Don't you get that? When people in England see you, they won't see *you*. They'll make snap judgements, they'll assume you're uneducated, they'll talk down to you just because of your colour.'

'But she's so light-skinned!' Bette retorted. 'And Bea's one of the most educated people I know.'

Millie grimaced. 'You think the English care how dark or light you are? Being light-skinned might bring us some kind of privi-lege in Grenada, but it won't work over there. All they'll see is a foreigner, some little island girl come to steal one of their own.'

'How could you know that?' Bette retorted.

'How could you not know that, either of you? Haven't you read any of the political books I lent you, any Fanon or Césaire? Any newspapers about life in England, at least?' Millie took a sharp breath. 'I need you to understand what you're walking into, Bea. It's not going to be easy, if you do decide to run off with this man.'

'Will you use his name?' Bea snapped, suddenly tired of Millicent proclaiming her superior knowledge. 'You've never been to England, so you can't know what it's going to be like. Don't try and put me off just because you'd be too scared to try.' She stood up and walked over to the empty suitcase. She picked it up and carried it over to her bed. 'Patrick loves me, and I want to give this a chance. I want to see what's beyond this island – the storms, the hurricanes, my job with nowhere to go but the filing cupboard. Whoever I ended up marrying, the bank would fire me the second they saw the ring anyhow. This way, I get to see the world.' She started to select books off the shelf above her bed, placing them in a row in the bottom of her suitcase. She'd have to repack properly, but she wanted to make a point to her sister.

Millie pressed her lips into a thin line, shaking her head and marching towards the door. 'This will all end in tears, mark my words. Don't come crying to me when he leaves you for a blue-eyed Brit.'

'Millie, wait!'

But Millie had already left the room. Suddenly exhausted, Bea pushed her half-empty case to the floor. Paperbacks clattered onto the floorboards, their pages splaying out like fallen leaves.

Chapter 11

26 Semaphore Road
Guildford
Surrey
England

10th September 1954

Dear Patrick,

    We are well, thank you for asking. I must say, however, we found your last letter rather confusing. You said you had met a local woman and intend to bring her home — but you don't speak of a woman local to the West Indian Islands, do you? You must be speaking of a missionary, or a businessman's daughter over to see that all is well on the islands. You would know better than to run after a local or threaten to bring back an island bride.

    Because if you did — especially without asking us first — you know there would be consequences.

    I must remind you of your place, Patrick. I understand what you young men are like, and I shan't go into detail, but it's understandable if you've become infatuated with someone over there. Now, however, you must return home at once and stop all this tomfoolery.

    I so hate to bring it up, but you have a responsibility to stick to your own kind: the sort of woman who understands precisely what it takes to be a Government wife. Consider what happened in your father's first marriage. It ended in fight after fight before she died, and those fights might have been avoided if they'd stuck to their own borders. To think your grandfather thought your father taking an Irish Catholic wife would be the biggest scandal this family would ever see! Don't make the same mistake as he did. Come home, and we can pretend this has never happened. Everyone makes mistakes when they're young.

With best wishes,

Moira

'You burning Commonwealth Office secrets?'

Patrick jumped in his seat, the charred letter blackening to ash as he held it over the flame. He'd written to his father and Moira the day he'd proposed, letting them know of his intentions not to return home alone. He knew they'd have their reservations, but he hadn't expected this. 'Sorry, Ron, didn't hear you come in.'

Ron laughed as he shut the door behind him. 'And I didn't mean to scare you. Coffee?'

'Please.'

Ron headed to the stove, setting the pot to boil. 'You gonna tell me what you're sending up in flames? If it really is a government document, my lips are sealed.'

'Ha, I wish.' Patrick sat back in his seat. 'You wouldn't believe me if I told you.'

'Try me.' Even with his back turned, Patrick could hear a wry smile in Ron's voice.

'It's my parents, you see. My father...' Patrick cracked his knuckles, shaking his head. 'He's putting all sorts of ideas in my stepmother's head, saying it wouldn't be right for me to marry Bea.'

The sound of bubbling water popped against Patrick's words, as Ron removed the pot from the heat and poured it into the waiting jug. The scent of fresh, bitter coffee wafted from the stove.

Ron raised his head, turning to face Patrick with a peculiar look on his face. 'And this is a shock to you?'

'To this extent, yes. Since I could walk, my father's been urging me to join the Commonwealth Office, talking about all these places I'd go.' Patrick met Ron's eyes as a steaming mug was placed in front of him, and Ron came to sit opposite. 'The way he used to talk about the empire, you'd swear he loved it more than any woman he'd ever met. But now, he's saying I'm not supposed to engage with anyone once I get to an empire country. How would he expect me to get by, if I acted as though I was above everyone I met?'

'Engage with anyone,' Ron said, smiling. 'No pun intended, I'm sure.'

'You know what I mean. It's just not right, them reacting like this. The English government is inviting empire subjects over to rebuild the country, so I might have met someone like Bea even if I'd stayed in England. They're being ridiculous.' Patrick ran his hand through his hair, and took a sip of hot coffee. It scalded the roof of his mouth, and he jerked the mug away.

A memory, long buried, clawed its way to the surface. When he'd gone back to his father's after Palestine, Mr Anderson had been less than comforting at the way Patrick had stayed so quiet, hardly slept, aimlessly wandered the corridors at night. *The things I saw, the atrocities from both sides, so many lives lost.* Patrick had been through a phase of never sleeping without nightmares, his mind constantly replaying the scene when he'd been the only one to wake up after an attack on their tank. *Crying over a mess of Arabs and Jews blowing each other up,* his father had scolded. *It's not as if you saw real tragedy. Your generation don't know what it's like to see your own men shot down in the trenches.*

Patrick blinked away the images, pushing them back into the depths they'd crawled from. His father had only said that to shock him back to life, surely. And besides, that was war talking; it always got his father whipped into a frenzy.

All this letter proved was that his parents still thought of him as the motherless little boy with odd socks and a runny nose, in desperate need of a kind of guidance that wore the same false smile as control.

Patrick glanced across the room, his gaze falling on the swaying trees knocking at the kitchen window. An almost ripe breadfruit was causing a large branch to bend, and Patrick wondered how many shakes it would take to get it to fall. 'My parents are being ridiculous,' he said. 'They're just upset I didn't speak to them about it first, I bet. You know Bea can recite all the kings and queens as far back as Alfred the Great? I hadn't even heard of him. In some ways, she's more British than I am.'

'Maybe you're right, and they're mad you didn't ask them first,' Ron agreed, his tone diplomatic. 'And I can recite the kings, too, you know. Or I could, when I was at school.'

'And we need more solicitors in England, surely,' Patrick replied, hitting his hand on the table. 'What's stopping someone like you heading over there?'

'Do you really need me to tell you that?'

Patrick scowled. 'But the English have been crossing borders for centuries! It's only fair the people whose land we stole can have some of ours. The war was meant to put an end to this sort of prejudice. Who cares about background, or colour?'

'Come on, Pat.' Ron leant forward, placing both hands on the table in front of him. 'We both know that everyone cares about colour.'

'But it doesn't make a difference. I've met Europeans, Africans, Arabs, Central Americans. Colour has absolutely no bearing on whether someone is or isn't a decent person.'

Ron stretched back, leaning so his chair swung. 'And that's an honourable point of view, Pat. But surely you see it's all about tradition, the order of things, with people like your parents.' He brought his chair back to the ground, landing hard. 'Just from what you've told me about your family, I mean.'

'But Bea's different.'

Ron paused for a second. 'Everyone thinks their girl is different. What's actually different about Bea?'

'Well, for one thing, she's so well educated.' Patrick sat up a little straighter. 'And her family name is respected. It carries weight.'

'On the islands it does.' Ron paused. 'But you're honestly telling me, you think all that – all the opportunities that girl's had – has nothing to do with the fact she's as light-skinned as Dorothy Dandridge?'

'Now that's not what I—'

'But it matters — colour matters even here. And over in the motherland?' Ron took a long sip of coffee as he paused. 'I've heard what it's like from a couple of local fellas who went straight after serving, even for people as pale as Bea,' he continued. 'The English just don't treat us right.'

'If it's that bad, wouldn't they have come home?' Patrick turned his attention back towards the window. He believed what he was saying, yet knots of frustration still curled up his spine. 'I think times are really changing.'

Ron sighed. 'I don't wanna knock your enthusiasm, I'm just saying. I don't think your parents are in the minority, judging you for choosing Bea.'

Patrick reached for his mug, needing something to do with his hands. 'But once they meet Bea, there's no way they'll turn us away.' He could picture the scene: all of them laughing over his parents' misunderstanding, swept away by Bea's charm and wit. He clung to the image. 'Can you imagine someone not liking Bea?'

At that Ron snorted, and drained the last of his coffee. The evening dusk was settling around them in the kitchen, moonlight beginning to pool through the window. 'Now on that, we can agree. If anyone can make someone change their mind, it's Beatrice Bell.'

'Exactly.' Patrick brought his coffee to his lips, brushing away the small ring it had left on the wooden table. 'So I won't tell her everything my parents have said, then. Just give her the basics — *they're a bit concerned, our different backgrounds, think it's too fast* — but nothing too detailed. No need to worry her when they'll change their mind as soon as she's through the front door.'

'You sure you're not worried she'll change *her* mind?'

'I'll always worry she'll change her mind,' Patrick admitted, doing his best to keep his tone jovial. 'I'd have been panicking about that however my parents reacted. She could do so much better, let's be honest.'

Ron stood up, heading for the sink. 'Do yourself a favour, you aren't so bad. Here's to you, eh?' He turned and lifted his mug to Patrick in a mock cheers, making him laugh.

'Thanks,' Patrick said, mimicking the gesture. 'And my parents will come around. I'm sure you're quite wrong about them. And everyone back home.'

Ron raised his free hand. 'Hey, for the record – I hope I am wrong. Just wanted to give you fair warning.'

'Thank you. But really, I know we'll be welcomed.'

Chapter 12

Beatrice

The air at Port Louis Marina was salty and bright, with familiar faces darting among the crowds of well-wishers. It seemed to Bea that people had been smart about what to bring along with them, waving brightly coloured rags and handkerchiefs high in the air. To attract attention, wave someone off so they could see you right until their ship dipped below the horizon. She wished her family had thought of that.

Through the crowd, Bea saw a familiar hand waving. Patrick pushed his way through the hubbub, emerging to greet her family with handshakes and smiles. Mercifully, her parents had given their approval after Patrick had visited for supper; he'd charmed them with talk of the motherland, let Bette beat him at a hand of rummy, praised Mrs Bell's beautifully kept home and cooking skills. He'd taken a long walk into the garden with Mr Bell, both returning with smiles on their faces.

'No Millicent?' Patrick asked, glancing at the crowd. 'That's a grand shame.' Millicent had also absented herself from the supper, leaving an empty chair at the table that made Bea's chest ache.

'I'm sure she'll come around,' Bette said firmly, giving Patrick her best attempt at a broad smile. She'd packed Bea a 'snack bag' of dried mango and slices of rum-soaked black cake, handing it over on their short drive to the port. *In case they don't have real fruit where you're going. I hear England's cuisine can be quite primitive.* The thoughtful gesture brought tears to Bea's eyes, and she glanced once more at her younger sister. Standing in the crowd, Bette looked far younger than her eighteen years as she stood backlit, her hair escaping its bun. Bea felt a lump rise in her throat.

'They're calling for final boarding,' Mr Bell said softly.

'I'll walk you over.' Mrs Bell guided Bea by the elbow just past the crowd, as Patrick gathered up their bags and shook hands with each remaining family member. Bea raised her chin, hoping it wouldn't start to wobble.

'I want you to know that we meant what we said,' Mrs Bell said in a low voice. 'There's no shame in coming on home if things don't work out. If he isn't the man you thought he was,' her voice wavered, 'or if it isn't the right sort of life for you, you can come right back.' Without breaking eye contact with Bea, she pressed a padded envelope into her daughter's hands. 'Keep that just in case you need it, and we'll say nothing more of it.'

Bea couldn't speak in response, just nodded her thanks and pocketed the envelope.

Bette and her father were suddenly back upon them, Bette drawing Bea into a warm hug. 'I can't believe you're really going!'

Mrs Bell's arms wrapped around the two of them, and they stood that way for a minute. Bea let the full weight of her decision consume her just for a second, panic rising in her chest at the thought of not seeing her family every day. What was she doing?

Patrick placed his hand on Bea's lower back and she automatically relaxed. This was her decision, and she was going to stick with it. 'It's time to go,' he said.

Finally pulling away, Bea composed herself as Patrick collected up her bags. 'You all take care now,' she said. 'I'll be seeing you.' She wouldn't be – not any time soon, at least – but no one had the heart to make a joke.

The whistle blew for embarkation, and Bea's family took a step back as she and Patrick headed towards the gangplank.

'Good luck, Bea!' came a muffled cry from far at the back of the crowd. Bea turned to see Millicent running towards the boat, darting through the crowd like a gecko running on hot sand.

Bea tried to turn back, to run down to see Millicent one last time, but the porter standing behind her blocked her path. She craned her neck past the porter, waving at Millicent. 'Please, sir, I must say goodbye to my sister.'

He shook his head, pointing towards the deck. 'We're already going to be late setting off at this rate. You'll have to wave from the deck, along with the others. Move along, miss.'

Bea felt Patrick's hand take hers, and she found herself being carried along the current of other travellers towards the top deck. She leant over the bow of the ship, waving both arms above her head. Millicent was standing with her parents and Bette, waving a bright orange handkerchief above her head. The wind whipped away Millicent's words, so Bea couldn't hear what she was saying, but she could see her big sister's lips moving and knew they were words of kindness.

She mouthed back that she loved her, and after a final wave to the shore peppered with Bells, Bea felt the wind whoosh past her hair as they set sail for the Mother Country.

Without realising she had started, Beatrice cried until the shoreline became nothing more than a speck on the horizon's edge. She clutched the envelope stuffed with banknotes that her mother had given her, and prayed she wouldn't need to use it.

NOTE INSIDE ENVELOPE

Dear Beatrice,

We truly wish you all the best for this adventure, and hope your marriage brings you great happiness and prosperity. If it doesn't work out, you can always return home. We'll be here.

Love,

Mom

2015

THURSDAY

No matter how fast moonlight runs, daylight catches up –
West Indian proverb

'Only me,' called Amelia, pushing the front door open with her shoulder and hauling both bags of shopping into the kitchen's cool shade. She took a moment to catch her breath and ease out the tension in her knees, casting her eyes back across the yard.

Built into the side of the hill, stilts propping up the front of the once-white house, pale green shutters opened out to views Amelia could sketch from memory. The modest front lawn never needed a fence to mark the boundary, thanks to the soursop and grapefruit trees swaying overhead, with roofs of the houses lower down the hill forming terracotta stepping stones leading out towards the sea. Its bright stretch of blue glittered towards the horizon, always reminding Amelia of the time she'd asked her father, back when she was a little girl, if he'd ever thrown a pebble from their porch so far out to sea it had dropped off the edge of the world.

Now, the white paint peeled in patches, and her father's roof was in desperate need of new tiles. The steep steps up to the front door never got easier, either. She turned her back to the view, her heart aching at the sight of the FOR SALE sign she'd hammered into the lawn a few weeks previously. With every hit she'd levelled at the sign – erecting it herself, having saved fifty dollars – she'd expected a sense of release, even closure. But the sign had just hammered right back at her, reminding her it was almost time her childhood home would become someone else's.

The estate agent had promised a sale within days: *prime location, excellent holiday home potential, overseas buyers desperate to snap up real estate like this.* But every email had been deleted, Amelia's buyer checklist refusing a viewing to anyone considering their family home as a holiday hideaway. Or worse, as somewhere to rent to partygoers who treated the island as one big resort for their personal entertainment. Memories sang from each dent on the floorboards, each dripping tap or broken shutter, ghosts of late-night conversations and early-morning arguments whispering from every corner.

Amelia had made her conditions for sale quite clear to the green-eyed estate agent: locals only, preferably families. *This house has seen three generations, and it's not about to become some playboy's bolthole,* she'd barked at the salesman. He'd switched to texts shortly after that.

Checking her phone, pausing on the porch while her breathing returned to normal, Amelia swiftly deleted another two messages which opened with the request that she 'keep an open mind'.

She wiped her brow with the back of her hand, the heat of the afternoon drawing beads of sweat from her hairline and threatening to cloud her eyes. A misty haze was descending over the garden, and Amelia groaned at the thought of a storm brewing. She'd warned her out-of-town family that August was a terrible month to visit – let alone that she was moving her father in with her, and did she mention her daughter was expecting? – but they'd insisted on arranging a holiday for that week. Something to do with school terms and flight prices, which she hadn't been able to argue with.

And so Amelia found herself with five missed calls from a distant aunt, three unpacked suitcases for her father, two unread emails from caterers with the subject line 'dietary requirements – urgent', and a copy of *What to Expect When You're Expecting* still on her car's back seat six months after her daughter had announced her news.

'Pop?' Amelia called again, softer this time, as she bustled the shopping into the kitchen. She placed both bags on the counter, sweeping the pile of unread mail into her handbag in one smooth motion. Her father's lone name waved at her from the front of each envelope, the lack of her mother's initials beside his still causing the back of Amelia's throat to constrict. She shook herself down, massaging her temples for a brief moment. Her books on grieving had warned her it would hit even years after, but it still felt fresh every time.

To distract herself, she cocked her ear to listen out for her father's response to her earlier greeting, and could just about make out a muffled snore from upstairs. Satisfied, she set about pulling open the blinds and letting early evening sunlight flood the spacious, wood-panelled kitchen-diner.

Before pulling out the pressure cooker for their evening meal of lambie souse – juicy lambie still in their conch shells, Scotch bonnets, sweet peppers, garlic, onions, limes and leafy chadon beni – she reached into her back pocket to check her phone again. Maryse had said she'd be here by now, but her daughter had never been famed for her punctuality.

Amelia's daughter was often a little late, a habit that she'd grown into in her teenage years and seemed to solidify while Maryse had been away at college. Amelia shook her head, a sigh escaping.

House clearance coming at midday sharp tomorrow. Anything we don't pack, they're throwing out! You on your way?

Just as Amelia pressed *send* – taking a moment to click on her daughter's profile picture, showing the two of them waving at the peak of Sugarloaf Mountain – a number flashed up on the screen.

'Barkley, hi,' she said, her brother's return greeting landing heavily through the earpiece. She winced; he always spoke way too loudly over the phone. 'You'd better not be calling to cancel.'

'Not exactly—'

'For God's sake, Barkley! We've been planning this reunion for months. There are relatives flying internationally, and I am sure as hell not facing them all alone.' Amelia placed the phone into the crook of her neck, reaching to pull out the pressure cooker and grab a chopping board. She grimaced at the picture she made:

bent over the cooker with a to-do list the length of her daughter's beautifully braided hair, all while her little brother strolled through a faraway city on his way to a fancy preflight dinner. His biggest worry was probably the stains he'd get on his new suede shoes on the subway. How did the youngest in the family always get away with it? 'Do you remember second cousin Patience?' Amelia couldn't help but add. 'She spent all of last Christmas telling me about her bunions! In such detail I could pick them out of a line-up!'

Barkley's oak-barrel laugh echoed through the phone and Amelia instantly softened. She wished she could stay mad at him. 'I said I was sorry at the time. I couldn't get out of a Christmas at Aidan's, but I did miss you and Maryse. Can you put her on?'

Amelia switched the phone to loudspeaker and placed it on the counter, filling a bowl of cold water to soak the lambie. She placed the garlic and pepper on the chopping board, roughly chopping off the ends. 'Maryse isn't here yet. Did she send you her latest ultrasound picture? The baby looks like it's waving at us.'

'She did. Aidan is obsessed. You know he wanted to print it out and put it on the fridge?'

Amelia cackled, her knife slicing through the ingredients in a well-rehearsed chop. 'You absolutely cannot, that's so strange. Any guests to yours would think you'd cracked and hired a surrogate.'

'We are quite all right with the dogs, but thank you.' Amelia kept her opinion on keeping two dogs in a loft apartment to herself as her brother paused. She could hear his husband speaking just out of range.

'Is Aidan there with you? Ask him if he's bringing the puzzle I lent him when you guys were last here. I've promised it to a family at work.'

'That's the thing...' Barkley hesitated, and Amelia's skin prickled with irritation. 'I've been called in to surgery, so we'll miss our flight tonight. Don't shout at me,' he added hastily as Amelia drew a sharp breath. The knife clattered onto the chopping board, narrowly missing her finger. 'I've looked online and we can get an early flight over so we arrive the day after tomorrow. I'll bring loads of duty-free liquor to make up for it.'

'Barkley, you promised—'

'I know, but I can't help if I have to work. We'll be there as soon as we can.'

Amelia rubbed her temples with her free hand. She felt guilty for the frustration that now coursed through her. This had happened so many times, she should be used to it by now. 'Fine. Text me when you set off.'

'I will.'

They said goodbye and Amelia hung up, wishing she were allowed to tell her little brother off, like she used to when they were growing up.

Before she could type out a passive-aggressive message about how his work always seemed to drag him away from family events, Maryse's muffled voice called through the screen door. 'Ma? Can you come give me a hand with this, please?'

Amelia threw the washed lambie, chopped garlic and peppers into the pressure cooker and switched it on. She'd make the sauce later.

Maryse was leaning against the door handle, half in and half out of the kitchen. Salt water still glistened on her skin after her afternoon shift, with sand just visible beneath her fingernails.

Amelia glowed with pride when she thought of her daughter's success as the hotel's lead tour guide at just 25, using the language skills she'd gained at university to charm visitors from French- and Spanish- and English-speaking nations. Amelia had been worried when Maryse had chosen to study languages that the wide world would snatch her little girl away from her. But after a few months abroad, Maryse had come floating back to their island.

'What's all this?' Amelia moved to open the door and ushered Maryse through, collecting up the dozen or so shopping bags looped over her daughter's arms.

'Party bags.' Maryse's eyes sparkled as she straightened up and placed the bags heavily onto the kitchen table. She started opening the brightly coloured gift bags and pulled out a mini bottle of

Westinghall rum, a sleek bar of dark chocolate, Spice Isle Hotel and Spa notepad and matching pen set. 'We had loads left over from a corporate event at work, so I thought we could give some gifts at the family party.'

Amelia picked up the bar of chocolate, its gold wrapper reminding her of a childhood story. 'Do work know you've taken these?'

'Of course! It was Cedella's idea. I've been telling her for weeks how stressed you've been organising everything for the reunion, and sorting Grandpa's move. I was hoping she'd give us a free spa day, but she just gave me these when I was leaving earlier. That's why I'm late.'

Amelia managed an 'Mm-hmm', an eyebrow arched in response. Maryse was definitely late because she'd been gossiping with Cedella or taking one last dip before heading over to her grandfather's, but Amelia decided to let it slide. She knew she had a tendency to be too soft on the girl – having to be both father and mother to Maryse – but she couldn't help it. Amelia could never resist sharing a secret or a piece of gossip with her daughter, something she wished her own mother had done more of with her when she was alive.

Maryse surveyed the kitchen. 'Grandpa not home from his walk yet?'

'I think he's resting upstairs. I'm sure I heard him when I came in.' Amelia sighed, placing the chocolate back into the gift bag. 'I'll give him another five minutes before we wake him. We've got to get everything packed up today, or we'll never move him in before the weekend.'

'Shall we just get started without him? We know he just needs to pack up the last of his things in Grandma's old dressing room, and he'd probably rather not go in.'

'That's true.' Amelia reached over, giving Maryse's shoulder a squeeze. 'When did you get to be so smart?'

Maryse shrugged. 'Probably got it from my father.' Her eyes glinted with mischief, and she narrowly avoided a swipe from her mother.

'Got your attitude from him, too, I'll say.'

'Nope.' Maryse stood up, jutting out her hip. 'That's all you, I'm afraid.'

'Agree to disagree.' Amelia slapped her hands on the kitchen table, the cool wood making a satisfying thud. 'Come on, then, let's get on with it. We'll wake Grandpa later.'

The two of them walked upstairs to the old dressing room, which had once been Amelia's bedroom and then Maryse's play-room for the years before they'd moved into a home of their own. Amelia could swear her mother's perfume still floated on the air – a floral jasmine echo reverberating through the room. The scent-memory caught Amelia behind the eyes, and she took a second to steady herself. She looked over at her misty-eyed daughter as she headed for the wardrobe, and could tell she was feeling it, too.

'Oh, Ma, I can do this if you want. Why don't you go and wake Grandpa, and see if he wants a drink of something?'

'Thank you, love, but I'll be OK. It's good to be in here.'

The room hadn't changed since her mother had died two years ago, its whitewashed walls and pale wooden floorboards still creak-ing and cracking in all the same places. Amelia kept meaning to fix it, but hadn't managed to find the time. 'And besides, I can't leave you to do the heavy lifting. It's just this last shelf I need to clear in here.'

She gestured to the wardrobe, and asked Maryse to fetch the dressing table chair. 'Hold it steady while I reach in the back.'

'What's back there?'

'Just old clothes, I think,' came Amelia's muffled reply. She threw down some old shirts and scarves, her fingers grasping at scraps of cotton and crêpe de Chine. 'I want to give this wardrobe away while we have the movers, so I need to completely empty it. I have a family we've just placed in a new home, but they're sharing a wardrobe between eight of them. I said we had one spare, and Grandpa said he wanted it to go to a good home.'

'The family with the triplets?'

'No.' Amelia was impressed Maryse could still hear her; she felt one more stretch would send her toppling into Narnia. 'Although I did give them the old bunk beds. It's the family whose private landlord refused to sort the sinkhole problem out back.' Even without an audience, Amelia shook her head at the thought. She loved her work for the housing and family department in the council building overlooking the harbour; enjoyed sitting at her poky desk strewn with pictures of the families she'd helped over the years. She just hated the things she discovered about human nature, mostly through the tricksy landlords and two-timing husbands after whom she had to pick up the pieces.

'I think that's everything,' Amelia called behind her. As she shifted to try to face Maryse, she felt her foot slip from beneath her. To stay balanced, she threw both hands out in front, expecting them to slam against the back of the wardrobe.

Instead, her left hand jammed against a hard, heavy shape.

'Ma! Are you OK?'

'Fine,' Amelia replied, winding her wrist in a circular motion. She withdrew, but then reached her fingertips to clasp at the shape she'd discovered. She yanked it out, feeling Maryse steady the chair beneath her feet.

In her hands lay a large wooden chest, coated in thick dust. Amelia stumbled as she stepped down from the chair, placing the chest on the dressing table.

Amelia brushed away some of the dust, revealing ornate twists carved into the sides of the chest. The design gave the old wood a belt of detail cutting through its middle. A padlock held the lid down, but it fell to one side, unlatched.

'What's this?' Maryse asked, her voice soft with intrigue. Amelia shook her head, taking a step back to survey it properly.

The chest sat in the centre of her mother's dressing table, framed by the dust-coated mirror behind. 'I have no idea,' she said.

Amelia caught her reflection, seeing her confused expression beside Maryse's open-eyed look of wonder. Maryse's long braids were so elegant beside Amelia's close-cropped curls, their reflections only just visible through the thick coating of dust on the mirror.

The dust annoyed Amelia. She'd meant to have a word with the cleaner; she'd noticed a few things were dropping off. Anger sparked like static as she ran her finger along the dressing table's lacquered top, finding a thin layer of dust there, too. Just because her father was old and a little confused, he still deserved a clean house.

'Well, shall we open it?' Maryse peered over her mother's shoulder, her hand resting absent-mindedly on her belly.

Amelia looked back down at the chest, making a mental note to call the cleaners on her way to her meeting with the party caterers the next day. She should probably have made a physical note, but had left her notepad downstairs and didn't trust that she'd remember to look at her phone again.

'I don't know what this could be.' Amelia sat down at the dressing table, her fingers tracing the chest's outline.

'How exciting!' Maryse cried. 'What if it's jewellery?'

Amelia gave Maryse a sideways look. 'I wouldn't get your hopes up.'

'One day I'll discover a secret family fortune,' Maryse said with a dramatic sigh. 'Or win the lottery.'

Amelia laughed. 'Maybe don't quit your day job just yet.' She turned her attention back to the box in front of her, her curiosity piqued. The chestnut box looked as though it had once been expensive – precious, even. It had a tired shine to it despite the dust. 'Besides, I'm pretty sure I have all Mom's jewellery.' She peered at it more closely, as though its contents would announce themselves to her if she stared hard enough. 'I haven't seen this before.' She took the broken lock in between forefinger and thumb, twisting the clasp to let it fall open. The lock snapped, falling in two pieces onto the tabletop. The noise made Amelia jerk her head up, locking eyes with her own reflection again. Unease knotted its way up her back, as though she'd overheard something not meant for her ears.

Amelia reached out to open the lid, but stopped short.

'Ma? You OK?' Maryse shuffled around to lean against the table, her back to the mirror, one hand on the lid. 'I'm sure it's nothing important, or Grandma would've told us about it when we were sorting her will.' Maryse's voice softened. 'I was only joking about the jewellery. It's probably some old clothes, or hats, or hairpins.'

Amelia sat back. She knew Maryse was right, but the idea of finding something of her mother's that she hadn't seen before – and couldn't ask her about, no matter how small – caused her chest to tighten in the all-too-familiar clutches of grief.

'You're right, it's probably nothing,' she said eventually, rolling back her shoulders. 'And we need to get on.'

Amelia took a deep breath and prised open the lid, unease still tapping along the length of her spine. She tilted her head and looked inside.

Staring back up at her were sheets upon sheets of writing paper, thin and curling at the edges like leaves in need of water. Pencilled and inked handwriting darted its way across the pages, some faded and mostly scrawled, in part obscured by face-up picture postcards. Ink-blotted newspaper articles lay folded along one side on paper so thin it looked as though it may tear just by glancing at it, and tiny blue cards announcing themselves as *telegrams* propped up the outer edges.

Amelia's breathing quickened, a smell similar to old library shelves filling her nostrils. A scrap of faded, monogrammed material lay tucked beneath a fluttering of letters, and she moved it aside to discover more.

Too many names ran from page to page, unfamiliar faces beaming up at her from the postcards' frozen images. *Wish you were here! Thinking of you! Greetings from ...* The box seemed to call out to Amelia, faraway voices filling her ears.

'This is amazing,' Maryse said. Amelia hadn't noticed Maryse reaching over her, but before she could say anything, her daughter's hands were riffling through, unsettling what must have been decades of grime and memory.

Amelia had no idea how Maryse could look so unfazed, so at ease, reaching into this graveyard to a time long lost. Maryse reached to pick up the material – a handkerchief? – but Amelia's hand rested on hers mid-motion.

'We should mind our business.'

'Really? If Grandma wanted this gone ...' Maryse trailed off, evidently remembering her grandmother's strict instructions to donate or recycle everything that could go when she knew her time was drawing to a close. 'Do you think she meant for you to find it?'

Amelia frowned: her mother had never seemed the type for hidden messages or mystery. 'There's no note or anything. You'd think she'd leave us a letter if she intended for us to find ... whatever this is.' Amelia glanced back into the box, noting the signatures across postcards and letters and telegrams.

A photograph caught her eye, and she couldn't help but retrieve it. Smiling back up at her were her parents, standing in front of church steps. *How beautiful they were.* 'Oh, look at that dress!' Maryse exclaimed, bending forward to get a better look. 'So this must be Grandma's memory box, or something.'

Amelia felt sick, grief snaking its arms around her waist for just a second. Here was her mother, able to speak to her once more through letters and postcards and pictures. Raw emotion tightened its grip on Amelia's body as she pictured her mother's hands packing away each artefact, folding up pieces of her history and diligently jotting down names on the backs of photographs. Even with all that her mother had achieved over the years, at heart she had remained a girl clinging to the stories and letters of loved ones that rooted her home. But why keep it hidden from the ones she loved most?

Amelia blinked hard, willing herself not to cry. She couldn't let grief's cold grip pull her under, not with so much to be getting on with. 'If this is a memory box, we have no business prying.'

'It's not prying,' Maryse said decisively. 'This is our heritage.'

'I'm not so sure.' Amelia shook her head, noticing her hands were trembling. Concern pinched at Maryse's cheeks, and Amelia knew she needed to get a hold of herself.

'What's wrong?' Maryse asked again.

'I'm fine. It is just a shock, to see Mom's handwriting and a new picture after all this time.'

'Of course it is,' Maryse agreed, turning the photo over in her hands to read the inscription on the reverse. *Our wedding day.* 'I wish I could've known her when she was younger, don't you?' Maryse began tracing her fingertips along each beaming face in the wedding photo. 'She was so cool.'

'She really was.' Amelia sniffed, putting the lid back on the box. 'Why don't we put it away, and worry about this after Grandpa's moved in? And this big reunion is out the way.'

'Good idea. Can I keep this, though?' Maryse asked, gesturing to the photo she still held. 'I might show it to Tommy, start putting the pressure on.'

Amelia rolled her eyes, pushing down on her knees to stand. 'One thing at a time, child. You have a baby to bring into the world.' *And the last thing we need right now is a wedding to plan.* Amelia surveyed the space around her, rooting herself back into the present.

This room was supposed to be cleaned and ready to host some distant family members, but with her father's decline she'd asked the families to book into hotels at the last minute. With Maryse's family and friends discount at the Spice Isle, this hadn't caused too much offence. Amelia knew the neighbours would judge her for not putting up her family herself, but between getting her father settled with her and starting to baby-proof the house, there was no more space or hours in the day to consider relatives she hadn't seen in years.

At the thought of all she still had to do – visit the caterers, talk timings with the venue, confirm the removal van for her father's house, finish the stacks of paperwork on her desk – Amelia felt a helpless anger that her mother wasn't there to lend a hand. So many sympathy cards drawled on about friends and family being *there if you need us*, but no one could be there for her the way her mother had been. No sympathetic messages, however well meaning, could undo the drowning sensation that overwhelmed Amelia every time she reached to dial her mother's number, only to remember why there would be no answer.

Amelia moved to pick up the box and swallowed a wave of

sadness, her eyes scanning the room for where to stash it away. *Out of sight, out of mind*, as her mother had often said.

She felt her cheeks flush as she reached to close the box, a sensation close to shame tapping at her shoulder. Her mother clearly hadn't wanted her to see this, or she would have said something. Yet Amelia couldn't help but feel it might hold years – decades – of correspondence, a way to hear from her mother one more time.

Her mother had always valued telling the truth, but whether or not she'd always been entirely honest was a different matter. Amelia knew herself that truth and honesty weren't the same thing: she'd been able to say 'I love you' to a man, while at the same time knowing 'I don't want you to be my future'. The two things were both true, but only one was honest.

And if Amelia was being honest, she was done second-guessing her own past.

'You know what – maybe we could take a look,' Amelia finally said, 'just to see what Mom thought was worth keeping?'

'Yes!' Maryse's face lit up. 'I bet there's loads of old-school names I can get inspiration from, too, if there are letters from old family and friends. Vintage names are all coming back around now. We've had two Dorothys under four in the kids' club at work recently.'

'I thought you were settled on Bianca for a girl? Or Stewie for a boy?'

Maryse shrugged. 'I was, but I like to have options. It might be nice to choose a name after family.'

A warmth spread through Amelia's chest. 'Whatever you choose will be beautiful.'

'I hope so.' Maryse motioned back to the box, her eyes gleaming. 'Shall we take a look, then? See what's inside?'

Amelia nodded. 'Let's do it.'

Amelia picked up the box and carried it to the double bed, her back protesting yet again. Maryse joined her, propping herself up against the pillows. She pulled her long legs up onto the bed, tucking them under herself, and watched expectantly as Amelia lifted the lid once more.

'Meli?'

Amelia and Maryse jumped in sync, Amelia's head turning sharply to the doorway at the sound of her childhood nickname. Her father leant against the door frame with one hand, his brow furrowed in anguish.

'Sorry, Pop, did we wake you?' Amelia asked, rising so quickly she almost tripped on her way to her father's side. It pained her to see him this way, his broad shoulders drooping and thick lines etched across his skin. Threadbare pyjamas were his loungewear of choice these days, something he would have chortled at when he was fully himself. Amelia could swear she hadn't seen him out of a shirt and tie her whole childhood, the tie loosening whenever it was time to kick a ball around the garden with her and Barkley. They'd joked he'd wear a three-piece in the sea if he could find a waterproof suit.

Sometimes, his spark would come back and he'd want to go flying kites or jump over waves at Grande Anse. How cruel an illness was to offer him half-memories; he was either his old self but trapped in this ageing body, or a ghost before his time. Amelia could never decide which was worse. So she just said *yes* to his requests, held his hand in hers while she let the line spool from her fingers and watch the kite soar in summer winds, pretending she couldn't hear when he asked her where her mother was.

'How about a crossword, Grandpa?' Maryse asked, appearing beside Amelia at a speed impressive for someone in their second trimester. 'I could always use your help. Today's is a tough one.'

After a second he nodded, reaching to take Maryse's outstretched arm. Amelia exhaled: he was OK. He knew where he was, who he was.

Maryse turned back, her eyes wide as she cocked her head towards the box. But Amelia had had enough surprises for one day. Exhaustion washed over her. Instead, she stuffed the box under the bed and headed into her father's bedroom to finish packing, her eyes landing on the three empty suitcases lying on their sides like hollowed-out fruit.

Is Barkley really working tonight? Be honest with me.
... Aidan Davies is typing

Aidan?

Aidan Davies is offline.

Amelia huffed; the last of her father's favourite outfits was stashed away in the final suitcase beneath as many paperbacks as she could stuff inside the case. She sat back on her father's bed, allowing herself a second to close her eyes. It was a dangerous game, but exhaustion was slowly wrapping its arms around her midriff and making its way up to her shoulders.

Her phone buzzed: her eyes flew open.

He is

. . .

But I don't know if he was called in or if he volunteered for the shift

. . .

Come on, you know what it's like for him to go back.

Amelia's fingers hovered over the virtual keypad. *But he promised* felt whiney and childish; *But he always loves it once he's back here* seemed too dismissive, as she'd learnt from previous conversations.

Her brother's life in New York felt freezingly far away at times, and was one of the few things that ever caused tension between them. She understood why he'd had to leave, yet she couldn't help hoping that one day he would return for good. Things were improving a little on the island, after all; she went to the marches, signed the petitions and even tried to use her position in the council to lobby for a change in the law against homosexuality. She planned to keep going, and knew she wouldn't give up until her brother could finally come home. She refused to believe he didn't want to, deep down.

Contrary to the statistics declaring that adopted siblings were whatever per cent more likely to drift apart, particularly in adult-hood, she and Barkley had stayed firm friends long after their days of exploring rock pools and grazing their knees playing street cricket.

Amelia had met a couple of others who'd been adopted as children, and always found it strange that their fantasy had been their birth parents coming to get them. To her, it had been her biggest fear.

She vividly remembered the morning she'd run back from school in floods of tears, after an older girl had teased her that she would be sent back now that Barkley had arrived. *They're replacing you, don't you know. They'll send you back to wherever you came from.* Amelia's mother had held her close before kneeling down to face her, brushing Amelia's curls from her face. Her mother's scent of jasmine and cooking spices tinged the memory, the weight and warmth of her mother's fingertips on her cheek a visceral reality. *Now you listen to me,* she'd said. *You are right where you're supposed to be, and you are not going anywhere. You and Barkley belong to us and to each other, and that's all there is to it.* Her mother had marched to the school, and the older girl had apologised soon after. Amelia had returned to this memory time and time again whenever she felt cast adrift, using it to anchor herself back upon these shores.

How Barkley could choose to go so far from their island, to somewhere so cold and overgrown with buildings and train lines and people, was beyond Amelia. She knew he faced hardship on the islands just for being who he was, but he always seemed so vibrant when he came back to the West Indies. She wished he could be here, marching beside her, signing his name beneath hers to bring the island into the twenty-first century. Amelia always felt ashamed to admit it, but she also wished he could be here to help with their parents and support Maryse as she entered the adult world. Yes, Amelia wanted society to welcome him with open arms, but was it so terrible to admit that she also wished he could be around to shoulder some of the familial burden? From New York, he could just about remember to send flowers that quickly wilted in the heat.

At least his move had brought her Aidan: the kind of brother-in-law who remembered birthdays and sent gifts for work events you didn't even think you'd told him about.

> Just remind him he promised he'd come, please?

I will.

> Thanks, A.

She paused, before adding:

> I really need the extra help before the relatives all start arriving.
> So much still to do.

How many days before they get there?

> Three. Most are coming next Tuesday, but the keen ones arrive Sun.

Damn. You and Maryse got your work cut out. I'll speak to B, don't worry.

> Thank you. Have you booked your flights already, or just getting them at the airport tomorrow night?

... Aidan Davies is typing.
Aidan Davies is offline. Last seen 18:21.

Amelia let her head flop back, her phone dropping onto the bed sheets. She was about to bring up her legs to lie down for a second, to let sleep whisk her away for just a few blissful minutes, but the sound of the kettle whistling in the kitchen broke through the settling silence. It had been a gift from an England-dwelling relative a few years ago, and her father had become part man, part tea ever since. She heaved herself to her feet and bent forward to zip each suitcase closed.

'Tea, Amelia?' called her father, his voice warm and inviting. She checked the time again, lifting each bulging suitcase so it stood to attention. She'd leave them there, and strip the bed as the last thing before house clearance arrived the next day. She nodded to herself: at least one more task checked off the ever-growing list.

'Supper's almost ready,' Maryse said as Amelia entered the

kitchen. Steam already clouded the room, the lightly spiced scent of her father's ginger tea mingling with the fiery peppers and salt water lambie. Amelia's father settled himself at the table, the crossword spread out across the worn wooden top.

'Thank you, love. I'll do the—'

'No, no, you sit yourself down.' Maryse waved her hand towards the table, picking a knife from the block to begin slicing into chadon beni and more hot peppers. 'You need a break.' She'd lined up the vegetables in height order beside the chopping board, just as Amelia always did. It was one of those tableaux that brought a surprised smile to Amelia's lips: *When did my baby get so grown?*

She knew some of her friends were curious – jealous, even – how she and Maryse had stayed so close. Girls were supposed to despise their mothers as teenagers and young adults, but Maryse and Amelia had kept to their strictly beloved routines: dawn sea swims every New Year's Day; Sunday afternoon hikes; Friday nights spent bent over a barbecue with cool lemonade – or weak beer, once Maryse got older – as friends drifted in and out of the frame.

When Amelia had finally saved enough from her government job to take Maryse abroad, they'd visited Barkley up in New York. She'd expected the trip of a lifetime, but they'd arrived to dirty sidewalks and shouting strangers, rattling trains and nothing but concrete buildings in places they'd been promised a 'view'. *'Ma,' Maryse had asked, tugging at Amelia's coat hem, 'why is the sea that yucky colour?'*

Barkley had insisted they'd love the city by the time their springtime fortnight was up, and embarked upon a movie-worthy 'I heart NY' montage: hot dogs from street vendors in Central Park, all three of them licking ketchup and mustard from their fingertips; window shopping in Fifth Avenue, Aidan joining them to lift Maryse high up so she could see past the mannequins; dollar slices of pizza with extra cheese in Times Square; trips to the Natural History Museum, where Maryse insisted on spending three hours running between exhibits; dancing to buskers at the Union Square subway station; walking along the Brooklyn Bridge at sunset until Maryse got tired, and Barkley carried her all the way home. By the time they boarded their return flight, Amelia could just about understand the hold the city had on her brother: it gave you a sense that you were surviving something, that you lived at the world's edge.

They'd returned to the city throughout Maryse's childhood and teenage years, graduating from the airbed on Barkley's Brooklyn studio floor through to the guest room in his and Aidan's Upper West Side loft. The magic of the city rubbed off on Amelia a little more each time, and yet the second she heard her final boarding call at JFK Airport, peaceful relief always flooded through her.

'How much longer do the lambies need?'

Amelia checked the kitchen clock. With a start, she noticed it had stopped: another job to add to her list. She checked her phone instead, ignoring the notifications flashing up at her. 'Only another five minutes or so.' She stretched and stood up, her limbs having stiffened a little. 'Here, let me take over.'

Amelia bustled past her daughter, who was busy stuffing the chadon beni and peppers into the blender. It was a squeeze with two of them at the kitchen counter, the food preparation area always having been Amelia's mother's lone domain.

As Amelia released the valve on the pressure cooker, Maryse reached over her to grab a leftover slice of lime. She tore off the skin, and popped the slice in her mouth as though it was a fresh clementine.

'Maryse!'

'Eh?' Maryse chomped the lime, a satisfied smile spreading across her face. 'That's better.'

'Are you trying to give yourself acid reflux?'

Maryse laughed. 'I've been craving limes like there's no to-morrow. It's been getting worse in the last couple of weeks.' She reached for the last slice, and Amelia resisted the urge to swat her hand from picking before dinner. 'Tommy's stocked our shelf of the fridge full of them. And you know they make lime juice? Not cordial – I mean juice in a carton. Like orange or grapefruit. He bought it online.'

Amelia frowned, lifting the lid to check the lambies. 'Maybe don't drink something you found on the internet.'

'Oh, Mom, you worry too much. Amazon wouldn't poison me.'

'You never know.'

Maryse grinned and popped the second segment in her mouth, dropping the rind in the bin. She began to collect plates from the cupboards as Amelia finished the final preparations.

'Did you crave anything with me?' Maryse asked as they sat at the table.

Amelia folded up her father's newspaper, replacing it with a steaming bowl of souse. They should have left it to marinate for a while longer, but as usual, there weren't enough hours in the day.

'I did. God, that's going back a way.' Amelia sat down, tucking into her own bowl. It lacked the flavour it would have had with longer, but the saltiness and peppery heat reminded her what the meal was supposed to taste like. 'For me it was hot sauce. I had it on everything, even kept a bottle in my handbag and in my desk at work. Put it on chocolate, cereal, everything.' Amelia leant forward, propping her elbows on the table. 'Barkley sent me a hot sauce invented by some crazy Californian that Christmas – best gift he ever got me. We'll have to ask him to bring some over this weekend.'

Maryse laughed, her beautiful brown eyes crinkling. She swished her braids behind her, leaning back so far in her chair Amelia worried it would snap. 'I bet Tommy would prefer I was after hot sauce, he loves it. Limes make his tongue feel fat, apparently.' Maryse's eyes glinted as she took another mouthful. 'All the more for me, I say.'

'What do you think, Pop?' Amelia asked, turning slightly to face her father. 'Would you rather a fridge full of limes, or one full of hot sauce?'

He cocked his head, steepling his fingers before him in the thoughtful way he'd done since Amelia could remember. 'I think neither.' He leant forward, gesturing for them both to follow suit. After a beat, he added, 'A fridge full of chocolate is far more my speed.'

Amelia caught Maryse's eye and laughed, knowing she felt the same gratitude for a Good Day. Her father grinned, satisfaction at having made them both laugh written across his face.

Amelia tucked into her food, avoiding the empty chair at the end of the table as best she could. Maryse began regaling her grandfather with a story from that morning's tour: something about an English family who'd asked if they could snorkel without getting their blow-dries ruined.

Amelia let herself drift from the conversation, her mind homing back in on the box she'd found upstairs. She didn't have time to start rifling through her mother's old correspondence; she knew that. But something nagged at her, the names and addresses and newspaper headlines coaxing her to go back. A voice she thought she'd silenced was whispering in her ear; a ghostly past self reaching out to poke her in the ribs. With her father moving in and her daughter's due date marching towards her, Amelia wondered whether it was finally time to let herself wonder: *How did I get here?*

'When you were pregnant, did you ever wonder what your birth mother craved? Or, what she was like?' Maryse reached for another dish, drying it on the tea towel she'd brought back from a holiday to Cuba. The writing was long-since faded, but the outline of Havana still traced its way along the white cotton.

Amelia leant back against the sink, bringing her hands out of the soapy water. Her fingers were wrinkled, the way they were whenever she and Maryse got out from the sea after an early-morning swim, and she turned her hands back and forth for a second. They were becoming more wrinkled these days, like an old lady's hands.

After they'd finished eating and got her father settled in front of the seven o'clock news, she'd drafted an email to the house movers, instructing them not to clear the box from under the bed in the spare room. She still had so many more to answer, from caterers, servers, hotel staff, relatives, doctors' offices trying to arrange appointments for three-and-a-half generations. She wished she'd never put emails on her phone: she was tempted to drop it right into the washing-up bowl, where it could take its chances beside the spoons and glassware.

'Ma?'

'Sorry, love. I don't think of her much, really. Why do you ask?'

'Seeing Tommy getting ready for the baby, getting all excited when he finds the baby books on special offer or watching YouTube to learn how to change a nappy or build a crib...' Maryse trailed off. 'I hope you don't mind me saying, but it's got me thinking about my dad. Like, I know he was a deadbeat and we've never needed him or anything.' Her eyeline dropped, her hands fidgeting with the glass she was drying. 'But why didn't he want to stay?'

'Oh, baby.' Amelia's heart sank, and she reached out to squeeze Maryse's shoulder. It left a soapy mark on Maryse's T-shirt, bubbles popping. 'That man was only ever good for one thing, and that was bringing you into the world. He barely stayed for the first sonogram, just carried on with his bullshit worldwide Eat Pray Love trip.'

'Do you know where he is now?'

'Last I heard he was living with a woman somewhere back in the States. That was years ago, though.' Amelia was proud for rarely having googled Maryse's father – a smarmy Midwestern American who'd come to Grenada to find himself. Instead, he'd found her. They'd had a movie-esque romance, running around the island and exploring every cave, every waterfall, every grain of sand. From the start she'd known it wouldn't last, but she'd been in her twenties and prone to conflating newness with love. When she'd discovered in his last week that she was pregnant, it had felt like fate. *So that's what it was all for.*

Amelia pulled back, holding Maryse's elbows. 'I can help you find him, if that's what you'd like?'

Maryse shook her head so violently it seemed it might spin all the way around. 'No, that's not what I mean. I guess I just wanted to know if you felt it, too.'

'Felt what?'

'I don't really know. Curiosity?' Maryse placed the last glass in the cupboard and stood back, wiping her hands on her jeans. 'Not like you're missing out on anything, but like … there's a spare space in a photo album you'd like to fill before you start a new one.' Maryse seemed pleased with this comparison, and straightened up. 'You know, before you close the book.'

'Right.' Amelia considered this slightly convoluted metaphor, draining the water from the sink. Maryse moved towards the stairs and Amelia followed, the two of them heading back up to the spare room. 'I haven't really thought about my birth mother for a while,' Amelia said as they arrived on the landing.

This was, of course, a lie: since Amelia had lost her mother and discovered she'd soon become a grandmother herself, the ghost of the woman who'd given her life had started haunting her. Should Amelia be more curious than she was? Finally admit it would be interesting, if nothing else, to discover the truth? Should she find out, once and for all, whose genes her grandchild would hold?

But these worries weren't Maryse's concern; Maryse would soon learn that once you were someone's mother, you rarely told them the whole truth.

Amelia paused in the doorway, her eyes landing on the chest. *Reading those letters will make it all too real, too final.* She hesitated, turning to face Maryse. 'You know what? Let's leave it for today. We have enough on our plates.'

Maryse's face fell. 'Are you sure?'

Amelia nodded. 'Whatever's in those letters will still be there tomorrow, and the days after.'

'But—'

'I said leave it, Maryse.' Amelia hoped her daughter couldn't hear the shake in her voice. She turned around and headed back downstairs, relieved to see her father sitting comfortably in his favourite chair, with the framed photograph of Maryse's graduation behind him. This was her priority: she didn't have time to exhume the broken bones of her mother's history. *What's past is past, and that's all there is to it.*

'Fancy a game of dominoes, Pop?' Amelia asked, settling herself into the chair beside him.

PART TWO
England and Ireland, 1954

United Kingdom of Great Britain and Northern Ireland
/ Republic of Ireland. Sketch in pencil.
P. J. H Anderson, September 1954.

Chapter 13

Beatrice

12 Claverdale Road
Brixton
London

19th September 1954

Dear Bea,

I can't believe you're really coming to England! I'd so love to host you here at the boarding house. In fact, perhaps I can come for your wedding? Did you say it would be in Sussex? Send me a telegram when you know!

I do hope this letter reaches you before you make your own crossing to England, as I realise I didn't give you much practical advice in my last note. Bea, prepare yourself for a cold like you've never felt before. It tunnels right through your clothes, even your underwear will be freezing to the touch. I swear, when you use the bathroom in England, you can see steam rising up from the bowl! It is so funny, even in a bleak sort of way.

When you arrive, make sure you're extra polite to anyone you speak to. They can be a bit funny here about us 'darkies', as I've told you before, so we really have to watch our step.

But Bea, guess what? I've met someone who really looks out for me. His name's Gordon, he came over here as a teenager with his family from Jamaica. He was invited – well, a lot of them were – to take a ride on the SS Windrush and set up a whole life here. Did you know there was a ship dedicated to bringing lots of us over after the war to help rebuild? I can't believe I had *to get a cargo ship to come across! I love that name, Windrush. If I ever get a cat, that's what I'll call it.*

Anyway, this Gordon, he's been taking me out and we've started going to the pictures together on Saturday afternoons, a couple of dance halls of an evening. He's even shown me a couple of market stalls in Brixton with spices and the like so that we can have real flavour in our food again – I swear, you ask an English person what seasoning they've used and they say 'salt' as if that's a full sentence.

Good luck on your journey, and I do hope to see you soon. It sounds like your mind is made up that you're going ahead with this – so I can only say that I hope it all works out. Or if it doesn't, I hope it's a wild fun ride for you.

All my love,
Nella

The salty air of Southampton port slapped Bea's cheeks like an overexcited hound wagging its tongue for attention. She blinked in the sunlight, emerging to the sound of gulls squawking with such vigour that they sounded choked.

She blinked again, her eyes adjusting to the weak light of the port.

Colourless. That was the only way Bea felt she would be able to describe it: cold, flat, grey. Not just cold, but freezing, even in her warmest of jackets. Nella's letter – which had, by a stroke of luck, arrived the day before Bea's own trip across the sea – had not warned her well enough just how flavourless the whole land seemed to be.

In all the books she had read, the films she had seen, England was a bustling, bright, brilliant place, full of adventure and whimsy. She was expecting something superlative; if it was going to be dark, then she'd expected the deepest of the dark, the winding backstreets of Dickens' *Oliver Twist* or the howling gales crying across Emily Brontë's moors. At the very least, she'd expected the picturesque greenery of Hardy's county landscapes to form the backdrop to her grand entrance.

But instead of coldest and darkest, she realised that it was quite chilly, and fairly grey. Some of the people even looked grey; their pale skin was ashen as they hurried about their business, filling the pavements to capacity, not stopping to check their watches or to take in the day. *Where could everyone be rushing to on a day such as this?*

'Ready?' asked Patrick, his kind face bobbing into view. He held her suitcase in one hand and a heavy jacket in the other, which he draped around her shoulders. 'You'll need this,' he said. 'The weather's turned.'

'But what will you wear?'

Patrick shrugged. 'I'm a bit more used to it. We won't be out in the cold long, we can get a taxi from here straight to the station. From there, it's only one change to get to Surrey.' He seemed to stiffen at the thought of his parents' hometown. 'We'll arrive in no time.'

'And we should get there around the time they're expecting us?'

Patrick coughed. 'Mm-hmm. Sure they'll be ready and waiting, should have the fire lit so we can warm up.'

Bea wasn't sure she agreed: Patrick had confessed, on the boat over, that his parents had expressed reservations about the match. *They said they're concerned we're too different, but I think they're just angry I didn't consult them on the matter. They need to meet you, and then they'll love you,* he'd promised.

At the look on Patrick's face as they began their descent, Bea brushed off any creeping unease and attributed the sensation to the long journey. Of course his parents wouldn't be anything other than cordial to their only son and his soon-to-be wife; there was nothing to worry about. She just had to keep calm.

She thanked him for the jacket, pulling it tight around her shoulders and trying not to care that it clashed with the pale green skirt suit she'd worn for the occasion of her First Day in England. At least the jacket would help her blend in with these flavourless people.

'The taxi rank is just this way. You ready to go?' Patrick squeezed her arm, hastily kissing her cheek. 'If anything's overwhelming or you need a minute, just say. I know what it's like being new in a country. We can take it at whatever pace you need.'

She smiled, breathing out heavily. 'Thanks, Pat.'

'Any time. You'll be great,' he said, squeezing her arm.

Just as they descended the gangplank and headed towards the front taxi in the queue, a stout, sweaty man leapt out from the front seat of the car. 'Sorry, guv, can't take you.' He kept his eyes averted while he spoke, without even glancing in Bea's direction.

Bea felt as though she'd taken a punch to the gut. For a split second she considered grabbing Patrick's hand and running back to the boat, returning to the civilised shores of her homeland where people knew how to speak to a judge's daughter. Was this what Millie had meant, when she'd warned Bea she'd be stripped of the soft padding of privilege that had kept her warm all her life? Bea shuddered at the thought, the cold whipping through her jacket's thin material.

At the thought of her sister, Bea racked her brains for what either of her sisters would do in this situation. She channelled Bette's determination, Millie's self-righteousness. Taking a step forward, she ignored the nagging sense of danger creeping along her spine. *Don't let anyone accuse you of poor comportment*, her mother's voice said in her head. *You represent more than just yourself, you know.* Millie had been right: here she was, being judged before she'd even spoken.

She took a deep breath and gave Patrick's arm a light squeeze. 'Sir, we are paying customers,' she said to the taxi driver, as calmly as she could manage. 'I don't think you can retract your services when we are willing to pay the fair price in exchange for a ride.' This overweight, pasty man would not ruin her first day in the country she'd heard so much about, she was sure of it. Not after such a bleak introduction to the so-called seaside. 'Look at all these bags. We can't walk all the way to the station with these. We have to catch a train.' She enunciated that last sentence in slow, clipped sounds, just in case his English wasn't quite up to standard. The whole time that she had been speaking, he had looked as though he hadn't understood a word she had said. Despite the cold, the darkness in his eyes made her break out in a sweat.

'Look, love, just find someone else. I'm not driving you two, all right?'

Bea took another step towards him, as Patrick opened his mouth to object. 'Pat, don't worry, I will sort this out,' she stated, not letting her eyes leave the face of the charmless taxi driver. A purple vein was bulging from his forehead, his skin like tracing paper. 'I don't think you understand what I am saying, sir. I am not walking all the way to the station. My shoes have a heel, it's far too far to walk.' She picked up her bags, walking defiantly towards the car. Blood was pounding in her ears, but she kept her steps even, her voice level.

'You heard her. We'd best be off,' Patrick added, picking up the bulk of their luggage and placing it in the car's boot. 'Thank you kindly.'

The man looked as though he was going to protest, but before he could say anything else, Patrick helped Bea into the passenger seat and slid in beside her. She tried to hide her shaking hands, distracting herself by looking out the window as Patrick made idle chit-chat with the disgruntled driver. She reminded herself over and over that she had every right to be here, in her supposed Mother Country.

'What an introduction! Bea, I'm ever so sorry,' Patrick said, pulling her into a hug as soon as the driver had sped away.

Bea shook her head. 'He can't treat people that way, it's unseemly.' She kept her composure, remembering Nella's and Millicent's warnings. She'd prepared for this. 'Not everyone is going to be welcoming, but that's their loss. Someone else's ignorance is not my concern.'

'Too right,' Patrick said, kissing her cheek. 'I am sorry, though.'

'Don't be. It's not your fault.' Bea rolled back her shoulders and smiled up at him, hoping it would put them both at ease. If that was the worst she was going to face, maybe she'd be fine. She could already imagine how she'd spin it in a letter back home: *We had the funniest taxi driver pick us up in his cab, you wouldn't believe ...*

'Let's get you out of the cold, anyhow,' Patrick said as he linked his arm through hers, their bags slung over his shoulder. 'Come on, I'm starving. Let's get something to eat.'

They carried their bags into the railway station, escaping the drizzly afternoon. The station was bigger than Bea had pictured, and had more connections across the south of the country than she'd expected to see. She recognised place names from her atlas: trains to Portsmouth, Brighton, Weymouth … The list went on.

Bea realised then that she, too, was getting hungry, and pulled Patrick towards the nearest café door. It was painted a faded English tone of red, and looked as though it was entirely made of plastic. Inside, the chairs were a white plastic, and the sticky tables were covered with red and white plastic tablecloths. The menus even felt like plastic to the touch when the two of them sat down.

While marvelling at the sights around her, Bea tried her best not to look too out of her depth. *I can do this.* Food, after all, was something Bea very much understood.

'I had quite a big breakfast, so I might just get fruit or something,' she said, trying to sound flippant. She couldn't see any fruit on the menu, but assumed they had some kind of basket or bowl she would be able to look at.

Patrick looked amused. 'I'm not sure that this is a fruit kind of place, Bea. What about something simple while you find your land legs? Maybe some soup?'

She thought about it for a second, supposing that she could try some soup. In the books she had read, the English characters were often raving about leek and potato soup, beef stew or chicken broth. It had a particularly English tone to it, so she buried the quick flash of longing for her mother's perfectly salted and spiced oil down stew or lambie souse. 'Yes, I guess I could try some soup. I'll still ask about the fruit, though. I still can't believe there wasn't any fresh fruit on the boat for the whole journey. Thank goodness for the supplies Bette gave us.'

Patrick agreed, and soon enough, a waitress appeared at the table. She did a double take at the pair of them, a reaction that irritated Bea a little. She just wanted some food, not to have to lecture yet another English person about manners. Once could be laughed off, turned into an anecdote, but twice?

Nella's letters had warned her of the briskness of the English – their ignorance of what other subjects of the Crown actually looked like – but Bea hadn't realised she'd come face to face with it quite so soon.

In an attempt to win the waitress over, Bea smiled warmly at her. 'Do you have any fruit today?'

'You what?'

Bea took in a short breath, composing herself. The woman's accent was thicker than the taxi driver's, and at first Bea had no idea what she'd said. 'I would like some fruit. What fruit do you have, please?'

The waitress looked at Patrick, raising her eyebrows at him, before turning back to Bea. 'Oh, fruit! Your English isn't too bad, you know, I got it that second time.' If her smile hadn't looked so genuine, Bea might have knocked the little notebook clean out of the waitress's hand.

'I graduated top of my class in English, thank you,' she replied smoothly. 'And we actually speak English in Grenada. All of the West Indies speaks English.'

'Where?'

Bea sighed. 'Grenada. West Indies? Caribbean Sea? We are British subjects, you know.'

The waitress shook her head, looking over at Patrick. 'Well, I never. Learn something new every day, don't you! My milkman's from Jamaica or somewhere round there, I think. Maybe you know him? Nicky Bain?'

Bea gave her a tight-lipped smile. 'I can't say that I do. I've never been to Jamaica, although my sister has taken holidays there from time to time.' She turned back to Patrick, rolling her eyes at him quickly. She just wanted to order, and yet she was somehow teaching elementary level geography instead. 'May we order some food, please? I would like some fruit, if you have any.'

The waitress snorted, already losing interest. 'No fruit here, darlin'. We might have something tinned, I can check if you want.'

'What? No, no, that's all right. I'll just have the soup, thanks.' The waitress wrote this down, took Patrick's order, and left the two of them alone again.

Bea could tell Patrick was trying not to laugh, clearly engrossed in the dirty menu he held in his hand. 'You...' she hissed. 'You never told me that you tinned fruit in this country! That should be for emergencies only!' He was audibly laughing now, his cheeks blushing and eyes shining. Bea felt herself starting to giggle, too. 'This is sacrilege!' she managed to whisper, before they were both laughing so hard her whole face ached.

When the waitress returned she looked confused, but smiled nonetheless. As she placed down their meals, Bea looked over at Patrick and a new wave of laughter rippled through her. 'Pat, what is that slop you are about to tuck into?'

He grinned up at her, already grabbing his knife and fork. 'This is one of the most English dishes, my darling bride-to-be. As a matter of fact, I think you're going to love it.'

Bea looked at the swirl of orange and red lumps that Patrick was now covering in brown sauce from a bottle, its label starting to peel off. She had never seen anything so unappealing. 'I think I'll stick with this soup, but thank you. And what is that you're covering it in?'

'It's brown sauce.'

'Brown is not a flavour, Patrick. What's even in it?'

He cocked his head to the side, studying the bottle. 'Do you know, I haven't the foggiest. But it's delicious, whatever it is. Just give this a try! You are looking at what the Ministry of Food declared as essential during the war.' Patrick nodded to his plate, piling his fork with the orange-red abomination. 'Beatrice Bell isn't scared of a few baked beans, is she?'

She kicked him lightly under the table. 'I know what you're doing, Patrick. I see right through your games.' She put down her own spoon, and stood up, stepping around the table so that she was beside him. 'But it's working. Give me a taste!'

Patrick Anderson continued to surprise her; the beans were absolutely delicious.

Chapter 14

Beatrice

Standing at the Andersons' front gates, Bea felt Patrick's hand curve around the small of her back. She let herself exhale. She hadn't realised she'd been holding her breath, but suddenly felt light-headed.

Looking at the expression on her face, Patrick gave her a re-assuring smile. 'I'm sure there's nothing to worry about,' he said, the words far more confident than the tone of his voice. 'Like I said, they're going to love you.'

'Only one way to find out,' Bea answered, swinging her handbag onto her shoulder and handing Patrick her packing case. Anxiety crept up her back, making her flush hot despite the freezing temperature. She was no fool; she knew they'd have their concerns, even before Patrick had confessed on the boat over.

Regardless, Bea had still done her best to prepare. After she and Patrick had retired to their separate sleeping compartments, she'd stayed up and rehearsed what she would say and how she would say it, her shoulders back and tone clipped. She'd planned to explain how she understood their reservations; her parents had also been concerned that two people so different could make a life together. But she must assure them she'd make a dutiful and confident government wife, and was equipped with all the skills required. Did English women know how to load a shotgun, or calculate profit and loss?

After only a day in this country, she could also add that her manners were impeccable: a darned sight better than those which had been levelled against her so far.

But as she stood, one hand resting on the wrought-iron gates, she felt the urge to run back to the civilised shores of Grenada. A place where people knew how to welcome the schoolteacher's sister into their home, offer the bookkeeper a cup of hot tea on a cold day, make small talk with the map-maker's betrothed.

Patrick stepped towards the gate, and Bea flinched at the rustle of his steps crunching over dry leaves. 'Why would they keep the gates locked?' she asked. She craned her neck, as though his parents might emerge from one of the thick hedges that flanked the road. 'You did tell them what time to expect us, didn't you?'

'Of course, I called the housekeeper from the station.' Patrick joined her in her search, his gaze sweeping across the grounds. Bea pressed her hands deeper into her coat pockets, suppressing a shiver as best she could.

Patrick reached up to ring the bell, but just before he could, Bea's hand shot out to block him. 'Are you sure this is a good idea?' she asked, her doubt swelling.

'Well, not exactly,' Patrick admitted. 'But once they see us together, they'll see reason.' He squeezed her hand, the determination stronger in his voice this time. Bea sighed. She wished she could believe him, but a nagging sense of dread was tugging at her hem.

The two of them stood for another moment at the house's grand entrance, its manicured lawns soundtracked by birdsong and the breeze through evergreen leaves. The flower beds lining the path up to the house were pristine, rows of colour-themed blossoms the neatest Bea had ever seen. She hadn't realised flowers could bloom in weather as cold as this.

She took a second to cast her eyes around the grounds and marvelled at the scale of it all. It was no wonder the Andersons thought highly of themselves in a place like this. Who needed this long a driveway? This many trees all to themselves, this much garden to tend and to look at? For just two old people rattling around the house?

Bea wished her sisters could see the garden, imagining their reactions. Bette would go charging straight on to the lawns, crane her neck to see the top of the house and beyond the trees, asking a thousand questions. Millicent would stand with her arms crossed, eyebrows arched. *The English with all their green lawns and orchards and forests*, she would say, *and what did they leave us with? Bet they couldn't last a day in a house built on stilts! Who laboured to make the money to pay for all their grand homes, anyway?* It made Bea's stomach churn. She hushed Millicent's ghost-voice, reminding herself that she had just as much right to be here as anyone else.

'Really, I don't want you to be worried.' Patrick's voice drew her back into the moment, grounding her to the cold earth beneath her feet. 'They'll give us their blessing before we know it. I'm sure they're just held up with something.' He gave Bea's hand another squeeze, pulling her towards him and planting a quick kiss on her cheek. Warmth spread through her body, and Bea let herself relax into him. She hoped against hope that he was right.

Chapter 15

After a beat, Patrick glanced at his watch. He'd definitely given the housekeeper, Aisling, the exact day and time frame to expect them. Every other time he'd returned home the gates had been flung open, a little 'welcome home' card sometimes perched between the railings. The card was from Aisling, he knew, but its absence concerned him.

He smiled at Bea, hoping he looked as though he believed what he was saying, and reached up to ring the bell. This time Bea let him, a determined look on her face.

A few seconds later, a figure was running up the driveway. Her dark blue skirts flew behind her as she ran, one hand clinging to her head to stop a white cap from blowing away.

'Aisling!' Patrick called, waving at the housekeeper his father had employed for the past fifteen years. He'd met her a handful of times, on sporadic visits home from school and, later, his international postings. 'How are you?' he added as Aisling slowed to a walk and put both hands on her knees to catch her breath.

Patrick could sense Bea's shoulders tense up, and he reached over to place her hand in his. 'Would you be so kind as to unlatch the gate, so we may speak with Father and Moira? I believe they're expecting us.'

Aisling straightened up again, her face bright red from the run. To Patrick's horror, her eyes were wide with alarm. 'I'm sorry, Mr Anderson, but I can't let you in.'

Patrick flinched, feeling Bea's grip tighten on his hand. The autumn air whipped around the two of them, forcing its way beneath his shirt. 'Whatever do you mean?'

Aisling shook her head, her hands coming to rest on her hips as she puffed in the cold. 'Mr and Mrs Anderson really aren't happy about this. Running off with this coloured bride – no offence, sweetheart. It's not what someone of your position is meant to do. Your father's beside himself, Mrs Anderson's barely eating. I tried saying about the Chinaman we've got down the village, he's as good as gold. Said yours would likely be the same, genteel-like, but they weren't having any of it.'

Despite making a comment aimed at Bea, Aisling hadn't even glanced in her direction. Patrick shook his head, dismissing the housekeeper with a wave of his hand. 'Aisling, why are you talking about a Chinaman, for goodness' sake? Just let me in.'

Her wrinkled face softened ever so slightly, her eyes dropping to the floor. 'I don't want to be turning you away, Patrick, you know I don't. But you've got to understand, it's just not right. And it's not my place to be telling your father what he should and should not do. It's his house, and there are rules.'

Patrick dropped the packing cases to the floor and reached to unlatch the gate. 'If you won't let us in, I'll have to do it myself,' he declared as Bea took a step back and he lunged towards the lock.

With a flick of his wrist, Patrick managed to slide the hook off the latch and, triumphant, pushed back the gate. He took Bea's hand once more, but when they moved to step into the grounds, Aisling's arm blocked their path.

'Did you say "us"?' Aisling's voice was strained. 'Patrick, I must implore you. Under no circumstances are you to let your island bride onto these grounds.' She lowered her voice. 'Mr Anderson said he'll give me the sack if I let her in.' Finally, Aisling's eyes darted to Bea, who stood motionless.

Patrick looked from Aisling to Bea, every muscle tense. Bea opened her mouth to say something, but shook her head at the last moment. 'Bea, I'll go in there and I'll explain—'

'You will do no such thing,' Bea whispered, the words ragged as she visibly fought back tears. 'They've made up their minds before they've even met me. And for what?' She turned to Aisling, who looked on the brink of tears herself. 'They think my colour impacts my education level? My numeracy? I speak better English than half the people we've come across since we've been here, and probably achieved higher grades than all of them put together!'

'Really, miss, I must ask you to—'

'Oh, now you will address me?' Bea locked eyes with Aisling. 'Now that I'm raising my voice? I came all this way ...' She stopped for a beat, catching her breath and turning back to direct the words at Patrick. 'I came all this way, and what? They think I'm not good enough for them, without even setting eyes on me? They hear I'm coloured, an islander, and that's it? They think something as mundane as the colour of my skin tells them all they need to know about me?' She looked back up at the house, her shoulders slumping. 'I thought we'd get to know one another.' Her voice shrank. 'I thought we could at least try and be civil.' Shaking her head, Bea threw up her hands in frustration. 'But what's the point? Why should I try twice as hard for people who will decide I'm some rough little island girl, without so much as one conversation with me?' She took a deep breath and turned her back on Aisling, so she stood eye to eye with Patrick. 'I can't face this, Patrick. Maybe I shouldn't have come here.'

Her last sentence cut straight through him. 'You mean to Surrey?' Bea's expression darkened, and Patrick reached for her. He pulled her close, the warmth of her body against his granting a small comfort in the biting cold. 'Bea,' he said, rushing to get the words out, 'you know I will choose you a million times over. You know that, don't you?'

Patrick could feel her hesitate. 'But what happens now? You never see your parents again? I can't ask you to do that for me.'

'But you aren't asking anything, Bea. I asked you to come here, to marry me, remember?' His eyes bored into hers, their foreheads almost touching, as he made his decision. 'You're my family now, and that's all there is to it.' They stood that way for a moment, his arm around her waist.

'If you're sure,' she replied. 'But how can they do this?'

'Let me find out, talk to them. I'm sure I can make this right.'

Bea let out a hollow laugh. 'Their minds seem pretty made up, Pat.'

He shook his head. 'But they're wrong. I'll tell them, I'll say—'

'I think we should just go.' Bea cut him off with a hand on his chest.

Patrick looked back down the road they'd walked up from the village centre, kerbside daisies wilting in the wind. 'And we will. We can go to Ireland to stay with my Aunt Nancy instead.' He paused, pulling in her jacket so it sat snugly around her waist. 'But you can't marry a man who doesn't stand up for you. Wait here – just give me five minutes.'

Patrick could feel Aisling struggling to keep up with him as he tore down the driveway. She'd clearly been eavesdropping, so he felt no remorse at making her sweat a little.

Patrick threw back the front door, marching straight into the sitting room.

His father sat by the bay window, in a dark wood room filled with Victorian furniture. A vast painting of Patrick's grandfather adorned the wall above the fireplace, his hard gaze boring into the back of Patrick's head. He'd always hated that painting.

'Patrick! What on earth are you doing, bursting in like this?' His father didn't even stand up from his leather armchair to greet him, and simply placed down his cup of Earl Grey on its waiting saucer. Patrick wondered how it would feel to smash the cup to the floor.

'What am I doing?' Patrick struggled to keep the anger and hurt from his voice, hearing the words crack in his throat. 'What are you doing, banning Beatrice from the house? She will be your daughter-in-law soon, and you treat her this way?'

Charles Anderson got to his feet, hardly looking in his son's direction. 'Patrick, that island girl will never be a part of this family. Because if you know what's good for you, you won't marry her.' The steadiness of his voice made Patrick even angrier, his heart racing.

'Father, see reason.' Patrick ran his hands through his hair in frustration, his eyes glancing back and forth to the painting watching over them. 'You've forced me to leave Bea out in the cold. I thought we could have a civilised conversation and sort this whole thing out.'

Charles sneered, finally locking eyes with his son. 'Don't you even say the word "civilised", boy. You're making this family a laughing stock. We can't even show our faces in the Officers' Club any more because of this.' He shook his head, taking a step towards Patrick. 'I see you've had your fun, let off some steam, but you have a place in the world. In society.' His eyes shot over to the overbearing portrait, nodding curtly in its direction. 'And there is no space for an island girl – a *coloured* girl, Patrick – in this society.' He clasped his hands behind his back, as Patrick's skin burned with rage. 'Now, go outside and tell her you made a mistake, and that she needs to get on the next boat back to where she belongs.'

Charles pushed his thick-framed spectacles up the bridge of his nose and nodded, as though in agreement with himself. His gaze wandered back to the window, from which he could see the orchard's bare-branched apple trees clawing the October sky. 'Because if you don't – if you go ahead with this marriage – you shan't ever set foot in this house again. You shall say goodbye to everything coming your way. The inheritance, this house, the land in Ireland, the Mayfair flat – all of it.' The smile that crossed his father's lips tormented Patrick, and he knew he'd be seeing it in his nightmares for years to come. 'This is who you are, Patrick, and don't you forget it. I raised you better than to turn your back on your responsibilities.' Charles finally turned to face Patrick, his eyes narrowed.

Patrick stood tall. 'Raised me?' he said, spitting out the words. He'd never talked back to his father, not once in his life. 'You sent me to boarding school when I was five, Father. You didn't even have me back for the summer holidays, or even for Easters, let alone for weekends. And you think you raised me?'

Patrick wanted to continue talking, to explain to his father how happy Bea made him, how smart she was, how he wanted more than just a pretty face to sit opposite, in silence, night after night. How the fact she'd lived a life shaped so differently from his own repressed, rainy upbringing captivated him, teaching him there was more to life than officers' clubs and country houses.

But the cold stare Charles levelled at Patrick told his son all he needed to know: none of that mattered. All he wanted was the son he could roll out at officer dinners, but never truly know; a son to show off – as long as the achievements listed stayed well within the confines of what others like him found interesting – and grandchildren he'd never see, for sending them to boarding school before they could form complex sentences. A son to walk the exact same line, trodden by generation after generation, which had led Major General Charles Anderson to his lonely cup of afternoon tea and an empty appointment book.

Before Patrick could deliver a final goodbye, a voice screeched into the room and ricocheted off the parquet floor. 'After all we've done for you, Patrick! After taking you in as my own, your father sending you to that fancy school, getting you into the Commonwealth Office, and this is how you repay us?'

Patrick turned towards the sound and came eye to eye with his stepmother, Moira. Her beet-red face popped from the collar of a blouse so tight it looked as though she'd been sewn into it. 'And I'm grateful, Moira,' he replied. 'But just because he gave me a good start in life doesn't mean he can control who I marry. I've done everything else exactly as you both wanted.' His eyes switched from parent to parent, galvanised by the image of Bea waiting, alone, at the gate. 'But the first choice I make for myself, the first time I decide to choose happiness instead of duty, you want me to throw it all away.' He wished Bea could hear what he was saying, to show her that she'd made the right choice. 'This is my life, one to which neither of you have paid a shred of attention until I dared to do something you don't approve of. And if choosing someone I love means I lose all this,' he gestured around the room, the weak afternoon light casting shadows across the floor, 'then I suppose this is goodbye.'

Moira brought her hand to her chest and collapsed dramatically onto the chaise longue in the corner of the sitting room. If the situation had been different, Patrick could almost have found the image funny. 'For God's sake, Charles, talk some sense into the boy!' she cried. She turned to look at Patrick, her eyes narrowed and spit frothing at the sides of her mouth. 'You'll ruin us, Patrick!'

Patrick looked from his stepmother to his father, then back out through the door. Without another word, he turned his back on the overbearing oil painting and strode from the room.

The sight of Bea standing alone, her back arrow-straight, made his feet move faster. He pounded the cold, hard ground as he ran, her expression softening at the sight of him. Without speaking, he swept her into a kiss, holding her so close he could feel the blood pump through her body.

'Let's get out of this place,' he said.

Chapter 16

J. M. W. Boarding House
Riverside Drive
Liverpool

26th October 1954

Mom, Pop, Millie, Bette,

I hope you're all well – and you're enjoying the Grenadian sunshine! I miss it almost as much as I miss all of you.

I don't want you to be worried, though – I'm having a marvellous time here in England already. Patrick's parents were unfortunately taken down with the flu right when we arrived, and they don't want us to postpone the wedding on their account. So, we're heading over to Ireland to marry at Patrick's Aunt Nancy's church. It's Catholic, of course. Can you imagine – seeing two new countries in such a short space of time? I feel ever so lucky, and have been made to feel welcome by everyone we meet.

I can't write for long, as Patrick is taking me to a play this evening. We don't sail until tomorrow, so he's promised me some English traditions before we leave again. So far, I have ridden on a train up to Liverpool, seen a working dock, eaten some delicious baked beans in a tomato sauce, sipped on hot English tea and nibbled a crumpet. I believe after this play – I think it's Treasure Island – we will have fish and chips overlooking the sea.

I'll write soon with more stories of my travels. Please give my love to everyone back home.

Love, Bea

Bea sniffed, hoping no tears had dropped onto the letter. She hadn't told a complete lie; she really had eaten all those new dishes, and Patrick had surprised her with the theatre tickets almost as soon as they'd got to the boarding house.

She rolled back her shoulders as she signed the letter, determined that this wouldn't be in vain. Things would get better, because they had to. She wouldn't have to lie to her family again. She was sure of it.

Dublin, Ireland

Chapter 17

Beatrice

Reaching up her fist to rap on the doorway, Bea took a moment's hesitation to gather herself together again. She'd been lucky on the journey over to Dublin and had been able to stay above deck, unlike Patrick, who'd spent the entire voyage in his cramped cabin with seasickness. It had given Bea time to prepare, to steel herself to come face to face with Patrick's family for the first time.

Nancy's house was one of many of the same houses, knitted together in row upon row of straight-backed bricks. Hers had white lace curtains trimming the window, with an empty, frost-dusted flower basket hanging beside the front door.

'Ready?' Patrick asked, his hand coming to rest on the small of Bea's back.

'As I'll ever be.'

She steeled herself. It was just a door, and it was just a house.

She knocked. The door opened.

'I thought you said she was black?'

Then, for a second, silence.

'Well, I never saw someone so coloured before, of course, but I was expecting more of a *black* black. Are you one of those half-and-halfs, dear?' Without taking a pause, Patrick's aunt smiled, ushering the two of them through the front door. Her greying blond hair was cropped just below her chin, framing a wide smile and hazel eyes. 'Well, don't just stand there, I've made nice cups of tea for you both! I assume you take sugar, Beatricia, was it?'

'It's just Beatrice, actually.'

'Right, right, Beatrice. Lovely name, so it is. Can I call you Bea?' Nancy didn't wait for a response, only squeezed Bea's arm as she guided the slightly affronted couple towards the front room. 'Well, Bea, I couldn't be happier to welcome you to my home. Who would've thought Patrick would get such a beautiful girl, and smart, too, so he tells me! You'll have to tell me what that bank of yours was like, never worked in one myself. Always been the shop floor for me.' Her voice sang as she led them through the crouched hallway, its alarmingly yellow wallpaper slightly peeling at the top. 'I've been just ecstatic to have the two of you married here, just delighted to host you both. Haven't stopped nattering about it to anyone who'll listen!'

Nancy bustled them into what could only be described as the loudest silent room Beatrice had ever entered. The wallpaper was practically screaming, green and orange floral patterns haphazardly collapsing into one another. A thick cream rug, the texture of a large dog, took up the centre of the carpet. Patrick didn't pay it any notice, stepping across it and sinking right down onto a sofa on the other side of the room.

Nancy carried on talking in her sing-song accent that sounded like the wind whistling. 'The priest couldn't be more thrilled, you know, he says you two will be his first. Would you like saucers with your tea?'

Nancy motioned for Bea to take a seat beside Patrick, upon the sinking yellow sofa, and started to pour out hot cups of steaming tea. Bea took a deep breath, preparing herself for an answer to a question she really didn't want to ask. It was dawning on her that she'd have to get used to this sort of thing if she was going to get by in Europe. But she'd prove Millicent wrong, and if Nella could do it, then so could she.

'We are the priest's first what, may I ask?' Bea made sure to pronounce all her consonants, clipping them a little. She shot Patrick a warning glance, not daring to pick up her own cup in case her hand started to shake and cause it to run right over with too-milky tea.

Nancy looked confused at first, her leathery white brow knitting together as she reached across and patted Bea's hand. A sympathetic look soon spread across Nancy's face, yet a twinkle remained in her eyes. 'Well, his first English person, dear! He's a lot more at ease with the idea of a fellow *colonisée* educated in a faith school like yourself, but a man raised and schooled in England without so much as a habit in sight, let alone a nun…' Nancy leant closer. 'It took some convincing, I'll tell you that for nothing.'

She grinned at her nephew, who frowned and shook his head. 'But I was baptised! Wasn't I baptised?'

'Never made it over for your First Communion, though, did you? Practically turned Protestant on us all at that boarding school! It was quite the scandal, Bea, honestly.' Nancy winked at Bea, reaching out her hand with a plate laden with sugared treats. 'Biscuits, both?'

Bea accepted a chocolate-covered biscuit so she wouldn't have to reply. She didn't have the heart to admit to Nancy that she was mostly Catholic on paper, only sticking with it for the food-related celebrations and the excuse to drink wine on a Sunday.

'Bea, are you in there, love?' came Nancy's melodic voice, with a gentle tap at the door.

Bea reluctantly pulled herself up from her seated position by the bedroom window, allowing the blanket she had pulled around her to fall away to the floor. Patrick had popped out to visit the church, leaving Bea to unpack. She picked up the blanket and folded it over her arm, opening the door to find Nancy's beaming face.

'I hope you don't mind, dear, but I took the liberty of digging this wedding dress out from storage. It's only been worn once, of course, and you're about the same size as my neighbour's daughter, who wore it last. I told her you were coming at our tea last week, and she was insistent you have it. Hates things going to waste, so she does, and what does her Ciara need with it? Even if she got married again, she'd hardly need a white dress.' As she spoke, she swept into the room with billowing white satin pouring from her arms. 'I wasn't sure whether or not you already had a dress. Do they wear wedding dresses where you're from?' Bea went to say that yes, she believed most countries wore a form of wedding dress, but Nancy was already talking again. 'I couldn't resist bringing it to show you. I think you'd look just darling in it, wouldn't you say so? I can run up any adjustments on my machine, you see, it's no trouble.' Nancy held it up, angling it towards the winter's sun, which was streaming through the glass.

The dress had a wide neckline, with sleeves down to the elbows and a hem which would sit just below the knee. A lace sash ran around the waistline, and the satin skirt fell just beneath, in a gracefully elegant cut.

Drinking in the sight of it, Bea reached out one hand to lightly stroke the skirt's material. She herself had never owned – never even seen – such a luxurious-looking gown. Even though the hand-stitching across the waistband was a little crooked if you looked closely, and the hem would need dropping a touch to fit her tall frame, Bea felt a childlike lump rise in her throat. 'Are you sure?' she asked quietly. 'I have a dress which would be quite practical, but it's nothing like this.'

'Oh, nonsense! Who wants to look practical on their wedding day?' Nancy dismissed the notion with a wave of her hand, as she laid the dress across the bed and made to leave the room. 'You just give it a try at least, and call me when you need some help with the buttons at the back.' Nancy flashed her a grin, shutting the door behind her.

As thrilled as Bea was to try on the dress, the thought of having to remove her clothes in such freezing conditions made her hesitate for a beat. Before she could let herself get too worried about whether it was possible to catch frostbite in a damp Irish terrace, she kicked off her shoes, stepped out of her travelling dress, and pulled the gown up over her hips. The fit was a little loose around the waist, but the sleeves sat nicely above her elbows and the neckline ran just below her collarbones. She smoothed over the skirt, and called for Nancy to help button up the back.

Within seconds Nancy was back in the door frame – clearly

having stood right outside, waiting for the call – and, before darting across the room to help Bea, she put her hand to her chest
and smiled. 'Goodness, if my sister could see you now. Isn't my
Patrick a lucky man?'

Bea smiled self-consciously, as Nancy marched behind her and
began working away at the buttons along the back of the bodice.
'I hope you don't mind me saying, dear, but it's a very brave thing
you're doing.' Nancy continued to work her way down the length
of the dress, penny-sized buttons hooking into place. 'A lot of
people wouldn't take such a chance. I've never lived anywhere but
Dublin myself, can't imagine what it would be like to disappear
halfway around the world to a place where no one would look like
me, where I wouldn't know a soul. And you could go anywhere
with my Patrick ...' She grew quiet, gathering the loose material
at the waist and pinning it, lifting fine silver pins from a box on
the bookshelf. 'He's had a tough old time of it, losing his mother
so young, left with that father of his.' Nancy lowered her voice.
'Between you and me, you're both better off without that man.'
She added a final pin, and spun Bea around to face the mirror that
hung beside the bed. 'I'm glad Patrick's found someone so brave,
is what I'm trying to say.' Nancy stepped back, leaving Bea alone
in the mirror's reflection. 'What do you think?'

'It's perfect.' Bea couldn't help but gush. She did a little twirl,
letting the skirt float around her. 'I don't know how to thank you.'

'Just be good to him, but don't let him get away with any
mischief,' Nancy said with a smile. 'Although if you really want to
get me a gift, I could always use a new hat.' She laughed, heading
for the door. 'I'll leave you for a moment, but give me a shout
when you want the buttons undoing. Don't know whose idea it
was to make them so fiddly.'

The kindness was almost too much for Bea to bear, and she
stood in front of the mirror to lock eyes with her own reflection.
We'll be better off without Mr Anderson – quite right, too.

Chapter 18

Patrick

To calm Patrick's pre-wedding nerves, he and his best man, John Coleridge, had drunk a little too much whiskey the night before the wedding. Walking towards his friend at the end of the aisle, Patrick hoped Bea wouldn't notice the slightly grey tinge to his skin.

'And you're sure this is the right woman for you, Pat?' John had asked him, his fourth glass of whiskey swilling around the bottom of his tumbler, the ice long since melted. 'You definitely wouldn't want to just go back to your father's house and pretend this never happened? You can still cancel if you want to, you know.' His words slurred into one another, sounding as though they had all become sick of queuing up to be said aloud.

Draining his own glass, Patrick had shaken his head, picturing as he did so how beautiful Bea would look the next morning. He had organised a surprise for her, and couldn't wait to see the look on her face as she arrived at the church. 'John,' Patrick began, his confidence soaring higher than his blood alcohol level. 'Have you ever met someone who makes you forget to breathe?' He raised his chin as he spoke, his eyes becoming misty. A corny line, he knew, but the closest he could get to putting into words the monumental shift of perspective and sense of vitality that spending time with Bea gave him.

'Really though, Pat. She'd be fine without you, you know, definitely meet someone else who'd take her on. She's a lovely girl, of course she is, but why does it have to be you?' John looked down into his glass, avoiding his friend's eyes. 'I've watched you lose a lot of people over the years, Patrick. Your mother, those boys in the year above us at school who went away to the war and never came back, your entire squad in Palestine. I'd hate to think she might be taking you for a ride.' Despite the expression on Patrick's face, John pressed on. 'You could do what I've done – just have your parents introduce you to someone. My Sally is wonderful, from a fine family, and it's kept my parents happy. You're absolutely certain that Bea's worth all this? That she isn't just using you for the passport, like a lot of those foreigners do?'

Patrick looked at John, wondering at that moment how well the two men really knew each other. They knew each other's drink orders, how they voted, what their fathers did. But maybe John wasn't the kind man – the reasonable man – Patrick had considered him to be. 'Damn my father, John! You aren't listening to me. Times are changing, and you do realise it's her who's taking me on, not the other way around? She could've had anyone, and she chose me.'

Patrick drained the last of the fiery liquid from his glass, savouring the burn as it trickled down his throat. 'Also, Grenadians essentially are British citizens. They have the right of abode, just like all Commonwealth subjects do. If she'd wanted to move here that badly, she'd only have to book a ticket. She wouldn't have needed me at all.'

John had shaken his head, said a few more words about his soon-to-be-fiancée Sally, but had pestered Patrick no more. They'd exchanged some pleasantries about their next postings – John's in New Zealand for at least two years, Patrick's to be confirmed after his wedding – and made half-hearted promises to apply for the same city in years to come.

Now, Patrick glanced around the church and felt that familiar pang whenever he took part in something momentous in his life: receiving his exam results; getting called up for National Service; embarking on his postings abroad. The ghost of his mother loomed at all these occasions, the lack of her warm presence chilling any room.

He knew Bea would understand a little of what it felt like to be missing family on a day like this, but not for the first time, he wished he knew someone who'd lost a parent in the way that he had. Just so he could hear it explained to him, without having to come up with the words himself.

'Look at me now, Mother,' he whispered under his breath, picturing her settling down next to his aunt Nancy. With a start, he realised he wasn't missing his father one bit.

Chapter 19

Beatrice

True to form, the maid of honour did not arrive quietly; the sputter and roar of a motorbike filled the peaceful silence of the churchyard, and Bea blinked hard to make sure her eyes weren't deceiving her.

'Look at you, a bride! You look breathtaking, my girl.'

'Good Lord, Nella! Is it really you?'

Nella rose from the back of the motorbike, shaking her halo of hair out of the helmet and placing her hands on her hips. 'You didn't think I'd let you get married without seeing the bloke for myself, did you?' Smiling to reveal all her teeth and lighting up her eyes, Bea threw back the veil she and Nancy had sewn and ran right into the waiting arms of her closest friend.

Nella felt thinner, but somehow sturdier than Bea remembered. A sensation close to relief flooded through her at the feel of a familiar body hugging her own, and Bea struggled to hold back tears.

'I can't believe it!' Bea exclaimed, pulling away to hold Nella by the elbows. 'How did you ...?'

'I have to give it to you, Bea, you found yourself a good man.' Nella gestured for her companion – the driver and owner of the motorbike – to park up so the two women could talk. 'Pat tracked me down from our letters, I guess. Even sent me over strict instructions of what colour dress I should wear, but he has no idea what looks best on me, so I chose it myself. Isn't it glorious?' She twirled on the spot, the deep blue satin spinning around her like ripples in midnight waters. Bea clapped her hands together.

'It's stunning! But, Nell, you really shouldn't have spent your wages on something so lavish, not for me. It's only one day.'

Nella arched an eyebrow. 'Let's just say that your fiancé is a generous man. And I'll wear this until I'm bursting out of it, so he made a good investment. Although do not let him pick you out a dress any time soon. Do you know he had the audacity to suggest I wear a lime green?' Nella cackled. 'He couldn't remember what colour flowers you'd chosen, so he wanted me to match the stalks!'

'He didn't!' Bea laughed.

'He sure did. Anyway, I can't believe you didn't ask me yourself!'

'I didn't want you to have to go to any trouble,' Bea replied sheepishly. 'It's just a ceremony really. I didn't think you'd have any leave!'

Nella's eyes twinkled. 'If it's for a family wedding, christening or funeral, they give us special dispensation.' She winked, her lips curling as she over-pronounced the words. 'If anyone asks, we're sisters, all right? They always say that the likes of us all look the same, so I thought I'd use it to my advantage.'

Bea nodded and laughed, pulling her friend in for another hug. She looked over Nella's shoulder, clocking the tall stranger dismounting the motorbike behind her. 'And this would be...?'

Nella stepped back and gave a short wave of her arms. 'Gordon, meet Beatrice. Bea, this is Gordy. Now there's no time for chit-chat, let's get you married!'

Gordon smiled at Bea and greeted her politely, shaking her hand. 'I've heard so much about you, Beatrice.'

'Please, call me Bea.'

'Well, Bea, we'd love to invite you over to London. There's plenty of room at Nella's boarding house.'

'Oh, yes,' enthused Nella, checking Bea's dress and veil were secured properly as she spoke. 'We were talking on the ferry over. You must come for a honeymoon!'

'That's a lovely idea! I'll tell Patrick.'

Nella grinned. 'I knew you'd be up for it. We'll show you all around, take you to a dance, a few of our favourite bars.' She clapped her hands, gesturing for Gordon to head inside. 'But no time for all that now – let's get you married!'

As Gordon strode ahead of them to find a seat in the church, he passed an expectant-looking Nancy waiting in the doorway. 'Room for a little one down that aisle with you, Bea?' she said.

'Of course.' Bea smiled, extending her arm. 'Thank you, Nancy.'

'It always helps having someone to lean on, when you do the walk. Longer than you'd think, it is.'

Linking her arm through Nancy's, Bea nodded for Nella to step out ahead of them. Nella grinned, and pushed open the church doors.

'Ready?'

'Let's do this.'

Chapter 20

Patrick

Foreign and Commonwealth Office
King Charles Street
Whitehall
Westminster
London

12th November 1954

For the attention of Patrick Anderson MRICS,
Many thanks for informing us of your recent change in marital status.

We write to acknowledge receipt of your letter, and to inform you that your next posting has been agreed.

Following two further weeks' leave in which to get your affairs in order, you are instructed to ship out at 07:00 from Southampton docks to your posting in Lushoto, Tanganyika, 29/11/54. A local and Commonwealth department representative from the Surveying and Ordnance team will greet you on arrival at Dar es Salaam port, Tanganyika, from whence you'll be transported to Lushoto.

As is customary for wives and children, your wife will be offered a room at the lodging house in the town. We estimate that you will spend two days there upon arrival, and following this will be moved to the base camp at West Usambara.

Kind regards,

Timothy Cumberbatch, Directorate of Overseas Surveys (Sub-Saharan Africa division)

2015

FRIDAY

'You want sugar?'

Amelia shook her head. 'Just as it comes, thank you kindly.'

With four hours before the movers arrived at her father's house, and two days before relatives began to descend upon the island, Amelia allowed herself a moment to breathe. She accepted the cup of iced coffee the vendor, Joe, was handing her, his fingers brushing hers. She reached into her pocket for a couple of notes, but he waved her away. 'You save your money for the grandbaby you got coming. When's she due?'

Amelia took a sip, the cool drink just the perfect level of bitter on her tongue. She smiled back at Joe. 'Not until November. I warned her, if she goes late she'll be too close to Christmas, but what can you do?'

'They do what they want, these young people.'

'Isn't that the truth?'

Amelia nodded a goodbye to Joe, heading down the street from his stall towards the main market centre. His coffee stand was perfectly placed at the top of the hill down to the market square, a queue always snaking along Grenville Street from his brushed copper cart. Amelia wasn't sure whether his name really was Joe, or whether it was a branding exercise, but she never questioned him.

His was some of the best coffee in St George's, and she wouldn't want to risk offending the man. He rarely let her pay, and it gave her a little thrill to feel his eyes on her. She sometimes felt as though she was fading as she got older, and relished every moment that proved otherwise.

She took another sip of coffee, mentally running through her shopping list. She mostly needed fruit for the desserts she would make for Barkley and Aidan when they arrived, acting as taste-testers for the full family reunion. She'd make her father's favourite grapefruit pound cake, which apparently needed to be gluten-free for a cousin's wife. She'd use her mother's recipe, substituting the flour for whatever Maryse could find her as a replacement. The pound cake always had just the right balance of sharp and sweet, the sugary glaze that coated her teeth transporting her right back to childhood. She'd wanted to make a traditional, fruit-stuffed black cake, but a good one needed to soak in spiced rum for months. As usual these days, she'd run out of time.

'There you are!' Maryse called, waving at her mother from the coconut water stall. 'I thought you'd started without me.' Other market stands on rickety wooden legs propped up each side of the street, shaded by multicoloured canopies and umbrellas. Maryse leant one arm on the stall, causing the table to bow ever so slightly beneath her. Amelia hurried over, concerned she'd need to pay for the whole thing if her daughter caused it to topple.

'Didn't we say 8.30?' Amelia countered, one eyebrow arched. 'I assumed you'd be late getting here. You were still sleeping when I left earlier.'

Maryse took a sip from the young coconut clasped between her hands, a purple umbrella sticking out of the side. 'You have such little faith. Good walk this morning?'

'Fine, thank you.' Amelia didn't burden her with the fact that she'd barely been able to enjoy her usual early-morning walk along Grande Anse: she'd been running through every possible scenario that the box they'd found could conjure. She'd hardly taken two steps before she'd had to take out her headphones to let her thoughts speak for themselves. Curiosity spilled from one thought to the next as she pondered what the chest's contents may reveal, what secrets they may unearth. What secrets she even wanted to unearth. Either way, she knew she'd built it up to hold all the secrets of the universe she'd ever wanted answers for, so she'd be disappointed whatever the outcome.

'Did you say you're doing a lemon pound cake?' Maryse asked, her eyes scanning the stalls ahead.

'Grapefruit – your great-grandma's recipe,' Amelia replied, pushing thoughts of the chest to the back of her mind. They walked further into the market's centre as noise bubbled up around them.

'Right, I always loved that one,' Maryse said, narrowly avoiding a collision with the fishmonger. 'A shame she never wrote down her gingerbread recipe.'

'I think she took it to her grave so no one would ever be able to rival it,' Amelia said, making Maryse laugh as she rolled her eyes.

'Typical great-grandma. Kept her cards so close to her chest she hardly played the game,' Maryse agreed. Amelia tightened her hold on her daughter's arm, weaving through the growing crowds of sunburnt tourists and morning shoppers and stallholders. Amelia knew it was wicked to mock her elders with her daughter, but the temptation took over on occasion. Her grandmother – Maryse's great-grandmother – had been appalled when Amelia had had Maryse 'out of wedlock'. Amelia was convinced the hidden gingerbread recipe had been her revenge.

It was becoming harder to hear each other as the market thickened towards the centre: stallholders fought to be heard above their neighbours, each call of 'nutmeg', 'apricots', 'cassava', 'coconut water, delicious coconut water here', blending together in a chaotic, colourful song. The scents and sounds of the market always comforted Amelia, the salty air seasoned with fresh spice.

Amelia haggled her way from stall to stall, weighing her shopping bags down with golden apples, papaya, grapefruit and guavas. She had enough for a test batch and a final dessert with each; alongside the grapefruit pound cake would sit a zesty papaya pie and guava stew, all with home-made golden apple juice to wash it down. She thought wistfully of the black fruit cake, but reasoned that even if she had found the time to make it, it wouldn't hold a candle to her mother's version. They followed the same recipe to the letter, but Amelia's never had the same depth of flavour.

She and Maryse waved at neighbours and friends as they meandered through the crowds, stopping to accept good wishes for as long as the flow of bodies would let them stay in one place. They forced themselves to march past the chocolate stalls and the jewellery, promising they'd have a full shopping spree once the party and house move were all complete.

Amelia did her best not to get carried away, yet still found herself ordering some sugar cane as she and Maryse emerged from the other side. Maryse took hers with a shriek of delight, munching on the cane as they turned left out of the market and headed along the harbour wall. The calls and haggles fell into the background, yet the air still hummed with scents of nutmeg and cinnamon, coffee and coconut.

'Will the baby get a sugar addiction if I eat too much of this? Tommy thinks I'm going to make it love sour things with all the limes, so I'm trying to balance it out.'

Amelia chuckled. 'I think you should've paid more attention to science at school.'

'You're just saying that because you don't know, either.' Maryse narrowed her eyes, but kept her lips curled in a smile. Amelia swatted her away with her spare hand, her sugar cane already finished and discarded in one of the shopping bags.

'And you and Tommy, you're still getting along all right?' Amelia asked without looking at Maryse. They'd only been together a year when Maryse had found out she was pregnant, and Tommy had moved in with them straight away.

'All good, thank you. He's going to Grandpa's this morning, to help him sort the last of his things and move all the heavy stuff.'

Amelia nodded. 'That's nice of him.' Tommy was a nice enough boy – good job at the high school admin office, good grades, good haircut – but Amelia couldn't help but wonder if he'd be the one Maryse would choose in different circumstances.

Maryse took a final bite of sugar cane, and reached out for Amelia's as they passed a bin. She cocked her head as she disposed of both husks of fruit, twirling a braid in her fingers. 'I think "nice" is such a boring way of describing someone. I'd be so offended if the only way someone could describe me was "nice".'

Amelia scoffed. 'What are you saying? What's wrong with nice?'

'It's just so …' Maryse massaged the air in front of her, as if trying to reach out and grab the word she wanted. 'Vanilla?' She shrugged, reaching into her pocket to retrieve her car keys as they entered the car park. They'd walked the length of the harbour wall, a seagull almost keeping exact pace with them as it skimmed slowly across the water's surface. Only a few sailing boats bobbed in the water; the scent of fresh fish wafted over the ripples and waves.

'And you hate vanilla all of a sudden?' Amelia reached for her own keys, clicking her car open and reaching to lift the boot.

'I'm just saying, there are much better things to be. Interesting, funny, kind.' Maryse's eyes sparkled. 'Outrageous, even!'

'You are being outrageous,' Amelia said, lifting her bags into the boot and instantly feeling she might float away once they'd dropped off her arms. Maryse cackled, opening her two-door hatchback by placing the keys in the passenger side lock and twisting them with a jolt. Amelia kept meaning to take her car-shopping, and reminded herself they needed to sort a date.

'Thank you, Ma. Much better to be outrageous than nice – at least I'd have made an impact.'

'It's quite safe to say that you will always make an impact, my girl,' Amelia replied, laughing as Maryse gave a dramatic wave and ducked into her car. They continued the conversation through open windows as Amelia turned her key in the ignition, agreeing when to meet and what to bring, shouting above the rumblings of starting engines.

Amelia watched Maryse back out of her space first, before following suit. She cast a longing glance back towards the market, dreaming of a fortnight's time when she'd be free to wander it as long as she pleased. All day if she wanted. She'd buy fruit for breakfast and scoop out the seeds of a sugar apple, followed by juicy orange segments. Then she'd stay right there, her legs dangling over the harbour wall, and she'd order plantain with grilled chicken, licking the salt and jerk spice from her fingertips. She might even stay until close and finish up with a hot curry – so spicy it would make her eyes water, but so delicious she wouldn't care. Then she'd call her friend Didi, and she and her daughter Cedella would come to meet Amelia and Maryse, and the four of them would go to a beach bar and—

A car horn alerted her to the fact she'd just sat through a green light, watching it turn through amber and red. Amelia waved an apology and shook her head to herself, turning up the radio.

Amelia found herself hesitating outside her father's house. Maryse's car was wedged beneath the breadfruit tree, so Amelia could only just fit alongside it on the narrow driveway. They should have just shared a lift.

She'd managed to take two phone calls on the short drive up to her father's house, confirming start times for the party and final numbers for the hotel. The hotel had been so good to put up such a large group and offer a sizeable discount, so Amelia hoped they'd all be gracious guests. She'd only spent a handful of summers and the occasional Christmas with the cousins and aunts and uncles and all their partners who were arriving from overseas, so she couldn't really attest to how they'd behave in a hired space. They'd always crammed into one another's houses, pull-out beds and inflatable mattresses and pillows on the floor when nothing else would fit. She and Barkley had loved these international sleepovers, hopping from island to island near and far, craning their necks to watch the rest of the world press its nose to their aeroplane window.

Amelia got out from the car, the wind already picking up and whipping her short hair around her ears. The sky was still a watery blue; no storm clouds threatened them yet. She began ascending the steps, glad to hear a gentle hubbub from indoors already.

'...arriving in three hours. Tommy, can you take Grandpa back to ours? Mom and I can finish up here.' Amelia opened the door to find herself eye to eye with Maryse, who leant against the kitchen counter as she called out instructions. 'Eh, how's that for good timing,' she said.

Maryse bustled Tommy and her grandfather from their seats, the abandoned playing cards on the table a hint at how they'd spent their morning. Amelia was relieved to see her father looked calm – peaceful, almost. Today was another Good Day.

'Will you join us for dinner?' her father asked, stepping out of his slip-ons and looking around for his shoes.

'It's not quite lunch yet, Pop,' Amelia replied, her tone gentle.

Her father's brow furrowed, but his shoulders stayed relaxed. 'Is it not? I must have been up with the birds this morning, already thinking of my supper.' His eyes gleamed, though his gaze seemed not quite to land on anything specific. 'Always thinking of food, am I?'

Amelia nodded, as Tommy reappeared holding her father's shoes. 'We can have an early lunch, if you like? I make a great omelette.' The open, kind expression on Tommy's face as he bent towards her father, helping him through the door, was almost too much for Amelia to bear.

'Yes, that will do nicely. Will you join us, Meli? Maryse?'

'Not just yet, Grandpa, we have to finish packing.' Maryse stood up from her leaning spot, throwing her arms around her grandfather. 'Are you excited to come live with us?'

He chuckled. 'I'm worried I won't get a moment's peace with you all.' He threw up his hands in mock despair, and Maryse mirrored the gesture.

'Not a moment, and that's a promise.' She dropped a kiss on his cheek, and Tommy reached over to squeeze her shoulder. It was a tight spot in the doorway, but somehow the three of them fitted. Amelia reached for her phone to snap a picture, the light just dappling their faces, but they'd all moved and started waving goodbye before she could open the camera app.

'Right.' Maryse shut the door behind them, turning to face Amelia. 'I've stripped the beds and emptied the bathroom cupboards, so the only thing left to pack is that chest.' Amelia's stomach dropped. 'So can we open it today?'

'I still don't know—'

'Ma, you've been distracted all morning. It's obviously all you can think about, because it's all I can think about, and don't go telling me we've finally fallen out of sync.'

Amelia attempted a withering look at her daughter, but stopped short. She hated to admit it, but Maryse was right.

★

'It just feels wrong, like I'm reading my mother's diary,' Amelia confided. She sat at the dressing table again, avoiding her reflection in the mirror. She let her gaze track towards the open window, the thin white curtains rising and falling in the wind. This room faced the back of the house, with a view over the peak of Morne Jaloux Ridge. She couldn't see it from the window, but the Seven Sisters Waterfall at Morne Jaloux had always been one of Amelia's favourite places to swim. She'd made up stories for Maryse as a child about waterfall-dwelling mermaids and nymphs, and even after she'd grown up, the forest and water had always held a sense of ethereal magic. There were a few young children attending the reunion, and Amelia had already added 'Seven Sisters Waterfall' to her tour-guide list.

'I guess we have to be prepared for the fact that the letters might not make much sense,' Maryse said, bringing in a stool to sit down beside her mother. 'It will be like only reading half an email chain, with fewer "Please find attached" and "Kind regards".'

The room was completely bare, save for the dressing table, unmade bed and empty wardrobe; all the other possessions were packed up and ready to go. The movers would take the furniture to the families listed in the spreadsheet Amelia had sent them, each name and address typed up in neat, precise lines.

Amelia nodded, her hand hovering over the lid. 'Exactly.' She steeled herself. 'What's the worst that could happen?'

Maryse raised an eyebrow. 'Or it might be something good, you never know. Love letters between Grandma and Grandpa, letters from family asking after you and Barkley.'

Barkley. 'I'd better give him a call, actually. Let him know what we've found, now we have a minute to breathe.'

'Will he want to see it with you, do you think?'

Amelia hesitated. Her brother had gone through a rough couple of years with their parents, right after he'd come out and emigrated for good. They'd refused to let him tell their grandparents when he'd got together with Aidan, and Amelia knew it still hurt her brother that he'd been living a lie before they'd passed away. *At least Grandma and Grandpa were mad at both of us for never getting married,* she'd tried to joke. He hadn't found it funny.

Barkley had moved to New York for medical school in the late 1980s, and Amelia had convinced herself it would be temporary. They'd always talked about what it would be like to grow older on the island: him setting up his medical practice while she climbed to the top of local government. Both helping the community, in their own way.

The summer he returned after graduating – the year Maryse turned four – Amelia had had the breath knocked from her body when he'd announced his plan to accept a permanent job in Brooklyn. She couldn't work out what was more hurtful: that he was leaving, or that he hadn't told her he'd applied.

The family had barely spoken that year, Amelia and her parents struggling to understand why he'd leave the island for somewhere so dangerous. Somewhere he may face racial prejudice on top of homophobia. He'd become misty-eyed explaining about the multifarious community he'd found, the way his friends rallied around one another and spoke so openly about their dating, desires, dreams, their heartbreak as the AIDS epidemic blazed on.

When Amelia and Barkley did find the time to speak, both using shaky landlines, his voice had gained a new edge, and Amelia had become convinced he was hiding how hard he found it. How could he bear to be away from his niece, who loved him more than anything in this world, and instead, choose to build a whole life that didn't include them?

Despite her sadness, she'd refused to let him stop speaking to their parents, coaxing the family back together as best she could across time zones. First it had been through intermittent phone calls she orchestrated like a work conference: agenda item 1, Barkley's New Job; Agenda item 2, Pop's Retirement; and so forth. Eventually they could move on to Barkley's Love Life, Amelia's Lack Thereof (by choice, thank you very much), Mom's Volunteer Drive, Pop's Latest Project, the books they were all reading.

It became a weekly call as the years ambled on, Amelia and Maryse hunkering down on a Sunday evening and dialling one house down the road and another across the sea. They mostly discussed books these days, or albums that had just been released. Amelia looked forward to it every week, even after her mother had died. She did her best not to resent her brother for his carefree life, his lack of phone calls and visits, even as both parents began needing more care. He was where he needed to be, in a supportive community. Despite knowing this, she couldn't help but wish – after a particularly exhausting day driving her mother to hospital appointments, arranging shopping for her father and losing her temper with Maryse – that she could slip her hands through the phone and yank Barkley back to the island. *You've had your fun, now get back here and help me.*

'Barkley's in a good place with Pop, with Mom's memory, too. I'd just better let him know. There might be all sorts in here he'll be interested in.' Amelia withdrew her phone from her pocket, dialling Barkley. 'No answer.' She opened WhatsApp instead, and hit *record*. 'Hey, I guess you're working. Or packing – don't you fly later? Anyway … Maryse, am I still recording? OK, good, yes.' She drew a deep breath, wishing she'd just left a voicemail. 'We've been sorting through things at the house and it's all packed up, but we've come across some kind of memory box. It has loads of letters and postcards and all sorts. From a quick glance they're almost all addressed to Mom, so I'm checking if you want us to wait for you to get here before we go through it all? Let me know. OK, thanks, bye.'

She exhaled, falling back into her chair. 'That was exhausting. Whatever happened to voicemails?'

'No one uses voicemail any more, Ma, I've told you.' Maryse shook her head, though not unkindly. She flopped down onto the bed, rolling her neck left and right. 'He won't really mind if we look without him, will he?'

'Let's just– Oh, hang on.' Amelia's phone was buzzing, hopping across the dressing table in fits and starts. 'Hi, Barkley. You're on speaker.'

'Hey, Uncle Barks,' Maryse called.

'Sorry I missed your call, loved the voice-note, though.' Barkley's voice was muffled; cars and sirens whined in the background. 'I'm just leaving work now. Flight's not for a few hours, we leave around nine. Changing at—' The sound of a horn blaring in the distance cut him off.

'So you're definitely coming now?'

'I was always going to, just got called into work.' He paused, catching his breath. 'What's this about a treasure chest?'

'Memory box,' Amelia corrected. 'We think it's Mom's old correspondence. Do you want us to wait for you to look through it?'

She could hear Barkley's mind working, his breathing heavy through the phone as he darted along crowded sidewalks. 'I think I'm good,' he said eventually.

Amelia frowned. 'Really?'

'Yeah. Thanks for checking, though. Send me pictures of anything interesting.'

'You really don't want to—'

'I said I'm good.' His tone was firm, tired. 'I've been really working on my unresolved issues with Mom, so I don't know how healthy it would be to dredge up old questions.' Amelia resisted the urge to roll her eyes: her brother had barely been in the USA five minutes before he'd enlisted the support of a therapist, whom Amelia pictured as one of those old white ladies with a penchant for wearing patterned cardigans even in the height of summer.

'OK, well, we'll let you know if there's anything interesting.' She couldn't resist. 'Or, you know … anything about you.'

'Hey, I am interesting!'

'I think it's old love letters between her and Grandpa,' Maryse cut in. Barkley's laugh echoed down the line.

'You think everything is fresh out of a romcom.'

'Do not!'

Amelia grinned. 'You can't see it, Barkley, but she's threatening you with a pillow.'

'Sounds like my cue to leave. I'll let you know when we set off tonight.'

'All right, then. See you tomorrow. Safe flight.'

They hung up, and Amelia turned back to the box. She felt a

little deflated by Barkley's reaction – disappointed he didn't want to share this with her. Perhaps she was being silly after all, worrying over things she probably wouldn't understand and couldn't ask her mother to explain.

'I guess Barkley has a point,' Amelia said slowly. 'There's no need to dredge up the past. We've all made our peace with it.'

'Are you sure about that?'

Amelia turned to face Maryse, one hand still resting on the box's lid. 'Of course I'm sure.' She reached up to run her fingers through her curls, avoiding Maryse's gaze.

'Really? Now I'm not trying to be disrespectful.' Maryse threw up one hand in defence. 'I just think, maybe, you're scared that this holds something new from Grandma. And once we read this, she's really gone.' She stood up, coming over to sit beside Amelia.

Amelia startled, as though she'd reached out and put a wet rag in an electrical socket. 'But she's been gone for years. I should be OK with finding something like this.'

'You're allowed to not be OK, you know.'

Amelia's instinctive reaction was to deny it – to prove to Maryse that she was perfectly fine. But her shoulders slumped, and she closed her eyes for a few moments.

'For years, I've wondered if there was something like this. You know, I even once searched for my own adoption record in the council offices?' Amelia opened her eyes and smirked at the memory, her foolish attempts to open long-closed files. 'There was nothing, but every time I asked Mom or Pop about it they'd just clam up. Mom would get so upset if I asked why they couldn't have children of their own, who my "real" mother was, but I was just too young to understand the terms I should've been using. Birth family, that sort of thing.' Amelia finally held both hands around the box, tracing the knotted design from left to right as though it spoke a language comprehensible through touch. 'I was never even that curious. I didn't want to go and find my birth family or anything. I just wondered who I'd come from.' She paused. 'Eventually I just stopped asking. I tried to accept I'd never know how I got here, if any birth parents would ever show up looking for me. I thought one day Mom might tell me, but then she got ill so quickly, and now Pop isn't his old self...' She trailed off, and Maryse sat back down beside her. She placed one hand on Amelia's back, the softness of the gesture causing Amelia's chest to ache.

'Grandma probably thought she had more time.'

'And I don't blame her for that. We all always think there's more time.'

Maryse gave her an encouraging smile. 'Speaking of...' She said. 'We only have a couple of hours or so before it gets crazy busy in here with the movers.'

Amelia stopped stalling. She opened the box and, one by one, began to pick out the letters. She took a deep breath, her gaze avoiding the words on each page. *One step at a time.* 'Let's be practical about this,' she said. 'We shouldn't dive in before we know how it's all ordered. Shall we sort by date, or by format?'

Maryse turned up her palm to accept whatever her mother would give her. 'I think by date. They might be from decades apart, for all we know. And we'll keep an eye out for your birth year, and Barkley's, too. Who knows what might be in here?'

'Fine,' was all Amelia could manage to say. It felt as though her hands weren't her own as she and Maryse sifted through the box, their touch of the artefacts as delicate as if they were handling baby birds.

Amelia's nerves burned as she lifted letter from telegram from postcard, doing her best to read only the date. The first line of each one was always the same – well wishing, thanking for the last letter – so, luckily, she wasn't distracted by the contents before she needed to reach for the next one.

'Eh? What's this?'

Amelia looked up from the patchwork quilt of letters, postcards, news stories and telegrams which blanketed the table. She'd been engrossed in finding the dates, pinning together a timeline and laying it neatly on the dresser.

'What have you found?'

'Some kind of book.'

Amelia placed down the christening photo she held – trying to work out if it came before or after a letter about a wedding in the same year – and turned her attention to Maryse.

A leather-bound book lay beneath the faded orange hand-kerchief, gold lettering along the book's cracked spine just about making the title and author's name visible.

A Midsummer Night's Dream and Selected Sonnets. William Shakespeare.

'It looks like the cover might come off if we try and move it,' Maryse warned, running her fingers along the book's cracked spine.

Amelia could see she was right; the cover had clearly been lifted so many times that it almost hung loose, the pages curled and dry. 'It looks like it's been dropped in water or something,' Amelia agreed. 'Let's leave it where it is, and work around it.'

Maryse nodded, but kept one hand on the book. 'There might be something underneath, is the only thing. I'll just give it a try.' Before Amelia could stop her, she pulled back the cover.

Inside, a handwritten inscription caught Amelia's eye.

To my love,
  We are such stuff as dreams are made on.
  Yours, P

'*P*? Who is *P*?' Amelia asked aloud. 'Is that a quote?'

'I'm on it,' Maryse replied, and Amelia turned to see her daughter tapping away at her phone screen. 'Here – "We are such stuff as dreams are made on" is a quote from Shakespeare's *The Tempest*, said by Prospero to his daughter and her fiancé.'

Amelia's brow furrowed. 'So *P*... must mean "Prospero". Some kind of nickname?'

Maryse pulled a face. 'Who would have been Prospero? Grandpa?'

'Must be,' Amelia replied, trying to keep her tone level. 'They did a few plays with the amateur dramatics group when they were younger. Must have been to do with that.'

Amelia hoped Maryse couldn't hear the uncertainty that clawed at her throat. Her parents had never once mentioned theatre-based nicknames. They'd been far too practical for such things.

Nausea caused Amelia's stomach to flip. What if all this was the remnants of some secret affair? A lost love from her mother's past? Perhaps Amelia was being foolish, selfish, to think these letters would revolve around her. Her mother had every right to keep secrets, to have a part of her life which hadn't been under the label of Wife or Mother.

Amelia leapt to her feet, causing a ripple to run over the carefully laid tapestry of letters, postcards, telegrams and news articles, turning them all askew.

'Enough of this – I've seen enough for today.' Her skin felt as though she'd been pricked with needles, but she didn't want to reveal her new suspicion to Maryse. *Let her believe it's just between her grandparents.* It might well have been, after all. But then why keep it hidden under lock and key? 'Leave that book where it is, and pack up all these others. We'll tell the movers not to touch this.' She scrambled to her feet, almost twisting her ankle in the process. 'I have to go.'

Amelia could hear the wind before she could feel it, the rustling leaves and snapping branches announcing its arrival. She was glad for the warm air wrapping its arms around her, its presence cooling her sweating brow and lifting her shirt from where it had started sticking to her back. She needed to think.

She was almost at the waterfall in Morne Jaloux Ridge after leaving Maryse at the house, the dulcet sound of flowing water coaxing her to keep picking her way along the rocks. She could have taken an easier route than the slick rocks she traversed, but the burn in her thighs helped centre her as she strode on.

She could have gone to many other places on the island to feel closer to her parents as she'd known them growing up: the old Central Bank building, which was now a library, funds for which her parents had helped raise; the little community centre with its makeshift theatre and ageing photos adorning the walls, where she and Barkley had spent many hours under their drama teacher's watchful gaze; the museums and galleries dotted across the island, a wing even bearing her family name in the Island Community Art Nook; the bay at the underwater sculpture park, where her parents had insisted they pay a visit every year, swimming down to see the concrete and steel-clad bodies representing lives lost to slavery and the endurance of their people.

But her feet had carried her here, to the site of her childhood fairy stories.

Amelia's breathing came hard and fast as she finally ascended the last rock pool, rewarded with the sight of cool water cascading from stone. She'd been so fixated on her parents' memory that she could swear time rewound before her eyes: a scene of her and Barkley splashing in the water, with her father snapping pictures on his beloved Kodak, floated into life. She saw her mother running to jump in with them, keeping her hair tied back in a multicoloured scarf, taking turns to help each of them tread water.

Amelia closed her eyes, leaning back into the memory. All four of them huddling on a towel as they dried off, her mother pulling one of them onto her lap to tell stories of the water nymphs and mermaids who dwelled in the pool's deeper crevices and beneath the rock face. The memory swelled and bled its colour, morphing into the sight of Amelia as the adult, with Maryse held close on her lap. Her parents were still there, but in this version, they kept their line-free faces and youthful, bellowing voices. Baby Maryse squealed in delight at the stories swimming around her, Amelia unable to tell whether the words she remembered were spoken by herself or her mother.

A splash caused her to snap open her eyes, the memory dissolving into the pool at her feet.

The people in these memories were the parents who had loved and raised her; no discoveries of secret affairs or forgotten loves would change that.

What am I doing, mining my mother's memory for information I don't need?

Amelia gazed down into the pool, blinking back tears of longing.

Longing to freeze her father in a Good Day. Longing to shield Maryse from the heartbreak which may come her way, to keep Barkley here at home instead of his faraway continent. Longing to speak to her mother one last time, to ask, *Who were you, really? What were you hiding?*

PART THREE
Tanganyika, 1955

Tanganyika with border countries. Map sketch in pencil.
P. J. H. Anderson, 1955.

Chapter 21

Beatrice

West Usambara Base Camp
Mkuzi
Nr Lushoto

14th January 1955

Dear Millie & Bette,

Happy New Year! I hope you're both well, and the children in school are behaving for you, Millie. Bette, how are your university applications going? I'm ever so proud.

As for us – we made it to Africa! Sorry I'm only now getting around to writing.

It took us almost three weeks of travelling to get here: over two weeks on the boat over from England to Dar es Salaam in Tanganyika, then two days driving through the country. Christmas on the boat wasn't so bad, they did a lovely roast chicken.

We arrived at camp last week, and there are four other men: locals Athumani and Chene, a surveyor, Henry, who is from somewhere I can neither spell nor pronounce in Wales, and the captain, Simon. Or Captain Parker, as he insists on being called.

They all took some convincing that I should be allowed to live out here on base camp with them, but I stated my case the way Pop would have expected in his courtroom. I was calm, provided strong evidence, and had an expert witness (Patrick) to prove I would be an asset to the camp.

I'd like to say I convinced them through my persuasion skills, but I think all it took was finding out I'm a qualified bookkeeper. I am now helping to match government budgets with the realities

151

of government spending for their monthly reports. Moral of the story: be careful what you wish for.

Luckily, I have made firm friends with the camp's maid, Hawa, about whom the men neglected to tell me when I was lobbying to live at base camp. She's married to Chene, and while the men are out during the day, she's teaching me plenty about the landscape, all the fruits we can and can't eat, how to brew coffee on the fire, how to sneak a little brandy when the men aren't looking. It's ever so exciting.

Write back soon! I want to keep hearing how life is going back home. I do miss our island.

Love,

Bea

Bea put down her pencil, gazing out of the plastic film that acted as a window in her government-issue tent. It felt good to write the truth to her family after having to lie back in England. She'd already written to Nella, thanking her for their honeymoon stay in London and asking after her nursing exams. She wanted to send her parents a more detailed update, too, but had other work to be getting on with.

She had a pile of laundry to her left, folded neatly on the bed, and the balance book sat at the makeshift desk – a reclaimed, sanded plank of wood from a crate that sat atop an old bedside drawer, worksheets and letter-writing paper kept in place by a few of Patrick's paperweights.

The tent was large, its ceiling held high by a complex infrastructure of poles and pegs, and their furniture was basic but well made. A thin rail held their clothes; their bed was a thin mattress raised by a metal and wooden frame. It was only four feet wide, a stark difference from the double they'd shared on their London honeymoon, but Bea loved falling asleep pressed close together.

She was surprised how quickly she'd grown accustomed to life in the faraway outpost. Letters had to be sent to the Post Office box down in town and collected once a week; food was freshly supplied, water was pumped from the source. It was just comfortable enough to still be exciting, just busy enough to distract from homesickness, living on the brink of wilderness.

Now this, she'd thought the day she'd arrived and been shown around her canvas lodgings, *is what an adventure is supposed to feel like.*

'Are you ready?' Patrick poked his head around the tent's door, his forehead almost brushing the canvas ceiling.

Bea leapt to her feet: putting away their laundry would have to wait. 'Almost,' she said, pulling on the heavy lace-up boots she'd been waiting weeks for. They were already caked in a thin layer of earth, and she'd only worn them around the camp for a couple of days.

'No rush, Hawa's just finishing up the dishes from breakfast.' Patrick came to encircle her waist, tucking in the back of her shirt, which had come loose from her shorts. They were an old pair of his, held up by a belt she'd had to poke new holes in. She felt strangely stylish in them, her dresses reserved for evenings and a rare trip back into town. 'Excited for your first visit to site?'

'Of course,' Bea replied. 'Although I do need to finish up the month-end balance.'

Patrick nuzzled into her neck, kissing her so her cheeks grew hot. 'Don't worry about all that,' he said softly. 'I can't believe how good you look in those shorts.' He began to pull her shirt back out from her waistband, running his fingertips along her waistline.

'Do we have time?' Bea whispered, her mind slowing as he grazed her bare skin. The heat between her legs intensified as he kissed her collarbone, and she began to unbutton his shirt and tug it from his shoulders.

'Bea, Patrick? The jeep's here!'

Hawa's voice cut through the canvas walls, and they broke apart reluctantly. 'Later,' Patrick promised, and they shared a laugh as they hastily re-dressed.

'This is what they were worried about – having a wife at camp becoming too much of a distraction,' Bea teased, keeping her voice low, looping her arm through his as they left the tent. The sun was already beating down, despite the early hour, long shadows cast from shrubs and trees and tents dotting the green-brown landscape.

'Let them worry,' Patrick whispered back, a smile in his voice. 'And besides, it's a small price to pay for having our own book-keeper keeping us in line.'

'There you are,' Athumani scolded lightly. 'You two took your time.'

Patrick shrugged, and Bea avoided looking at him in case she started to laugh. 'Just checking a couple of expenditures,' she said, her chin raised high.

'Sure you were,' Athu replied, a glint in his eye. 'We all set?'

'All set,' called Chene from the driver's seat. The rest of them climbed into the back of the jeep, shuffling around to make room on the bench seating. They trundled away from camp, the wind whipping through the open windows. As they neared their destination the wind slowed, its whistle mingling with sounds of birdsong and the crunch of tyres over weather-beaten earth. Bea took a calming breath, allowing herself to catch Patrick's eye when they came to a stop.

'Right,' the captain barked as they all clambered down from the jeep. 'Get in line, everyone, let's be having you.' He had an ancient rifle strapped across his front, leaving his arms free to clap at the small group. 'Quickly now, right you are,' he snapped.

At camp Bea did her best to avoid Simon as much as she could, with his bad breath and disdainful expression whenever he spoke to her or to Hawa. He clearly lumped them both together as Distractions, Inconveniences – these women so beneath him in race and ranking. Bea was determined not to let him get to her, working twice as hard to prove her books were perfectly balanced, her meals deliciously seasoned, her laundry scrubbed until it shone. She didn't let herself wonder whether a white wife would have faced the same scrutiny; there was no pleasing men like Captain Parker, whatever you looked like. At least he never paid her unwanted attention, which would have been ten times worse.

'You must all know how to handle yourselves around a firearm out here,' Captain Parker continued, marching up and down as if he were an army general, 'as we may come under attack from any number of beasts and predators at a moment's notice.' *Is he going to ask if any of us already know how to shoot?*

Holding the old rifle, Parker barely waited for the group to be assembled before he began his roughly prepared speech. He droned on about how to load the gun, how to hold it up so you could see what you were aiming at, how to pull the trigger and take a stance that wouldn't blow you off your feet.

'You hear that?' Patrick whispered, leaning sideways so Bea could hear. 'You have to take a stance with legs wide and arms up. None of your funny business and twirling about here, missy.'

Bea tried to suppress her smile, nodding seriously along with the captain's instructions.

'Patrick, you served in Palestine, so why don't you give us an example shot?' Simon handed the rifle and ammunition to Patrick, who accepted it carefully.

'Thank you, sir, but I have it on good authority that there's a better shot among us.' He turned to Bea, his eyes bright with excitement and mischief. 'Bea, would you care to demonstrate?'

Parker's expression darkened. 'Don't be ridiculous, Patrick—'

'I suppose I can give it a go,' Bea cut in. 'What's the target?'

She rolled back her shoulders, narrowing her eyes at Patrick when Parker's back was turned. *Go on*, Patrick mouthed, looking gleeful. Bea pulled a face at him, but kept a spring in her step. This could be fun.

'If you insist. Best stand back, everyone,' the captain ordered, and the line dutifully marched back so many paces Bea was almost offended. 'If you bring the gun to me, Beatrice, I can show you how to load it.'

'I already have.'

Parker arched an eyebrow. 'Right you are.'

Bea ignored his whispers to Henry – *'This ought to be good.'* – and the sniggers that followed. *You represent more than just yourself, you know*, her mother's words echoed, and Bea picked up the gun and took a moment to steady herself.

Bea took her shot while standing, obediently, just the way the captain requested. She closed her left eye, bringing the butt of the rifle to sit snugly at her shoulder so she could look through the scope. Locating a hanging seed, she adjusted her position until the seed sat right at the centre of the cross hairs.

She pulled back the trigger in one smooth, well-rehearsed motion, and the seed sliced to the ground.

Patrick clapped her on the back, running to stand beside her. 'Told you, you should've been a sniper,' he said, grinning. Bea turned back to the line to see Hawa beaming at her, the other men looking confused.

'Who's next?' Bea asked sweetly, putting on the safety catch. Without looking, she could hear Patrick stifle a laugh as Parker, Chene and Athumani all took a step forward and raised their arms to volunteer.

After an evening meal of an unrecognisable meat stew, which Bea told herself was chicken, she sat down to write a P.S. on the letter to her sisters.

> *Remember how we used to say 'Why would Pop teach us to shoot instead of something useful?' Well, turns out it might be an important skill after all.*

'Any chance that can wait?'

Patrick's head poked around the tent doorway, a glint in his eye.

'That depends.' Bea straightened up at the makeshift desk, noticing her lamp was burning low. 'What's my alternative?'

Patrick nodded his head in the direction of outside. 'Come here, and I'll show you.'

Bea glanced down at the blank page, pausing only for a second. She'd finish writing tomorrow. Anticipation sparking in her chest, she followed Patrick outside, taking care to mind the guy ropes in the dusky light. The sun had dipped its head behind the mountains, the moon clear and full in a cloudless sky.

Bea could now make out what Patrick was carrying: under his right arm he'd tucked a couple of blankets and firewood, a small book clutched to his chest.

She reached for his free hand as they walked, careful to avoid jagged rocks and cracks in the earth as they strolled to the camp's boundary. They ducked out of sight, Patrick laying out the blankets with a flourish.

'The stars here are like nothing you've ever seen – no lights for miles around. It's incredible.' He smoothed out the blanket and gestured for Bea to take a seat. 'We could make a fire, but I thought we could lie back, watch the stars a while first.'

Bea lowered herself to the ground, the uneven earth softened by heavy cotton. Tipping back her head, she felt a deep sense of peace wash over her. The stars above gave the evening sky a bejewelled glow, sparkling clouds of faraway galaxies drawing her up and out of herself until she felt as though she was floating.

Patrick's hand found hers as he lay by her side, the rise and fall of his breath the only sound in her ears.

'This is beautiful,' she whispered. 'It makes me feel so small, but in a good way. The world has never seemed so wide.'

Patrick rolled on to his side, his hand brushing Bea's waist and coming to rest on her lower back. 'I have my whole world right here.'

Bea felt her cheeks flush. She swivelled to face him, so close their noses touched. She noticed the book he'd brought out with them: *A Midsummer Night's Dream and Selected Sonnets*. They'd read it so many times it was becoming worn, the cover fading already. She could quote Patrick's favourite poem about the stars – something to do with truth and beauty – but now wasn't the time for words.

She lifted her chin and kissed him, pressing her body into his. He responded, pulling her in closer. She kissed him more deeply, an urgency overtaking her as she reached for the buttons of his shirt. Her dress was pulled over her head, cool evening air caressing her bare skin as her body arched at his touch.

Afterwards, they lay looking back up at the stars beneath the blanket, their clothes in a discarded pile covering the book. Bea felt as though she was glowing, part of the constellations above.

Chapter 22

Patrick

Patrick stepped back from the theodolite, reaching into his pocket for a handkerchief to wipe his brow. They tried to get out to the site as early as they could, always leaving camp at first light, around 6 a.m., but the mid-morning sun was already starting to bear down on him.

Since Bea's success at target practice the month before, he'd felt far more at ease leaving her at the camp with just Hawa and the balance book for company; she seemed to be more sure of herself as days had rolled into weeks, settling into life at camp. He'd been worried, at first, what she'd think about his whisking her away from her fine dresses, intricately cooked meals and seaside idyll in exchange for a camp bed, earthen plains and stews prepared over an open flame. But to his delight – and hers – she seemed to relish it. An adventure, just as he'd promised.

He returned his attention to the theodolite, the cumbersome piece of equipment which made his job possible. It was essentially a telescope on a tripod, with multiple levers and discs allowing the user to calculate external angles between fixed posts. He, Athumani and Chene had spent all morning hammering down the posts so they could calculate the distances from their camp to the mountain's base, negotiating the undulating terrain.

That morning, he just wanted to finish calculating the incremental change in elevation before the mountain began its towering ascent. To the naked eye, the ground looked completely flat, but looking through the theodolite's cross hairs told him there were subtle contours. He just had to calculate their exact angles, and he'd crack it.

This was his favourite part of the job: after physically getting the site ready, fixing posts at even sections and setting up the measuring equipment, he got a moment of peace. His notebook was full of scribbled calculations on trigonometry, determining various changes as the ground rose and fell beneath his feet.

He looked through the theodolite's viewfinder and reached just below the telescope, checking the centring plate was correctly levelled. Satisfied that it was, he moved his hand up to centre the vertical axis so it was level with his first fixed post. The cross hairs marked the exact centre of the point in the distance, and he checked the levers either side of the telescope to find the angles between each. Just as he'd thought – there was a $1.5°$ elevation. Small, but significant.

'All right, I'm done here,' Patrick called to Chene, without looking up from his notebook. He'd write up all the distances and angles on graph paper, so they could be sent into the central office to be translated by a cartographer. People often assumed cartography was his area of expertise when they heard 'maps', but he'd never been a precise enough artist for the cartographic sciences. To Patrick, these maps were living, breathing spaces in which to spend an afternoon. The perfect combination of numbers and nature.

'We're all set up for tomorrow, too,' Chene replied, louder than Patrick had expected. He looked up, to find Chene right next to him. 'We're getting through the work faster than I expected. It's only the eleventh, so we still have all month to finish this area.'

Patrick's stomach lurched. 'Today is the eleventh? Of February?'

Chene looked puzzled, and nodded slowly. The sun lit him up from behind, casting a long shadow over Patrick. 'Yes. It's also a Friday. If we're lucky, Athu will break out his good supply of banana beer. He's been brewing it for weeks.'

Patrick hoped Chene couldn't see his hands shaking as he put back his notebook. 'Right, that sounds great. Shall we get ready to head back?'

Chene nodded, and began to help Patrick disassemble the theodolite. The eleventh of February: his father's birthday.

As he, Chene and Athumani headed to the jeep, ready to retreat to the shade of their camp during the midday sun, Patrick thought back to the last time he'd truly celebrated his father's birthday. Charles Anderson had never liked a fuss, but on his fiftieth, he'd insisted Patrick come over from his station in Belfast to celebrate. The evening was seared into Patrick's memories like a hot poker mark, because it had been the only time in his life he remembered his father saying he loved him. Granted, they'd had so much whiskey Patrick could hardly have spelt his own name at the time, but it had still happened.

The jeep lurched forward, and Patrick snapped back into the present. The camp came into view as they meandered their way past ravines and jagged rocks, shrubs and swaying baobab trees. It was too late to write and wish his father many happy returns of the day now, anyway. What would he even say?

Patrick hesitated, getting down from the jeep and collecting up his equipment. He wouldn't burden Bea with this, he decided. No need to bring up someone who certainly wasn't giving them a second thought, who had cast them away like yesterday's newspaper.

'Good day?' Bea was suddenly before him, wringing a tea towel in her hands. 'Lunch is on the go. Spiced bean stew. I think Hawa's just doing a roti to go with it.'

'A roti? Sounds very Tanganyikan.'

Bea swatted him with the tea towel. 'You'd be surprised. Hawa said she used to work for an Indian family when she was first in service. She has a proper tandoor, like the Indian families back home, so she's making the roti authentically.' She paused for a beat. 'My mom always just used to fry them.'

'I'm sure it will be delicious,' Patrick said, pulling Bea in for a quick kiss. This was his family now; he didn't need the one he'd come from.

'Come on, let's get washed up to eat.' Bea took his hand and led him to the wash station, beside the well and water pump. She'd already pulled up a couple of bucketfuls, and the two of them washed their hands in time to the song of an ashy starling which had come to perch on the baobob tree behind them. 'Are you sure you're all right?' Bea asked again. 'You seem quite quiet.'

Patrick sighed. Did he tell her, risk bringing her down? 'It's ... It's nothing. Just a long morning.'

Bea dried her hands and handed him the tea towel. 'If you say so.' He hoped that wasn't disappointment he detected in her voice. 'Athu's finished brewing that beer he was telling us about, so maybe that will cheer you up tonight.'

'Now you're talking,' Patrick said, forcing enthusiasm into his voice so it came out far louder than he'd meant. Bea cast a sideways look at him, but shrugged. She headed back towards the camp's centre, Patrick following close behind. He shook his head quickly, desperate to dislodge thoughts of his father. Charles Anderson had already almost cost him his wife, and he wouldn't let him get between them again.

'Bea, wait,' he called, running to catch up with her. He caught her around the waist and lifted her up, spinning her around until she cackled with laughter. 'Sorry, I think I've just been out in the sun too long. I love you, you know.'

Bea grinned. 'I know.' She lowered her voice, encircling his waist and pressing her body into his. 'Maybe we can stop by the tent before lunch, after all?'

Patrick grabbed her hand and broke into a run, the delighted sound of her laughter ringing in his ears.

Chapter 23

Beatrice

2nd March 1955

Dear Bea,

Thank you in advance for mending my shirt, I can't believe I tore it again – and on the same hanging branch. I promise I'll be more careful when I get back.

It's strange, but the thought of being away from you for seven nights feels like I'm missing a sense: my fingertips touch without feeling, my eyes view without seeing. I'm counting down the hours until our work at the mountain's peak is complete, when I can be back beside you, laughing with you, reading our favourite lines aloud from well-worn books. How I used to do these trips without you, I do not know.

Stay safe back at base camp. I've ordered you two more titles which should arrive this week – My Cousin Rachel and Lady Chatterley's Lover. Act surprised when I return, as I'll have to retrospectively write the inscriptions. I've a new tradition to uphold, after all.

All my love,
Patrick

Bea reread the note Patrick had left her, after using it as a bookmark in *Lady Chatterley's Lover*. She was greatly enjoying the scandal of the book, and found herself getting through her work quickly so she could get back to it. It was one of those books which felt as though it was continuing to happen without her the minute she closed the cover.

Patrick was due back that day, after a fortnight spent out at the mountain's peak. Bea had longed to go with him, and had tried not to be too disappointed when Captain Parker had told her, firmly, that the hike would be a gruelling few days, only fit for the men required for the work.

'Coffee?' Hawa offered as the two of them sat by the fire to take a break from that morning's laundry.

'Please,' Bea said gratefully, accepting the cup to warm her hands. They were starting to chap from the laundry – having to use an old-fashioned mangle, the like of which Bea had never seen. At first Bea had found the manual laundry strangely therapeutic, but the last few days had made her hands sore. She curled her fingers around the sweet coffee to bring them back to life, swilling the liquid in her tin cup.

'How are your hands?'

'They're not too bad, thank you.'

Hawa smiled kindly. 'You will become more accustomed to it.'

Bea nodded, returning her attention to the food and drink before her. After sorting out the day's washing, she and Hawa had breakfasted on a porridge-like bowl of uli and fresh mango. The sweet brightness reminded Bea of home.

As much as she enjoyed this strange new world, the word 'home' still conjured images of swaying palm trees and a blue-shuttered house on stilts. It was taste which catapulted her back to her childhood home more than anything, and she hoped the longing in her gut would quieten the longer she was away. She was on an adventure, as she'd always wanted. So why did her dreams still taste like breadfruit and smell like salt water?

'Do they always do this?' Bea asked, after a beat of silence. In the distance, she could hear an unfamiliar birdsong. 'I mean, go away for weeks at a time.'

Hawa nodded. 'It's harder for the wives who live in town, but yes.'

'Do you know any?'

Hawa shook her head. 'Not this time. We move around a lot,

too. Chene has been a guide in this part of the country for seven years now. We've only been based at this camp for the last year.'

Bea nodded, ashamed to admit she'd assumed Hawa had always lived this way. 'And you don't mind Chene going away so much?'

Hawa took a sip of her coffee, leaning back in the deckchair in which she reclined. She tucked her legs up beneath her, surveying the land around her. 'When we were first married, he would go away for months. My job was in Dar es Salaam, as a housemaid. And one day he came back and I said, *let me come with you.*' She paused. 'At least this way, we're together more than we're apart.'

Bea nodded. 'I guess that's true. My alternative would be living completely on my own in town, and seeing Patrick … what? Once or twice a month?'

'That's right.'

Bea considered this, draining the last of the coffee. She was glad for Hawa's company, and refused to dwell on the loneliness that had started to creep up on her each night Patrick was away. This was the life she'd chosen, and the price was being on her own from time to time. Surely, that was worth waking up somewhere as majestic and beautiful as this.

After mornings helping Hawa with light chores and running through that week's budgets, Bea found her afternoons unfolded before her in vast, empty hours. She did her best to fill her time with reading and writing letters to her sisters, parents, to Nella. She didn't admit to them, of course, that she was feeling a little faded. It would pass, as soon as Patrick was back. And besides, she had Hawa, her books, her old letters: she didn't need Patrick to have a good time. *If I keep telling them this was worth it, I'll believe it myself.*

'And I hope you don't mind me asking, but how are you managing?' Hawa asked, breaking through Bea's thoughts. 'I mean, in your condition?'

Bea frowned. 'I know I'm here on my own, but I hardly think loneliness is a condition.'

Hawa's brow furrowed, but she still curled her lips into a smile. The sun hit their tin mugs to make them sparkle, and for a second it looked as though Hawa was holding a beam of pure light. 'I meant the baby.'

'What baby?'

Hawa's eyes bulged. She stood up, fidgeting with the wrapper she wore. 'I'm sorry, Mrs Anderson, I didn't mean to speak out of turn.'

'Call me Bea, please, Hawa.' Bea put down her empty mug, confusion clouding her head. She felt woozy, wondering whether she'd drunk the coffee too quickly. 'What are you talking about?'

Hawa sat back down, turning to face Bea in her fireside seat. The fire had long since burnt out for the morning, its coals just smouldering. 'Please forgive me, I must have made a mistake. It's just...' Hawa looked pained as she continued to speak. 'You haven't asked me for any... advice – for anything to use to protect your clothes from monthly blood. And I do most of the linen laundry, and there's been nothing on your sheets...'

'You've been spying on my laundry?'

'Of course not! I've been in service long enough, Mrs And– sorry... Bea... that I can't help picking up on things such as this. And this is your third month at camp...' Hawa trailed off.

Bea's face grew hot. So she hadn't been alone, after all. She'd been so distracted by her travels, she hadn't realised how much time had passed.

'What do I...? Is there a way I can find out for sure?'

'We can wait for the jeep to get back tonight, and drive into town tomorrow. The hospital is only two hours away.'

Bea winced, and Hawa's hand came to rest on hers. 'Or, you can wait. But this... break. Is it normal for you?'

Bea hesitated. 'No.'

'Let me make you something to eat,' Hawa said softly, departing from her seat beside Bea. 'You'll feel better. I didn't mean to shock you.'

But shock wasn't the sensation Bea was experiencing; if any-thing, it felt closer to relief. She wouldn't be alone at camp, filling her days when the men were off on site by reading stories of other people's lives. She pictured a little face like hers, chubby arms reaching to be held, eyes blinking up at her, expecting to be shown the world. Bea could teach him or her about Grenada, about England and Ireland, show them the world was theirs for the taking.

She smiled to herself, her hand coming to rest on her abdomen. She'd been feeling a little sick, but thought it had just been the new diet and lifestyle in long, hot days. 'Hello, little one,' she whispered as Hawa scurried away. 'How shall we tell your daddy?'

Chapter 24

Patrick

'Surprise!' Patrick called, beaming up at Bea. He'd wangled the afternoon off as soon as he'd got back to camp, promising he'd be on water-pumping duty for the next week if he could have a few hours alone with Bea. He'd missed her more than he thought he would while he'd been away, and he'd woken each morning to find himself reaching for her, only for his hands to land on hard ground.

He savoured the look on her face as she came to sit beside him in the makeshift 'mess hall' – a collection of three bench-seat tables beneath a large canopy – enjoying how her eyes widened at the scraps of material he'd laid out on the table.

'The wind's picking up, so I thought we could fly kites.' For a second, he worried this sounded childish. A week apart, and he wanted to play a game?

'How lovely!' Bea exclaimed, her eyes darting across the colours and prints on the table.

'I did a whip-round for some unwanted shirts, worn-out clothes, that sort of thing,' Patrick said, revealing the almost-finished kite he'd been working on while he'd been away. He pointed to the collection of sticks and twine that spooled across the table and held his construction together, shrugging sheepishly. 'This, I took from the supplies tent. I'm sure no one will notice.'

'Just don't tell the bookkeeper, eh?' Bea replied, leaning towards him with a mischievous grin. 'God, I've missed you.'

She looked as though she might say something else, cocking her head to the side as a smile danced across her lips. He leant forward to kiss her, his lips lingering on hers. 'I missed you, too.'

They broke apart when Hawa walked past, offering them both a pot of tea. She and Bea seemed to share a look, and Patrick wondered what he'd missed.

'So, what's left to finish?' Bea asked, turning her attention back to Patrick. He began to lay out the finishing touches: scraps of material to form tails on each of the kites he'd been working on; the last of the twine and string to attach. He worked diligently, narrating what he was doing as his hands knotted and tied in familiar motions. The technique must have lodged in his brain from childhood, rearing its head now he had someone to share it with.

'It's quite simple, really,' he said, feeling a warm sense of pride at being able to show her something new. 'We're almost done with this one. You just take the string here and tie it to the frame.' He showed her how to loop the strings together and round the kite, forming three separate lines that would make the kite soar.

'Where did you learn how to do this?' Bea asked, fastening the knot on the frame of the kite just as he'd shown her.

'Aunt Nancy taught me. We used to fly kites all the time on our summer trips. Apparently my grandad used to be a dab hand at this sort of thing, he took Nancy and my mother out to fly them all the time.'

'It's a good skill to have,' Bea agreed, her tongue poking out as she concentrated on attaching the kite's tail.

Patrick laughed. 'It's hardly one I can take to the bank. But it's a nice craft.'

'And how nice that it was handed down,' Bea enthused. 'And, Pat, I have something to tell you, actually.'

'Oh yes?' Patrick said absent-mindedly, engrossed in checking the base and the tow line were correctly attached to each kite. He wanted this to be perfect for her, making up for the days they'd been apart. 'Can you just hold this out for a second,' he asked, 'so I can see if the strings are all the right length?'

Bea stood up, dutifully taking the kite from Patrick's hands. He ducked his head to kiss her just as their hands met atop the kite, before striding back to hold out the strings and make sure they were equal in length. 'So if you just stand back there, I can—'

'Patrick...'

'That's right, I can still hear you. A bit further?' He waved, needing just another few inches. 'Only a couple of steps.'

Bea pressed her lips together as though she were trying not to laugh. Patrick's brow furrowed. This had to be precise, otherwise it wouldn't work.

She took the final few steps required, holding the kite above her head. She tried to call something out to him – something about knowing? Going? – but the wind swallowed her words.

'Sorry? I can't really hear you. Did you say we should go?' Patrick looked from right to left, surveying their camp surroundings. 'You're right, the wind is picking up. Let's be off!'

He collected up Bea's kite from the table, grinning at her and beckoning for her to follow. He practically skipped towards the camp's exit, humming a tune under his breath. He couldn't help himself.

Bea caught up with him and he took her hand as they picked their way over the guy ropes, across the uneven ground and around pockets of shrubbery and trees bearing swollen fruits. They stood just outside the camp's boundary, the sun still high above the mountain's peak.

'I'll run them both down if you hold the string?' Patrick said. 'We'll do yours first.' There was no stopping him; he leapt up and ran, the kite held high above his head, energy coursing through him. He hadn't had someone to fly a kite with in years. 'Ready? Lift the strings!'

A gust of wind billowed through the camp and Bea's kite took off, flying above their heads. Its patchwork of faded materials let just enough light through to give the kite an ethereal glow, sunshine coating it in honey. 'Pull the baseline!' Patrick called, frantically waving his arms. He hoped she remembered which was which, although he wouldn't mind taking the time to show her again. At the gleeful look on her face as the kite took off, his heart soared.

Bea must have done as instructed, as her kite's movements became less jagged. It ducked and swooped, the tail twirling beneath. 'All right, can you manage both for a second?' Patrick called again. Bea nodded, and soon enough he'd thrown his kite high above his head. He sprinted back beside her, taking the second kite's strings from her hands just as it began dipping back down to earth.

'Thank you,' he said, panting. He wound one of the strings around his hand and pulled the second and third at exact intervals, making his kite cut colourful loops in the sky. Bea laughed as their kites bowed to each other and began to dance, their music windswept and fresh.

'Look at you go!' Patrick cried, moving closer towards her. 'A natural.'

Bea smiled back at him, her voice low. 'Pat, we need to get a third kite.'

Patrick frowned. *Whatever can she mean?* 'I can't really manage more than one, but we can make you another if you want to try a different shape?'

'No, Pat.' Bea placed her hand on his arm, and he whipped his head around.

'Careful you don't drop the string—'

'We need a third kite. One for me, one for you...' Her smile widened, and she placed her free hand on her abdomen. 'And one for the baby.'

Patrick's eyes lit up and, forgetting himself, he dropped his kite strings and pulled Bea in towards him. 'Are you sure?' he whispered into the crown of her head. He felt as though his heart was about to stop.

'I think so, yes.'

'But this is amazing!' He swept her into his arms, causing her to drop the strings.

'The kites!' Bea protested.

'Forget the kites! This is wonderful!' He pulled her in closer, and over her shoulder he saw his kite land in a nearby tree, a flash of red among the green. Hers fluttered all the way to a patch of bare earth, and from far away it resembled a pile of fallen leaves. In that moment, he didn't care a jot. What a moment, what a life. *I can't believe I found you.*

'So you're happy?' she asked.

'Couldn't be happier.' He pulled back, cradling her elbows. He couldn't dream of putting into words what this felt like. *Happy* was an understatement, surely. They needed a new word to encapsulate this feeling. After years — decades — floating around with the occasional friend and acquaintance, never really belonging to anyone, here he was. About to belong to a whole team, instead of sitting on the bench or waving from the back of the stands, hoping someone would wave back.

He sniffed, trying to keep his voice level. He didn't want to frighten her with all this. He locked eyes with Bea again, feeling his own crinkle as he smiled. His whole world, here in his arms. 'How are you feeling? How long have you known?'

Bea smiled. 'I wanted to be sure, but I realised last week while you were away. I'm a little nauseous, but nothing too bad.'

'Right, yes.' Patrick nodded. 'And I mean, are you excited? Nervous?' He ran his hands through his hair, raw emotion overtaking him. 'We're going to be parents!'

'Lord, hearing it out loud feels crazy. We're having a baby!'

Patrick laughed, pulling her in for another hug. 'I can't believe it. I mean, I can, but ... You know what I mean.' Words failed him. 'Wow.' He paused, running one hand up and down her back. 'If it's a boy, can we name him John?'

Bea snorted, wiggling free. 'Baby John? Of all the people we know, why choose to name a baby after your old school friend?'

'It was John who recommended the West Indies to me,' Patrick mused. 'Without him, I might never have been given the Grenada posting in the first place.' He grinned as the wind whipped his hair around his ears. 'I'd like to name the baby after the person who led me to you.'

'You old softie,' Bea teased. 'We're not having a girl called John, though. No way.'

'Who's to say it's only one baby, anyway?' Patrick added, pulling her towards him again and nuzzling her neck. 'Couldn't it be twins, for all we know?'

Bea laughed. 'Maybe it's triplets. Maybe it's four babies. What do they call it when there are four of them?'

'I don't know, but if we ever have four babies, I think the term would be "outnumbered". Can you imagine?'

Patrick fell quiet for a second, his arms going a little slack. His mind began to wander, and Bea leant forward to bring her eyes level with his. 'It won't really be four, you know. I don't think that sort of thing actually happens to regular people.'

Patrick hesitated for a second, unsure how to explain the shadows his mind had led him into. 'No, of course. I'm just...' He'd just come out and say it. 'I don't think I know what to do – how to be a father. I've spent so little time with my own father over the years, I've never really seen how it's supposed to be done.'

'Oh, Pat.' Bea took his hand. 'We'll figure it out. I'm sure there's a lot we don't know, but there's plenty we do.'

Unease churned Patrick's stomach. He wished he could get back to the elation he'd felt only moments ago. 'I'll write to Aunt Nancy, see if she remembers what my mother was like. She might have some tips.'

'That's a lovely idea.' Bea dropped a kiss on his cheek. 'We'll have a lot to learn, especially with the baby being mixed. But we'll manage it together.'

'Oh, of course.' Patrick nodded, trying not to feel out of his depth. 'You can teach me all about how to do their hair properly, and—'

'That's not what I mean.' Bea paused, and a flash of irritation crossed her features. 'You'll be raising a coloured child. In Grenada things might have been different, people wouldn't mind so much. But if we stay in Empire communities in Africa, or we go over to England? The baby will be treated differently, all because of its skin colour.'

Patrick slumped back a little. He felt as though he'd been winded. 'But surely, times are changing?'

173

Bea's expression clouded. 'Not if my welcome in England is anything to go by.'

'But that would be so unfair.' Patrick felt sick. 'Surely with our connections, we'd be fine?'

'Connections?'

'You know ... I could get any child of ours into a decent school, set them up for a job wherever they wanted, all that sort of thing.'

'Like your father did for you, you mean?'

'Oh.' Patrick took a step back, shocked at his own words. How easily they'd come tumbling from his lips, expectations for a child he hadn't even met yet. Was this how easily, insidiously, lives were mapped out without a second thought?

He felt furious with himself. Bea opened her mouth to speak, but he raised one hand. 'Wait, no. I'm sorry. That's not what I want at all.' He moved back towards her, hoping she couldn't hear the desperation in his voice. 'I don't want to just throw our child down the same path I was sent, without even asking if it's what they want.' Another thought occurred to him, twisting the spike in his gut further. 'I don't want them growing up feeling like they're half from one place and half from another, like I did. They'll be a full person in their own right.' He thought back to the taunts and jibes he'd faced at school – the way he'd buried his accent so deep he didn't recognise his own voice. 'It's a strength, to contain multitudes. We'll teach the baby that, won't we?'

'We will,' Bea said slowly, still eyeing him strangely. He wished he knew what to say to change her face back to her earlier expression of joy. Without his realising, they'd strolled further back towards camp, the kites abandoned. 'We'll teach the baby to be proud of where they're from. And that means teaching him or her about Grenada, as well as England and Ireland. Teaching them about their whole heritage, not letting them ever think the colour of their skin should change how they see their place in the world.' Bea sighed. 'I learnt the hard way how the world sees people like me, but maybe the baby won't have to.' Her eyes tracked out along the plains behind them, gazing towards the mountains. For a second, Patrick feared she'd walk off and leave him, alone on the edge of the wilderness.

'Of course they won't have to,' Patrick said. 'We'll do everything we can to make the baby's life easy, won't we?'

'I don't know if easy is what we should aim for,' Bea replied. Her fingertips slipped from his grasp, wounding him. How was he getting this so wrong? 'Is that what you'd aspire to? Ease?'

'I don't mean that,' Patrick replied. 'I suppose I mean ...' He thought for a second. What did he mean? He wouldn't say he'd had an easy life, but he'd never had to give any thought to what to do next: doors were always open, seats were pulled up for him at any table if he wished to sit. No one questioned his roots, no one had mocked him since his early school years. He'd always been able to get what he wanted with – he could admit – fairly minimal effort. The thought his child wouldn't have that same access, that same privilege, made cold dread pulse through him. 'It's tough to think my child might have a harder life than I had.'

Bea winced. 'Not in all ways. For one thing, this baby will be surrounded by love, at home with us.' Much to Patrick's relief, she stopped walking and turned to face him. The wind had settled to a breeze, sending her skirt rippling around her calves. His pulse quickened. 'And we'll both be around to take care of the baby, to raise him or her, to teach them all the joys that come from being a child with a rich heritage.'

'I like that,' he said, feeling back on even ground. 'Love is all that matters.'

'Right,' Bea agreed. 'Love, understanding, a safe home. All that matters.'

He stepped towards her, the heat of the afternoon sun beating on the back of his neck. 'And you'll tell me if I'm out of line with anything? You won't let me mess this up?' He hoped she couldn't hear the tremble in his voice. 'You won't let me turn into ... him?'

'You won't mess this up, Pat. You aren't your father.'

He tried to smile at her, but knew it didn't reach his eyes. He hoped she was right. 'No, I'm not.'

'Do you think you're going to tell him? And your stepmother?'

'I don't think so.'

Bea nodded. 'Right.'

The wind dropped and left the two of them standing in the quiet afternoon. Patrick caught his breath, letting out a long sigh. 'Now come on,' he said, suddenly desperate to get back on an even keel. 'We need to get back and get ready for dinner. You're eating for two now, don't you know?'

As she chuckled, Patrick felt his shoulders relax just a notch. *We'll be just fine. I'm nothing like my father.*

Chapter 25

Beatrice

POSTCARD

Wish you were here – Eau Piquant, St Lucia

14th September 1955

Dear Bea,

Congratulations on your news! A baby is always a blessing.

Julien and I have been enjoying our honeymoon here in St Lucia – it's such a stunning island. Bette was so jealous when we told her of our travels; she claims she's desperate to fly the nest now you've gone. She keeps talking about the USA and Canada.

Julien and I may travel further afield in future, but for now we are hoping to settle in Springs, back in Grenada. We'll send you our new address once we get home.

Write soon and let us know the goings-on in Tanganyika. The news services give such poor coverage of the rest of the Empire, telling us only of London as though it's the centre of the universe. You're a far more reliable source for what's happening in faraway corners.

With love,

Millie

Bea picked up her pencil to write to Millie, to begin a lengthy explanation on the latest updates from Tanganyika. Having stayed bed-bound for these last few weeks of her pregnancy, Bea had found the most joy in three things: her books, which Patrick often read aloud to her; her past letters and postcards from St George's and London; and, oddly enough, the newspapers.

She'd become enthralled with local updates on which politician had said what, how the British had responded, who was going to take their next seat. A legislative assembly had recently been formed in Tanganyika, with representatives from the three major racial groups all taking their seats and having voting rights on policy development.

The more she read, the more Bea felt the winds were changing, not just in Tanganyika, but across so many African countries. With little else to do, she'd found she had become thirsty for knowledge about how each nation would tread the path away from the war, even looking towards independence. She'd tried to order a couple of the books Millie used to recommend, but hadn't been able to find them through the local library service.

Growing up, she'd always dismissed Millie's political rantings as pie in the sky; they'd never see the British monarch removed from the money or the white faces removed from business, so they may as well learn to live with it. But if independence was on the cards for African nations, it might just work on the islands, too. Her pulse raced at the thought, a mix of unease and excitement at what it might mean. She'd never realised politics could be open to faces like hers, but now that it was, words like 'policy' and 'legislation' made her want to read on. Perhaps it wasn't just her and Patrick who thought the future looked brighter, more open. Perhaps one day Patrick's father would realise his mistake in cutting them off. She didn't risk saying this to Patrick, in case it upset him.

Bea eased up from her perch on the camp bed, her gaze drifting out of the plastic window as she reached for her notepaper. She wanted to ask Millicent about her plans to lobby the local council, to ask if she was taking a leaf out of Tanganyika's book in ensuring equal representation.

But, while she was tearing out a new sheet, a ripple coursed through Bea's stomach and caused her to sit back down with a thud.

'Patrick!' she called out, raw fear suddenly pulsing through her. This wasn't supposed to happen for another two weeks. 'Pat, it's happening!'

The twinges of the last few days had been easy to ignore, to pretend they were something else. As waters seeped through her skirt and onto the bed sheets, Bea knew it was time.

Like an injured child, Bea wanted her mother to stand by her side and tell her that everything was going to be all right as she began to sweat, pain twisting from her stomach and creeping through her back. She needed to hear her mother give her a stern word, get her to steel herself for what was to come. *I did this many times, you can manage it this once. Motherhood is pain, you may as well learn that right from the start.*

When he finally did rush in, far later, Patrick looked even sweatier than Bea was. 'And where the hell have you been?' she snapped. 'This has been going on for too long already! Where is the taxi? The car? Or am I going to cycle into town while pushing this baby out?'

Patrick's face lacked even a lick of colour. 'I'm so sorry, I've been trying for almost an hour.' He raked his hand through his hair and began to pace. 'We couldn't get a driver to come out at this hour. We've radioed all over town, but no one can make it. They weren't expecting us for another two weeks.'

Bea looked up at her wild-eyed husband and wanted to slap him. 'You mean I have to do this here?'

Patrick nodded slowly, not daring to take another step closer. Letting out an almighty groan, Bea snapped her head up. 'Well, then, where's the midwife?' Her eyes narrowed. 'You called the midwife, didn't you?'

'We can't reach her.' Patrick's words were dripping in guilt; panic bulged from his eyes. He stumbled to her side, kissing her forehead and speaking in a low voice. 'I'm so sorry, we'll get you through this. I promise.'

He squeezed her hand, but Bea swatted him away. 'I did not,' she groaned, 'fight tooth and nail to be allowed onto this base camp, only to go into labour two weeks before I'm scheduled into a hospital! I can't give birth in here, Patrick! Our bag is all packed for the clean, professional hospital, not some government tent!' She tried to even her breathing, feeling her ribcage expand

and contract all too quickly as the panic truly began to set in. 'I can't do it here, Pat! I can't!'

'Yes, you can.' Hawa stepped into the humid space, her voice level and cool. 'Mr Anderson, I think it's best you wait outside. This is women's business.'

As a long, low moan escaped from Bea's lips, Patrick backed out from the scene once more and returned to pace up and down. Bea could just about make out his shadow, blurred through the window made thick with condensation.

After fewer hours than she had been assured it would take for a first birth, Bea's contractions began getting closer and closer together. Another wave of pain ripped through her body, tearing her in two. In that moment, she hated Patrick for doing this to her.

Hawa rubbed her back and told Bea to pant. She had no idea whether Hawa had even done this before, but not being in a position to complain or contest, Bea obeyed every piece of advice she was offered.

It suddenly started to happen all at once, as the smell of blood mixed with something worse filled the air. Bea's instincts must have kicked in, because she felt the urge to push and push and pursue the pain in a single-minded determination she had never experienced before.

'Head, madam! His head is coming!'

Another burst of pain.

'Please … don't … call … me … madam,' Bea managed to wheeze between panting and gulping for air. 'Bea. It's B—'

She cut herself off with a deep-seated groan as it felt as though her body and heart were tearing in two.

A rush, a squeeze, and cries that were within and without her own body. Blood spotted the threadbare mattress and her vision blurred.

'Here. *Binti*,' Hawa whispered, breaking through the exhausted cloud of relief that had descended upon Bea. She'd picked up enough Swahili to realise that Hawa had said *daughter*; her *binti* was here, and she was so small, far too small to have caused the earth-shattering pain and fear that had gripped Bea moments ago.

Hawa took a quick look over the baby, wiping her down and severing the line which connected mother to child. She presented the baby to Bea, wrapped up in a blanket which Bea noticed with sudden affection had 'PA' embroidered in its corner.

'Can I come in now? Is it over?' came Patrick's hopeful voice, sounding so small from outside the tent's canvas walls.

Bea's head became woozy, her arms growing worryingly slack around her precious bundle. She thought she was calling for Patrick, but no sound rose from her throat.

'Madam. Madam? Mrs Anderson? Can you hear me, Beatrice?' Hawa called, sounding as though she was underwater. Bea felt an arm on hers as her vision spotted again, and the baby was no longer on her chest. Someone was pressing on her stomach; a faraway voice was repeating the words 'blood' and 'afterbirth'.

'Stay with me, Bea. Stay with me,' pleaded Patrick's voice, another underwater sound to Bea's ears. He was saying something about salt and sugar, but she couldn't make out what he meant.

His voice was becoming more and more urgent as Hawa's hands moved from Bea's abdomen to between her legs. Patrick was still whispering in Bea's ear as he rocked the baby in his arms, his words disappearing before she could take them in.

Blood spattered the floor, and Hawa sat back with a triumphant look on her face. 'Now it is over,' she said, getting to her feet. 'We'll get you to the hospital as soon as we can. They will want to make sure you have not lost too much blood.'

As Hawa began to clean up, Bea's nostrils were suddenly filled with the sharp scent of ammonia. Her eyes snapped open with a painful jolt.

'Smelling salts! I knew it.' Patrick said triumphantly, his voice clear as the sea. 'They always work in a pinch.'

'Only you would describe childbirth as being "in a pinch",' Bea replied groggily, reaching to take their little one back from him. Patrick guided the baby into her arms, keeping a close hold around mother and child.

Pulling their little bundle close, Bea became overwhelmed with an equally warming and terrifying sensation of love and pride and something she couldn't quite put her finger on. Looking at the inquisitive little face with big fiery eyes, soon to turn a deep dark brown, Bea knew, even in her misty-minded state, that she never wanted to let her go.

'*Imara*,' Hawa said as she returned with some hot, sweet tea and tipped it to Bea's lips. *Strong, powerful.* Bea nodded in agreement, gratefully accepting the drink. Her eyes went straight back to the most beautiful face she had ever seen, a tight mass of curls already sprouting from the cone-shaped head. The baby's skin was surprisingly pale, almost translucent in the evening light.

Patrick was whispering something to the two of them, planting kisses on Bea's forehead and marvelling at the beauty in her arms. It took Bea until Hawa had left the room to realise that Hawa had been talking about her.

Father, Moira,

I write to announce the birth of Nancy Eve Anderson, born 19.09.55.

Since holding my daughter the day she was born and each day since, I cannot fathom how any parent could turn their back on their own child for the sake of some outdated, unfounded beliefs. Shame on both of you.

I will follow your wishes and will not send any further updates, but wanted to write and inform you that she is here, healthy, and as beautiful as her mother.

Patrick

TELEGRAM

20 September 1955

Mom Pop Millie Julien Bette – [stop] – baby Nancy Eve Anderson has arrived – [stop] – healthy and beautiful – [stop] – only stayed three days in hospital – [stop] – send love to all – [stop] –

Bea and Pat – [stop] – ///

Chapter 26

Beatrice

Bea had known there was a problem when her telegram home went unanswered. At first she'd put it down to the postal service, the confusion as she'd been in and out of hospital straight after the birth while she and Patrick awaited a change of address to move into town. She'd let herself get swept up in the rush of love and lack of sleep, marvelling at the life she'd grown, who filled her with a complicated mix of dread and angst and adoration every day.

As the sun rose and set on their new family over the next fortnight, days blending into one, Bea became more and more aware of the distinct lack of contact from her parents and sisters.

Until an uncomfortably hot morning, when word finally made it to camp.

The West Indian News
1 October 1955

Hurricane Janet wages war on West Indies

Most powerful cyclone on record sweeps across the islands.

Formed from a tropical wave starting at the Lesser Antilles on 21 September, Hurricane Janet has claimed over 1,000 lives to date.

The Category 5 hurricane is the ninth hurricane and eleventh tropical storm of the year, with winds travelling up to 175mph. In the West Indies, an estimated 8,100 homes have been damaged.

All bridges on the island of Grenada have collapsed, spice crops damaged, and buildings unroofed. St Vincent has been ravaged with multiple homes and buildings destroyed, while St Lucia has suffered the most coastal damage.

Small crafts are still advised to remain in port until further notice from the Weather Bureau. Storm warnings have been lifted since 25 September, however islanders are recommended to remain vigilant.

Communication lines are returning shortly to Grenada, Barbados, Trinidad and Tobago. To report a missing person, please contact your local police force.

The article had clearly been torn from the paper, its edges jagged and uneven. The telegram which accompanied it, however, had been typed out in painfully neat text.

TELEGRAM

8 October 1955

Bea – [stop]– please send money – [stop] – Millicent hospitalised – [stop] – urgent treatment needed – [stop] – Mom Pop too proud to ask – [stop] – aid not enough – [stop] – Bette – [stop] ///

'I'll drive into town and sort out an international wire. I'll go right away,' Patrick promised, pressing a kiss onto Bea's cheek as the two of them sat on the bed. She nodded, mute.

'This … This can't be right. We aren't the kind of family who relies on *aid*. We're the ones who provide it.' She turned the telegram over in her hands, its faded blue-and-black print mocking her with its brevity. She felt dizzy, the heat scratching at her skin. 'The British will go over and sort it all out, won't they? Grenadians are British subjects.' She continued, in a smaller voice, 'We have rights.'

Patrick paused, a pained expression on his face as he stroked Bea's cheek. She hadn't noticed her eyes had begun to stream. 'If Bette says they need help, whatever help they're getting mustn't be cutting it,' he replied. 'We'll get them as much as they need. I'll send the last of my savings and fix this.'

'No,' Bea said, sitting bolt upright. The envelope her mother had pressed into her hand over a year before sprang back into her mind, and she leapt to her feet with more energy than she'd felt in weeks. 'We'll use this,' she said, rifling through her precious box of letters and postcards and telegrams. She found the envelope, holding it out like a beacon.

'Are you sure? We shouldn't spend your savings, Bea. We can use mine. It's the least I can do,' Patrick insisted, standing beside her and gently rubbing her back. 'I know you want to fix this, but—'

'I have to try.' *I can't abandon her again.*

Bea felt her face crumple into a sob as she pictured her parents' house in the storm and aftermath, imagining the fruit trees torn from their roots, the shutters ripped from walls. She struggled to keep her breathing even. 'That telegram doesn't even say what's wrong with Millie. I never told her that I was sorry for how things … What if she's …?' The words trailed off, the air squeezing out of Bea's lungs.

She gasped and gulped, air refusing to fill her lungs. Her heart raced, trying to outrun her pulse, sweat pricking at her forehead. She could feel Patrick's arms encircling her, but his voice was too far to reach. Her body began shaking to the point of convulsion, deep-seated fear strangling her throat.

Before she lost consciousness, Bea wondered whether this was what it felt like to die of a broken heart.

Bea woke to find Patrick fussing over her, Nancy strapped to his chest in a dangerously loose sling.

'What do you think you're doing?' Bea scolded. 'It has to be more like a swaddle.' She raised her head and found that Patrick must have moved her so she lay down on their bed.

'If you can tell me off, you must be feeling better,' Patrick quipped back. He sat beside her, dutifully tightening the swaddling around Nancy and the material lashed to his waist. 'How did you learn to do this?'

'Hawa showed me. And I don't know, I just sort of worked it out for different positions.'

Bea rubbed her temples, gazing around the room. There was a pile of laundry to do, and her desk was a complete mess.

'Hey,' Patrick said as if reading her thoughts. 'Stop worrying. Just rest.'

'How can I rest when my sister is ... is ...' Bea couldn't say the word. She screwed her eyes shut tight, willing the panic in her body to slow. She felt as though needles had pricked her blood, her whole body awash with fear.

'It's all right.' Patrick rested his free hand on hers, his other cradling Nancy from outside the sling. 'I've sent the wire transfer, it's all in order.'

Bea's eyes flew open. 'I wanted to use my savings – my money.'

'I know you did, but that's yours. You should keep it.'

'What ... in case I want to run back home like Mom said?'

Patrick looked stung. 'You know that isn't what I meant.'

'I know.' Bea collapsed back onto the bed, her heart pounding. 'You should have asked me, though.'

'You'd have only told me not to, but you can save your money for yourself. I wanted to help. Millie's my family, too.' Patrick's voice was small when he said those last few words, but Bea heard him clearly enough. A cold shame washed over her; she knew she was behaving like a child. *I wanted to be the one to save the day.*

'Thank you,' she grumbled. She took a deep breath, feeling her breathing even out.

'It's all right. We'll get Millie all the help she needs and she'll get better.' He reached for her hand again, and this time she let him take it. 'It's going to be all right, Bea.'

They sat in the quiet, Bea fidgeting with the thin blanket she lay on. 'I just can't believe I wasn't there. Everyone I know was impacted, and what was I doing?' She shook her head, the taste of guilt thick on her tongue. 'It's not right.'

She gave Patrick a sideways glance, a thought occurring to her. 'How do you do it?'

'What?'

'Never settle.' Bea paused, before adding, 'Always leave.'

Patrick gave a short laugh. 'Some people say the Irish were made for leaving.'

'I'm being serious.'

'Right.' Patrick cleared his throat. 'I ... I suppose I know Dublin is always going to be there, no matter how far I go. And it stopped being home a long time ago, if I think about it.'

'So where is home?' She wasn't sure why she clung to this, but she pressed on. 'Why can't you settle?'

'I've never needed to settle before. I've never thought further ahead than my next posting.' He gave her a sad smile. 'And now, I feel like home is wherever you are. And Nancy.'

'And maybe you're worried it will all be taken away from you if you really commit to a place. Like when you were a child, thinking you were moving to Surrey but you got sent to that school instead.'

The look on his face was as though Bea had found a bruise and pressed it. She felt another flash of guilt; she'd only been trying to understand. 'Maybe that's it.' Patrick went to stand up, but hesitated. 'I think you should write to Nella about this. She'll give a better answer than I will.'

'You think I just want answers?'

'You want reassurance, don't you? That the guilt you're feeling for missing such a disaster at home, for surviving—'

'That's enough.'

'I want to comfort you and tell you Millie will be all right, because I know we'll do everything we can to get her the help she needs.' He swallowed. 'But if you want reassurance on how you're feeling, I don't know what to say. When I was the lone survivor of my regiment in Palestine, it kept me awake for weeks. Months. I kept replaying it over and over again.' He shook his head. 'You should feel grateful you weren't there, that you didn't have to see it. You're one of the lucky ones.'

'But didn't you feel so helpless? Wonder if you could have done something differently, and been able to help them?'

'Of course.' He locked eyes with her, continuing to rock Nancy. Bea's arms felt too light without her. 'But nothing you could've done would stop a hurricane, Bea. Just like nothing I could've done would have stopped enemy fire. You can't blame yourself.'

'But if I'd been there, maybe I would've seen Millicent, or warned her not to go out or something.' The fear in Bea's body intensified, panic scratching the back of her throat. 'I can't help thinking I should've been there, with my family.'

'Your family is here, too,' Patrick said in a low voice, cutting Bea to the core. Nancy started to squirm, and Patrick's face fell. 'I think she needs feeding,' he said, turning his attention to unwind the material that held her to him. He handed the baby over, with as much care as if she were made of glass, and dropped a kiss on her cheek, then Bea's.

Bea exhaled, shifting so she could feed Nancy on her lap. God, she was exhausted. 'I'm sorry,' Bea said. 'I'm just so angry. And scared. And you're the only person here to hear about it.'

He came to sit beside her once more. 'I know, I get it.' He reached his fingertips to her chin, raising it slightly. 'But none of this is your fault, all right? Nothing you could've done would change what happened.'

Bea rocked Nancy in her arms, the weight and warmth of the baby drawing her back into the present moment. She knew Patrick was right, but guilt still tasted fresh on her tongue. 'Maybe I will write to Nella,' she agreed after a beat. 'See if she feels the same.'

'All right, I'll leave you to it.' He straightened up, tickling Nancy's back in a tender gesture that squeezed at Bea's heart. 'I'll get you some food, we need to keep your strength up.' He turned back as he headed out of the door, looking over his shoulder. 'Millicent will get better, I promise you.'

Oh, Patrick, she thought. *Did no one ever teach you it's bad luck to make promises you can't keep?*

Bea's existence became shadowed, angry guilt and fear boiling down to melancholy. She woke only when Nancy woke, eating just enough to give herself the strength to feed her daughter. She knew there was more she should be doing – reading Nancy stories, walking her through the great outdoors and filling her little lungs with warm air, showing her off in the market or at the Government Club in Lushoto – but at each opportunity to leave the tent she simply handed the baby to Patrick, her features slack. She'd even insisted they delay their move into Lushoto town, fearing she'd miss another letter if she left camp.

'Can I get you anything?' Patrick would ask, bringing her fried sweet potato and crispy plantain in a bid to keep her eating.

When she needed to cry, he held her; when she needed to sleep, he took Nancy to be cooed at by their fellow camp-mates. They knew to leave Bea well enough alone, no words capable of providing her comfort.

As Bea lay with Nancy on her chest in the early afternoon, the two of them falling in and out of sleep, Hawa's voice broke through the tent's walls. 'Miss Bea, are you in there? A letter has arrived for you.'

'Where is it from?' Bea sat up, doing her best not to disturb the baby.

Hawa didn't falter. 'The postmark shows Grenada.'

Bea scrambled to her feet, throwing back the tent door. She managed to smile at Hawa, her hands shaking as she opened the seal.

'I'll send word for Patrick,' Hawa said, her tone reassuring and firm. 'They aren't far today. He'll be here in no time.'

Bea could only nod, a silent thanks, as her eyes scanned the page in her hands.

St Augustine's Medical Centre
St Paul's, Grenada, W.I.

20th October 1955

Dear Bea,
I want to start by saying thank you. I know it was you who paid for the surgery, Bette revealed all as soon as I woke. I don't know how I'll ever repay you for such a kindness. Bette also said she sent another telegram the day the surgery was over, telling you

it had been a success. But your reply never came. So I knew I had to write.

I can't bear to write out how it happened, as it is something I hope to forget one day. All you need to know is that I was gravely injured in the hurricane – I took far too long to secure the schoolhouse, and by the time I stepped into the road to head for home, the sky and the sea had turned on me. I was found pinned to the ground by glass and broken shutter boards, surrounded by beheaded roofs and dislodged bricks and fallen trees. By the grace of God, it is a miracle I fell where I did. Had I been just a few yards in either direction, I wouldn't have woken up.

The doctors have done all they can for me, but there was one thing they couldn't save. Bea, I've been told that I will not be able to bear any children. The debris that struck me left multiple, severe wounds to my abdomen and shattered my pelvis. The doctors actually used that word: shattered. As though I were made of glass.

I do not tell you this for you to feel sorry for me – I am still here, one of the lucky ones.

It hurts deeply to have the chance for children robbed from me, but perhaps this will free up my hands to work with the daughters of others. I've recently learnt of a group doing just that: they call themselves the Soroptimists, working to better the lives of women and girls here on the islands. I plan to offer the West Indian chapter my support, as soon as I'm well enough to walk.

Write to us soon, and please don't hold back. I may not be able to have a child of my own now, but I still want to hear every detail about yours.

All my love,
Millicent

2015

SATURDAY MORNING

Grandma's grapefruit pound cake

- 9 oz plain flour
- 9 oz granulated sugar
- Large pinch of baking powder
- Large pinch salt
- 6 tablespoons lard or butter
- 7 oz yoghurt or cream cheese
- 2 large eggs
- 2 oz canola or sunflower oil
- Grapefruit rind from 2–3 grapefruits (depending on size – you want about 2 tablespoons' worth)
- Few drops vanilla extract
- Few drops milk
- Juice from 2–3 grapefruits (for drizzle)
- 5 oz powdered sugar (for drizzle)

Method
- Grease your tin (I like a rectangular baking tray but a Bundt cake tray also works), then combine dry ingredients and stir well. Set them aside.

- Cream together granulated sugar, butter, and cream cheese or yoghurt until light and fluffy. Add the eggs and beat into the cream and butter mixture along with the oil, grapefruit rind, and vanilla extract.

- Combine your dry and creamed mixture, add milk if it's a little stiff.

- Pour mixture into the baking tin once smooth, and cook for 1 hour or until a fork comes out clean.

- While cooking, make the drizzle by combining grapefruit juice with powdered sugar. You can either use this fresh, or cook into a syrup (I prefer the syrup). If too sweet, add a small pinch of salt.

- When your cake is cool, puncture cake with a fork and drizzle over the syrup mixture. Serve with iced tea.

Amelia beat the creamy mixture with her whisk, her forearms burning. She'd hardly slept, the inscription in the book she'd found playing over and over in her mind.

Its words had dripped in a level of romance only suitable in a film script: it had clearly been sent from a lover and kept tucked away for so long that three generations had walked right past it.

To my love,
  We are such stuff as dreams are made on.
  Yours, P

Thinking about it again made Amelia roll her eyes. Surely, if her mother was going to have an affair or keep a token from a long-lost lover, she wouldn't have kept the book by a dead white man? If anyone knew her mother properly, they'd have given her something far more modern, or a classic with substance and tragedy: a Toni Morrison, a Maryse Condé, a Jean Rhys. Yes, her mother had loved Shakespeare when she'd been younger. But she hadn't known her mother to read – or watch – one of his plays for years before she died.

Amelia would unlock the honest truth, and she knew that chest of letters was the key. She just wasn't sure she had the strength to read them.

Amelia had to distract herself, and there was still plenty to be getting on with. Barkley and Aidan's plane was due to land later that morning after flying through the dawn, so she had a few precious hours to prepare the desserts, stay in touch with the movers as they carted her father's furniture across the island, help her father settle in.

The movers were under pain of death not to move the dressing table, or to upset the materials strewn across it. Amelia blinked away the image as she sifted powdered sugar into grapefruit juice, a pan already heating on the stove, ready to turn sugar to syrup.

'What time can we get back into Grandpa's house today?' Maryse asked, reaching into the fridge to find the milk. She had a shift that afternoon, despite it being Saturday, so she'd volunteered to go in early and speak to the hotel about party plans.

Amelia glanced down at the oven clock. 'Not for another hour or so. The movers will be going back and forth today, finishing off deliveries.' She kept her tone bright as she spoke. Amelia was determined not to show Maryse just how rattled she was by the box they'd found; she was the mother, at least for a little while longer. 'Why do you ask?'

'All those letters – I haven't stopped thinking about them.' Maryse reappeared from the fridge, opening the milk to give it a sniff. 'I know you said to leave it be, but I think we should read them all properly.' She gave the milk a short nod, handing it to Amelia. Neither one had to move from their spot, as their kitchen was even smaller than Amelia's parents' had been: a little nook of three countertops and crowded stove just off the dining area. Theirs was a three-bedroom ground floor apartment, which Amelia could hardly believe had once felt cavernously big when she and Maryse had moved in shortly after Maryse turned two. Their views were mostly of the passing road and surrounding trees, their home nestled into a valley's ravine, but sunlight still streamed through the shadows.

Amelia poured a few drops of milk into the cake batter, stirring it in slowly. 'Maybe.' She avoided Maryse's eye as she spoke, hoping to avoid an argument on the subject. 'Can you hand me the wooden spoon?'

Maryse did so, before reaching for a glass from the shelf and filling it with lime juice from the carton wedged into the fridge door. She took a grateful sip and moved to sit at the dining table just outside the kitchen nook's door frame.

'Don't sit down, I need a hand here. Can you hold the bowl while I scoop the batter into the tin?'

Maryse got back to her feet, slower than she had been in recent weeks, and shuffled back into the room. Her belly was pushing its way through her polka-dotted dress, causing the material to strain at the waistband. 'We need to get you some new clothes,' Amelia observed, glad to have the option of a different conversational avenue. Perhaps if they could make plans beyond the reunion party, she wouldn't have to think about facing family while questioning her own roots. 'These bigger sizes aren't cutting it, you need proper maternity outfits.'

Maryse made a face and lifted the bowl her mother had finished stirring. She raised it over the tin, as Amelia scraped the batter from the sides so it all poured into the tray in a gloopy, citrus-scented heap. 'Maternity clothes are all so ugly, Ma. It's like they think you become a mother and immediately forget how to dress.'

Amelia chuckled. 'No offence meant, I'm sure.'

'I wasn't talking about you. I mean the people who make the clothes! Just because something has an elasticated waistband, it doesn't also have to be in some horrendous print. I saw one the other day with dinosaurs all over it, no word of a lie. For a grown woman!'

Amelia cocked her head, putting down her spoon and lifting the full tray. 'I'm offering to take you shopping, Maryse.'

'In that case, forget I said anything. Somewhere's bound to have a decent maternity range, right?'

194

Amelia smiled. 'Right.' She placed the cake in the oven, turning the timer on. In an hour, she could sort her father out with breakfast and get started on the guava stew. She had a few emails from work she wanted to check, but even Amelia disliked office admin on a weekend.

She straightened up from the oven, stretching with her hands on her lower back. 'So after the party, we'll have a shopping day.'

Maryse's smile faded, and she lowered her voice. 'You're feeling OK about the party? Is there anything else I can do to help?'

Amelia tied her apron tighter around her waist, smoothing it down. She shook her head. 'We just need to get it over with. And once it's done, we won't have to host one again.'

'I would've liked to go to the States for it myself,' Maryse said wistfully. 'Somewhere we hadn't been before. Don't you have a cousin somewhere like Texas?'

'Tennessee,' Amelia corrected. 'But that's Laura, she's a second or third cousin, I think. This lot are all my first cousins, Mom's nieces and nephews and their families. You remember the last time you saw them – they came with you to the sculpture park?'

Maryse groaned, returning to sit back at the kitchen table. 'Everyone's going to do that thing, aren't they? "Lord, you're so grown, child!", and pinch my cheeks.'

Amelia snorted. 'You've got that right. You'll be saying it soon enough, just wait until you're a mother yourself.'

'Surely you don't say it to your own kid.' Maryse took another long sip of her juice, draining the glass and setting it back on the coaster. It had once been part of a sea glass set, but they'd lost all the others. Now, only the conch shell pattern in bottle green remained.

'Well, no, but you'll be surrounded by other people's kids all the time.'

Maryse grimaced. 'But I hate other people's kids.'

'Very few people like other people's kids, but it's the price we pay to spend time with our own.' Amelia took a rag from the sink, wiping down the counters.

She scrubbed at a hardened spot of batter, working away until the sink counter gleamed. If she could keep focusing on what she could control – what she knew how to do – perhaps she wouldn't have to deal with that book, those letters, party planning and house selling. 'Now, shall we get started on the guava stew?'

'There's guava stew?' Amelia's father appeared in the kitchen, a well-worn paperback tucked under his arm. The sight of his dark hair grown floppier with age and his large, kind eyes brought the metallic taste of guilt to Amelia's tongue: how could she wonder about her birth parents when she had all she needed right here? Perhaps she wouldn't look inside that box after all, tell the movers to pack it all up. *What's done is done, and knowing how a story starts doesn't change the ending.*

'Morning, Pop,' she said, waving him to sit down at the table. 'How about some fruit and yoghurt for breakfast?'

'But you said guava stew,' he teased. Amelia tried not to show how relieved she was: he was making a joke, so it was another Good Day.

'Grandpa, that much sugar in the morning would give you a heart attack! Let me fix you some peaches and honey over that Greek yoghurt you like.' Maryse swept back towards the fridge, a look of delight brightening her grandfather's features.

'I could get used to this treatment, girls,' he said, sitting back in his chair. Amelia grinned at him, hoping he couldn't see the bags under her eyes.

'This is delicious, Amelia. Your best yet. A triumph,' crowed Aidan, his feet up on the coffee table as he chomped through a large slice of grapefruit cake. He and Barkley had come straight over when they'd landed, renting their usual Prius from the fancy car hire place beside the airport. Amelia had poured fresh coffee as soon as they'd walked through the door, her chest swelling at the sound of their car tyres crunching over dry earth.

Aidan and Barkley were each other's physical opposites; Aidan was a slight, pale man with round spectacles, almost always wearing as much colour as he could cram into one outfit. Somehow on Aidan, a pink silk shirt looked effortlessly stylish when paired with tangerine-orange trousers. Amelia knew if she tried the same thing, people would ask her when the circus was leaving town.

Aidan was dwarfed beside Barkley, whose stature regularly got him confused with NBA players when stateside. Barkley spent almost as much time at his gym as he did in the hospital operating theatre, his broad shoulders filling out a relaxed band T-shirt that Amelia didn't recognise. He wore cut-off denim shorts down to the knee, which Amelia knew Aidan hated. *If I had his thighs,* Aidan would say, *you think I'd hide them beneath baggy shorts like that?*

'Well, thank you, Aidan. Have I ever told you you're my favourite guest?' Amelia replied, breaking off a piece of the moist cake with her own fork and popping it into her mouth. Even she could admit she'd got the balance of sweet and tart just right; the syrup was thick without being cloying, and tangy without being sharp. She savoured the mouthful, its taste made even brighter by the company she now kept.

As Barkley asked Maryse about how her work was going – when she was starting her maternity leave; could she lead snorkel tours right up until her due date? – Amelia let the cogs of her mind slow. Barkley was here, and even if they were making nonsense small talk, he always knew what to say. He'd help her to face what was in their mother's memory box, regardless of his therapist-speak. He was a man of science, so she refused to believe he didn't want answers as much as she did.

Amelia cast her eyes towards her father, now dressed in his favourite smart-casual polo and slacks. He seemed at ease, if not entirely present. He was leaning back in the armchair, his eyes following the conversation as it batted around the room like a cricket ball.

'We used to go snorkelling, didn't we?' he said, cutting into the conversation between Maryse and Aidan about the last group she'd taken out.

Maryse hesitated. 'I guess we did. You bought me my first goggles, didn't you?'

He shook his head. 'No, your mother gave them to you. Her sister had sent over a set, but they were too small for your mother so she gave them to you.' He sat back, a proud smile spreading across his face.

'That was me, Pop,' Amelia replied, trying and failing to meet his gaze. She stood up and began busying herself collecting the plates from everyone's outstretched hands. 'But you bought Maryse's first snorkel set, didn't you? It was blue, with white stripes along the mouthpiece.'

'With matching flippers,' Maryse added. 'Remember?'

Amelia took her father's plate, his face clouding. 'Eh, what am I saying? Yes, I remember.' He thrust his plate at Amelia, and she could hardly bear to look at him. She rushed into the kitchen, dropping the plates into the sink with a clatter. She took long, deep breaths leaning over the sink, with her head angled down in case she started to cry and needed the tears to drop straight into the sink – a trick an old boss had taught her, which had served her well when working on particularly heart-wrenching cases. Apparently, she had become one herself.

'Do you want to head out?' Barkley appeared behind her, leaning past to pick up the plates and stack them properly. 'Aidan and Maryse can entertain Pop. Why don't we go for a drive, and you can tell me what's up.'

Amelia nodded, afraid to say anything in case it caused the tears to start. She was too old to be sobbing over her kitchen sink, for goodness' sake.

'All right then,' he said. 'I'll tell them we'll be back in a couple of hours, that we're off to check on Pop's furniture deliveries and make sure the house is all clear.'

'We need to do that anyway.'

'We'll get round to it, but for now let's just… be.'

Amelia straightened up, smoothing down the front of her dress. It was a bright yellow smock that fell just above her knee, so close to resembling a tent but so comfortable she didn't care. She resisted the instinct to scold: *Be what? Quiet?* She rolled her eyes but agreed all the same.

The storm clouds were thickening overhead, and yet Barkley still drove them out of town and inland, towards the hilly district of La Borie. 'This has to cheer you up,' he said, turning up the stereo as an old Madonna track blasted from the speaker.

Amelia let out a short laugh. 'You've been in New York for too long.'

They pulled up just at the side of the St Paul's Road, and Amelia realised where he was taking them.

'This is what I miss most, when I'm back home,' he confided, getting out of the car and walking towards the dirt path up through the trees. His strides grew longer and his shoulders dropped, the landscape welcoming him back with each step. A lump rose in Amelia's throat.

'You don't miss the beaches most?' she managed to ask.

Barkley shook his head. 'It's all the greenery, we just don't get anything like it. New Yorkers see a dead tree and think it means their neighbourhood is gentrifying.' He pulled a face, and despite herself, Amelia laughed. 'I miss being able to pick some fruit and eat it just as you're walking along, being surrounded by all this life.'

'You got plenty of life in Manhattan,' Amelia countered.

Barkley laughed. 'People are too noisy, too messy. I just miss being out in nature sometimes.'

Amelia almost went to ask if now was the time he'd finally come on home, but stopped herself. He'd mentioned over the years about moving further out of town, particularly as he got into his forties, but he could never quite bring himself to take the leap.

They'd only fought about his emigration once, the day he'd revealed his plan to leave. The argument had blazed and crackled, scorching them both into silence for weeks. Amelia had never asked, definitively, if he'd ever move back to the island since. *I lived a whole lifetime being made to feel there was something wrong with me. I'm never going back to that,* he'd said the day he left. That had stuck with her as the moment she'd realised that perhaps she didn't always know what was best for her baby brother.

These days it wasn't simply that she missed him, and genuinely thought things had improved in recent years: since the loss of her mother, Amelia felt his absence like a physical pain. He could make such a difference to the community and to their family, if only

he was here. She found herself mourning the life that could have
been if he and Aidan had made a home near her and Maryse, near
her parents, providing that extra helping hand when it all got too
much. Whenever she tried to explain that feeling – the absence
of Barkley and Aidan, so visceral she could almost hear it taunting
her – she could never get the words right.

'Central Park is lovely,' she managed to say, wondering what
they were really talking about.

Barkley nodded. 'Sure is. Just not quite the same as here, you
know?'

Amelia made a non-committal sound in agreement and they fell
into step beside each other, beginning the hike up the winding
road to the hill's peak. They'd be rewarded with sweeping views
of forests and valleys and stretches of beach, made all the more
worthwhile after the long walk up.

They hadn't come to these gardens much as young people, it
being too far to walk from their home and full of fussy, beautiful
things. It was only after they'd reached and graduated from their
thirties that they finally understood the joy to be gained from
tending a garden and watching things grow.

Barkley had to make do with the roof on his building, lined
with well-tended plant pots once he'd wanted a greater challenge
than cacti on windowsills. Amelia never had as much time as
she'd like to be out tending her own backyard, but loved to lose
herself among the brightly coloured plants and flowers adorning
the Botanic Garden in which she now stood. Its greenery would
be referred to as *exotic* and *tropical* by foreigners or travel guides,
much like the way they described fruit that tasted of anything
other than water.

They arrived at the garden gates, slightly out of breath and knees
twingeing. It had ornate iron railings even taller than Barkley,
shrubs and plants and trees beckoning visitors down winding stone
paths. They took a left, cocooned in the shade of a silk cotton tree.
Amelia reached out, running her fingers along the smooth bark.
'Do you think I should speak to Pop?'

Barkley slowed his pace. 'And say what?'

'Maybe just ask if he knows what's in there.'

'The treasure chest?'

'Memory box.'

'Right.'

They walked on a while, sunlight finding its way through the branches overhead.

'He's pretty delicate. Bringing up the past might confuse him even more.'

Amelia raised her eyebrow, but didn't turn to look at her brother. 'Is that how it works?'

Barkley gestured to take the path further up the hill, and Amelia followed. They were led out from the tree-lined path and into an open grassy plain, flowering shrubs and fruit trees sprouting haphazardly in a patchwork of colour. 'It's not my area of expertise, and some people think it can actually help to trigger memories. But I think you'll be disappointed if you want answers, 'cause he'll probably just have more questions.'

'I wish we could know how much longer we'll have with him like this. He still has mostly good days.' Amelia's pace picked up speed, and she made a beeline for the natural wood bench at the crest of the hill. 'Is there a study we can read? Research that can tell us what to look out for?'

'I wish there was.' Barkley sat down beside her, facing out to the clouded view of the valley below. 'But we just have to take it one day at a time.'

They sat in the quiet for a beat, distant bird calls their only interruption. She could have said, *One day at a time is the luxury attitude of a child-free surgeon who has two PAs.* But she just smiled at him and nodded. No point getting into anything now.

Amelia took a deep breath, allowing herself a second longer before they'd have to leave and go to check on the house, call Maryse to tell her to take the stew off the heat, make sure Aidan was settling in.

'He won't be able to tell you what you want to know, anyway,' Barkley said after a minute or two more. 'Our adoptions will all have been down to Mom. You know what she was like.'

'So what are you saying?'

'If you want answers, you'll have to find them yourself. Piss or get off the pot, Amelia.' He sighed, a glint in his eye. 'You've been going back and forth on whether or not to read these letters, I'll bet.'

'It's a big discovery!'

'It is and it isn't. Nothing changes the *now*, you know?'

Amelia resisted the urge to roll her eyes at him. 'It might do. We can't know that.'

Barkley leant back on the bench, just as a white-breasted dove came to land on the ground in front of them. It pecked around, clearly accustomed to visitors bringing seeds and treats. Barkley smiled, but shooed it away. 'If it's making you this irritable, just do us all a favour and look inside the box, hey?'

'I just... I don't want anything I find to change how I think of Mom. Or Pop.'

Barkley continued to wave at the bird pecking near their feet. 'But it's bound to. No one ever likes to think of their parents as real people, do they?'

'I don't just mean I'm worried she'll be writing about personal things.' Amelia hesitated. 'I don't know what I'm about to unearth here.' She lowered her voice, despite the two of them being alone. 'I found this book with a really romantic inscription, and I don't think it was from Pop.'

She thought Barkley might look shocked, or even angry. But a bemused smile spread across his face. 'That's it? You found something from one of Mom's old boyfriends?'

'Well, when you put it like that...' Amelia shifted on the bench, watching the bird fly away.

Barkley placed his hands on his knees and stood up, chuckling. 'So Mom kept something from a long time ago. So what? If you want to go dredging up the past, you'd better be prepared for it to tell you that Mom was just a person.'

'I know she was just a person,' Amelia replied, irritated. 'I'm just scared I'll find something that will change how I think of her, and I don't want that.'

'It might not be the worst thing in the world, to realise she had her flaws just like everyone else.'

Amelia stood up, too, marching on ahead as they began their descent back down the hill. 'Oh, don't worry, I know how flawed you think Mom was.'

'Hey,' he called, jogging to catch up with her. 'Don't lash out at me because you're mad.'

'It's true, though, is it not?' The words spilled out before she could stop them. *So we're finally getting into this.* 'You ran off, abandoning us all.'

She didn't know why she'd chosen this very moment to pick the fight they'd avoided for two decades, instead of just admitting, *I'm sorry, I'm stressed, I need you and you're never here. I don't know how to do this on my own any more.*

To Amelia's surprise, her brother didn't seem angry. 'That is not fair. Moving away isn't the same as abandonment.' Barkley studied her and took a deep breath. 'It was never about leaving you all, it was about getting away from... here.' He glanced around them, his eyes tracking the intricately planted flower beds overflowing with colour. 'I needed to go towards somewhere where there was a real community, where I don't have to hide who I am. And where I don't have to pretend my husband is my room-mate. Don't act like you've forgotten.' Amelia winced at the memory: her parents insisting that Barkley introduce Aidan as no more than a friend when the two of them first returned to the island. *Your grandparents just don't understand things the way we do,* their mother had pleaded. To Amelia's surprise, Barkley hadn't become angry or defensive. She'd simply noticed a light extinguish in his eyes, his gaze withdraw. He'd done exactly as their mother had asked, and poor Aidan had to sit through their grandmother waxing lyrical about the importance of finding a 'good wife'.

'I know it's hard for you doing everything by yourself, and I'm sorry I've missed so much of Maryse's childhood and left you to deal with Mom, now to look after Pop. It hasn't been easy being so far away for it all.' Barkley shook his head. 'But you know I can't live somewhere where my husband isn't recognised as my partner.'

'But isn't it getting much better?' Amelia asked, desperation coating her words. 'If you were here, you could spend more time with Maryse and you could join our campaign group, help stand up for the cause, advocate for—'

'It's not just a cause to me,' Barkley snapped, cutting her off. 'It's the reality I live every day. Don't you get that?' He broke eye contact, gaze falling to the grassy path ahead. 'Where I am now, it sure isn't perfect, but I don't have to fear these insane laws. I can be completely myself.'

'As a Black man in the United States?' Amelia couldn't help but ask. 'Really?'

'Yes, really,' Barkley hit back. 'New York isn't like the rest of the country.'

'The Upper West Side certainly isn't.'

Barkley arched his eyebrow, kicking a loose stone at his feet. 'I still get mistaken for the janitor in the hospital, despite wearing scrubs, have to deal with folk addressing Aidan instead of me. I flinch whenever a cop car drives past, even if I'm just walking home after a long shift.' He shut his eyes for a moment, pain wrinkling his forehead. 'You want me to focus in on that? You think I should let it bother me? I'd lose my mind. Do you know just last week, the new doorman asked me if my boss would be back soon. He thought I was Aidan's housekeeper.'

Amelia's mouth fell open, indignant anger rising from the pit of her stomach. 'Are you serious? And all that – it's really better than what you'd have here?' Her voice softened. 'People love you here, you have family.' *You have me.*

Barkley gave a sad shake of his head as he opened his eyes. 'Aidan's my family, too, and his whole life is New York.' A smile curled at his lips. 'And besides, everyone pays a price for love. This is mine, and it's worth it.'

Amelia turned away, watching a dove circling overhead. When her brother spoke of love, the only face that came to her mind was her daughter's. Many would say she'd paid a price to raise Maryse by herself, but she wouldn't change her empty dating calendar for the world. There was more she wanted to say to Barkley now the floodgates had opened, but could tell from the way he walked on ahead that their conversation was over. 'I suppose so,' she said eventually.

The two of them continued in silence. *He's never coming home.* The knowledge hit Amelia like the swollen drops of rain that fell before a hurricane raged.

'It makes you think, doesn't it?' she said after a few more moments of quiet.

'About what?'

'Whether Mom had to pay a price for love.'

They strode on, descending through the gardens as clouds thickened overhead.

At the thought of her mother, Amelia swallowed down the rising mix of panic and frustration filling her chest. *How could you leave without explaining yourself?*

Leaving all desserts cooling in their kitchen and sending Aidan and Barkley to unpack, Amelia found herself, Maryse in tow, back in her mother's spare room. Barkley was right: she couldn't just let this go.

Maryse sat back down at the dresser, diving straight into the task at hand. 'I bet there's some amazing stories in here, Ma.'

Amelia nodded, determined to see it through this time. She only hesitated for a moment before joining her daughter, but Maryse had fallen quiet. Her eyes were popping open, the letter in her hand trembling.

'What is it?' Amelia asked.

'I didn't mean to read it,' Maryse protested, her eyes darting back to her mother. 'But I couldn't help it. I only moved the handkerchief out of the box to see if there was anything underneath and this was here. It had Grandma's name on it so I thought...' She handed Amelia the letter, her hands trembling. 'The handwriting in this one is the only one I can properly read, and I thought it looked just like yours, and I ... I think you should read it.'

The letter Maryse proffered was addressed to Amelia's mother, in handwriting Amelia couldn't quite place; the looping script danced along the page, becoming spidery as the writing went on longer. The paper on which it was written was threadbare, like a much-loved comfort blanket worn until light could flood straight through.

Amelia took a deep breath, and started reading.

It started out addressing her mother by name, a return address Amelia didn't recognise scrawled at the top.

The first paragraph gave general health updates from faraway places. Amelia frowned. What is Maryse so upset about?

A phrase jumped out at her, and she read on.

I'm sure by now, you've spoken to Mom. I'm writing to let you know that I think her idea is our best option. It might be our only option.

I think you'd make the most wonderful mother, and it would bring me such joy to know I'd given you that gift. I've always looked up to you, and think it would be an almighty shame for you to be denied the privilege of raising a child as your own. The world needs the kind of son or daughter you would bring up.

Amelia read on, as logistics were discussed in great detail. Her birth mother would fly over – despite the extortionate cost – and stay on the island for a month.

She realised she was reading it with an analytical eye, the way she would a case file at work. She read it through again, doing her best to drop the act. *Just read it for yourself. This is all you've ever wanted to know.*

Amelia felt as though her body was being pulled underwater as she read on, her lungs struggling to draw in air. She blinked, but couldn't get rid of the dark waves blurring her vision.

Here it was: the truth, in black and white. The first sentence in her story, the first domino to topple and fall.

This letter held everything she'd wanted to know: the who, what, where, when. So if this was all she'd yearned for, why did it make her feel so desolate?

'Ma? Are you OK?' Maryse's hand rubbed Amelia's back, and for a moment, Amelia let herself break.

She'd been given up – given away so willingly that her birth mother had got a holiday out of it. How could she? Bring a baby into the world and hand it straight over, her mind made up before meeting the child?

The thoughts catapulted her back to the day Maryse had been born. Amelia had been about the age Maryse was now, squeezing her mother's hand and screaming bloody murder on the island maternity ward. She'd wanted to have Maryse at home – had even made a mixtape to play during the birth – but complications had sent her flying through the doors of the emergency room and straight up to the ward.

She could almost sense her mother's hand gripping hers, feel the damp cloth dabbing at her sweat-soaked forehead. *You're almost there, keep going. Motherhood is pain, you may as well realise that from the start.*

And then Maryse had burst into the world, screaming her own song. She'd been so small and so light-skinned, taking after her absent father. But Amelia didn't care who she resembled: all she saw was the child she'd carried, she'd loved, she'd wanted so deeply from the day she'd found out about her. She'd reached for Maryse, already cooing her name as the nurses had placed her on Amelia's chest. She'd looked down and instantly understood what *I will always love you* was supposed to feel like.

Over the years that followed, Amelia had tried not to think of the woman who had gone through that exact pain of childbirth – only then to hand the baby over. She'd come across so many women in impossible positions through her job, many of them desperate to keep a child but having little choice in the matter. She'd told herself her birth mother might have died, might have been young, might have been forced to give her up.

But now, here was the proof she'd always wondered about. It had been a choice – an active, meticulously planned choice. She read it back again, her stomach churning.

Becoming someone's mother is a blessing, and I know that you'll be the kind of mother this child deserves. A mother who can love the baby with all your heart, who will have hours in the day and money in the bank to give him or her everything they desire. The dark thoughts that have descended upon me in recent months are becoming too much to bear – giving up this baby feels my only choice, and a child of mine growing up in Grenada feels right. Especially if you'll be the one to love them.

I'm yet to tell P of this plan, but know this: my mind is made up. Millie, I know you and Julien are meant to raise this child.

'I can't believe it was Beatrice and Patrick, all along,' Amelia whispered, her voice barely audible. 'Beatrice was never my aunt, she's my birth mother.' Amelia looked up at Maryse, whose eyes were brimming with tears. Amelia wished she could comfort her, but what was there to say?

Her mind stormed with flash images and half-memories, landing on the last time she'd seen Bea: at her mother's funeral. Bea had been inconsolable as she sat beside Amelia in the front pew. The bereft look in Bea's eyes had mirrored Amelia's own as Bea had whispered about it being *too late, never enough time*, and Amelia had nodded along, thinking they were speaking the same language of grief.

Yet their mother tongues could not have been more different.

All this time, Amelia's birth mother had been alive and well. Amelia's grandparents had even been in on the whole thing, orchestrating it from their hilltop house where you were never allowed to wear shoes indoors or raise your voice or play music too loudly. Or tell the truth of who you were, in Barkley's case. The thought made Amelia sway with anger.

She paused, her mind whirring with unanswered questions and unfinished sentences. This letter showed no emotional turmoil, no heartbreak at the thought of giving her up. Had it been really that easy for Bea, simply seeing her as a logistical problem to be solved? And what of her mother, taking a child from her sister?

A deep-seated ache fell upon Amelia and she blinked back tears of anger, sadness, heartbreak and shame. One thought lodged itself in her mind, and without thinking she reached up to fix her hair.

Amelia stayed quiet for a moment, studying her reflection in the dressing table mirror. She finally knew who was looking back at her, but it felt distorted. As though she'd been staring through glass, only to reach out and feel it flow away as water.

'I can't believe I'm not ... what I thought I was.' It sounded insane, said aloud. 'I always had this ... this feeling I had to be fully Grenadian, or at least from the islands. Like I knew it deep down.' She felt so stupid, shame brushing her cheeks. She'd known she had to be some kind of mix given her skin tone, of course, but assumed she was another ambiguous islander formed from generations of secrets and second families and island-hopping. The idea of being associated with anywhere else in the world not only confused her; it frightened her. Going on fifty years as a proud islander, and what? Had she been lying, without realising it?

Maryse's cheeks went slack. 'Oh, God. Does this make me more white than Black?'

'I don't think we can split hairs like that,' Amelia replied quickly. 'We're of this island, that's all there is to it.' She screwed up her eyes for a moment and took a deep breath, too many thoughts crowding her mind.

'No. I mean, yes, you're right. This is home.' Maryse pulled her braids forward over her shoulder, before her hands moved to cradle her bump. 'I cannot imagine giving a baby away. It must have been such a big decision for Great-Aunt Bea.' Her hand tightened around her stomach, tears threatening to spill down her cheeks. 'I can't even remember why I was so upset when I found out, and now I feel awful for ever considering ...'

Amelia softened. 'I know, love.'

'And there has to be more to this, doesn't there?' Maryse asked, her tone desperate. The wind had finally picked up and was hammering at the spare room window, the shutters knocking like a ghost asking to be let in. 'There must be more letters, more explanations.' Her eyes flashed. 'That book. It must have been left for you.' Amelia's heart lurched. *Love, P.*

'So she must have convinced him – Patrick,' Amelia said. 'He must have agreed to it, too, sent her over here to relieve them of their inconvenient child.' She practically spat the words. She knew she was masking fear with anger, but she couldn't help it: easier, in the moment, to burn with indignant fury than to let sadness drown her.

Amelia felt as though she was watching her own reactions from afar, surrounded by the ghost-memory of her cousins as children. They'd been fun and rowdy, grown taller and more distant with visits that grew further and further apart as the decades went by. Should she not have felt some sort of kinship with them, seen her reflection in their faces? They'd always got along, but surely she should have felt a connection that went beyond shared memories of sandbox playtime and late-night gossip?

'Do you think Patrick ever agreed?' Maryse replied, her gaze locked on the book's faded cover. 'A decision like that … it could've really torn them apart.'

'Who knows?' Amelia slumped back where she sat. She didn't want to think about what happened to Beatrice and Patrick, to spend any more time thinking of the people who'd discarded her like a forgotten toy. Her eyes pricked with hot tears.

It all felt too much. Amelia slammed the wooden chest closed, letting the letter from Beatrice fall to the floor. She ran to open the window, despite the weather, pushing back the shutters so they clattered against the outside wall. She needed to feel the air on her skin, gulp in as much as her lungs could take. *This isn't happening.*

'If she left you the book, she must have left you something else. That can't be it,' Maryse insisted. 'There must be another note, something that explains what happened. Something from Bea.'

Amelia could hear Maryse opening the chest back up, start to rifle through the postcards and letters and newspaper clippings.

But it was no use; Amelia knew it. They'd seen everything there was to see, read all the evidence they could gather.

Besides, she couldn't focus on the words in these faded letters; one thought pierced her mind, repeating itself louder and louder.

Her adoptive mother, the revered Millicent Mallalieu, had been a liar.

How could Bea do this? And how could Mom have kept it hidden?

PART FOUR
Tanganyika, 1956

Chapter 27

Beatrice

The West Indian News

15 June 1956

<u>School-mistress wins seat in Grenada's Legislative Council</u>

Less than a year after a catastrophic injury during Hurricane Janet, School-mistress Millicent Mallalieu has become the youngest woman to be elected to Grenada's Legislative Council at the age of 31.

Mrs Mallalieu, who married Bank Manager Julien Mallalieu in 1955 and has no children, won the seat to represent the St David region. A card-carrying member of the United Labour Party, and volunteer with Soroptimists organisation aiming to improve the lives of women and girls, Mrs Mallalieu is well-known across the island for her support of Independence – which has caused some to disagree with her ascension to the Council seat.

The new Councilwoman said: 'May this demonstrate to women and girls across the West Indies that whatever path you desire, it is open to you.

'I will continue to teach the boys and girls in my classroom to believe in their own capabilities, and to take every opportunity that comes their way. I look forward to serving the community, and working towards greater prosperity for our nation.'

Mrs Mallalieu received the endorsement of many members of the local PTA, her Soroptimist West Indies chapter members, and most notably, Mr Matthew West of Westinghall Industries. The business tycoon recommended Mrs Mallalieu in his most recent speech to the Chamber of Commerce, calling her 'one of the island's greatest minds'. The two met at a recent fund-raiser for the local children's home, of which Mr West is a patron.

'She did it!' Bea clapped her hands and dropped the newspaper article onto the table. It had been sent through alongside a letter from Millicent, explaining how she'd gone about gaining the backing of the Soroptimists before joining the United Labour Party. She'd written in depth about how Mr Matthew West had supported her, joking that she'd thanked him for his kindness by introducing him to Bette. The two were now stepping out, even taking trips to Westinghall's new North American base in Toronto, and made a beautiful couple. *I wonder what Bette found so attractive about the richest man in Grenada?*

Bea leapt to her feet and picked up the article again, taking it over to the pinboard they kept behind the kitchen door.

Their house in Lushoto, Tanganyika, was starting to get tired around the edges, having hosted countless government families over the years. No one had lived there for more than five, maybe six years at a time, the transient lives hinted at in the dusty corners of old-fashioned drawers, long-folded curtains, faded wallpaper in last season's pattern.

The compound was nice enough – neighbours either side who came in for coffee from time to time, bringing their babies over to kick up their feet and wave their fists beside Nancy – but moments like this made Bea long for home. Or rather, for someone to share these moments with; someone who knew the exact cadence of Bette's voice, or the way Millicent's eyes would crinkle when she delivered good news. 'Your aunt is ever so clever,' Bea cooed to Nancy, who sat on the woven mat at her feet. Nancy had to be watched at all times, as she loved to pull herself up to shuffle or crawl over any surface she could find. Just the week before, Bea had only stopped watching her for a second in the garden as she'd pruned back the blood-red frangipani flowers. She'd heard a wail, as Nancy had crawled right into the leaves of a spiky fern. Bea had gifted the fern to a neighbour, replacing it with a border of orange impatiens that framed her garden's barely there grass.

'Auntie Millicent is going to change things back in Grenada, make it a fairer place to live. Have I told you the story of the time Auntie Millicent made us all march, all day, holding up signs saying we deserved the vote? That's the kind of person she is. Always taking action.' Bea scooped up her daughter and checked the time; Patrick wouldn't be home for another couple of hours, and it was the housemaid's day off. Bea knew she needed to get a dinner on the go, but she had to celebrate Millie's win. She wished they had a phone installed, or that the party line wasn't so expensive.

For a second, she slumped in the kitchen doorway. Millie was running for political office, Bette was finishing up her university studies while travelling to and from Canada with her rich new beau, and what was Bea doing? Telling stories of times gone by to a nine-month-old, the government balance book long abandoned in favour of early learning puzzles and picture books. Some days, it felt as though the only person who noticed her was the one who couldn't even speak yet.

'I wish Daddy didn't have to work so late,' Bea whispered.

She couldn't bear to say it any louder – to admit to the isolation that hugged her close day in, day out. The neighbouring women were nice enough, but they kept themselves to themselves, asking only after the children and offering tepid cups of tea. There was nothing Patrick could do about it, busy as he was with his work; best to bury it deep.

Besides, Bea often felt better after reading her letters from family and friends. Nella's letters were becoming her fast favourites, enveloping her in the bright lights of London. *In London, I bet they never have to switch to the backup generator or shoo geckos from the house. Never have to check clothes for tumbu fly eggs ready to burrow under your skin.* In Bea's mind, it was a city with more and more people like her, building communities and sharing music, food, customs, fashions. She often pictured herself walking down a Brixton street with Nancy tucked into a fashionable pram, sashaying in a long coat that cinched in at the waist, waving to friends and neighbours.

Even saying the word *Brixton* conjured somewhere glamorous, somewhere with excitement at its core.

Bea shook out her shoulders, beaming down at Nancy, who'd started to squirm in her arms. 'We're all right here, aren't we, darling?' She nuzzled the top of Nancy's head, the scent plugging that empty well of loneliness that had started to ache within her. She took one last look at the newspaper article on the pinboard, making a mental note to show Patrick when he eventually got home. 'It's not Daddy's fault he has to work late sometimes. These countries need maps if they're going to try and make it on their own, don't they?' She paused. 'Although saying that, I don't know if Tanganyika is pushing to be independent any time soon. We should take a trip to the library and find out, shouldn't we?' She nodded, chucking Nancy under the chin. 'Let's go tomorrow.'

Bea began to walk again, making a beeline for the garden. She'd sit out in the sun just for a moment or two, and make up a story for Nancy about the flowers that grew in Grenada and in London and here in Tanganyika. She'd spin a wild tale that combined Grenadian ghost stories with old English folklore, throw in a couple of the mythical characters Hawa had taught her about back at camp. Then, she'd start on dinner. They could investigate Tanganyikan politics tomorrow – possibly chat to some locals at the library. Engage her brain in something other than recipe cards and nappy orders.

Perhaps, she thought wryly, *I'd be less lonely if Nancy had a sibling.*

The Tanganyika Standard

10th February 1957

Birth announcements

DAUGHTER BORN
Mr and Mrs Patrick and Beatrice Anderson (née Bell) are proud to announce the birth of their second daughter, Rose Cornelia Anderson, born in Lushoto Hospital.

Weighing 7lb 8oz, Rose is great-niece to Nancy Alexandra O'Shea of Dublin, Ireland, and granddaughter to Mr and Mrs Gabriel Bell of St George's, Grenada, niece to Mr and Councilwoman Millicent and Julien Mallalieu of Springs, Grenada, and niece to Mr and Mrs Bette and Matthew West of Toronto, Canada.

Like her older sister Nancy Eve Anderson, the new arrival holds British citizenship as registered through their father.

Rosslare, Ireland

Chapter 28

September 1957

Three months after Rose is born

'Smile for the camera, Nance!' Patrick called, lifting up his squealing daughter as the flash went off.

'And here I thought you were talking to me, the cheek of it,' scolded Aunt Nancy. 'I'm smiling wider than any of you!'

Bea laughed, signalling for the photographer that they were done. The five of them – Bea, Patrick, Aunt Nancy, and the little ones, Nancy and Rose – stood on the windy seafront at Rosslare, getting their photograph taken by a man with a Polaroid camera who would probably charge them *an arm and a leg and a pint of Guinness*, as Nancy said, to keep the printout.

Still, Bea was determined they'd enjoy this holiday. The Commonwealth Office had paid to ship the family 'home' – so long as home could be accessed via Southampton port – and from there, they'd headed straight across England and Wales and over to meet Aunt Nancy. *I must meet my namesake!* she'd declared, and insisted on paying for their boarding house in the Irish seaside town. Bea had been so touched, she hadn't pointed out that Nancy was now great-aunt to two little girls, not just one.

They were planning to stay in London for a couple of days before sailing back, so they could see Nella and Gordon and meet their new baby girl, Hortense. Nella had promised a night of babysitting so Bea and Patrick could go out dancing together, claiming that *'One of us may as well get out on the town.'* Bea could hardly wait. She couldn't remember the last time she and Patrick had been anywhere ... just the two of them.

But for now, she was relishing everything about this Irish trip: the drizzle coating her and her girls' hair, which would leave them with candyfloss frizz; the scent of salt water mingling with frying fish and chips; seagulls calling to one another and waves slapping sand. She felt as though she'd stepped into a picture book.

'Shall we stop somewhere for a cuppa? Positively gasping, I am,' Nancy proclaimed. Patrick nodded, returning from the photographer and wiggling his eyebrows.

'Not half as expensive as I'd have thought, actually,' he said, shaking the photo in his hand with a grin. He bent down so he was at eye level with little Nancy, who'd waited dutifully at Bea's side. 'I think I still have enough money ... for some penny sweeties.'

'Sweets!' Nancy threw up her arms for Patrick to lift her, and Bea's heart swelled at the sight of him hoisting their daughter onto his shoulders. *Nancy will be two next month. Where has the time gone?*

'To the sweetshop!' Patrick declared. Aunt Nancy linked Bea's arm, and they pushed Rose's pram – another gift from Aunt Nancy – towards an open door on the seafront.

'Let's have a tea after,' Bea promised, and Aunt Nancy grinned.

'I'll hold you to that, Bea. A teacake as well, we'll deserve it.'

'That we will.'

Inside stood rows upon rows of sweet jars, and Patrick held little Nancy up so she could see the contents of every jar before making her choice. Brightly coloured gobstoppers were stored beside sugar-coated pear drops, multicoloured lollipops, jet-black liquorice sticks, aniseed balls, shiny brown toffees.

Bea could feel the eyes of the shopkeeper, and the couple of other shoppers, tracking every move she made. Without looking, she knew the shopkeeper was staring at her daughter as she squirmed and shouted in Patrick's arms. Patrick wouldn't notice – he claimed he never did – but Bea knew. These people were all staring, not even pretending to hide their fascination.

That was the only downside of this trip, which she'd realised as soon as they'd arrived and been quizzed on 'where they'd all come from', or worse, 'what are you, then?'. At least in London, there would be many other faces which resembled hers and her children's. Nella said there were entire shops owned by African, Caribbean, Asian people who didn't bat an eyelid when she and Gordon walked in. Here in Ireland, Bea felt as though the family were the hired entertainment for the locals. Whispers followed them around every corner.

Africans, they must be! No, no, they're American. Can't you tell from the accents?

That second baby is white as they come. She must be the maid, not the mother.

'Have you decided, Nance?' Bea asked, keeping her voice light. Rose stirred in the pram, clutching the woollen blanket Aunt Nancy had knitted over the previous winter.

Nancy nodded, gleeful, as Patrick made the order with the shopkeeper. Bea felt a pang; her little girl had no idea, was blissfully unaware of the beady eyes tracking her. Bea plastered a smile on her face, feeling Aunt Nancy's arm squeeze hers.

As Patrick chatted to the shopkeeper – an ageing woman with cobweb-white hair – Bea held her breath. *Please don't reach out and touch Nancy's hair*, she willed. But the old lady said nothing out of the ordinary, and just weighed out the toffee pennies before handing over the red-and-white striped bag to Patrick.

'What do you say, Nance?'

'Thank you, miss,' Nancy said sweetly, and the shopkeeper's face broke into a smile.

'Her English is marvellous,' said the old lady, which promptly broke the spell.

'Yours isn't bad, either,' Patrick replied shortly. The whole family swept out of the shop, leaving the old woman to look as though she'd been slapped.

Bea's cheeks burned hot, but Patrick tried to catch her eye with a smile.

'How about that cuppa, then?' Aunt Nancy reminded, melting

away the tension. 'I know a darling little café just around the corner from here. Get us out of the wind.'

Little Nancy started to wriggle to be put down, and they slowed their pace along the promenade. True to Aunt Nancy's word, a greasy spoon café awaited them, its exterior painted a sunny yellow, windows framed with candy-pink curtains.

Bea braced herself yet again, hoping the stares wouldn't be too heavy. One more week, and they'd have a night to themselves in London. She let her mind wander to the dance hall they'd visit, the dark corners she and Patrick could escape to, the night that would be theirs alone.

'Bea,' Patrick called, snapping her from her daydream. 'They have beans on toast!' He pointed at the menu stuck in the grimy window. 'Shall we get some?'

Bea cracked a smile. 'We have to,' she said, and pushed the pram past the door he held open. His hand rested on the small of her back as he guided her to the table, and Bea caught his eye. She truly couldn't wait to get him alone.

'So, Bea, how is your family getting on?' Aunt Nancy asked, settling her namesake down at the table before making herself comfortable. 'It must be a while since you've seen them.' Bea angled Rose's pram so she could see into it, coming to sit beside Patrick.

'We haven't made it back yet, but we're hoping my parents will be able to come over and visit some time soon.' Bea picked up the menu, sticky to the touch, and tried not to crinkle her nose.

'We did hope Bette and Matthew might come to London for an extended honeymoon this month, didn't we?' Patrick added. 'But the timings didn't quite work out.'

'You didn't say your little sister had married that man of hers, Bea!' Nancy enthused, her eyes lighting up. 'And he is some sort of business magnate? You'll be expecting much better Christmas presents from now on, so you will.'

Bea grinned. 'That we will. Matthew's family own the rum and chocolate exporter, Westinghall Industries.' Nancy's face didn't flicker with recognition, so Bea continued. 'They're hoping to expand over to Europe now that Westinghall is established in North America, so we might be able to co-ordinate a visit one day. It's a great organisation. I think Bette's leading on more of their philanthropy projects now she's taking on the role of chair-woman.' Bea swelled with pride at the thought of her baby sister at the helm of an international enterprise, swallowing down any bubbles of jealousy that threatened to burst. She wished she could have met Matthew properly before the two of them married, too. She'd only ever run into him in her bookkeeping days, on the rare occasions he would come into the bank.

Bea blinked away the thought as Nancy waved towards a waiter, a smile spreading across her face. 'We'll have beans on toast for these two, and teacakes for me and the little one, if you'd be so kind. Teas all round.' She turned her attention back to Bea, catching her eye and winking. 'Shame they don't have any champagne here, we could have raised a glass to your sister.'

Bea laughed. 'Bette would love that, us toasting her from so far away.'

'He must be a very wealthy man if they were thinking of honeymooning this far,' Aunt Nancy said, chuckling. 'When did they marry?'

Bea noticed Rose start to stir, and pushed the pram back and forth in a gentle motion. 'Right when this one was about to arrive,' she said, feeling Patrick squeeze her thigh. 'Your nephew insisted I stay in Lushoto. He was convinced if I tried to go back over for the wedding, I'd go into labour on the boat.'

'And was I wrong?' Patrick asked playfully.

Nancy's eyes bulged. 'You didn't give birth at sea, did you?'

Bea laughed. 'I did not. I went into labour the day before my boat would've left, so annoyingly, he was right.'

'A rare occurrence, to be sure,' Nancy replied, her eyes twinkling. Their food arrived, little Nancy clapping her hands in delight at the sight of her teacake. 'All worth it, though, for these little monkeys.' Aunt Nancy ruffled little Nancy's curls, making her chuckle. 'And you're probably done after these two, are you?' she asked quietly, as she reached over little Nancy to cut up her teacake for her.

'Never say never,' said Patrick, at the exact moment Bea replied, 'Yes, I think we're done.'

1958

Chapter 29

676R,
Lushoto,
Tanganyika

2 November 1958

Dear Aunt Nancy,

How are you keeping? Sorry I haven't written for a while, things have been rather hectic both at home and at the office. It's safe to say, I don't think we'll make it for a visit this year. Here, or to Bea's family.

It's not all down to the unsettled ground around us – the good news is that Bea is expecting again. This time, we believe it's twins! We're delighted, of course, and I certainly look forward to having a busier house. Bea's mother has promised to visit for the month they're born, so at least we'll have some help.

I'd love to spend more time at home and planning family days out before we're outnumbered, but things are heating up in the Commonwealth Office – not just in my department, but across the entire organisation. Deadlines are mounting, and we're under increasing pressures to demonstrate how valuable our work is. If independence treaties are brokered, jobs may be on the line; now that the Gold Coast's independence has been granted (I must get accustomed to calling it Ghana), many other nations shan't be far behind. I hear there are rumblings in Nigeria, in British Somaliland, too. Here in Tanganyika, independence is also on the horizon.

My work here is coming to an end, though, and I'll soon be moved up to Sierra Leone. John is based there. Do you remember John? Best man at the wedding. He has two daughters, too, and he and his wife Sally live in the compound which I believe Bea and I will be placed in. So at least there will be a familiar face in this sea of trouble.

I haven't worried Bea with all this, of course. She's perfectly safe, as are the children, and I'm managing to economise and take on extra hours so we can afford to stretch for the new babies on the way. It isn't up to Bea to worry about all that, is it? I hope you don't mind me complaining to you – I'd hate to upset Bea, so I just bury my head in my maps until the early hours these days. I'm sure things will ease up soon.

With love,
Patrick

January 1959

Chapter 30

Beatrice

18 months after Rose is born / 1 month before the twins are born

'Did you hear what I said?'

Patrick finally raised his head from the desk, where he'd sat down fifteen minutes earlier to 'just check something'. 'Sorry?'

Bea suppressed a sigh. They'd been packing for what felt like hours, preparing to leave for Freetown, Sierra Leone. She'd been hoping for somewhere further afield, but at least Freetown was by the coast. She reasoned she could teach Nancy and Rose to swim when they were old enough, enjoy a few more years somewhere with real sun. She'd get around to talking Patrick in to moving to the Mother Country one day, once the twins were here and his work took up less of his time.

The Lushoto house that had once felt cavernous, now overrun with toys and books and baby clothes hanging up to dry, was being dismantled and packed into labelled, taped boxes. Given that they didn't own any of the furniture, Bea was astounded by how much stuff they'd managed to accrue since arriving just over three years previously. 'I said, you have to pack up your desk. They're sending the cars round in ...' She glanced at her watch; it had stopped. She tried not to scream. 'Well, soon. Can you just hurry, please?'

Bea turned to leave the room, her hand coming to rest on her stomach. She should really be on bed rest this close to her February due date, the kindly doctor had said. But who had time to sit around in bed when raising two children and trying to keep the house from falling apart?

Perhaps she could start packing up around him, and then Patrick would be spurred into action. The girls would wake from their naps soon, and Bea had little time before she'd have to start entertaining them again. All hope of getting productive work done would have to be abandoned.

She began to remove the maps that were plastered across the wall; some were decorative – fully formed sketches of countries they'd lived in or visited, which Patrick had drawn *just for fun* – while, to the untrained eye, others looked like the ramblings of a madman. Graph paper covered in calculations of distances and angles between points fixed on land, with almost illegible notes written beside them – she assumed, to denote exact locations, or where land fell into cliff or became river. She folded it up, and placed the papers on the pile to which she added the sketch of the Usambara mountains, the outline of Ireland, the annotated drawing of Grenada. Her throat felt thick when she looked at it, notes of 'our first dance' and 'where we got engaged' scribbled along the island's outline in fading pencil. *I wish I had the time to be that sentimental.*

'What are you doing?' Patrick asked, his voice sharp. 'I need those.'

'Then you sort them out, if they're so important.'

'I will, I just have to get this finished first.'

'You said that almost half an hour ago!' Bea spun on her heel, the stack of papers in her hand threatening to fall to the floor. 'We have to get this sorted out before the girls wake up. It's the last room, and then we can relax.'

Patrick ran his hands through his hair, locking eyes with Bea. He looked tired, dark circles running beneath his eyes, and despite their argument Bea felt a surge in her chest. He was working such crazy hours, training up new team members in fieldwork and calculation before he left. *He's under a lot of pressure, he's doing his best.*

'Yes, you're right,' Patrick said. 'I'm sorry.' Bea reached for him, to place her hand on his shoulder, but he'd finally started to move. He picked up the document he was working on – some sort of trigonometry example for the new surveyor to learn from – and placed it, carefully, at the bottom of the empty box on his desk. 'I'll get this finished, if you want to see to the girls?'

Bea handed him the maps in her hand. 'Thank you,' she managed, and leant over to drop a kiss on his cheek. He stopped for a second, closing his eyes.

'Things will calm down soon, I promise,' he said, his eyes still closed.

Bea let out a laugh. 'Oh, sure,' she said, indicating her stomach. 'Nothing like two screaming babies to make things feel calm around here.'

Patrick caught her elbows, drawing her in as close as her belly would allow. 'I'm sorry, Bea. I'm really trying.' His tone softened, and Bea found herself leaning into his chest.

'I know. Let's just get the house sorted out, and we can relax.'

He held her for another second, dropping a soft kiss on her cheek. Bea felt a stirring within her, and she brought her hand up to stroke the side of his face. She thought of the annotated map – the notes Patrick had diligently added to his intricate drawing of where it had all started for them. She hoped he could feel what she was trying to say. *I'm sorry. I love you. I'm stressed. I don't know why I'm taking it out on you.*

Before she could put anything into words, a soft cry arose from the girls' bedroom. Bea pulled back reluctantly, rolling her eyes at Patrick. 'I'll go,' she said, not looking back as she left the room.

Instinctively Bea checked her watch, to see how long Rose had been sleeping, but saw its hands frozen in time. She yanked it from her wrist as she swept into the nursery, discarding it in a pile of 'to throw out' threadbare Babygros. She'd deal with it later.

SIERRA LEONE

GUINEA

NORTH ATLANTIC OCEAN

Rokel River

White Man's Bay

Makani

Sewa River

Taia River

Freetown

Bo

Kenema

Moa River

SOUTH ATLANTIC OCEAN

LIBERIA

*S.L. with border countries, map sketch in pencil.
P. J. H. Anderson, August 1960.*

June 1959

Chapter 31

Beatrice

Four months after the twins' birth

Waving at Nancy from the schoolyard, her little hand holding Rose's, Bea had to hold back a sob. How could her babies be in school, already?

Technically Rose was only in kindergarten, toddling in on legs Bea swore she'd only just learnt how to walk on. *How are you both so big?*

Bea knew that here, at least, no one would judge her for crying. Two government mothers from the smaller compound were dabbing at delicate tears as they waved to their little ones, wiping their eyes with monogrammed handkerchiefs. Bea let a few tears fall as she turned back the way she'd come, hoping neither of the girls had seen.

It was happening more and more, since the twins had been born: Bea would be going about her day, preparing a meal or sorting out the laundry, dressing the twins or playing with the girls, and she'd feel a wetness on her cheeks. Her appetite was waning, too, her stomach constantly looped in a sailor's knot.

She hadn't told Patrick what was happening – how her body was turning on her. She'd tried once or twice right after the twins had arrived and her mother's visit had come to an end, but she couldn't articulate the heavy darkness that pressed down upon her while simultaneously spilling out from her insides. She'd hoped it would pass in its own time, but if anything, it was getting steadily heavier, casting longer shadows over her mind and body, choking her voice.

Whenever Patrick finally came home after increasingly long hours at the office, dropping an absent-minded kiss on her cheek before retreating to his study and tackling his mounting piles of paperwork, the idea of burdening him with talk of her darkening mind felt foolish. What was one woman's unexplained sadness compared to the negotiation of a nation's identity, its cartography, its independence? More to the point, what would she even say – I feel sad? I'm lonely? It sounded so childish. Everyone had down days. *I'll snap out of this soon, and everything will go back to normal. We'll talk again, we'll dance again, I'll be happy. I'm fine.*

'Come on then, boys,' Bea cooed into the tops of the twins' heads. They were both strapped to her front in the sling, the way Hawa had shown her back in Tanganyika when Nancy was born, and she'd adapted to create two cross-body harnesses. They were getting far too big to both fit on her front, even at four months, so one would soon have to rest on her back. She'd seen African women with one on each side, so one day she'd have to stop someone and ask how to do it.

They gurgled back up at her, James giving her a gummy smile and William raising a fist towards his mouth. She tried to smile back, but the knot in her stomach tightened. She ran her hands up and down the boys' backs, hoping the familiar motion would keep them more soothed than she felt.

She turned her back on the one-storey schoolhouse and headed back down the road, the school buildings being only a few streets away from the compound.

Patrick had suggested sending Nancy back to England to board: '*It's what everyone else does.*' Bea had had to resist the urge to sock him on the arm. '*And send her off to be educated by a stranger? Without any bedtime stories, or home-cooked meals? Because you had such a good time with that, didn't you?*' She had almost suggested they upped and moved the whole family if he wanted the girls to be schooled in England, but the only time she'd mentioned a move recently, he'd become twitchy. He thought she had no idea, but her starved mind gobbled up any scrap of news she could get these days; even she knew the country was reaching a tipping point. Those who stayed in government were rewarded, it seemed, far better than those who ran at the first sign of danger. And they needed all the reward they could get, with four children and mounting bills.

Arriving back at the house after her short walk from the school, Bea didn't bother to go inside; she'd only want to sit down for a minute, and she didn't have time. She bundled the boys into the bassinets she'd attached to the back seat of the car – their imported Pontiac shipped over the year before – and sat behind the wheel. She exhaled, taking a moment to steady herself.

What if she just drove? What if she didn't go to the market, didn't go through the motions, and actually tried to feel something? Go somewhere?

She'd recently had fantasies of walking out of the door and not looking back, the urge to go so realistic she could swear she could feel the weight of the doorknob in her hand, the turn of it beneath her palm, hear the click of the lock as she pulled it shut.

The previous week, she'd so nearly left the children with Sahr while Patrick was out working. She'd figured she could sit on the bus right to the end of the route, only to see where it took her. She could have packed up a bag, set sail from Freetown harbour all the way to the furthest port. Perhaps she'd finally get that Brixton fantasy, walking down a road where accents resembled hers and possibilities awaited around corners.

She could do that now. Just turn the ignition, and see where the road took her.

A wail caused Bea to startle, her head whipping around to see William's chubby legs kicking out of his bassinet. He'd kicked off his socks.

'That's all right,' she told him wearily. 'It's probably too hot for socks today anyway.'

She leant back in her seat, taking a few deep breaths. *You're not going anywhere, get a grip on yourself. You're fine, remember?* 'All right, boys, listen up.' She gripped the steering wheel, slipping back into character. 'Today, we need to find some ingredients they may not have readily available, so I need your eyes and ears open.' She turned the key, shifting the car into reverse. 'We're doing my mother's recipe for callaloo soup. Your daddy loves it, too. And Daddy has a lot on, he's working hard for us, so we'll treat him to one of his favourites.' Bea closed her eyes for a second, picturing Patrick's face light up when he walked into the room and saw her cooking the meal. 'So, shout if you see any callaloo leaves – baby spinach will also work – and then we need okra, onion and garlic, bell peppers, Scotch bonnet, pumpkin or sweet potato, and coconut milk.' She swivelled to face the boys in the back seat. 'Got that?'

As she pulled off the drive, she wondered whether she looked as though she were losing her mind. Any onlookers would certainly think she was crazy, speaking to babies as though they were grown-up sons. When did she become the kind of woman whose only joy came from silent children, or the imagined face her husband would make to see her standing at a stove?

'Been to the market, have you, Bea?' trilled Sally – John's wife and Bea's neighbour. Sally always managed to look pristine, her thin blonde hair scraped back into a bun to reveal a made-up face, despite her surely having to reapply it multiple times a day to keep up with the West African heat. She wore dresses which looked so sharply tailored and pressed that it must be an effort to get them on each morning without creasing. Bea was certain that if she could, Sally would iron her clothes directly onto her body.

Bea lifted the boys off the back seat and returned them to the safety of the sling, which had felt too empty without them in it for the drive back from the market. It was strange; she felt trapped when they were strapped to her body, but lost whenever they weren't.

Her shopping bags were growing heavy in her hands, but she knew she needed to stay and chat to Sally, as custom dictated. She tried not to let her eyes track the length of Sally's outfit – a starched lavender A-line dress – and did her best not to care that her smock hadn't been washed after two days' wear.

'Yes, just back from dropping the girls, too. Rose started kindergarten this week, she's still settling in.'

Sally clapped her hands. 'That's right, your girls school here! Remarkable.' She gave Bea a look that bordered between sympathetic and condescending. 'Ours are back in England, of course.'

Bea plastered on a smile. 'Of course. You must miss them very much, but I'm sure the standard of education makes it all worth it.' *Doubtful, given I saw you having to count on your fingers to pay the milkman last week.*

Sally nodded. 'Completely. But I'm sure the ...' She paused, scrunching up her nose as if the words tasted bitter in her mouth. '...village school is adequate for your children.'

Through the fog in her brain, Bea sensed an undeniable sneer as Sally said those words. She was no fool; she knew the judgement that surrounded the Andersons. She'd heard the mutterings of the white British wives, questioning whether Patrick could ever be sure the children were his, with their colouring all being so different. *Could be any of the officers, even a local*, she'd overheard at a party, once. The Andersons had only arrived in Sierra Leone in February 1959, right before the boys were born, and Bea had thankfully been too caught up with the children to attend the gossip-fuelled tea parties. She meant to visit with some of the African families living on the compound and working for the government, but still hadn't got around to making an appointment. Everything was so formal in Freetown.

'The village school is just lovely, thank you,' she replied, realising she'd left quite a gap in the conversation. 'But if you don't mind, I really must get inside and start preparing this evening's meal.'

'You do your own cooking? How quaint! You know you can get people for that, don't you?'

Bea gave a tight-lipped smile. 'We have Sahr, our houseboy, he manages the cleaning and laundry. I'm quite capable of cooking our own meals.'

Sally wafted her hand. 'Oh, of course. And you must be familiar with all these,' she winced, 'native ingredients. And the spices, those bitter herbs. I suppose it's all normal, for you?'

Bea could argue, but she could feel James starting to stir in the sling. She didn't have the energy to stand around and face off with Sally. 'Yes, perfectly normal when you take a little care. Anyway, I must dash.'

Sally waved, and Bea knew this conversation would be batted around and twisted into something ugly by the end of the day. Sally would run to the house of one of the other wives who'd been shipped over from some shire county in England, and ramp up the story until Bea was reportedly speaking in African tongues or beating Sally around the head with an unidentifiable vegetable.

She shook her head, hoping Patrick wouldn't be too late home for dinner this time. The callaloo soup would feel like home, she was sure of it. Freetown would feel like home soon, too. If only she could just untwist her stomach, stop the tears clouding her eyes without warning.

Chapter 32

House 6
Wilkinson Road
Freetown
Sierra Leone

10th February 1960

Dear Millie,
Do you ever think about how carefree we used to be?
How marvellous it was when we were all teenagers and
young adults, worrying only about where we'd go for drinks that
weekend, or who would play which part in the amateur dramatics
production.
Patrick and I try, of course we do, but our lights are so dimmed
between school runs and tantrums. Our conversations become so
fraught these days, if we find the time to talk at all. It certainly
doesn't help that we're falling out of step on the unsettled ground
beneath our feet.
Speaking of, I'm guessing that 'Wind of Change' speech from
the British Prime Minister was broadcast at home, too? He can
drone on a bit, Harold Macmillan, but I was pleased to hear
they're planning to honour independence agreements across the
African continent. I made a note of what he said, in case they
weren't broadcasting outside African countries. I thought you'd like
this bit:
'The wind of change is blowing through this continent.
Whether we like it or not, this growth of national consciousness
is a political fact.' I thought it a bit rich, acting surprised that

people want their own countries back. I wonder if Grenada will be
independent some day soon. What benefits would it bring, do you
think?

If I were less exhausted, I'd learn more about all this
independence talk and properly look into the economics of it all
– both here and back home with you. But my time gets washed
away in the laundry or dissolves into dish-soap these days.

I'll have to leave the politics to you, Councilwoman. I know
it's in good hands, and I'm sorry I wasn't more supportive in my
younger years. Will you send me a cheat sheet, so I can keep up?

With love,

Bea

'Mamma, why are you crying?'

Bea whipped her head up from the sink, scrubbing at her cheeks
in sharp, jagged motions.

Not again, not now.

The wet, soapy washing-up glove she wore smeared translucent
bubbles across her cheeks, making Bea curse under her breath. In
her haste, she'd forgotten she was wearing them. She often lost her
way when Sahr took a rare Saturday off, and it hadn't helped that
Patrick's site work had been delayed to drag over the weekend.

'What's that, sweetie? Why aren't you doing your jigsaw with
Rose?'

'I finished.' Nancy's eyes bulged as she took a tentative step
towards her mother, her hand coming to reach out and cling to
Bea's leg. Her bottom lip wobbled, causing a squeezing in Bea's
heart. 'Why are you crying? Do you miss Daddy?'

More than you know.

'Oh, love, I'm not crying. It's these bubbles,' Bea managed to
say, desperate to inject a brightness to her tone. She pulled herself
back into the room, scrabbling around for an appropriate lie. 'Some
people's eyes tear up when they chop onions,' she continued,
babbling. 'I can cut an onion without shedding a single tear, but
washing-up bubbles make my eyes all itchy.'

'All right, Mamma.' Nancy shifted her weight from foot to foot, worrying at the hem of her dress in a way that made Bea's throat ache. She noticed that the pocket on Nancy's smock dress was coming loose; she'd add it to the list, along with fixing the collar on Patrick's work shirt.

'Do you miss Daddy, Nance?'

Her little girl nodded, and Bea's body took over from her mind. She swooped Nancy up into a hug, her soapy gloved hands getting bubbles on Nancy's dress. 'He'll be home soon, I promise. He's just away one more day.'

For a second Bea wished, selfishly, that her daughter was older and could be someone to confide in. Or that Nella was here, or Millie, or Bette – even Hawa or one of her neighbours from Tanganyika. Anyone who would say, *Ah, it's you. Bea. And how are things with you? You must be missing Patrick. Let's cheer you up, go for a dance or a swim. Come on, Bea, take my hand.* Bea was so rarely addressed by her name, these days; always a variation on Mother, Mrs Anderson, or a formal Beatrice. Even Patrick called her 'Mother' in front of the children, if he managed to raise his head from his latest calculations at all.

'Mamma, my dress is wet,' Nancy said, touching the fabric of her smock where Bea's hands held her close. Her eyes looked just like Bette's had as a child: bright, more hazel than brown. Rose was growing into Nancy's miniature, the same heart-shaped face and almond eyes. Rose's curls were even bouncier, growing up and out, yet her eyes had turned a surprising shade of green.

Bea blinked as fiercely as she could, plastering on a smile. 'It's only a little water, it will dry soon.' She placed Nancy back down, stripping off the washing-up gloves.

'But it's wet now,' Nancy wailed.

Bea took a short breath, pinging off the gloves and dropping them into the sink. She reached for the washing-up liquid, topping it up with more water. It needed to last another week.

'Nancy, please. We need to go to the market, and your dress will be dry in two minutes if you go outside.' She bent down, guilt flashing through her. It wasn't Nancy's fault she felt this way. 'Can you go and play in the garden, and see if your dress is dry when I call you back in?'

Nancy gave her mother a wary look, but nodded. Bea exhaled, and ruffled her hair. 'That's my girl, thank you, Nance. I'll get Rose and the boys, and we can get you all a treat from the market.'

'What are you accusing me of, exactly?' Bea said curtly through the wound-down window. Heat rose from the cracked earth of the market road, hot light glinting off the gun slung over the soldier's shoulder. He still had teenage fuzz growing on his jawline, and he did his best to avoid Bea's gaze.

'No accusation, madam. But it is protocol that we search the cars.'

Search the cars heading back to the government compound, Bea thought.

The soldiers' presence had been steadily increasing as independence loomed over the country; they patrolled the streets and generally gave the British a tougher time. Nothing untoward, just a slow-burning reminder of turning tables. Bea knew they were just doing their job – their duty to the country they could soon call their own – but today she was done. She'd held it together when Nancy had toppled over an entire table of buttons, she'd used up change she could not spare to pay double for the plums Rose had licked, and she'd darted behind the shade of the car to feed William when he'd woken up screaming.

Now, she had a week's worth of groceries layered in the perfect puzzle in the boot and four children to get home in time for lunch.

'What crime would a mother of four possibly be committing, may I ask you? Illegal quantities of gone-off palm wine? Too many kanya cakes?' She could hear she was being needlessly rude, but couldn't hold her tongue. The melancholy that had clouded her all morning was replaced with bitter anger, sharpening her tongue to an arrowhead.

The soldier hesitated, arching an eyebrow. 'It's protocol, madam.'

Bea took a short, sharp breath before turning to the back seat. 'I won't be a moment, girls.'

She slammed the car door, marching round to open the boot. 'Look,' she instructed. 'You can check every item, but you're the one who'll repack it all.' She gestured to the canned beans, bags of rice, fresh vegetables and glistening fruit.

As if on cue, Rose started to fidget. 'Mamma, I'm hot.'

'Me too,' Nancy joined in, both of them turning to face their mother through the back seat.

Bea spun on her heel to face the soldier. 'Well?' *Just because my duty is to these children, it doesn't make it any less important than yours.*

He mumbled something about protocol under his breath again, but ushered her on. Bea let herself exhale a breath she hadn't realised she'd been holding. 'Thank you,' she managed, the knot in her stomach growing even tighter despite the vindication. She scrambled back into the overly hot car, wondering why she felt as though she was going to cry despite the small win.

'Let's get home,' she said flatly, watching the soldier's hunched outline recede in the rear-view mirror.

In historical records of coups and insurgencies, Bea found reports never captured the mundanity of war for those fortunate enough to exist on its peripheries. It so often looked like too many checkpoints, women dealing with tinned food shortages, and arguments with underqualified soldiers clutching guns they didn't know how to shoot.

She couldn't go on like this. Something would have to give.

Chapter 33

Patrick

The overhead lamp in the office swung low, its thin cable threatening to snap above Patrick's head. He hadn't noticed how the hours had continued ticking by, but upon looking up from the grid-paper upon which he was calculating border distances, he realised he was one of the few left at work.

John had headed out an hour or so ago, trying and failing to coax Patrick to join him for an evening drink. Patrick had grunted a general goodbye in his direction, absorbed as he was in the calculations on his desk. He'd been doing his best to show his commitment lately; rumour had it that more cuts were around the corner. And those fleeing back to England were being relegated to the most tedious of administrative tasks, if they were permitted to keep their government jobs at all. The fear of this happening to him lodged deep in his stomach, leeching pure panic and spurring him to work that extra hour, pick up just one more project whenever he could.

Blearily, Patrick checked his watch. His stomach told him he'd missed the evening meal, and he sighed at the thought of another night of leftover rice fried with pounded vegetables. He grimaced, and stood up to pack away his compass, protractor and pencils. The temptation to join John in Quentin's Bar – their favourite haunt – and spill soured palm wine on the sticky tables was compelling. It had been a painfully long week, and he longed to blow off some steam.

But as he headed for the door and waved at the security guard, the image of his family flashed into his mind. Guilty for staying out long past sunset yet again, Patrick unshackled his bicycle from the nearby railing and set his sights for home.

'Daddy... Daddy's home!' Nancy's sing-song voice called, and the patter of her bare feet on the tiled floor made Patrick's heart lift. She appeared in her polka-dot pyjamas, her thick hair braided off her face in preparation for sleep. Behind her ambled three-year-old Rose, her adorable curls spilling from pigtails and tickling the tops of her ears. Patrick scooped them both up, planting big kisses on each cheek.

'Where's Mother?' he asked, looking from daughter to daughter. *There she is*, he was tempted to add; each girl's smile was the glowing copy of Bea's.

'Eatin'!' Rose exclaimed, a gleeful look on her face for having got the answer first.

Patrick grinned, buoyed by the adoring looks of his daughters, and carried both girls into the kitchen. Bea sat, shoulders hunched, over a bowl of stew. They were attempting to get the twins to sleep through the night, but one of their heads poked out from the sling wrapped around her chest. Bea's eyes were sunken, dark circles beneath, and her skin looked sallow. Patrick swallowed hard, but tried his best to keep his tone bright. 'Girls, why don't we get you into bed? I can tell you a story, if you're very good.' He tried to catch Bea's eye, to signal that he'd be back down in a few moments, but her gaze was cast on something unseen on the table.

Promising to continue the 'fairy story' he'd been telling them off and on for the last few bedtimes, Patrick ushered the girls upstairs. The story was a reimagined version of *A Midsummer Night's Dream*, but he wouldn't admit it wasn't his original work. 'Do a made-up story, Daddy,' they often insisted, refusing the confines of books with endings already decided.

As he poured all his remaining energy into a tale of faraway lands and fairy glades and woodland creatures, with Nancy interrupting only once to request a scene change, he spoke until their chests rose and fell in the even breath of sleep. He dropped a kiss on each forehead, tucking their bunk bed blankets up to their chins and fastening the mosquito nets around each bed. He paused at the doorway, looking back at them. When had Rose's hair grown that long? Had Nancy's dimples disappeared? He shut the door with a tired reluctance, retreating back downstairs.

'You won't believe what the girls drew today,' Bea said, after he made it back to the kitchen. Her bowl was half empty with the spoon discarded to the side, her hand lightly patting James's back as he stirred in the sling. Patrick felt a pang, wishing he'd been back earlier to see his boys awake.

He sat down beside her and took her free hand. Even in her exhausted state, her beauty still floored him. 'What did they draw? Something from the fairy story?'

Bea shook her head, careful not to wake James with her movement. 'Take a look. Just there, on the table.'

Patrick drew his eyes from her and reached towards the crumpled sheets of paper, smoothing them out to see. Even for five- and three-year-old artists, their subject matter was clearly depicted: one showed a house surrounded by towering walls, and the other showed a shakily drawn car beside a stick man. In the stick man's hands was, unmistakably, a gun.

'They think this is normal, Pat, seeing soldiers every day.' Bea's eyes grew wide as she spoke. 'I've tried to make light of the situation here, face it as it comes. I know it's all above board ... but the girls can't see guns in the street and think it's normal.'

Patrick paused, inspecting the drawing. 'I saw guns all the time in Ireland. It didn't do me any harm, growing up.'

Bea's lips curled. 'Do you think that might have had anything to do with spending most of your time in an English private school with round-the-clock surveillance?'

'You know what I mean. Besides, we can hardly keep them indoors all day, can we?' He looked back down at the drawings, stiffening when he noticed the man with the gun was smiling. God, he really didn't have the energy for this tonight. 'What do you think we should do?'

'I think there's only one thing for it,' Bea said, locking eyes with him as an earnest expression spread across her face. 'I think we need to leave. Nella says London is safe, you and I both have rights of abode there.' He wasn't sure, but she seemed to perk up as she spoke. *When was the last time she looked at me like that?* 'We've enjoyed our visits to Brixton, and you'd find a job easily in the capital.' Bea sat back in her seat, readjusting the sling's straps over her shoulder. 'Maybe I could even find some work there, who knows. We have the children to think of.'

Patrick faltered, unease settling in the pit of his stomach. 'We might struggle to cover the crossing right now, let alone the full cost of relocation. You know it isn't as simple as my just finding another job. It doesn't work that way.'

'Yes, I know, they'd shove you in some boring clerical role.' Bea sighed. 'But wouldn't that be worth it for the children? Can't we at least try and make it work?'

Patrick hesitated. Shame burned his cheeks as he dropped his gaze from hers. 'As I said, it's not that simple,' he began, keeping his voice steady. This was exactly the kind of conversation he tried to avoid: the reason he'd stopped mentioning money at all since the twins' arrival had caused them to tighten their belts.

He hadn't given a thought to his father in months, but with each mounting bill he felt renewed embarrassment flush through him. His father's bigoted views were costing them in many ways, and without his inheritance or any sort of stipend, Patrick was already working more than anyone else in his department to keep their heads comfortably above water. It wasn't Bea's fault she'd married the only Commonwealth officer whose pockets weren't lined with generational gold, and admitting the truth – *We'd have nothing to fall back on if we left. I can't just abandon my government position* – would be nothing short of humiliating. For Patrick, and for Bea.

What would she think of you, if you let her down like that? He simply couldn't do it.

Patrick sighed, continuing his explanation. 'If I left, they'd slash my pay, leave me with nowhere to progress. And besides,' he added, hoping to move the conversation on, 'It will be worth sticking it out here, I'm sure. Independence should be a smooth process and we'll get moved then anyway. Most likely, back to England. And the government would put us up in a house again, so we'd only have to cover bills.' *Which we're barely covering as it is.*

Bea let out a short laugh. 'Or, independence could bring danger. I know it's all being negotiated properly, but you can never predict what might happen.' Her eyes grew distant, and Patrick realised with a sinking feeling that the conversation was over. 'London can be a new start,' she added eventually. 'We can make it work with the money.'

Patrick murmured something non-committal, his stomach churning. He couldn't stand the hot shame boiling his insides yet again.

He would find a way to solve their money troubles; there was no need to worry Bea. He shrugged, getting to his feet. 'If moving is truly what you think is best, I'll ask around about the sort of jobs I'd be qualified for.' He kept his tone light, but he was already calculating how many extra projects he could pick up to cover the relocation fees. A scrap of overheard conversation fell into his mind, and he added, 'Teaching could work for me, at the polytechnic colleges. They always need lecturers with field experience. I'm sure someone mentioned it just last week.' What did professors earn? He'd ask around, subtly, see if it was feasible. He extinguished the sadness that flickered at the thought of telling stories of his adventures instead of living through new ones. *We all have to grow up, one day. It would be for the best.*

'I think you'd make a fine teacher,' Bea answered, her words kind but her eyes glazed.

'Thank you.' He stretched out, subtly checking his watch. It was still early; he could make it to Quentin's Bar after all. Feelings of shame returned, but he swallowed them whole: he was working hard, he deserved to blow off some steam. He'd just go out for an hour or so, calm himself down. No need to worry Bea. 'I think I'll just nip out quickly. I won't be long. Do you need anything?'

But Bea didn't answer, her face turned to study the girls' drawings once again. For an instant, Patrick thought about dropping to sit beside her, taking her hand, asking why her eyes were so distant.

Yet, he did not: that creeping shame returned as he reached for his hat and closed the door behind him. If he stayed, they'd only argue about money or the children or countries of residence, and he needed time to figure out what to do. One drink wouldn't hurt.

Chapter 34

Beatrice

Despite priding herself on her renowned punctuality, for only the fourth time in her life, Bea was late.

Not even a couple of hours – sorry-I-missed-teatime – late.

Bea stared down at the bowl she had grabbed and hauled into the pantry, her only option for escape. Sahr had hardly even noticed as she'd leapt into the tiny space, leaving him alone to clean down the kitchen after the girls' breakfast. Thank God the army truck had started doing house stops to take the children to school, so she no longer had to walk them the three blocks in the morning's rising heat.

Bea braced herself, her knuckles turning white-brown as she gripped the edges of the bowl. Sweat began to pool behind the backs of her legs crossed beneath the bowl, which was now swirling with salty liquid. Her neck grew hot despite having piled her hair hastily on top of her head, a deep pink silk scarf keeping it wrapped in place.

Doing a quick calculation in between waves of nausea, Bea knew she couldn't be more than four or five weeks gone. At an absolute maximum, she could have hit the six-week mark.

Getting to her feet, she fixed her gaze on to the fresh bowl of mangoes that she and Patrick had harvested from the tree at the end of the garden. Only now did she appreciate their swollen flesh, fit to burst out of their own skin.

Where love should have swelled from her heart and filled her body from top to toe, there was a gap of sheer nothingness. Bea felt she had taken a step on the staircase to find that all the steps were done; she'd reached the landing, her foot falling like lead to the floor. She felt no anger, yet neither did she feel joy. She closed her eyes, letting her hands drop to her sides.

She couldn't share her suspicion with Patrick, not yet. After all, what if she was wrong?

Or, rather, what if she could solve this herself, without him ever needing to know?

She must have options, that much she knew. She'd heard whisperings of methods to stop a pregnancy in its tracks: housemaids suddenly made un-pregnant, or wives whose would-be child would not be the spitting image of her husband. It was the kind of act Bea was aware happened to other people, and so it must be a possibility for her.

She stood up slowly, emerging from the pantry and waving to Sahr through the window. 'Can you watch the boys for a moment?' she asked, emptying the bowl and filling it with soapy water. Before Sahr could reply, Bea headed for the front door and, without changing from her house slippers, ran across the sun-baked ground. The party line phone gobbled up the last of her change, and before she could fully admit to what she was doing, she dialled the doctor's office.

'Please have a seat, Mrs Anderson.'

'Thank you, doctor.'

'Your notes here say you want to talk about family planning, is that correct?' Dr Johnson looked at Bea over her glasses, and Bea detected a sneering superiority in the woman's tone. Slightly overweight and sweating in the midday heat, Johnson had the trademark sunburn on her nose and cheekbones with which all the new arrivals were afflicted as soon as they stepped off the boat. Bea thought up a joke she could tell Patrick when she got home, but swallowed it quickly. He couldn't know she'd been here.

The doctor's surgery smelt of bleach and only had a tiny sliver of a window, so a glass bulb hung bare from the ceiling. It filled the space with a sickly, artificial glow.

Bea avoided the doctor's eyes, words escaping from her lips without her brain's intervention. *God, I'm tired*. 'I am in need of a termination of pregnancy.' It tumbled out almost as one word, the quickest Bea had spoken in some time.

'I see.' The doctor's tone was belittling, and Bea suddenly regretted coming in. What was she thinking, booking this appointment barely a week after discovering she was pregnant? 'I will have to ask you a few questions, as I'm sure you'd expect, Mrs Anderson.' The doctor lowered her voice to add, 'I'm sure you understand I could lose my licence if anyone knew we were even having this conversation, but there may be exceptional circumstances for ...' She paused. 'Women like you.'

Bea's head snapped up, her eyes finally locking with the doctor's. 'Like me?'

Johnson nodded. 'Women who have found themselves in a predicament ... Perhaps involved with a British man where they shouldn't be?'

The assumption hit Bea like a cold slap to the face. 'My husband is a British government employee. We've been married for ...' She did the maths quickly, her mind fogging. 'Six years.' She glanced down at herself, then back to the doctor. 'I'm not ... I don't even sound local.'

'I'm sure you understand it's difficult to tell the difference, to an ear like mine. All foreigners can tend to sound the same.'

Yet I'm sure you could tell a Spaniard from a Kraut? Bea wanted to ask, but her mouth couldn't quite shape the words. *Do doctors treat people this way in London?* She could write and ask Nella, but then she'd have to admit to what she'd done. She slumped back in her chair, wishing she'd taken the time to style her hair before coming in.

'Well, regardless, I still have to ask you some questions to establish whether this would be an emergency matter.' Johnson shuffled the papers on her desk, seemingly for something to do with her hands.

Bea could hear a muffled gargle coming from the pram out in the reception area, and she knew she was on borrowed time before the boys woke up. She'd had no choice but to bring them with her, leaving them under the receptionist's watchful gaze. Their pram had been fixed so many times since it had been shipped over after their trip to Ireland, and Bea was convinced one day soon the wheels would come off entirely.

'Are you unable to provide for the new child? Would it cause you and your children to go hungry, to be cast out of your home, if it were to arrive?'

Bea rubbed her eyes. 'Well, no.' She took a deep breath, clutching her hands in her lap. 'I just can't handle another baby, you see. I already have four children under five, two girls and twin boys.' The ache in her bones intensified at the thought of her children, and her lip began to tremble. 'They're such a handful, in constant need of attention, and we don't have any family here to help, so it is just me every day. Patrick – that's my husband – he doesn't even know I'm here. He thinks it's all great fun and games running around after children, but I tell you, it is exhausting, and I feel I haven't slept in years. If I tell him I'm pregnant again he'll just want to keep it, add to the brood. He has no idea what it's like looking after four children day in, day out.' She buried her face in her hands. 'I don't know what's happened to me. It's all just so damn hard. I'm not cut out for this.'

She wanted to tell the doctor that this broken woman sobbing in a public office wasn't her ... not really. Beatrice was the kind of woman who sought adventure and opportunity, who got on with any work that needed doing and celebrated its completion with a glass of rum punch and a jive about the room. Who had watched the sun rise over mountains that no one in her hometown had even heard of, who stayed up late into the night watching the stars come out across the plains. Who gave birth on a mountainside, and was back at her bookkeeping duties within a month.

Bea raised her head, swiping clumsily at her cheeks. 'Do you know what it's like, doctor, to walk past your own reflection because you don't recognise yourself any more? I used to be this life force, but now, everyone calls me Mother. Even Patrick calls me Mother, and he thinks it's endearing, but it isn't. You know, I can't remember the last time we had a conversation which didn't revolve around the children? We used to talk about books and films, art and travels, make jokes and share stories. Now I'm lucky if I remember to ask how his day's been, or if he strikes up conversation about anything other than the grocery list or the children's schooling or the damn independence treaty.' She paused for breath, her pulse racing. 'No one ever talks about how lonely it can get, staying at home with the children when there's no one to help. It's so, so damn lonely, and I don't know whether I'm supposed to talk to my neighbours about it, or if that will make it worse. Is everyone else just walking around feeling like this and no one is talking about it? Or am I going completely crazy? I see other women, in the market or the schoolyard or the street, and I just wonder – do you feel like this sometimes? Do you ever find yourself in floods of tears for no reason? Feeling like you've swallowed an anvil? Do you wish, one day, someone could sweep into your life and just make all the decisions for you? Because I would love that. For someone else, for once, to just tell me what to do and how to be happy and show me how to smile again, because I sure as hell can't work it out.'

The room sat silent for a moment after Bea trailed off, each of them waiting for the other person to speak. After a beat, Johnson returned to shuffling the papers. The sound sliced through the room. 'Would you harm the new child, if it came into the world?'

Bea jerked her hands up to her chest, the smell of bleach and sweaty desk chairs filling her nostrils and making her stomach lurch. 'Of course I wouldn't, what a ridiculous notion. What do you take me for? How can you even question that?'

'It's just the questions we have to ask, Mrs Anderson. I'm sure I don't have to tell you that termination without just cause is illegal in this country. In pretty much any country, I believe. Certainly in the Empire.' Johnson started to shuffle those damned papers again, and Bea felt panic rise in her throat. The conversation couldn't be over already, could it? 'And I must remind you,' the doctor was rising from her seat, setting her eyes firmly on the door, 'you would, of course, need your husband's permission in writing before I could even consider taking the steps required, and even then it would have to be an emergency situation in which your or the baby's life was in danger. You've already admitted that not only does your husband not know you are here, there is little to no danger involved in your case at all.' Johnson brushed down her neat white coat in one sharp swipe. 'I'm afraid I simply cannot help you.'

Casting her eyes over Bea in one more sizing-up gaze, the doctor motioned towards the exit. 'Try to relax a little, Mrs Anderson. So many wives would do anything to be in your position, I'm sure it's all just in your head. Forget about this loneliness talk, and concentrate on your family. You should try and be grateful. Maybe visit a friend for a glass of wine of an evening if you're feeling that isolated.' Bea refused to meet the doctor's eye as she opened the door and reached for the pram, both boys still snuggled soundly in its shade. 'Your husband will be wondering where you are by now. It's best you get home and get his lunch on the go. Need to keep your strength up in your condition.' The doctor paused as Bea noticed a dummy on the floor, and bent down to retrieve it. 'And speak to Marta on reception before you leave. She will book you in for an antenatal appointment with one of the midwives.'

Fighting back tears, Bea grabbed the pram and fled from the office. She couldn't stand to be in that stuffy room brimming with judgement for one more second.

Heading back down the road, Bea racked her brain for a new plan. Maybe her mother would know what to do, could help her to come up with a solution. She still shouldn't bother Patrick with it – not while he was so busy with deadlines, and independence conference dates loomed over his department. Bea could solve this herself, and he'd never need to know.

She turned back into the compound, making a beeline for her writing desk as soon as she got through the door. Her mother would help her; mothers always know best.

Chapter 35

Patrick

'Here, drink up,' John instructed, returning to his seat in Quentin's Bar with a slight sway. He and Patrick were sitting in the back corner booth – their usual haunt, with its cracked leather seats and a faded photograph of King's Yard Gate framed awkwardly on the wall. John slid the whiskey over to Patrick. 'What's got a bee in your bonnet, then? You're even quieter than usual.'

Patrick grimaced. He knocked back his whiskey, enjoying the burn it gave him. 'Bea keeps mentioning a move to London. I don't know what to tell her.' He couldn't bear to say what he really felt, deep within himself. *I'm scared I'm letting her down. I'm scared I can't be the man she needs me to be.*

John snorted. 'You can't leave now. They'll shove you in an admin job that barely pays enough for the milk round. If they even keep you on in government.'

'I know.' Patrick rubbed his temples. 'I thought I could look into teaching, maybe.'

'And give up all you've worked for? Don't be ridiculous, you can't leave the field. Besides, the director would crucify you if you handed your notice in now, not to mention the team you'd leave in the lurch.' John shook his head. 'You can't leave, and that's the end of it.' He paused, swilling the whiskey around his glass. 'And do you want to go back to England?'

'If it's what Bea wants, if it would make her happy.' Patrick paused, fiddling with a loose button on his jacket. 'I just want her to be happy, but I think I'm getting it wrong.'

'These women, there's always something more that they want. "I need new jewellery, Terence's wife has a new car, I want another housemaid, the girls' school fees have gone up."' John shook his head, his eyes glassy. 'It's as bad as dealing with the locals.'

Patrick frowned. 'What do you mean?' He could feel the conversation slipping away from him, any chance of sentiment or advice washing down with their whiskey. He certainly couldn't admit the full truth, now.

'Going on about wanting their own rules, these bloody Africans. They could hardly tie their own shoelaces without our oversight.' John slapped the table, leaning further forward. 'Did you hear that supposed "politician" that was in the office the other day? Prattling on about rights, democracy, self-governance. Who taught them the bloody phrase "self-governance"? And now they think they can run an entire country on their own? They'll all come crawling back to the Empire, mark my words.'

Patrick tried not to look irritated. He should have known better than to confide an ounce of emotion in John. 'I'm sure they'll be quite capable.'

'See, that's the problem with you, Pat. You always sympathise with the locals.' John gave a short laugh. 'You even went as far as to marry one.'

Patrick's head shot up. 'Don't you—'

'I'm not trying to disrespect you, old boy, you know I think Bea's one of the good ones. I'm just saying...' John chuckled; bolts of anger crackled along the ridges of Patrick's spine. 'You can't help yourself. You root for David instead of Goliath, despite knowing the Goliaths of the world always win in the end.'

'Goliath was killed,' Patrick replied shortly. Over John's shoulder, he signalled for the bill. 'Who reads that story and roots for the oppressive giant? What's wrong with you?'

'Oh, dear. I've upset you.' John's words slurred into one another, and he slumped forward over the table. 'Don't mind me. Just saying what we're all thinking.'

Patrick cocked his head and opened his mouth to counter John's argument – to ask who 'all' was. He knew he had a reputation around the office for his indifference towards independence; his dual citizenship hinted at his sympathies before his actions, or words, did. But on looking to his friend's eyes, he realised there was no point in trying to fight him. 'Come on, pal,' Patrick said, standing up and grabbing the table when a head rush threw him off balance. 'Best we stop now.' He didn't protest when John threw a fistful of notes on the table by way of apology, knowing it was John's father's money anyway. He tried not to let resentment pierce him, nodding goodbye to Quentin as he and John stumbled from the bar.

'See you, John,' Patrick called, delivering his friend to his front door after their long walk back. The stars were out, their outlines blurred. They shone dimmer than the stars which had kept him company in Grenada, or Tanganyika.

He fumbled in his pockets, wondering if he'd even remembered to bring out his keys. It was an old jacket, one he'd had to pull from the back of the cupboard after William spat milk all over his favoured one a couple of days previously.

Failing to retrieve the keys, his fingers clasped around a familiar shape: a small, leather-bound book, its pages now worn and its scrawled notes paling. He blinked twice, drawing the book out from his jacket and holding it carefully. Peeling back the cover, he kept his left eye closed and squinted with his right. He focused, as best he could, on the words in front of him.

Annotated pages of *A Midsummer Night's Dream & Selected Sonnets*, the copy he'd borrowed from Bea over six years before. He read his notes hastily scrawled in the margin, remembering the feel of Ron's kitchen chair on his back and the worn table beneath his palm as he wrote. How breathless he'd become when he'd given her the book in the little community theatre, hidden from prying eyes. How delighted she'd looked, handing it back to him with her own responses jotted between the lines. The way she used to look at him made him feel as though he was soaring. As though he'd found someone who did, truly, know him.

He held the book close to his chest, promising himself to do better. He'd solve their money problems, speak more openly with her, get her a home in London if that was what she wanted. He'd tell her, *I'm sorry, there's so much pressure. I love you. We are such stuff as dreams are made on. Please come back to me.*

He stumbled as he walked in, tripping over the bamboo mat. He cursed under his breath, righting himself and kicking it back into place.

As he did so, an off-white envelope poked out from one corner. He bent down, picking up the letter and turning it over in his palm.

The return address made the breath leave his body. *Guildford, Surrey.*

He stuffed it into his trouser pocket, his mind clouding. Five years without a word, and now a handwritten letter fallen beneath the mat. He rubbed his temples, clasping the book of poems even tighter.

'Not now,' Patrick whispered, his tone pleading. He shook his head, returning his gaze to the *Sonnets*. He'd throw the letter out without reading. He'd tear it up. He'd burn it.

He'd forget about it, drifting off in a whiskey-induced haze the minute his head hit the sofa cushion.

Chapter 36

Beatrice

As they stepped through the doors of the captain's house, Bea gazed around the room. She'd agreed to stay an hour – maximum two – at this drab government party, leaving the children with Sahr's sister. They'd driven over with just the radio for company, Bea's mind flipping between replays of her disastrous doctor's visit the morning before and thoughts of what advice her mother may give. She'd posted her letter to her mother that morning, filling a whole two pages with ramblings about the children, the army trucks, the compound walls, the baby she now knew she was carrying but did not feel she could mother.

She still hadn't worked out how to tell Patrick.

As Bea shrugged off her shawl in the captain's grand hallway, she took in the polite chatter and dainty hors d'oeuvres served from silver platters, the scent of expensive perfume dancing hand in hand with sickly-sweet wine. Bea was not the only non-white person in the room – the Koromas, Johnsons, and Cokers from the compound were standing beside the hosts – but she was certainly in the minority. The only others who vaguely resembled her were holding platters of delicate food and trays laden with the evening's drinks.

Somehow, Bea realised this was a feeling she'd grown all too used to in these government-sponsored scenarios, and that evening she felt weary of it. The ache in her body intensified, her arms feeling heavy at her side. Her throat clawed for a gulp of fresh air in the stuffy room, a flash of panic, *get out, run home* coursing through her.

'I'll take our coats through, if you want to start mingling,' Patrick offered, his voice anchoring her back beside him.

'No, no, you go ahead,' she managed to croak. 'I'll take these and catch up with you.'

Patrick shrugged, his eyes already flickering towards the laden plates. 'If you're sure. I'll grab us drinks and fix you a plate, too.'

Bea nodded. 'Thank you, that would be great. Nothing with—'

'Sardines? Of course not.' He squeezed her hand again, passing over his coat with a loving smile. 'We'll only stay a couple of hours, I promise.'

The metallic taste of guilt filled Bea's mouth as she remembered what she was hiding from him. She swallowed hard, plastering on a smile.

As she walked through the hallway, only catching snatches of conversation about houseboys and independence conferences and taxes, she let her gaze wander over to the paintings hung upon the captain's walls. Generations of uniform-clad men stared back at her, clutching guns, occasionally accompanied in the photo by a well-dressed woman slightly off-centre.

There were never any children in the photos, nor were the women ever pregnant. Yet, the dates beneath each frame clearly signified the forward march of generations. If she'd had the energy, Bea would have laughed: clearly, this captain only felt children to be worthy of displaying when they followed some kind of pre-determined path, joining their lineage upon the wall and Empire playing field. She wondered where he was hiding the daughters, and why she'd never noticed this on previous visits.

'Oh, good, you're here.' A voice cut through the twilight, and Bea's head whipped round. 'Hang this one up beside this, but place them on separate hangers. Do you understand?' Before Bea stood a brown-eyed redhead, her clipped tones matching the tap-tap-tap of her impatient, patent shoes. 'Can you manage that?' the woman bleated again.

Bea took a deep breath. 'You are mistaken, I do not work here.' If her clothes, made-up face, and what she'd considered to be quite an elegant hairstyle hadn't already given this away, her accent surely did. The woman frowned. 'My husband is inside,' Bea continued. 'Mr Anderson – perhaps you know him? In the surveying and ordnance division?'

'Oh, what? I, um ...' The woman's face grew red, her brow furrowing deeper in confusion.

Bea had learnt, over the too-many times this sort of thing had happened, that embarrassing the offending party was the most satisfying route to take. She'd tried berating, shouting, but it never got her a reaction quite as good as watching their faces burn with embarrassment at having insulted a fellow government wife. There was never anything to be gained from shouting, 'Do you realise that I am a British subject? That this actually is what British looks like?' They never listened. Given how much time and effort had gone into expanding the Empire, Bea was always surprised its far-reaching network wasn't common knowledge.

Bea continued to speak, uncaring who heard her. 'Might I suggest you hang up your own coats, if you have such a particular way you'd like to do them? And might I also suggest that you address me as Mrs Anderson, if you ever plan to speak to me again. Much obliged.'

The woman's cheeks burned a deep crimson, as she suddenly became engrossed in a button hanging loose on her coat. Bea brushed past her, hoping it wasn't obvious that her hands were shaking.

The rest of the evening stayed true to what Bea had promised, ending with a short dance, leaning her head on Patrick's shoulder. In between songs, she could hear the rude woman whispering to another thin-lipped lady, an indignant 'How was I supposed to know?' followed up by some kind of simpering reassurance.

Patrick held Bea close, and the two of them swayed in time to the imported tune of Cliff Richard. *Got no bags and baggage to slow me down, I'm travelling so fast my feet ain't touching the ground.*

The drawing room lights were a little brighter than Bea would have liked, the music a little too slow, but still she put on her best impression of Wife at a Party. She stepped forwards and backwards, holding on to Patrick tightly, desperate to feel a spark of something, anything. The music continued: *Travellin' light, travellin' light, Well, I just can't wait to be with my baby tonight.*

It had been so long since they'd danced, and Bea felt her heart crack that she wasn't fully present for it. Why couldn't her mind just focus, let her exist in this sweet moment without guilt and panic and stress gnawing away at her skin?

When the music paused, Bea watched Patrick head for the drinks table, and wondered whether it would be so bad to drag him with her and hide in the cloakroom after all. *I'm sorry, I'm stressed. I love you. I don't know what I'm doing. I don't know why I can't snap out of this.*

'Bea,' Patrick whispered as they shook off their coats and removed their shoes. The babysitter, Sahr's sister, had been paid and sent home, leaving the two of them in the rare position of having peace. Bea couldn't remember the last time that had happened.

She let him take her hand, lead her through to the kitchen. He poured them each a small measure of whiskey, its amber liquid catching the soft light of the kitchen lamp.

'Did you have a good time, tonight?' She could hear the trepidation in his voice and felt guilty for not being able to answer with the truth.

'Yes,' she lied. God, that was becoming too easy. 'It was a lovely evening in the end.' She considered whether to tell him the interaction she'd had with the red-headed woman, but couldn't muster the energy to live through it as a retelling.

Bea stretched her arms above her head, taking a long sip of whiskey and letting it warm her throat. She looked up at Patrick, his hands resting on the narrow wooden table at which they both sat. With a start, she realised she hadn't looked at him properly in quite some time: faint lines had begun to form where his eyes crinkled, and he had a nervous look about him. 'Is something the matter?'

Patrick shook his head, awkwardly reaching into his jacket pocket. He hesitated for a second, and then revealed what he held. 'I ... I found this, the other night. You've seemed a little down lately, so I thought this might help?' He phrased it as a question as he pressed the small book into her open palms.

The small weight and cool touch of the leather made Bea catch her breath; she was instantly transported back to the first moment she'd held it, the night Patrick had returned the book with his inscriptions and notes in the margins.

Hot tears pricked at the backs of her eyes, and Bea had to swallow hard to stop a sob from escaping. It felt as though he'd given her a token from a lost life, grief striking her.

She ran her fingers lightly over the cover, opening it with care. She traced along the indentations on the page from Patrick's handwriting, marvelling at the little notes they'd written to each other.

'Do you remember,' Patrick said, his gaze distant, 'reading lines from the play and the sonnets to each other on the boat over to Dar es Salaam? Back when we first came to Africa?'

'The storms got so loud.' Bea faked a smile, her stomach twisting itself into knots. 'Shakespeare becomes much less romantic when you keep having to ask, "Sorry, what was that last line?"'

Patrick grinned, pulling her hand towards his. She wished she was feeling the joy written across his face. 'And how we were planning to read out that poem about the twins at their christening?'

'It was a quote from one of the plays about twins, but I can't remember which. I remember the line, though,' Bea paused, closing her eyes. '"*Friends now fast sworn, whose double bosoms seem to wear one heart.*"' She faltered. 'I always meant to embroider that quote onto a keepsake for them.'

'No need, they'd only rip it to shreds.' Patrick waved his hand to dismiss the notion. 'The state of their christening in the end ... I still don't believe it.'

'I'd forgotten!' Bea exclaimed, the memory a beam of sunlight emerging through the clouds of her mind. 'When Rose had wanted to get into the holy water because she thought it was a bath, and then Nancy cried because she didn't want Rose to get wet—'

'And the twins were screaming the place down, and one of them managed to vomit right into the font.'

'And we still don't know which one it was!'

Despite herself, Bea found she'd started to laugh. It was as though her body was performing all on its own, putting on the display she needed to show but couldn't quite feel. 'There's no way they'll let us go back for Nancy's First Communion when she's old enough.'

Patrick shook his head, wiping the shining tears of laughter from his cheeks. 'We might be in a different church by then – a different country.'

'You think so?'

'I do. Independence is just around the corner, I can feel it. We'll be moved before you know it.'

Bea hesitated. 'Or, we could go sooner.' She didn't want to ruin the evening, but she couldn't help herself. She hadn't felt this close to energised in months, but thoughts of London spurred her on. 'Why don't I ask Nella if there are any suitable houses for rent near her and Gordon? Just to see what's out there?'

Patrick hesitated, before pulling her towards him. 'If that's what you want, I'll make it work,' he said, his smile not quite reaching his eyes.

'So you'd be all right, with leaving?'

'In time, I would,' he said hastily. He looked pained, as though he were about to say something more.

'Are you sure?' she pressed.

He nodded. 'It's just the money I'm thinking of, but that's nothing for you to worry about. I can get it sorted out. We might just need to hang on a little longer, that's all.' His voice sounded thin, far away, but the words were enough to lift Bea's spirits.

'It's the right choice, with all that's going on. A new start for us all,' she whispered, the only genuine thing she'd said all evening. Patrick squeezed her hand, but avoided her gaze. She wanted to ask, *What aren't you saying? Why don't you let me in?* But the hypocrisy felt too much to bear.

'Let's get to bed,' she said instead, pulling him in close for a kiss. There was something he wasn't telling her, she knew that much, but the strength to ask what was wrong dissolved into the quiet fog of her mind. She stayed awake long into the night as that fog turned to storm, her desperate thoughts swirling.

If I could shake this melancholy, if we had a home on settled ground, if I could just find a solution for this baby, perhaps we could bridge this chasm between us. What if we're already too far apart?

Chapter 37

Patrick

Patrick rubbed his eyes, taking another sip of cold coffee. If he could stay awake a little longer, he'd have this report finished by morning.

They shouldn't really have gone to the party at the captain's house the night before, but it was necessary to keep up appearances. He hadn't wanted to turn down the chance for a night out with Bea, either – a chance to give her the book he'd found.

He read over the last sentence and typed out END OF DOCUMENT, adding his signature. He'd hand it in first thing, and get straight on to the equipment review he'd been roped into. Hours of logging what various equipment did and how it should be used, before it got sent to various corners of the ever-shrinking Empire. *This report will be the making of you,* the director had promised. Patrick hadn't realised he still needed 'making', but rumours of golden handshakes were creeping through the department. If he could just stick it out a little longer, stay in the director's good books, perhaps he'd be able to give Bea everything he'd promised. He was so sick of letting her down. What sort of a man couldn't provide what his family wants, and needs? The way she'd come back to life when he'd said, If that's what you want, we'll make it work: he had to make London happen. If only they could hold on a little while longer.

He sat back in his chair, stretching out and winding his neck from side to side. He'd sleep on the sofa again, so as not to wake Bea. His stomach felt hollow at the thought of another cramped night, and at the thought of the letter from his parents. He'd remembered it that morning, but still hadn't been able to tear open the envelope and face what it held.

As soon as he'd remembered it, Patrick had shoved the letter to gather dust beneath the paperweight Nancy had sent him last Christmas. *You mustn't send such heavy gifts,* he'd scolded, even though he loved the Irish slate keeping his work in order. *I send books and puzzles for the children. You're still a child, too, in my eyes!* she'd scolded right back. Patrick always marvelled at how clearly he heard her voice whenever he read her letters.

That's what was putting him off, he realised: the thought of hearing his stepmother's or father's voice in his head when he read their words. It had been years, with nothing. Not a single birthday card for the children, not even a telegram to acknowledge a new decade beginning.

Patrick stood up, jittery. His bones felt heavy, but his muscles needed to move. It was just a letter. He could open it, see what it was, and then talk it through with Bea. As long as it was nothing that might worry her. With her concerns about moving and the rumbles in the streets, he wouldn't dare add to her burdens.

He breathed out heavily, and reached for the letter.

Dear Patrick,

I know it has been years, and I would not blame you for throwing this letter away as soon as you see who has written it.

I do hope you and your children are well, John's parents inform us you have four now. I wish I were writing under different circumstances, but the truth is

No. Patrick tore his eyes away; if he didn't read it, perhaps it wouldn't be true. He hated himself for caring.

the truth is, your father is unwell. He has one year, maybe less, and I cannot help but notice he's never been the same since you left. I know he grieves the loss of his son, and it would be remiss of me not to inform you of this development.

What was it with the landed English middle classes that they couldn't bear to reveal even a shadow of sentimentality? 'This development' made it sound as though his father had added to his investment portfolio or accepted the chairman's position at the golf club. Patrick shut his eyes, massaging his temples. In that moment, he felt so grateful his children had never met these people.

Do the right thing, and come home to see him. I'm sure he will forgive you, if you are apologetic enough. We all make mistakes when we are young, Patrick, even your father can attest to that.

If you need money, I can wire you the cost of the crossing. No need to bring the children, but I know your father would be most pleased to see you.

Regards,

Moira.

Patrick felt sick. Moira's erasure of Bea struck him hard, each jagged line of cursive cutting him deeper. How dare she speak this way, imply his marriage was a crime that needed absolution?

He needed to talk to Bea, right away. He'd hidden all his concerns from her long enough: something had to give. Bea would know what to do and how to respond – if they should respond at all. He stood up, the sharp movement making his back protest. He made for the door, glancing down at his watch, adrenaline pumping through him.

Quarter past three. In the morning.

Patrick faltered. He couldn't wake Bea at this hour. She'd be up with one of the children soon anyway, it wouldn't be fair.

He paced a second or two more in his study, taking a deep breath. He didn't have time for this. He crumpled up the letter in his hand, cursing under his breath. *To hell with him, to hell with this.*

Patrick opened the bottom drawer of his desk, reaching for the whiskey he stored for Emergencies Only.

Chapter 38

Beatrice

The Sierra Leonean

7 October 1960

Independence date set

Citizens of Sierra Leone are advised that the date for Independence has been set for 27th April, 1961. Public holidays shall be announced in the coming weeks.

After more than 150 years of colonial rule, Prime Minister Sir Milton Margai welcomes the independence talks. The Duke of Kent is due to visit the nation to formally begin independence proceedings at the beginning of April 1961.

Terms of independence were initially outlined at the Constitutional Conference held at Lancaster House, London, 30th April 1960. While Sierra Leone will be granted full independence from Great Britain, the country will become the 21st member state of the British Commonwealth.

All citizens will be automatically granted Sierra Leonean citizenship, providing they can prove at least one grandparent was born in the nation. Any child born after midnight 27.04.61 to a non-native must therefore apply for the right to hold a passport through the father's lineage and country of origin.

British and other "expatriates" will have the right to remain indefinitely with proof of income. Expatriates are reminded to remain respectful of local Sierra Leoneans during this time, and are invited to take part in independence celebrations at their own discretion.

Schools, libraries, and all public bodies are to remain closed for the next week while terms are being agreed.

Another school closure, another day full of meetings that kept Patrick in the office until past sunset. Bea had finally sent Nella word of their plans to move, although she still hadn't managed to pin Patrick down to a date, and was counting the days until Nella's next letter arrived to advise on available homes in the capital.

Homeschooling during lockdown days was bone-achingly tiresome, pushing Bea's patience to its already broken limits. She needed to know the girls would be in a London school before she had to start teaching them much beyond kindergarten level. She kept meaning to talk to Patrick about it and agree timings, but they seemed to be spending more and more time apart as his maps took over his office, and she grew ever more desperate to hide the new life making her belly rise and her feet swell. She barely had the energy for anything these days, running on cups of fruit juice and the memories of what happiness felt like.

That morning, as Bea began laying out pencils and writing paper and drawing pads for another day of homeschooling, she let her glance fall through the window. What if she just walked out? What if Sahr called Patrick, told him he had to come home and feed the twins, watch the girls? What if Bea – she was at the front door now – just turned the handle? What if she heard the click of the door close behind her – as it was – and what if she just walked over to the car? No, she couldn't take the car. That wouldn't be fair. What if she flagged down a ride from someone, asked to go where they were going? What if – she arrived at the end of the road – she just walked and walked, got to the beach, walked into the sea and swam away?

A sharp pain in her foot drew her attention, and Bea's gaze fell to the ground. She was standing right at the edge of the compound, behind the large gates which kept the rest of the world at bay. A small, jagged-edged rock had caught the ball of her foot, the flesh dented but not quite broken.

She took a deep breath, life returning to her body.

She was standing alone, at the edge of the compound, barefoot.

Panic flashed across her back and deep in her belly, nausea rising from her stomach. She turned and ran back into the house, her heart pounding in her chest. What was she doing?

'Mamma, where did you go?'

Bea could feel it again; the tears had started. She leant back against the front door and swiped angrily at her cheeks, not bothering to hide them from her daughter this time. 'I just had to get some fresh air, that's all,' she replied, ruffling Nancy's hair. 'We'd better get started with school today.'

'We aren't going to school?'

Bea shook her head. 'Not today.'

She ushered Nancy back into the kitchen where Rose sat at the table, her feet dangling at the edge of the chair. Bea's eyes darted over to where she'd left the twins, crawling over one another in the makeshift playpen she'd strung up beside the pantry door. Her heart rate slowed, and she took a deep breath. *You didn't actually leave. Everything's fine.*

As she began setting the girls up with drawing paper, blinking back the tears which still fought to be shed, Sahr bolted into the kitchen. 'I'm so sorry, madam!'

Bea froze. Had he seen her? She threw herself on to the attack, just in case. 'Sahr,' she said, her tone sharp, 'I don't know how many times I've asked you in the last couple of years. Please call me Mrs Anderson in my own home, won't you.' She swallowed hard as nausea bubbled up in her stomach, and took a couple of shallow breaths as Sahr continued to sweat in front of her.

She'd managed to make it through the week so far without a single bout of morning sickness, and prayed she'd be able to keep up her lucky streak.

'Sorry, Mrs Anderson, I'm sorry. I forget that you don't like "madam".' His face crumpled, his eyes bright and panic-stricken. Bea felt stabbed by guilt once again.

'What's happened? Is everything all right?' She lowered her voice, hearing it tremor. More panic filled her from the inside out. 'Has something happened to Patrick?'

Sahr looked to the window, pointing down the street. 'Mr Anderson is fine. They're taking the Koroma family. For questioning, maybe, we don't know. The Koromas have not done anything wrong.' Wringing his hands, Sahr grimaced. 'I hate to trouble you, but can you help?'

Bea took a step back, selfish relief washing over her. It wasn't her family in danger.

But still, the Koromas were some of the most honest people she'd ever met. Both spoke with accented English and had met at university in London, although Bea didn't know where they were from originally. She'd assumed it was Sierra Leone, and realised shamefully that she'd never asked.

'What do you think I can do?' Bea asked, warily. 'What do they want with the Koromas? And which "they" is doing the questioning?'

Sahr was becoming agitated, his hands jittering up and down. 'It is some breakaway group, we don't think it's anything official. Vigilantes, or similar.' His voice lowered. 'I just heard that questioning is starting, for any locals assumed to be spying or giving information to the British ahead of independence terms being agreed. This new group wouldn't do anything in front of you, though, it would be too dangerous. They know they're operating outside the law. Just taking their chances where they can.'

Bea shook her head slowly. 'I don't think some vigilante group will be intimidated by me.'

'But there is a chance, if you get some of the other wives to help, too.' He didn't have to finish the sentence, say, *Some of the British-looking wives.* She knew what he meant.

Sahr's gaze darted left and right, his lips pressing tight together. Bea hated to see him look so harried – he was usually so calm, so steadfast – and at that moment she just wanted to do something to get that look out of his eyes.

She steeled herself, willing her mind to come back to life. 'Can you watch the children? I can't promise I'll be able to do much, but—'

'Oh, yes, I'll keep them here in the garden so they're out back. Thank you, madam, thank you.'

Walking from the house with her shoulders rolled back, Bea relished feeling something other than tired apathy. Indignant anger rose from her feet through her body, her footsteps landing harder with every step. She knew tensions were running high in Freetown between the settlers and local countrymen on different sides – of course she did – but when your life revolved around grocery shopping, school runs and keeping house, it was hard to get too embroiled in the local politics. Patrick never gave her much detail, glossing over his days as *same as ever*, or *quite boring, really.*

Despite not knowing as much as she'd like, she hadn't been able to shake the feeling of unease creeping since independence was announced. The anvil in her stomach had grown heavier, the weights pressing upon her shoulders pushing down with more force.

'Good morning, Bea! You look like you're on quite a mission. Heading off to the market, are you?' Sally appeared, stepping down from her front door and falling into step beside her neighbour. She was actually wearing a string of pearls, on a Wednesday morning. 'If you are, you couldn't pick up some sugar for me, could you? John used the last of ours in his morning cuppa. Don't know what I'll do with that man.' Bea shook her head, and gestured for Sally to come a little closer. Finally, Sally's love of gossip and drama might actually play into Bea's hands.

'Sally, we haven't much time. Knock on every door on that side, and I'll take this side.' Bea motioned up and down the street, and continued. 'Apparently there are people coming for the Koroma family, some sort of local group accusing them of spying. A bunch of vigilantes wanting to take them away for questioning, most likely.'

The colour drained from Sally's face, and her eyes bulged. 'Who told you that?'

'It doesn't matter,' Bea said quickly, before realising how that sounded. 'All right, my houseboy mentioned it. But you mustn't tell anyone that, all right?'

'Of course.' Sally's eyes brightened, but Bea could see fear flashing just below her intrigue. 'But the Koromas are British citizens, they wouldn't get involved in anything untoward. Idi fought in the war, for Christ's sake. What would anyone be wanting with a pair of government workers? They can't be hauling in everyone who looks African in this bloody compound, surely?'

Bea halted. 'Has this happened before?'

Sally nodded, her face full of pain. 'My houseboy, I'm convinced of it. He disappeared in the night a few months ago and he never came back. He isn't even from Freetown, or Sierra Leone. He's Guinean.' Sally sniffed, and placed her hand lightly on Bea's arm. 'The girls loved him, you see, and they'll have to get used to the new one all over again when they're back from school. I don't even know if he was involved in anything. It's madness.'

'Oh, Sally, I didn't know. That must have been awful.' Bea gave her neighbour as sympathetic a smile as she could manage, and pressed on. She knew she meant that it was awful for the houseboy, but for once, Bea didn't mind that Sally would hear that it was awful for her. 'Dinnah Koroma, at House 2, she's just had a baby. There is no way she's talking to anyone about anything other than nappies and night feeds. These local groups are just trying to scare one another, get people to talk,' Bea continued as Sally began to fidget. 'It's madness, they'll get their independence soon enough anyway. No need to start infighting. Patrick says the paperwork is practically all drawn up.'

'But if they're going to start questioning the women, I could lose my maid, too,' Sally replied, ignoring Bea's last comment. Her face was now whiter than Bea had ever known a face could be. 'What can we do?'

Bea pulled back her shoulders, her older sister's face coming to mind. She'd channel Millicent – pretend she was the kind of woman who took charge and made things happen. 'Just get all the wives on the street to come out. I have an idea.'

Perhaps this is how I'll get back to myself, through small acts. She may not be able to change Government policy or influence business strategy, like her sisters back home, but she could still make some kind of difference. She might even, finally, make a connection with these other wives.

Bea pressed on, resolute.

True to Sahr's prediction, an unmarked van rumbled into the compound with more than enough space in the back. Bea had seen them occasionally driving through Freetown, housing a handful of too-young men with something to prove.

As the van lurched onward, from each house's front door stepped its matriarch. With arms crossed and heads held high, hair in silk wraps or curlers, wearing aprons or wrappers or blouses, each woman watched the van slow to a stop outside House 2. Their eyes bored into the back of the unmarked vehicle.

'If you lay a hand on him,' Bea called from the front of House 6, 'we will all see and we will report it. Every single one of us.' Bea could feel her hands trembling, but refused to let it carry through to her voice. *There isn't enough space in that damn van for us all, is there?*

Bea started to sweat, but Sally gave her a firm nod. Each woman kept her face towards House 2, as a single bald man stepped down from the cab and walked, his shoulders hunched, towards the front door. He was older than Bea expected, his forehead deeply creased.

Bea kept her eyes fixed on his every step. She had heard rumours of broken arms and bruised faces at these sorts of things: people being taken from their homes for questioning and never quite returned the same. It would not happen on her watch.

Despite knowing that most of the other wives were standing there for fear that they'd have to iron their own clothes and scrub their own toilets, at that moment Bea didn't care. This was her chance to be a part of something bigger than her own home – something to show she was still here.

Before she could say anything else, Bea heard a voice begin to rise from further up the street, a lone songbird singing into the breeze. Another voice joined in, and soon the whole street was singing along in time with one another. The man hesitated, seemingly unnerved by the sudden music surrounding him. *I once was lost, but now am found. Was blind, but now I see.*

Letting her own voice join the chorus, for a second Bea feared the man would step out towards each one of them and really give them something to worry about. *'twas grace that taught my heart to fear, and grace my fears relieved.* Their voices grew louder, each woman looking to one another and back towards House 2, not letting their eyes leave the intruder for long. *Through many dangers, toils and snares we have already come. This grace has brought us safe thus far and grace will lead us home.*

The man began to back away from the front door, slowly at first, and then he was running to his van and clambering up into the driver's seat as their voices grew louder. The women watched him grip the steering wheel, shake his head, reach for the gearstick.

After what felt like hours but was just a few ticks of the clock, the van rumbled into reverse and the women let their song drop, breathing a communal sigh of relief. Squeals of 'I can't believe it worked!' and 'That'll show them!' rose from outside each home, as they dispersed back to their laundry piles and shopping lists.

With a sick feeling in her stomach Bea couldn't fully attribute to morning sickness, she knew that the questioner in the van would eventually be back. She dared to wonder whether they'd still be there to see it, to help. This couldn't go on.

'That was quite terrifying, wasn't it?' trilled Sally as she turned around and headed towards her car. 'What a good idea to sing, it always calms my nerves. I think Mariama started it, she has the voice of an angel. All the Johnson children sing beautifully at our church, and now I see where they got it from.'

'Maybe I'll head to the market myself, now that I think about it. Do you think Dinnah will need anything?'

Bea nodded, turning to face her neighbour. Her hands were still shaking. 'I'd say she'll probably want some sugar after that scare. I'll drop her round something later – some cakes maybe, for the shock.'

'Jolly good. I'll do the same, take her some strong tea.' Sally waved to Bea, already back in her little bubble. How easy it was to slip in and out of such situations when you knew you could simply call your husband to come and get you, or hop on a flight back to your country house in Britain and pretend nothing sour had ever happened. 'Take it easy now!'

Returning to the house, Bea found that Sahr had already brewed her a hot cup of sweet tea despite the heat of the day. 'Thank you, madam – sorry, thank you, Mrs Anderson.' He placed the cup down in front of her, his hands trembling almost as much as Bea's.

'What is going on, Sahr?'

He shook his head. 'I don't involve myself in these things, but it's clear something is coming. It's supposed to be peaceful between my people, but every so often we get something like this. Accusations flying around about what the terms will be. People are concerned about who independence will really favour.' He shook his head, refusing to meet Bea's eye. 'There may be fighting, we don't know. Freetown may not stay safe forever. Especially not for you.'

Bea considered this, as she drew her knees up to her chest and took a sip of the sweet tea. She let it burn her throat, strangely grateful for the searing pain which centred her focus. 'Well, you have a home here for as long as we are here. You know that.'

'That is kind of you to say, Mrs Anderson. I'll get the girls inside, it's getting too hot out there for them.'

Bea smiled at him. 'Thank you.'

Bracing herself for her daughters to stampede into the room, Bea's glance fell to the table. A letter lay discarded beside the fruit bowl, the return address belonging to her mother. Bea grabbed it, rushing from the room.

What if her mother scolded her? Told her, *This is what you get, this is your penance for running away with the wrong kind of man. For abandoning your family. You've made your bed, Beatrice, and now you'd better lie in it.*

Bea blinked back the image, suddenly wishing she'd never said a thing. She threw herself into the bathroom, locking it hastily behind her. Whatever her mother would say, it couldn't be as bad as the words she was imagining. She opened the envelope, and began to read.

3 Lower Lucas Street
St George's
Grenada
West Indies

1st October 1960

Dear Bea,

What can I say in response to your last letter? Firstly, well done for being brave enough to tell the truth. You were always one of the brave ones, but we knew that the day you set sail for your new life so far away.

It is a difficult time to be thinking about children. You have been blessed with so many beautiful babies, Nella's momma tells me all about her Hortense over in London, our Bette is perfectly happy without any as she splits her time between here and their Westinghall base in Toronto, but Millicent is struggling very much. She does so much for children with her work in the schools and Soroptimist groups and her seat on the council, but behind closed doors, she yearns for a child.

I have an idea which may help you both come to each other's aid. This baby that you are carrying: what if it should be given a loving home right here in St George's, to be raised as Millicent and Julien's child?

It was most common when I was a child to have relatives raise one another's children. Grandparents would often take guardianship, or aunts and uncles may take in their niece or nephew if there was not enough money – or time – for the child's parents to raise them. It is a practice that still continues, of course, and one you would do well to consider.

You can come here and rest up for the last few weeks or months of your pregnancy, take a break, and give birth at St Andrew's hospital. We can deal with the legalities right here. Your father will know all the hoops we'll have to jump through.

I'm not saying this is your only option, but it is surely your best. Take some time to consider it.

With love, Mother

In the locked bathroom, the letter felt strangely light in Bea's hands as she held it up to the match pinched between thumb and forefinger. The little flame danced into life, and soon enough it was eating away at her mother's wise words. *No need for Patrick to see.* Not until she'd figured out exactly how to explain it away. Perhaps if she could just get the girls back in school, or get a full night's sleep, she'd feel better. Able to tell him, properly, what was going on.

She didn't know why this hadn't occurred to her before seeing it written in plain English; the solution now was so simple. Millicent wanted a baby, and Bea could help. What's more, Bea could dig out that envelope her mother had pressed into her palm the day she'd left Grenada. She could use that money to go back, after all. Patrick wouldn't need to worry one bit.

Bea took a deep breath and attempted to picture it: the act of handing over a baby to her sister.

She held out her arms, trying and failing to imagine the weight of a tiny newborn wrapped in a blanket. Could she do it, give birth to a child and give it away?

'Yes.'

She almost jumped. Had that voice belonged to her? It sounded as though a stranger had crept into the room and stolen her accent.

And yet, she agreed. Yes, she could do it. Free up her arms for the children she already had, free her mind from the lack of sleep, the constant tears, the foreboding sense of panic. Free her time to return to work one day, start a new life in London, build a community.

As she imagined handing over this baby, making it the responsibility of someone who had truly pined for it, she waited for grief to course through her. She stood with her arms outstretched, imagining the squirming weight wrapped tight in a bundle and saying, 'Take it away.'

She opened her eyes: not a flicker of grief crossed her tired mind. It remained empty, save for the ever-present, dull ache which pulsed like a ticking clock.

Washing away the ash from the sink, Bea knew that she'd need to take a little more time to work out exactly how to talk to Patrick. There was something he wasn't telling her; a heavier tension than the usual parenthood frustrations outlined their conversations, widening the gap between them even further.

As the sink drained, Bea found her hands fidgeting with her rings and she avoided her own eyes in the mirror. She and Patrick were both keeping secrets, deceiving each other in some way. She wondered who would break first.

Two Months Later

Chapter 39

Patrick

4 De Faux Road
Springs
Grenada

29th December 1960

Dear Bea,

We are well, thank you, and all is going ahead as planned for the New Year. Julien is finally taking over from that awful MacLean character at the bank, and I'm continuing my work with the council to improve the curriculum – particularly history and politics, teaching Grenadian ways instead of the constant stream of Anglocentric rhetoric our curriculum spouts. Bette hasn't been back here since the summer, she and Matthew have to travel through America for the business so she's staying put in Toronto. Ron is directing the next amateur dramatics production, I believe they've chosen King Lear. He sends his love.

I write of all this as I am struggling to put into words what it means to us that you'll trust us with your child.

I would never admit this to anyone else – not even to Bette, so please don't tell her – but all I want is the responsibility of a child. I crave the mundaneness of it; the excitement of it; the joy and the heartbreak.

I don't know if I've told you, but we did look into adoption only to be rejected. Can you imagine, me? Being told 'no', categorically?

*I would have to give up all my work to take on a child, they said.
Teaching, council work, even volunteering with the Soroptimists. Too
many people rely on me there, it would be so unfair to let them all
down. I now can't explain to you the utter relief I feel that I'll get
to be someone's mother, and it's all thanks to you.*

*I am so proud of all I've achieved, and I even feel shame that
those achievements seem dwarfed by my inability to carry a child.
It is a new decade: I shouldn't be so desperate for something so
primal, surely. And yet, here I am.*

*Write soon, and do let us know as soon as you have
confirmation of your new address and date for your move to
London. Will you travel from there to here, to give birth? Trust
you to take on an international house move while expecting! You
always were the strongest of us.*

All my love,
Millicent

'So you see why we have to do this?' Bea paced around the
kitchen, her smock dress swinging at her knees.

Patrick had been late at the office again, and the children were
already bathed and in bed by the time he'd finally managed to
escape, their absence giving the house an eerie silence. Patrick had
planned to sit down with Bea that evening, finally show her the
letter from Moira he'd kept scrunched in his bottom drawer. When
she'd greeted him with 'You need to read this,' he thought she'd
found it. A Grenadian return address, he hadn't been expecting.

The tick of the kitchen clock mocked him as he sat cradling
Millicent's written words, giving the tension in the room its own
heartbeat. He wished he could force back the hands, return to the
minutes before he'd been handed this letter.

So many questions appeared before him that he struggled to
get the words out. 'Why didn't you tell me you were pregnant?'

Bea's foot fell heavily to the floor as she stopped pacing. He
could hardly bring himself to look up at her, his mind racing with
anger at her decision, undercut with shame for not having noticed.
'I think I didn't want to admit it was truly happening.' Bea raised

her head. 'But now I need to face up to it, and I wanted to tell you that I've found a solution.'

'A solution?' Patrick hissed, the words burning his tongue. His anger grew heavier. 'Bea, there's so much we need to talk about here. Firstly, that you think a child of ours is a problem to be solved? What the hell is wrong with you?'

'Exactly, Patrick,' she retorted. 'What is wrong with me? Why don't I love this child already, like I did every other time?' She threw up her hands. 'You can't understand what it's like for me, Pat, alone with the children every day.' Tears escaped down her cheeks, pain etched into the thin lines around her eyes. 'I know you want a say in this and I'm sorry to have shut you out, but it isn't you who will have the extra mouth to feed every morning, the fifth – fifth! – baby to grow and to nurture, all while trying to raise the others.'

Her words grew louder, arriving faster and merging with the faraway sound of a car backfiring. Patrick flexed his hands, noticing he'd balled them into fists. 'You want to know all that's wrong with me?' Bea continued. 'I'm exhausted, all the damned time, and I miss the person I was before the babies. I love them, I love them so much.' Tears continued to fall from her eyes, her voice catching in her throat. Patrick hated his instinct to comfort her in that moment. 'But sometimes, I just want to walk out of the house and not look back. I want to be able to just *feel* something. I'm going through the motions and putting on a show, but nothing feels real any more.'

She sat down heavily on the chair opposite Patrick, and he could hardly bear to look at her. 'I can hear other people laughing at a joke I once found funny, and see the girls getting excited about a new game or the boys giggling, and you poring over your maps long into the night, and I just think, Ah yes, that's what happiness is. But I haven't felt the warmth of it in my own self for so long. I just have to make do with scraps from other people, and I'm scared of what will happen if I stop even being able to do that.' She stopped to catch her breath. 'What's wrong with me?

I already know I won't be able to love this baby. And that's not fair on anyone.'

'But every other time you were scared and—'

'Not like this, Patrick. I can't hope to describe what this has felt like, but this isn't just worry about how we'll manage the finances or mend old baby clothes. The thoughts I'm having...' Her eyes dropped to the ground. 'I almost left the other day. I almost left them, sitting in the house all by themselves apart from Sahr.'

Confusion mixed with anger began bubbling in his stomach. 'You did what?'

'That's what I'm saying, Pat. You haven't even noticed, and I've been going out of my mind.'

Patrick blinked, his mind swimming. Perhaps if he heard her out – or pretended to – he could talk her out of this madness. She hadn't left the house – he'd have noticed. He'd have sensed it, at the very least. 'How have you hidden the pregnancy for so long?'

Bea almost laughed, the sound clattering towards him. 'Hidden it? You're the one who brings work home almost every night. You haven't touched me in months. It's been three months since we've done anything besides a chaste kiss, did you notice that?'

'Well, you're always busy with the children,' Patrick spluttered, shame burning his cheeks. 'Or you're asleep by the time I get to bed!'

'Because you'd rather stay up with those godforsaken maps than come upstairs to me! Haven't these countries got enough borders without you having to draw any more?'

'Please don't turn this around on me, Bea. It's not my fault the political winds are changing. At least my work is honest.'

'What's honest about drawing up new boundaries for people who never wanted you here in the first place? This country is falling apart because of people like you!'

Patrick felt the breath had been knocked out of him. 'People like me?'

He'd thought, all this time, that Bea saw him differently; she just saw him as Patrick, map-maker, family man. Not some English government official, swanning around with an arrogance so sharp it could wound.

But here it was, her admission. *She thinks you're just like your father. She thinks you've let her down.* 'Is that how you really feel?'

Bea threw her hands up in despair. 'I feel like you're avoiding me. You've become so obsessed with this country, with this continent, that you've forgotten who you brought here.' She paused, her voice cracking. 'Don't you care what's happened to us?'

'That's not…' But he couldn't finish. He looked at her, properly, for the first time in weeks. He noticed the slight rounding of her stomach, her fuller cheeks, the creases at her eyes that hadn't been there before. His gut twisted: how could he not have noticed? 'I am doing all I can to keep this family together.'

'By taking on so much extra work that we never see you?'

'How did you know about that?'

'I know I don't have friends here, Pat, but I hear what goes on well enough.'

He couldn't stand the bitterness in her voice. 'What do you mean? You see Sally, and the Koromas, and—'

'How would you know who I see? You're always away, hiding in your study or at your office. It's not even safe to be here any more, but you refuse to commit to a date we can actually move to London. Why?'

'Why?' Patrick felt ablaze. 'I'm working myself to the bone to try and save up so we can make a life in London, and we still may not have enough once we've paid for the crossing. I'm keeping my ear to the ground so I can know exactly what's going on and how safe things are. I'm training up new staff. I'm writing manual after manual – which I hate, by the way – and while I'm doing all this I'm missing out on time with the children. And with you. It's killing me, Bea, but what choice do I have?'

'That's the thing – we always have a choice!' Bea took a deep breath. 'And this is what I'm saying. Let's choose the children we already have, let's choose to live in a country where the biggest threat is a big red bus coming too quickly around a corner.'

Patrick closed his eyes for a second. 'We just need to hold on a little longer—'

'I've held on long enough, Patrick! It's time we got out of here!' She paused, gathering herself. 'For once, why can't you just tell me what's really going on?'

Patrick felt sick. 'Because I don't want to let you down,' he admitted, his voice shaky. 'I don't want to admit that asking for a move back to England would mark me a deserter, and you know they'd shove me in some low-paid, low-skilled clerical position and we'd never be able to make ends meet. You keep saying we can make it work and economise even if I get sent to admin purgatory, but honestly? I don't know if we can. I've heard the stories, seen the figures, and they don't add up to supporting a family.' He took a sharp breath. 'Do you have any idea how humiliating that is to admit? That I might not be able to provide for us, to do the one thing a husband and father is supposed to do?' He pressed his lips together, closing his eyes for a second. 'What's more, there are more people who want reassignment than there are teaching positions available, and I can't guarantee I'd be the lucky one selected for the job. I just need to hang on until I get reassigned officially.'

Bea looked at him, her gaze inflamed. 'That's your problem, Pat. You're so focused on your assignment that you forgot about your family.'

Patrick dropped his head in his hands, despairing. Her words sliced through him, the truth of them scratching their outline across his heart. 'I'm sorry, Bea. I'm sorry I've been so focused on work. But I just want to give you the life I promised.'

'Nobody's life turns out the way they picture it, Pat.'

'You can say that again.' Patrick took a deep breath, attempting to steady his pulse. He couldn't shake the anger that surged through him, all of it cut with a bleeding sense of betrayal. 'You still should have spoken to me about the baby before now.'

Bea nodded. 'I know, but I couldn't bring myself to admit to what was happening. I'm sorry.'

Silence overtook them, punctuated by the sound of Bea's heavy breathing. This wasn't how it was supposed to go; they'd promised honesty, trust: *It's us against the world, now*. He refused to believe that could change without him noticing.

A darker thought clouded his mind, the image of his father dismissing him, with that God-awful portrait in the background. If he got up now, walked out, turned his back on his family, how would that make him any better than the parent he'd vowed never to become?

'I ... Bea, what's happened to us?' Patrick asked. 'When did we stop being able to talk to each other, properly?' He didn't move from his seat opposite her, but reached out one hand. 'You should always feel you can speak to me, all right? I never want to turn into the kind of man whose wife fears a conversation with him.' He ran his hand through his hair. 'I'm nothing like my father.'

'No, of course not,' Bea said, automatically reaching to take the hand he offered. 'You're nothing like him. And I need you to be on my side with this. Please, Patrick, we've got to have a new start. And giving the baby to Millie and Julien is our only hope.'

He looked up at her, his eyes bloodshot. He hadn't realised he'd started to cry, but it was all too much. He let the tears pool and fall. 'Can I have some time to think about it at least? You can't just drop this on me and expect me to be all right with it. There's so much we need to deal with ...'.

He cast his eyes back down to the letter from Millicent, wondering how to explain what was going on inside his head. 'You've put me in an impossible position here, can't you see how unfair that is?' He did his best to keep his tone level, though in that moment he wished he could scream. 'If I say no, I break Millicent's heart. But if I say yes, I have to give up a child?' He took a deep breath. 'It's all right for you, you have your parents and sisters and brothers-in-law.' His voice wavered. 'But our children ... you ...' His heart sank. He never thought he'd have to explain this to her. 'You are all I have. This is my only family, and I need to keep it together.'

Bea raised her hand and gently stroked his cheek, guiding him to face her. Sadness stabbed at his skin as she looked at him, his broken feeling written across her eyes, too. 'And you will keep your family. Can't you see, that's what I want, too? Please, Pat, we can't let this break us. I'm scared I'll fall apart if I keep this baby and we stay here.' She drew her forehead close to his, her hand cradling the back of his neck. 'Please just think about how this would help us all if we go through with it. I can't be a mother again, and it would mean the world to Millicent and Julien to become parents. We all need this.'

They sat for a moment, neither looking at the other. The tick of the kitchen clock grew louder, cutting through all that lay unspoken.

After a moment, Patrick drew back. He couldn't bear the images now flashing across his mind's eye: another beautiful baby arriving in the world and being snatched away before he got a chance to hold them close. Softly, he said, 'You can't force me to agree to this, Bea. And you can't ever hide the truth from me again.'

She paused. 'And you can't force me to change my mind.'

'But, Bea, there's more.' Enough lying by omission, enough burying the truth. He pulled Moira's dog-eared letter from where it sat stuffed in his shirt pocket. 'We have to stop hiding things from each other, don't we?' He placed it on the table in front of her and smoothed it out.

The way she looked back at him was strange; it was unsettling to see her wear an expression he didn't recognise. 'Do you want to see your father?' she asked after a beat.

'I …' Patrick trailed off. 'Honestly? No. But I feel like I should, one last time.'

'You owe nothing to your father, Pat.' Fat tears slid down Bea's cheeks, and despite himself, Patrick felt the urge to comfort her.

'No, you're right. But maybe when we eventually get to London, I can go and visit? Just to show them they were wrong about me.' Patrick paused: something shifted. 'I'm sick of running away.'

Bea raised her head. 'Then let's run towards something. Let's set a date for London, make it official.'

Patrick considered it: pictured handing in his notice and having his director read him the Riot Act about abandoning his team and the men out in the field. But he'd chosen the field for so many years now, and Bea was right. It was time he chose her, chose their family.

Perhaps if he did, she would, too.

'I'll apply for teaching jobs in London, I'll start researching it tomorrow. We need to put down roots somewhere, try and start again. The children need stability.' His throat caught on the words, going dry at the mention of his children. 'All the children.'

The way Bea shook her head cut him to the core. 'I'm sorry, Pat. Just think about it.'

'You can't keep something this big from me and expect me to go along with it,' Patrick said, exhaustion overtaking him. 'We have to be honest with each other.' *This can't be the end of us.*

She was sobbing by then, tears splashing onto the table. 'I know, and I am sorry. I miss you, how we used to be. I just don't know what else to do.'

Patrick stood up, squeezing her shoulder. He wished he could pull her close, soothe her, tell her everything would be all right. But how could he promise such a thing? 'I know. I'm sorry, too. I'll start applying for jobs in London, give my notice for the end of next month.' He looked down to see Bea wiping away her tears, but he couldn't bring himself to sit beside her. *This might be the end of us.* 'It wasn't supposed to go this way.'

'No,' Bea agreed, sniffing. 'It wasn't.'

Chapter 40

Patrick

The Sierra Leonean

15th April 1961

State of emergency – stay home orders announced

In the lead up to the independence announcement, the government of Sierra Leone has announced a state of emergency across the nation following an insurgency attempt from the opposition All People's Congress Party (APC).

The party has been urging the government to hold free, democratic elections ahead of independence, claiming a neo-Colonial rule shall befall the country without immediate action.

The public is hereby ordered to remain in the home, with only Parliament officials granted permission to leave. Stay at home orders will remain in place until independence proceedings formally take place 27.04.61.

Patrick hadn't meant to break the stay-at-home order: if he'd been asked, he'd planned to say he was a Parliament official. He'd spent many pre-lockdown evenings away from the house since Bea's decision about the baby, so it had seemed only natural to jump on his bike as dusk fell that evening.

He'd needed to retrieve his calculation document of the Tagrin Bay waterway anyway; the delivery deadline loomed ever closer. It would be one of his final deadlines before their move, so he found himself taking more pride than usual in his work. He needed all he could get for his teaching portfolio after securing a trial period at a London polytechnic, which had little to do with the reference from his director and far more to do with his family name. Even when they weren't speaking, it seemed Patrick's father still maintained a level of influence over his life. It sickened Patrick, yet he knew he had no choice but to accept it.

That night, he had planned to pedal through the official checkpoints while waving some government documents in front of him by way of excuse. Anything to get him out of the house with its suffocating silence, communicating over the children's heads and through conversations with Sahr, he and Bea only addressing each other to discuss their move booked for the end of the month.

Bea wouldn't even notice he was gone: since he'd given up trying to change her mind, they'd hardly spent time in the same room. He would only be away for ten minutes, so he reasoned he'd come to no harm. Besides, who would cycle in a national lockdown unless they had the right to do so?

'You there! Stop!'

Barely two minutes from the compound's gate, Patrick squeezed on the old bike's brakes and slowed to a halt. He tried to keep his breathing even. *Parliament official, just off to a late-night meeting.* His own naivety – and stupidity – suddenly astounded him.

A figure loomed large in the shadows, slowly emerging to reveal a tall man with narrowed, angry eyes.

'What did you say, English boy?'

Patrick heard himself stutter. As his eyes adjusted, he realised it was not one but three men – each one dressed in a khaki he didn't recognise as the National Guard's official uniform. His spine straightened, his mouth going dry. He could feel he was visibly sweating. 'I'm just nipping into the office, it won't take long.'

'The rules don't apply to you, hey, Englishman?' the second voice shouted. 'You didn't hear? We make the rules now.'

Patrick's eyes darted from each unfamiliar face to the other, their footsteps advancing ever closer. He couldn't risk turning round and starting to pedal away – they'd be too quick for him. He considered for a mad second whether to throw the bike at them and run, but with three against one, his chances of escape were shrinking.

'Look, if it's money you want—'

'Money? You think we come for your English money?' The largest man spat on the ground just in front of Patrick, the other two sizing him up and taking another step towards him.

As they crept closer, Patrick realised they weren't men but boys, barely out of school. Three knobbly-kneed teenagers with patchy tufts of hair at their jawlines stood before him. In the split second before he turned on his heel, Patrick could have sworn he saw desperation in the eyes of one of them, and wondered whether it would be worth attempting to strike up a bargain. They were just angry kids, and they were right. He wasn't above the law.

Time slowed: abandoning his bike and fleeing down the road, for the whisper of a moment Patrick thought he'd got away. His arms and legs pumped wildly, lungs burning. His mind homed in on the image of Bea's face, despite all that was happening between them, his ears ringing with the sound of his children's little voices calling out to him.

The thought of his children caused him to falter ever so slightly, one foot hitting the ground too soon. Hot fear flashed in his gut as he imaged Nancy having to run, teaching Rose how to hide. How arrogant he'd been to assume war wouldn't touch him or his children because of their precious British passports – if his job had shown him one thing, it was that the Empire wreaked havoc on all involved. Why hadn't they already left?

Just as he regained his footing, a hand grabbed him and slammed him into the ground. The air was thrown from his body and his vision blurred as a blow to the head landed hard. Punches and kicks exploded along his back and thighs; Patrick curled in on himself to become as small as possible.

'If you live here, you follow the rules.'

Through swollen eyes he saw them prise his watch from his wrist, and braced himself for a final blow.

His thoughts landed on Bea once again as he let his eyes fall closed, his head pounding. Memories crackled into life, their dark outlines taking shape and projecting in technicolour: Bea diving beneath the waves on Grande Anse Beach, the light catching her form as she glided through the water; her face lighting up as she danced in her wedding gown, motioning for him to join in; her arms outstretched as Nancy toddled towards her; her laughter as Rose cooed from her cot; both twins bouncing on her knee, all three of them beaming.

Patrick's bones became heavy, a drowsiness claiming him. He focused on his children, imaging the weight and warmth of each tiny palm resting in his. He braced himself for a final blow, an encompassing darkness.

But no further bruises came. Upon claiming their gold-plated prize, the thieves had exchanged a few urgent words and left, their footsteps retreating in time to the tick of Patrick's stolen watch.

In the silence they left behind, Patrick opened his eyes and glanced around as best he could. Shallow breaths returned the life to his body, tears dripping down his cheeks and snot streaming from his nose and onto his lips. He tried to stand up, but knew it was too soon.

He considered staying splayed there all night, but the fear that more thieves would find him propelled him to stand. He cursed his own entitled stupidity, shame burning through him.

Stumbling back down the road, the sight of his front door made tears of relief flood his cheeks. In that second, Patrick didn't even care as curtains twitched and lights in neighbouring houses were turned on as he fumbled to enter his home.

For the first time since independence talks had started, it hit him that they really would have to leave this life behind.

'Patrick? I thought you were upstairs! Why—' Bea stopped at the door and shrieked at the sight of him, running to take his body weight on hers. It was the first time they'd touched in weeks, and he leant into the warmth of her body. He tried to speak, but his jaw felt locked and awkward.

She poured him a whiskey in the kitchen as he sat slumped over the table, surprised to see a small pool of blood forming on the wood. He was vaguely aware it would stain, but made no move to wipe it away. He touched his face, trying to find the source, his hand coming away bloody when he ran his fingers along his nose. Now that he was home, he felt so drowsy.

'We're leaving.' Bea's voice sounded as though she was speaking through the wireless, her voice cracked and static. 'We're packing up the children and we're getting the next boat out. I have the timetable somewhere, I'll dig it out and we'll go tomorrow. They might've seen you come home, they might be waiting. We have to go, straight away.' Patrick tried to focus on her, but his line of sight was spotted.

She rushed to his side, her belly landing awkwardly between them. A waterlogged rag dripped in her hands, which she ran over his face and arms. The coolness soothed him, his breathing pattern returning to normal. He realised she was still speaking; perhaps hadn't stopped since he'd arrived back home.

'—and the police won't do anything to find them, and the hospital will either be closed or overrun. We should've left the day the Koromas were almost taken for questioning. We can't wait another minute.' Her words were becoming clearer, and Patrick blinked hard. 'Can you stand? Can you speak?'

He nodded slowly, wincing at the tension in his neck. 'Yes,' he managed to croak, Bea's face softening with relief.

'You need to rest. And we need to . . . We need to have a good long talk when you're up to it. We can't go on like this.' She helped lift his arm over her shoulder, and the two of them staggered towards the stairs. 'I'm so sorry, Patrick,' she whispered, helping him take the first step. 'The thought we could've lost you tonight, I—'

'You don't have to—'

'Really, I—'

'It's all right.'

When he slept, Patrick dreamt he was running and running, and woke with a jolt when he'd started to fall. He found he'd grabbed Bea's hand in the panic, and she hadn't let go.

Lying in the dark, anger still gnawed at him as his thoughts returned – as they often did – to Bea's decision.

He knew he was guilty of long days and late nights, of appearing for the highlights of childhood without getting bogged down in the daily detail of it all. But he wanted to shout that he was doing this blind: he had no real concept of how a father was supposed to act. Wasn't the fact he was there every day, had now chosen to give up his whole career and teach others to do the thing he loved most, enough?

And yet, at heart, he knew he couldn't talk her out of her decision. He would have to come to terms with what was happening, to accept that he had become so obsessed by his work he'd missed the borders hardening in his own family.

He stayed up late into the night, grief whispering in his ear and tugging at his nightshirt. He couldn't tell whether its voice was of the parent he'd lost, or of the parent he may have become with another baby.

Chapter 41

Beatrice

16th April 1961

Nella – [stop] –

SL not safe – [stop] – leaving earlier than planned on 16.04
– [stop] – arriving Royal Victoria Dock Port of London 22.04 –
[stop] – please inform landlord of earlier arrival date – [stop]
– I will go ahead with flight to Grenada for birth – [stop] –

– [stop] – Bea – [stop] – ///

LETTER ON NOTEPAPER

Nella,

*Thank you again for greeting us at the docks and helping to
get us settled. The girls were a little overwhelmed at first – hell, so
was I – but seeing you and Gordon and little Hortense has made
this change so much easier.*

*I'm sorry I couldn't stay long in Brixton, the last few days
have absolutely flown by. Patrick and I are only just on speaking
terms, so it's a miracle we got through the last few days of
unpacking and getting the house sorted. Thanks so much for
bringing round those curries, they were a lifesaver.*

*You've already done so much, but please can I ask one last
favour – will you and Gordon keep an eye on Patrick, as well
as the children? I know you've already said you'll help mind the*

little ones while looking after Hortense, working your shifts to fit with child care, for which I'm ever so grateful. But can I also ask that you check in on Patrick, from time to time?

I'm not asking you to babysit him — to be honest, he could do with some time to see what it's like trying to raise four children and keep house while he waits for his teaching contract to start at the college. But just ... I don't know. Keep an eye?

Love,

Bea x

St George's, Grenada

Chapter 42

The room was too quiet: the baby should have been crying. She should have been screaming to high Heaven to announce her arrival, telling the whole world, *here I am, what are you going to do about it?*

But she lay sound asleep, her tiny hand clasped around Bea's finger. Bea hadn't wanted to hold her, had wanted to give her straight to Millicent so she wouldn't have to look.

Only, Millicent still hadn't arrived; Bea's labour had come two weeks too soon and her sister was in the middle of a council meeting. Their mother had rushed from the hospital to find her, so Bea knew her time with her little girl was running out.

She wanted to leave her with something – a note or a token to try to explain it all away. A letter describing exactly what had happened, and why. She wouldn't be able to ask for forgiveness, but perhaps she could hope for understanding.

After all, she hadn't known how to love this baby until it was all agreed – until the baby was here, and it was too late.

For a mad second, she'd imagined cradling the little girl to her chest and making a run for it. Diving out of the room, finding the nearest phone, calling Millicent at work or at school and admitting, '*I can't do this, she should be mine. I'll make it work. I'll see a doctor and learn how to be happy again. She'll make me be happy. You can't have her, this was all a mistake.*' She pictured the scene: felt the cool weight of the phone in her hand, heard the winding of the phone number and the bleep-bleep of the dial tone.

But she couldn't stand, let alone walk. She fumbled to place the baby in the cot beside the bed, grateful they'd found a private room at the last minute. She could cry openly, let the tears fall for all that was happening.

The baby will be happier with Millie and Julien, there is no money for another baby. Bea just kept repeating to herself that this little girl wasn't really hers, as if that would make it any easier. The beeps and shouts from the maternity ward beyond her closed door seemed to mock her, as laughter and whoops of joy filtered through the room.

Bea tried and failed to ignore the sounds, reaching for the paper and pen that lay beside her bed. She tried to write something about what she wished for her little one: that she would be happy; that she would experience love in all its colours; that she would be free to become whoever she wanted. She could learn to sail the sea in a Grenada fighting for and winning its own independence, discover that her adoptive mother had been instrumental in helping their country find its feet.

In her sleep-deprived state, childishly full tears fell and made inky splotches spiderweb out on the page. Bea's stomach was gripped by nausea. This baby was hers, and that was all there was to it. How could she hand her daughter over, sail back to England and leave her here? How could she receive letters from Millicent through the years, sharing stories of a child Bea should be raising?

The problem was that no one had told her the child she'd be giving away – the moments she'd be missing – would be with *this* child. Each time the baby so much as blinked, Bea's heart constricted, a rip tide of love coursing through her.

Aah, it's you, Bea thought when she looked down at her daughter, still gripping on to her finger so tightly. *Well, I can hardly go giving you away, now, can I?*

But that was exactly what she'd agreed to do, and she wasn't the kind of woman to go back on a promise to her sister.

Realising this was really happening, she let herself cry for her own sake, for Patrick, for her children missing out on another sibling. *You will be formidable, my girl.*

She finished off the letter, and with a start, realised she also had somewhere in her handbag the worn book of Shakespeare that

Patrick had given her; she'd thrown it in at the last minute before her flight, keeping it close at all times. Even though she could recite almost every one of their favourites now, it still brought her soft joy to trace her fingertips over their inscriptions and little love letters to each other. She'd leave it with the baby alongside the letter, for Millicent to give to her when the time was right. Bea wiped her tears, forcing herself to think of how her sister would feel now she was someone's mother. She'd abandoned Millie once; she couldn't do it again.

Bea turned her attention back to the paper in her hands.

Her hand hovering above the notepaper, she paused at how to sign the letter.

She couldn't write 'Mother', as that wasn't what she would be to this child. Writing her first name felt impersonal, overly formal. She frowned, panic rising in her chest.

Time was running out: the constant beeping of the machine beside her maternity ward bed marked precious seconds passing, each one drawing her closer to the moment her child would become someone else's. Millie would arrive any moment.

She looked back down at the letter, not wanting to waste another second. Its page was already crumpled from having been screwed up in her hand and smoothed back out, the pencilled words creasing. She hadn't known how to address it – Millie hadn't revealed the names she'd chosen – and there was a slight smudge across the letter's opening. In the end, she'd simply opted for:

My dearest,

How can I explain what I'm about to do?

After reading it once more, she decided how to end the letter, signing it and tucking the note into the baby's blankets. She lifted the child from the cot, the baby's solid weight anchoring her. They would only be mother and daughter for a few minutes longer. She dropped a tender kiss on the little girl's forehead as she held her close.

She knew the baby wouldn't remember this – wouldn't remember her – but as she rocked the child to and fro, she repeated a lifetime of good wishes and I love yous and I'm sorrys under her breath.

A knock on the door startled her, her head snapping up and her arms instinctively tightening around the child. She willed the door to stay closed, to let her exist in this moment for a second longer. *Please, no.*

'One minute,' she called, the words stumbling out faster and louder than she'd intended. The baby stirred, doe eyes snapping open and locking with her own. Bea felt a tear snake down her cheek, and swiped it away before it could drop onto the baby. Her gaze darted back to the letter; she suddenly regretted her decision to even write it. The knock on the door started up again, sending ripples through the room's still waters.

As the door handle slowly began to turn, she felt something within her fray and snap: she reached back into the baby's blankets and grabbed the letter, stuffing it into the pocket of her hospital gown.

'I'm sorry,' she whispered to the baby she hadn't known how to love until it was too late. 'It will be for the best.' A sob threatened to choke her.

The door finally opened and Millicent's footsteps clattered into the room. Bea let her eyes fall closed, running her fingers up and down the baby's chubby little arm one last time. She prised the letter from her pocket, tucking into the folds of the book of Shakespeare. She placed both beside her bed, paralysed by indecision.

She'd meant what she said: this was for the best. Her daughter would be loved, and maybe this time, love would be enough?

'Bea?' Millicent's voice trembled in a tone Bea had never heard before. 'How are you doing? How is the baby?'

Bea couldn't bear to look up at her sister; she kept her eyes locked on the baby. *How can I let you go?*

'It's a girl, Millicent.' Bea lifted her gaze up to see her sister's face pinched with worry, eyes shining with hope. Bea's heart cracked in two. 'You have a daughter.'

Millie leant forward to give Bea a tender hug, no words capable of explaining the bond they now shared. Bea could sense Millie's desperation to hold the little one, and she nodded as her sister eventually pulled back. Millie's arms encircled the precious bundle, her face breaking into an expression of joyous relief. Bea tried to feel a hint of happiness at the look on Millicent's face, but her raw pain was too sharp. Millie rocked the little girl close to her chest. 'Hello, little one,' Millie cooed. Bea turned her face away, letting the tears soak her pillow.

There's no going back. You were never meant to be mine.

Chapter 43

Beatrice

9 *Craster Road*
Brixton
London

27th May 1961

Dear Bea,

I know you're still angry with me for how we left things. I would be, too; it was cruel of me to leave you at the airport so quickly. I just couldn't face watching you leave, or accept what it would mean for us. I've been holding in such anger about what you hid from me, and I've let bitterness almost consume me.

But it has to stop. I've had word from Moira again, and she's informed me my father has very little time left. When I read her words, all I wanted was to turn to you and talk about it. But with how I left things, and how I've been leaving you for all this time to cope with the house, the children, all on your own – I wouldn't be surprised if you stayed in Grenada.

Nella showed me some of your letters, told me how alone you'd been feeling. Bea, I never wanted us to end up like this – I hope you can believe me. Because despite everything that's happened and the decision you made without me, yours is still the face I picture before I fall asleep and the hand I reach for every morning. I love you, and I've loved you since I saw you on that beach and you caught my eye at the dance. I'll love you through the school runs and the change for the meter and the late-night fights and the blowing out of candles as each year thunders by. I've loved you as we've traversed continents and danced on the peripheries of war, and no matter the skies we've lived beneath, I've seen Heaven beside you.

But after all we've been through, I'm scared love isn't enough. I was naïve to ever believe it would be. Can we get back to what we once had, or has that tide already turned?

Regardless of what's next for us, please come home soon. The children miss their mother, and I need you. We have so much we need to say.

Love, P

'Who are you writing to?'

Bea glanced up from Patrick's letter, to see Bette sweep into the room. She walked with the quiet confidence of someone with money, her chin raised and hair expertly pinned up.

She glided over to where Bea sat, joining her at the kitchen table. *How many hours had we sisters spent here as children, sharing a snack or playing cards? Reading over lines for the next play, scribbling over homework?*

Bea swallowed. 'I'm trying to write back to Patrick, but I don't know what to say.'

The two of them were alone in the house, Bette having arrived the night before. Matthew had taken their parents for a tour of the new visitor attraction at the distillery – an obvious ruse to give Bea some time alone. She wasn't sure she wanted it, but no one had asked. She missed baby Amelia with every waking breath. Her arms kept reaching for the child she had barely held, falling short as she grasped at nothing. It had been over a week since her sister had rushed into the room and taken the baby away, cooing a name Bea hadn't chosen, but it felt a century.

Only Bette had seemed to sense Bea's glass-thin fragility, the way she felt as though she'd shatter if someone held her too close.

'What do you want to say?' Bette asked softly. She had a perfectly ripe guava in one hand and a knife in the other, placing both down carefully on her plate. She began to slice through the grass-green skin, revealing sweet juice and red flesh. She offered a piece to Bea, who shook her head.

'I don't know.' Bea hesitated. What would be the point in keeping this all to herself, as she'd been doing for the last six years? Loneliness is a terrible listener, as she'd discovered all too easily on her own. *Enough.*

'I feel broken, Bette. I wish the children were here.' She wiped at her eyes – which, of course, had begun to stream. 'I want Patrick to be here, too, but I don't know whether I want to run to him or scream at him.'

'But you still love him,' Bette stated, popping another slice of guava into her mouth. 'And you want to go back to London? That's what happiness looks like, to you?'

Bea nodded. 'I think so. God, I miss the children so much.'

'And that's it?'

'What's it?'

'Just Patrick and the children ... That's what happiness looks like to you?'

Bea scrunched up her nose, thrown by the question. 'Honestly? I thought giving up Amelia would bring some sort of happiness, bring me a sense of relief.' She paused. 'But without her, all I feel is empty.'

'But it doesn't have to be that way. Bea, you've got to remember who you are.' Bette shook her head. 'I don't know how you've been doing it, always waiting at the back of the line. I get that there's so much pressure to do right by your husband, by your children, and forget about your own desires and interests.' She looked wistfully out of the window, where a small sailing boat was bobbing steadily from the harbour towards open water. 'Why are we never encouraged to put ourselves first?'

Bea's eyes tracked along the boat before it sailed out of the frame. 'I wish I knew.'

Bette curled up her legs beneath her, taking the last slice of guava and picking at the peel. 'It doesn't have to be like that, I don't think. You could work if you wanted to. You could learn a craft or a trade. You're still a person, even if you're someone's wife. And mother.' As Bette spoke, Bea wondered which one of them she was really saying this for.

'You're right, but it's so much easier said than done.'

'So do it! Weren't you the one who convinced stuffy old Englishmen to let you be the first woman on base camp?'

Bea hesitated. 'That was before the children.'

'And weren't you the one who put a stop to that family getting arrested, in Freetown?'

'There were plenty of others.'

'But it all came from you! I know that version of you is still in there, even if you can't see it. You're the brave one, Bea.' Bette stood up, continuing to watch the boat as the wind picked up and whisked it over the whitecaps. 'You should do whatever it is that would make you happy. One evening class, or one annual trip home, or nights out with Nella. Or a job of your own, whatever you want to do. If you go back to London, you've got to be going back to something better for you.'

Bea's stomach dropped. 'But I don't know if I can go back.' *I can't leave my baby here.*

'What's all this?' Mrs Bell marched into the kitchen, making Bea and Bette jump. 'Bea, you will go back to London because that is your home now.' She cast a look at Bette. 'Your sister is right, you need to do something to stop these tears and make a life for yourself. I didn't raise you to wallow.' She dismissed Bea's dark thoughts with a simple wave of her hand, dusting them into the harbour below. Bea wished it were that simple.

'How come you're back so early?' Bea asked, not moving from her seat.

Mrs Bell ignored her. 'Bette is also wrong, you know. This isn't just about you.' She took a deep breath and walked towards Bea, her hand coming to rest on her daughter's cheek. The move was so maternal, so uncharacteristically tender, it made Bea's eyes prick with tears again. 'You'll go back to London because you're a mother.' She spoke softly, but her words had an edge to them. 'There are four babies going to bed with cold cheeks for missing out on goodnight kisses from you. You'll go back because you have a duty to those little ones. You know better than anyone that motherhood is pain. It's also joy, don't misunderstand me, but it is a whole lot of pain.'

Bea leant into her mother's touch, filling her lungs with air. 'What if I don't know how to do it any more?'

'Of all people, you know how to make things work.' Mrs Bell withdrew her hand and picked up Bea's empty mug. 'You are the one who has faced such terrible treatment from your parents-in-law, who has lived in faraway countries on the brink of war and raised four children, all while living to tell the tale.' She looked over to Bette, who nodded solemnly. 'You will get through this, Beatrice, because you're stronger than you think. When you get back to London, you've got to make this decision count.' She made for the door, still talking over her shoulder. 'And you must remember, this is a kind thing you've done. Do you know what other people would give for a sister like you?'

Before Bea could answer, her mother swept into the garden and pulled the screen door behind her.

'I can't take it back,' Bea said, not looking at Bette. 'I can't change what's happened, can I?'

Bette reached out and patted her sister's hand, the movement making Bea's stomach twist. 'I'm afraid you can't. But you'll see, in time, that this is a good thing you've done. For both you and Millicent.' Bette withdrew, standing up and stretching her arms above her head. Her engagement and wedding rings caught the sunlight, glinting a brilliant gold. 'You just need time, and you'll see this was worth it. You've given Millie the greatest gift you ever could, and now you need to figure out what you'll do for yourself in return.'

Bea sat back, closing her eyes for a second. She felt Bette's hand squeeze her shoulder before her footsteps retreated. Bea breathed in the familiar scents of fallen fruit and sea air, listened for the call of seabirds, the waves, the faraway buzz of the harbour.

There was no going back: Amelia would be staying here with the mother who'd yearned for her, who would stop at nothing to give her an incredible life. And Bea would have to leave. She'd have to face whatever was waiting for her in London, with or without Patrick by her side. She felt her heart break in two, the pain of it burning through her.

Amelia can never know. I'll never get to be her mother.

At the realisation, Bea let tears stream down her cheeks. She cried for her daughters and her sons and her crumbling marriage, for the version of herself she'd lost in time. She cried for the future she wouldn't have with Amelia, for all the moments she'd miss with the little girl growing up on the island. *She was never meant to be mine.*

Dear Patrick,

I know you're still so angry with me, but I wanted to write and explain myself a little more. Since Millicent and Julien took Amelia, I have been hollowed out. There's an emptiness inside me that I know now I'll never be able to fill again.

In spite of this feeling, this ache, I think you should know that a part of me doesn't regret this. Handing the baby over to Millie was the worst pain I've ever experienced, and yet seeing the love on her face each time she holds the child makes it tragically beautiful. They are besotted with Amelia, and she'll grow up surrounded by unconditional love. I want you to know that in this sadness, there is love.

There's always been love, and I'm sorry that we let ours fade. I say we, because I think we are both to blame.

I know I've hurt you with this decision, but you've hurt me, too. Your vision has become so distorted by border marks and contour lines and Independence Conferences that you missed the civil war in your own family. That's how it's felt: me against the world, me against the children, me against you.

You left me to fend for myself, burying your head in the sand. I can't ignore how that's made me feel, and I need you to promise you'll put more effort into your family. If we stay as a family, that is.

It's time we admit that the people we both fell in love with have long gone; the carefree bookkeeper, the adventurous map-maker. We're so different now. I cannot honestly say whether we'll make it through, but I'd like to try. Would you?

Love, Bea

Chapter 44

Beatrice

Bea reached into her old wardrobe for the wooden chest she knew would still be gathering dust at the back of the shelf. She probably shouldn't have been lifting things only a fortnight after giving birth, but she desperately needed to keep her hands busy – anything to distract them from the weight they should have been carrying.

Into the chest, Bea placed the small copy of Shakespeare, with the letter she'd written at the hospital tucked into the back cover. After two weeks without leaving the house, she had opened the shutters on her bedroom windows for the first time. She'd let in some light, breathed fresher air.

This was something she was going to survive, she'd decided that morning. Her mother and Bette were right: it would have to be worth it. Bea would have to make this mean something.

With just the book and the letter, the large wooden chest looked too bare. She wanted to leave Amelia with something beautiful, a token that said, *I love you, I'm sorry, it's all for the best.* Even though Bea knew, deep down, Amelia would probably never lift the lid.

They could never tell her the truth, after all. What would it do to a child to hear her mother hadn't known how to love her until it was too late?

Bea scrambled around trying to find something else to add, not wanting to leave too much empty space.

She yanked open a drawer, her gaze landing on a faded orange handkerchief. Her hand flew to her mouth as she realised what it was: the colourful scrap that Millie had waved at her, the day she and Patrick had sailed away from Port Louis Marina.

She reached into the drawer, plucking it out with such care she worried it would disintegrate at her touch. But it was stronger than it looked: the silky-soft material flowed through her fingers, its colour a little faded but still bold.

She folded it up gently, placing it inside the chest. The wooden box had a knotted pattern running through its middle, an old padlock still attached to secure its lid.

The front door opened, and a flurry of voices and gurgles entered the house. Bea fell over herself in her scramble to the door, her mood lifting at the sight of the little one in Millicent's arms. Instinctively she reached for the baby, and just a flicker of a shadow crossed Millie's face before she handed her straight over.

'Hi, little girl,' Bea cooed. 'How are you doing?' She leant down and breathed in the milk-powdery smell of her daughter's curly head, clutching Amelia close to her chest.

'She had a good feed this morning,' Millicent piped up. 'She's settling in so well.'

Bea eventually looked up to search behind Millicent. 'Julien not with you?'

'He had to go back to work, ran out of leave. He's coming by this evening, though.' Millie reached out her hand and placed it on Bea's upper arm. 'So you're really leaving tomorrow?'

Bea nodded. 'Right after we sign the papers. I have to get home to ...' She trailed off, unable to say 'my children' while still holding Amelia. She rocked the baby to and fro, turning to lead Millicent into the sitting room.

'I still feel like it's a dream, you know?' Millicent said, her voice velvet soft. 'She's just so ... And you've been ... Oh, I don't know what I'm trying to say.'

Bea couldn't help but laugh. 'I don't think I've ever heard you stuck for words.'

'It's probably the lack of sleep. Which I'm glad for,' Millie added hastily. 'Glad for it all.' She paused, her eyes lingering on the now-sleeping baby. 'I don't know how we'll ever thank you for this, Bea.'

'Giving her the best life you can, that's how you'll thank me.'

Bea couldn't believe the words she was saying, how composed she sounded. Since she'd let herself cry the day Bette had visited, she hadn't shed a single tear. She wished Bette could have stayed longer. 'I made a promise to you, and I want it to mean something. If we start breaking promises between family, where would that leave us?'

Millie moved to sit beside Bea on the sinking couch, their knees touching. 'She will be the most adored child on this island, and we'll give her every opportunity imaginable.' Her hand found Bea's and squeezed it. 'And you'll have the most wonderful life over in London. We can come and visit, and you can bring the children here, too.'

'But we mustn't tell them,' Bea replied, the words coming out so quickly they almost collided with one another. 'None of them can know. They have to think you adopted her from a mother who'd passed away or something, who was completely incapable of keeping her.' *Not a mother who'd forgotten how to love, and made a promise she'd never be able to take back.* 'Maybe we can tell them the truth one day, but while she's growing, we have to keep it a secret.'

'If you're sure?'

'I don't want her to think she was unwanted, or sent away, or anything like that.' Bea's voice was slowly breaking, and Millie's hand found hers. 'I want her to grow up feeling as loved as she is, feeling treasured.'

'All right,' Millie agreed, squeezing her sister's hand again. 'Whatever you want to do is fine by me. You're the bravest person I know, Bea.'

Bea could do nothing but nod, while she let the weight of her decision bear down upon her. She looked at the child's peaceful face, sound asleep, and carefully handed the bundle back to Millicent. This was it: the time stamp by which she'd judge the rest of her life, remembering either a *Before* or an *After*.

'How is Patrick getting on, and the children?' Millie asked after a beat.

'They're doing well. A letter arrived yesterday,' Bea replied swiftly, the lie coating her teeth. He hadn't written for weeks, had ignored her last letter. 'All settling into London well.'

'That's wonderful. You must be looking forward to seeing them again.'

Bea nodded, knowing the tears she'd been keeping at bay would finally fall if she spoke another word. She rested her head on Millie's shoulder, careful not to disturb the baby, allowing her sister to whisper comforting things about seeing her husband and her children.

'You'll be back with them soon, Bea, it's all right,' Millie cooed, offering Bea a handkerchief. Bea let herself be rocked for a moment, savouring that for once, it wasn't her being the mother.

Eventually, she recovered enough to turn her attention back to the wooden chest she'd been filling. She stood up, trying to ignore that too-light feeling she had after letting the baby go, and hurried to bring it into the sitting room. Dust still clouded along the lid and the sides, and Bea wiped it down with her sleeve after dabbing at her eyes. 'There's just one thing you need to do for me,' she said, swallowing hard. 'If we ever agree to tell her – although we probably won't – will you give her this?'

Millie prised open the lid, gasping at the sight of the faded orange handkerchief. She ran her fingers along the box's contents, her dark eyes shining. 'Of course, Bea, anything you like. We can decide whether to tell her when she's grown, when she's old enough to understand. We have so much time.'

England

Chapter 45

Beatrice

Bea's hands shook as she opened the taxi door, knowing the driver certainly wasn't going to get out and open it for her. Still, she thanked the man in the most polite tone she could manage, and glanced up at her front door.

She had to give Nella credit: the house she'd found for them to rent was beautiful. A three-storey, brown brick town house with white window panes and a pillar-box red front door. The street wasn't as tree-lined as Bea may have liked, and the paint was peeling in places along window frames, but it was where she needed to be.

She gathered up her bags and went to let herself in, but at the last minute pulled her key back from the lock. Patrick had been here alone for almost a month, and from the desperate tone of his only letter, she wasn't even sure if he'd be pleased to see her.

Perhaps this is how it ends: on a drizzly doorstep in the city I've dreamt of. One baby halfway across the world, four asleep upstairs.

Bea took a moment to steady herself, smoothing down her hair and rolling back her shoulders. She had every right to be here, in this city and in this house. Was she not a British citizen? Weren't these still her children, her husband?

She breathed deeply. She knocked.

The door opened.

'Bea.'

'Hi.'

'What are you ...?' Patrick's eyebrows rose. His face was dish-evelled; there was a dishcloth thrown over his shoulder and a stain down the front of his shirt. His hair was all over the place, his trousers kneed. 'I wasn't expecting you until tomorrow.'

'I think I got confused with the time difference.'

'If I'd known you were arriving I'd have kept the children up. They're all in bed.'

'Right. It's all right.'

They stood facing each other a second longer, uncertainty thickening the air between them, before Patrick sprang into action.

'Let me take your bags,' he said, reaching behind her for her suitcase. 'Come on inside.'

'Thank you.'

Patrick threw her a tight smile, turning his back and heading down the narrow hallway. 'I'll put the kettle on.'

Bea took a tentative step onto the black-and-white checked tiles, removing her raincoat and hanging it on a peg which Patrick must have installed while she'd been away. Beside it hung four tiny coats in varying colours, four pairs of wellies crowding the floor beneath.

Bea closed her eyes for a moment as pain rushed through her, repeating her mother's words in her head. *You've got to make this decision count.*

She let her fingertips trail over each raincoat, the hoods only just big enough to cover her clasped hands. She wished she could pound up the stairs and wake each child, cradle them in her arms and cover them with kisses.

'We're out of sugar, sorry,' Patrick whispered, reappearing with two steaming mugs.

'Oh, without is fine. Thank you.' She felt shy all of a sudden, an awkwardness wedging between them as she accepted the mug and they floated towards the front room. A version of her wanted to pull Patrick towards her and tell him to stop this nonsense and let them forgive each other already. Another version wanted to cry, scream at him, *How could you let it get to this?* Another wanted to apologise, beg him to forgive her. *I never meant for it to go this far.*

'Thank you for your letter,' Patrick began as Bea leant back into the sofa's second-hand softness. 'It... It really got me thinking.'

'What about?'

He turned to lock eyes with her, sending a flash along her body. How, after all this time, could his eyes on hers still do that?

'How I made you feel, so lost and alone. I can't believe...' He trailed off, shaking his head. 'After the way I was ignored as a child, I can't believe I let that happen to someone I love.'

Bea's stomach tightened. 'So you do still love me?'

'Of course I do.' He paused. 'And I'm so, so sorry I let it get as far as it did. That should never have happened, it's not what I promised you.'

Bea nodded, but Patrick wasn't finished. 'But love isn't always enough,' he said.

Bea felt sick, and she closed her eyes for a second. *So this is how it ends.*

'I needed to understand, to know I wasn't going to turn into my father,' Patrick continued, though Bea barely heard him. 'I went to see him, last week.'

'What did you do with the children?'

'I went when the girls were at school. I had to take the twins with me.'

Heartbreak became rage as Bea sat up straight. 'You took the twins to see a man who would deny their existence?'

Patrick ran his hand through his hair. 'I was just going to go and confront him, once and for all, have it out before he died. Tell him that he'd been wrong all along, that he didn't know me like he thought he did. That I was nothing like him.'

'And what did he say?'

Patrick let his gaze track back across to where Bea sat. 'I couldn't go in. I sat at the entrance to their drive for an hour, maybe two.' He finally looked back up at her. 'I said all I needed to say to him the day we left. I didn't want to give him the satisfaction of getting the last word.'

Bea willed him to look at her. 'And how did that feel?' she asked, the gap between them feeling larger than ever.

He shook his head. 'Do you know what? I felt completely empty. It just reminded me of the way you looked on that driveway when we were last there.' He finally moved towards her, his hand coming to rest on hers in a slow, almost apologetic movement. 'I never want to leave you out in the cold like that again. I want to understand everything that's happened, and I want to change. I don't want to miss out on time with the children ... with you.' He fumbled in his pocket, retrieving a dog-eared booklet. 'My trial at the college went well, so I've put my foot down on the timetable and made sure I can be home in good time and there's no weekend working, hardly any overtime apart from marking through the summers. There won't be any lecturing then, so I'll be home much more.' He showed the timetable to Bea, though the numbers and letters on the page made little sense. 'I want us to truly forgive each other, to find our way back.' His gaze was so earnest; Bea's mother's warnings rang in her ears. 'Do you think we can try?'

As she accepted his outstretched palm, she felt something that had eluded her these past couple of years. The feeling glimmered and shone, sparking into life at the pit of her stomach. Hope.

Bea hesitated, before squeezing his hand. Every decision they'd made up until this point seemed to be leading them to this moment, perched in a rented terrace in a south London suburb, with four of their babies sleeping upstairs and one halfway across the world.

But it all had to mean something; from heartbreak had to come joy. Perhaps they could move forward with their grief, and Bea could become someone new: not only known as the surveyor's wife, but as a person in her own right. Someone who her family described as brave and kind in earnest. Someone who didn't cry when she thought her children weren't looking, who was the kind of woman strangers in the park or at the train station or on the high street looked at and said, That's what happiness is.

'Yes, I think we can try,' she said. 'But there's no going back to each other,' she added, her tone decisive. She shifted so she sat closer to him, her eyes boring into his. 'There's only forward. There's only moving on, together.'

'I'll take it,' Patrick said, smiling in a way that reached his eyes. 'But before we do, will you do one thing for me?'

Bea gave a tentative smile. 'Of course.'

'Will you tell me what she was like?' he asked. And holding his hand in hers, Bea felt she finally had the strength to do so. *We will make this decision count.* For the first time without shedding a tear, she spoke of her youngest daughter. It hurt, but Bea knew she was where she needed to be to bear the pain.

Three Years Later

Chapter 46

Beatrice

'Are you sure you have everything you need?' Bea called over her shoulder, as Nella bundled her and Patrick out of the house.

'Yes, we're fine. Aren't we, girls?'

Three little faces appeared behind Nella's legs, as Nancy, Rose and Hortense nodded with enthusiasm. 'We're going to put on a play,' Nancy declared. 'The twins will be the knights, and we'll be the princesses.'

Nella whipped around. 'Why don't you lot be the knights, and save the little princes? That's far less cliché.'

'What does cliché mean?'

'I'll tell you now, but get inside.' Nella ushered the girls back down the hallway, turning for one last wave to Bea and Patrick. 'I don't want to see either of you until at least midnight, you hear me?'

Bea laughed, waving as Nella closed the door and her voice became muffled. She linked her arm through Patrick's, strolling down the street. Her faux fur coat kept out the chill; her scarf was tied up around her curls.

Their walk into Brixton was short and bitingly cold, their heads bent close together. The doorman at the dance hall waved them straight in, recognising Bea from Nella's birthday party the month before.

'I'll get us a couple of drinks, if you want to find somewhere to sit?'

Bea felt nervous, though she didn't know why. She spotted a table nestled towards the back of the dimly lit hall, a jazz band setting up on the stage at the very front. Spheres of light hung from the ceiling, thick velvet curtains framed the wooden stage. It reminded Bea, a little, of the stage back in Grenada. For once, the thought of the island where her youngest child was growing up without her didn't cause a spear through her heart. She was able to think of it fondly, to think of Amelia as she'd been in the photo Millie had sent over the previous month. She'd been a star in her Sunday school nativity play, and she'd looked radiant even in black and white.

Patrick returned, sitting opposite her. 'What does this remind you of?' Bea asked, graciously accepting the cocktail.

Patrick followed her eyeline towards the stage. 'It looks like the one in St George's, doesn't it?' he said with a smile. 'We should get tickets to something soon, don't you think?'

Bea laughed. 'I think we've used up our babysitting quota for the next year, at least. Poor Nella and Gordon have no idea what they're in for.'

Patrick raised his glass in a toast. 'To the last night off we'll have in a while.'

'Cheers.' Bea clinked her glass against his, the impossibly orange liquid swirling.

'It's called a sidecar,' Patrick explained, watching Bea take a sip. 'I thought you'd like it. It's meant to be quite fruity.'

Bea took another sip, enjoying the sweetness on her tongue. 'What did you get?'

'Manhattan.'

'Good choice.'

The band began to play, and the two of them held hands over the table.

Patrick's drinking had subsided to almost nothing since they'd arrived in England, particularly after they'd learnt of his father's death from liver disease. The following month, it would be three years since the funeral, to which Bea had refused to go. Patrick had gone out of duty, he claimed, but Bea sensed it was something more. Something between fathers and sons that she'd never understand.

She was getting better at accepting all that she couldn't comprehend: the way her sons communicated without having to speak; Nancy's unwavering confidence and Rose's brilliant mind; the fact that she could feel both heartbreak and happiness at the thought of her child across the sea, surrounded by the love of her family.

Bea glanced at Patrick, lost in the music, his drink pushed to one side. The tune from the band sounded like their early days as it meandered and crescendoed and found its rhythm once more.

'Whenever I hear jazz it makes me think of you,' Patrick said, without pulling his eyes from the band. The saxophone player was starting a solo which sounded as though it was being broadcast straight from a Caribbean dance hall. 'And whenever someone quotes Shakespeare.'

Bea smiled to herself. 'How often are people around you quoting Shakespeare?'

He turned to face her, reaching to sip his drink. 'Occupational hazard, sharing a building with the journalism department. Although I'm always thinking about you, really.'

'And the children?'

'Of course the children.'

The music grew louder, the rest of the band joining in with the sax.

'Are you ready for your present now?' Patrick asked.

Bea laughed. 'We said we weren't doing anniversary presents.'

Patrick's eyes glinted as he reached into his pocket and pulled out a glossy pamphlet, the name of the polytechnic at which he'd started lecturing embossed on the front.

'Are you trying to recruit me?'

'Just take a look,' he said with a chuckle. 'I picked it up yesterday. They do part-time courses. Some of them you can do as a correspondence course, so you hardly have to go in. Look.' He turned the page, the titles of various accounting and finance courses jumping out at her. 'Now that the twins are in school, I thought you might like to do something more for yourself?' His voice was tentative, soundtracked by the smooth melodies of the club.

'This isn't me pushing you to work if you don't want to,' he added hurriedly. 'You could do a course for free, you see, through my contract. You'd get the accountancy qualifications they recognise here in a couple of years, and I've been around so much more to help with the children, what with having summers, Easters off from lecturing.'

Bea finally raised her eyes from the leaflet, facing Patrick's pinched expression. Her heart felt so full. 'I ... I love that idea, Patrick. Thank you.'

As it often did, Amelia's face came to Bea's mind. In her head, she thanked Amelia: *I'll get to take this opportunity because of you. I'm a more resilient person, a braver person, because of you. Thank you, my love. Will you ever forgive me?*

'Do you ever wonder what it would've been like if we'd kept her?' Patrick asked. This often happened: one of them would be thinking of Amelia, and the other would somehow sense it. It had been hard at first, skulking around the subject and only bringing her up on her birthday or when Millie sent a letter or photo. On Amelia's second birthday, they'd unspeakingly taken a step forward. Patrick had returned home with flowers for Bea, and together they'd baked her mother's grapefruit pound cake recipe. Bea had cried herself to sleep that night, Patrick holding her close. Something had shifted between them after that, connecting them in their bittersweet heartbreak.

Tonight was the first time Patrick had asked such a question, and finally, Bea felt she could reply.

'I wonder what it would've been like to keep her all the time,' she said. 'I think of her every day, think of what could've been.'

Patrick let out a long breath, as though he'd been holding it for a while. 'I didn't realise how long I'd waited to hear that,' he said at last.

'What do you mean?'

Patrick shook his head. 'I don't really know. I thought it was just me, wondering how things could've been different.' He looked away for a beat. 'I forgive you, for making that decision without me. I hope you've known that.' He ran his hand through his hair, leaning in closer. 'I understand it was what you felt was right for our family.'

Bea nodded, slowly, unable to speak.

Patrick fiddled with the strap on his watch, the only thing he'd been left in his father's will. 'Have you forgiven me, do you think?' he asked, so quietly his words were almost drowned out by the final notes of the band's set.

The music quietened as the band took a break, the lead singer starting to talk to the few dancers who swept across the floor. 'Of course I forgive you,' Bea answered, her eyes gazing around the hall and landing on Patrick. 'You've put our family first, and that's all I've ever needed.' It was true: he'd been home on time every night, planned trips and holidays, taken the girls to ballet every Saturday morning so she could have a break with the twins. She felt him choosing her – choosing their family – each morning, when he woke her with a cup of sweet tea. His maps remained scrolled in the lecture hall, his study now adorned with drawings from the children and thank-you notes from students.

Could they have kept Amelia, with this lifestyle? Bea couldn't bear thinking about it. Amelia was Millicent and Julien's child now, and that was how she forced herself to frame it. Breaking a promise to her sister would have been unforgivable. *How could I have denied my sister becoming the mother she always dreamed she would be?*

'Thank you,' Patrick said, lifting her clasped hand and kissing it. 'I'll always put our family first. I love you, Bea.'

'I love you, too.'

She felt something inside her shift, and she pushed her chair closer to his. She looked back down at the college leaflet, ideas sparking in her mind. 'I could really do it, couldn't I?'

Patrick planted a kiss on her forehead. 'You could do anything you set your mind to. You, my love, will be the best bookkeeper this lovely city's ever seen.'

Bea grinned, hope surging in her chest. 'I think I will.'

'Then we must celebrate.' He stood up, reaching for her hand.

'Here's to you, Beatrice Anderson,' he declared, raising his glass. 'Future British bookkeeper extraordinaire and smartest in her class. Not to mention, the most beautiful wife a map-maker could ask for.' He took a small sip as the band started up again, and he pulled Bea up from her seat. 'May I have this dance?'

Brixton Gazette

7th February 1974

Grenada declares Independence

Grenada, West Indies, has today (7th February) announced its independence from Great Britain under the leadership of the United Labour Party.

Following the party's success at the 1972 elections, Grenada becomes the 36th country to join the Commonwealth of Nations and retain Her Majesty the Queen as Monarch. The island nation will rule from its own Senate and Legislative Assembly, with the next free elections to be held in 1976.

Locals in the Brixton, Clapham and Camberwell neighbourhoods marked the event with street parties and partial business closures.

At the celebration on Trent Road, Brixton, bookkeeper and owner of Brixton Finance Ltd, Beatrice Anderson, said: 'Today is a special day, and marks a step towards a more equal and fair relationship between Grenada and Great Britain. Rights to self-governance have been recognised, and we hope this brings greater prosperity to Grenada and inspires other Commonwealth countries to follow suit. We must leave imperialism where it belongs – in the history books.'

Mrs Anderson's sister, Senator Millicent Mallalieu, takes a seat in the Legislative Assembly with the United Labour Party. Her photo was displayed at the street party, pictured overleaf, alongside photographs of Grenadian icons past and present such as journalist Alister Hughes and trade unionist and newly elected Prime Minister Eric Gairy.

2015

SATURDAY AFTERNOON

Amelia hadn't realised where she was headed until she'd arrived.

When she'd first sat behind the wheel of her beat-up Nissan Micra after telling Maryse she needed to 'just get away for a while', she'd automatically shifted into gear with her eyes set towards work. While she had often found comfort in the order of things in her office – her paperwork piled by order of importance, the photos keeping her company at her desk, the constant ringing of the phones – the office would be shut up for the weekend.

Letters from Beatrice, postcards from Bette, articles torn from newspapers and telegrams typed in faded text, all lay folded in her handbag. She needed to read through them all once more, but for now, she desperately wanted to try to just... be.

The afternoon sun was still high in the sky, and she pulled out of her parking spot and headed left, driving up the west side of the island with the radio turned up to maximum. She wanted to drown out her thoughts and found herself tuned into the too-bright sound of the local DJs playing the latest hits interspersed with pop classics of the noughties. The songs reminded her too much of when Maryse had been little and her parents had helped out on road trips and holidays, so she jabbed at the dial to switch stations. A smooth dance hall beat made the steering wheel vibrate, and she rolled down the windows so the afternoon air could rush through and underscore the soundtrack. The DJ's voice crackled over the music, wishing everyone a 'fine start to Saturday night'.

Then she ran out of road. Amelia hit the brakes, blinking out at the view just before her.

The sea mocked her from below, waving up from where it

rolled onto hot sand. Mercifully the beach was almost empty, save a couple of walkers and young families strewn across the sand.

Sugarloaf Mountain jutted out from the water a mile or so out to sea, its windswept outline blurring in the afternoon wind. Years of storms and sea winds had formed every tree on the mountain into a lattice of bending branches and interwoven leaves, all leaning across one another in an attempt to become flat against the earth. The leaves rustled; a storm was certainly on its way, and at that moment Amelia wished it would rain down and swallow her up. Wash her away, so she wouldn't have to think about what came next.

What does come next? Beatrice and Patrick had arrived early for the reunion, giving her the perfect opportunity to confront them for the decades of lies. But what would that solve? Who would that help, really? No amount of shouting or questioning would turn back the clock and bring back her mother.

She locked the car door and stepped onto the sandy ground, palm and coconut leaves padding her footsteps. Hers was the only car at the beach on the island's tip, and she leant against the bonnet. She stretched her neck from side to side, rolling it in smooth circles.

It was no surprise she'd ended up here. While Barkley favoured concrete metropolises cut off from the rest of the world by a snaking river, and Maryse sought out the most hidden caves or rock pools, this spot on Levera Beach had always made Amelia feel as though she was standing on the edge of the world.

Tourists always came here to snap greedy pictures of Sugarloaf, pointing their cameras and smartphones out to sea. Amelia preferred to emerge from the road thick with trees, take a few steps onto sand so fine it felt like silk, and rest up against one of the lone coconut trees surviving out on the shoreline. The view to the mountain surrounded by sea was undeniably beautiful, but the sight when she turned to face the island had so much more colour, more contrast – more shadows and patches of light.

She remembered the first time she'd brought Maryse to this beach, when she was still a baby. Her father had insisted on driving, and her mother had sat in the front seat screaming at him to slow down on every corner. 'If he goes any slower the car will keel over,' Amelia remembered teasing. They'd arrived with far too much stuff to carry: beach chairs and towels and brightly coloured umbrellas, one for each of them, all spread out as though they were expecting a party of forty instead of four. Her father had brought a red-and-white striped beach ball, which he bounced upon the towels, much to baby Maryse's delight. Of course, Maryse had cried when sand got in her eyes, and kicked off her towel so many times Amelia gave up trying to cover her. Instead, Maryse had lain on her back to marvel up at the light streaming through coconut leaves, reaching up her tiny fists as though trying to take hold of the sun.

As Maryse had grown older, they'd continued to visit for picnics packed with as many games as snacks, carting cricket bats and tennis balls and boules and swimsuits. Maryse had first learned to swim on Grande Anse, but had always threatened she'd one day try and swim as far as Sugarloaf from Levera Beach. To Amelia's knowledge, this hadn't ever been attempted, although they had taken a boat ride over to the island for her parents' fortieth wedding anniversary. How happy her mother had been to visit after so many years waving at it from the shore. 'How easy it is to overlook what's right in front of you,' her mother had said.

Amelia took a step away from her car, kicking off her sandals. She thought about leaving them strewn by the wheel, but couldn't resist; she reached down, and tucked them neatly beneath the driver's side door.

The sand beneath her feet brought a rush of calm, and Amelia began to wiggle out of her shorts and pull her dress over her head. The shorts were a little big on her slight frame, and they fell easily to her ankles. The smock dress – an old one she'd found for a bargain on her last trip to New York – was a little harder to escape from, but she threw it along with her shorts onto the back seat. Her underwear was dark, and could just about pass for a swimsuit. She patted down her hair, and broke off in a run towards the water.

★

327

Amelia had no idea how long she'd swum for, but her limbs were screaming at her to stop when the sun began its descent towards the waterline. For a mad second, she'd considered braving the swim across to Sugarloaf. She'd started pulling the water towards her in long, deep strokes, her lungs complaining while she pushed on. She'd kept her eyes focused on the mountain's peak, the salt water causing her eyes to stream. But she paid it no mind. She'd kept going against the waves, the swell low and undulating so water broke just over her shoulders and down her back. The wire in her bra started to dig into her ribcage, and her legs soon tired of relentlessly kicking a way through the wake.

Now her breathing grew heavy, so she let her arms slow to a stop until she was floating on her back like a starfish. She couldn't avoid it; she had to start playing over and over the conversation she'd have to have with Beatrice and Patrick.

She tried to get into Bea's head. These days, the 'dark thoughts' Bea referred to in her letters would be considered some kind of post-natal depression. Was that an excuse, a justification?

Amelia had been fortunate not to suffer with Maryse, but her friend Didi had become unrecognisably low when she'd had Cedella. Amelia had spent hours on the phone to Barkley, who kept insisting it wasn't his area of medical expertise, but offering advice all the same. It had been awful having to coax Didi to take a shower, to feed herself as well as the baby. But Amelia had never considered that Didi might have given the baby away entirely.

What of the other side – being the sister who wanted a baby more than anything? She had tried, but Amelia couldn't fathom it. How could you take a child from a sibling, and expect everything to be OK?

When Amelia eventually emerged from the water, hoping she still had her towel stashed in the boot, she picked her way back along the sand, deep in thought. She had to speak to Bea and Patrick – she knew that much. Even if she couldn't quite put in to words what she was feeling, Amelia knew she owed it to Maryse to find out more about their shared heritage. Maryse deserved to know who she came from, how it might impact her own child.

The anger Amelia had been pushing down finally burst from her, and she kicked at the sand until it billowed up in a cloud around her. The beach had stayed empty while she'd been swimming, and she let out a howl from somewhere deep, primal.

The release was instant: she did it again, throwing her head back and keening into the wind. She must have looked like a wild animal, but she felt like a bird.

She took a deep breath, making her way back towards her car. As the sun set behind the beach and over the island, cartoonishly long shadows spilled from the roots of bending trees that stood thick at the sand's edge. Dark shell-shadows ballooned in Amelia's path, their peaks reaching back towards the tidemark. The early evening was still warm and clear, the moon already visible despite the sky remaining dusty blue.

When she got back to the car, realising she'd left her keys in the ignition, Amelia reached for the towel on the back seat and dried herself down. There was only one person she wanted to hear from, and without thinking, she took out her phone from the driver's side door and dialled into her saved messages.

Hi, Meli, only me. Maryse tells me nobody listens to voicemails any more, and I need to learn to send voice notes instead. I won't be bothering myself with any of that newfangled technology, thank you, and I know you won't mind. I'm just calling to say I can make that Soroptimists lunch even though I said I wouldn't make it. Bette isn't flying in until next week, so I am available. Anyway, I'll let you go. Call me back if you want, or just come on over when you can. Remember you still have my casserole dish, the big blue one. OK, bye.

Amelia pressed *play* again, lulled by the cadence of her mother's voice. She wished she could call her and ask for answers.

But then, didn't she already have them? She had the letters; she had that tiny book of Shakespeare – a gift from a father who couldn't even have held her.

She turned off her phone, discarding it on the passenger seat, and turned her back to the sea, letting the sounds of the evening wash over her. Wind whispered through leaves and branches; water lapped in a steady beat upon the shore. From a distance she could hear the faint bassline of a party just starting up, or perhaps it was the soundcheck at one of the hotel entertainers in a grand building set further along the coast. Life was continuing round her, and she wished she could give it a good slap.

But breakdowns were the reserve of the rich and the unencumbered, Amelia knew. She didn't have time to spend her whole night screaming into the wind on a beach that had felt her footsteps for more than fifty years.

She pulled her clothes over her still-damp underwear, reaching to set the radio on low. As she turned the key in the ignition, she faltered with such force the car stalled on the spot. In all her thoughts of what she'd say to Beatrice and Patrick, she hadn't even considered how she'd face her father now she knew the truth.

She sat for a moment, dumbfounded, before pressing the clutch and starting the car once more. No matter how much it caused her stomach to twist in on itself, she had to admit that her father was fading from the man he once was: this would only confuse him even more. Some days he was so clear-headed it was as though nothing was wrong, but others, she knew he was saying 'Millie' instead of 'Meli' when he addressed her.

She swallowed the lump in her throat, shifting the car into gear. There was no time for a meltdown. She'd head on home, and she'd deal with this the way her mother would tell her to: with a good night's sleep, and a logical plan.

SUNDAY

'And you're sure you don't want me to come in with you?' Barkley asked, pulling into the car park of the Spice Isle Hotel. He and Aidan had filled the car with decorations and photo albums for the reunion party, the irony of which was not lost on Amelia.

'Thank you, but no.' Usually she'd have been thrilled that Barkley was stepping up to the familial plate, but not today. 'I think I need to do this myself.'

'Maryse is all right with that?'

Amelia hesitated, undoing her seat belt. She'd been up half the night reading every letter, every postcard, newspaper article, long after Maryse had retreated to bed. Calmness still eluded her, but her grief had become less sharp after spending a few quiet hours with her mother's voice in her head. 'Maryse was pretty cut up that I wouldn't let her come with me, but I worry she'll get so angry. And they're old.'

'Age doesn't give you a free pass out of owning up to your actions,' Barkley said, leaning forward from the back seat.

'No, you're right. But ...' Amelia sighed. She didn't really know what she meant.

Aidan placed his hand on Amelia's, giving it a squeeze. 'I get it. Some things you need to do for yourself, not as a parent to someone else.'

'Right.' Amelia clicked her seat belt open and pushed back the car door, stretching in the warm morning air.

'They're in room 277,' Barkley prompted, jumping out beside her to start unstacking boxes from the back seat. He placed some on the roof and some on the ground, before pulling Amelia into a close hug. 'You've got this.'

'Call us if you need us, OK?' Aidan added, emerging from the driver's side.

'OK.'

★

Before Amelia could reach up to rap her fist upon the door, her phone buzzed.

'Ms Mallalieu?'

'Speaking.'

'So glad I could catch you. Is now a good time?'

Amelia paused, taking a step back down the corridor. 'Sure.'

'It's Terrence, from TLM Sales and Lettings. I noticed my emails had been missed, so thought it was easier to call.'

'Have you found a buyer?' Amelia clutched the phone tighter, unsure what she wanted the answer to be.

'I believe I have, Ms Mallalieu.' She could hear the sales rep grinning, and it caused her skin to prickle with irritation. *Smarmy so-and-so.*

'Who are they, if you don't mind me asking?'

'They're an international family who are just moving back to the area. She's local, he's ... maybe Canadian? Palest fella you've ever seen.'

'Right.'

'They have a little girl, you see, and they're expecting a little boy so they want a bigger place. And to move back here.'

She could tell he was waiting to be praised, and did her best to muster the energy needed. 'That's great, thanks, Terrence. Send me their offer and their details, and we'll go from there.'

'Finally! I knew we'd find you the right person.'

'Just as long as they sign a contract never to use it as a holiday home, it's fine by me.' This was an understatement; if it were up to her, she'd interview every potential buyer and choose the most deserving, the kindest, those who'd been through tough times and needed a beautiful home. But her father would need more care than she and Maryse, and even Tommy, could provide soon enough – they needed the money from an easy sale, and out-of-towners always paid over asking.

'Yes, yes, it's a contract of sale. Must be a primary residence. So I'll send you the information, and you can accept the offer today if you're happy with it.'

'Great,' Amelia said, her over-correction making her sound sarcastic. 'I mean it – that's fantastic. Thank you.' Somehow, gushing made the sarcastic tone sound even bolder, so she gave up. She said goodbye, agreed to review the offer by end of play, and wondered instantly why sales people couldn't just speak normally.

As she hung up, another notification caught her eye. The movers had completed her father's house clearance, all deliveries made.

Despite everything going on, she felt comforted by the knowledge that all that furniture was going to families who needed it most.

Attempting to buy herself a moment more, Amelia clicked open the Find My Friends app. There were Aidan and Barkley's icons, waving at her from so near. It felt good to see them so close to her own icon, when usually they were marooned on a little faraway island. There was her father, his icon bobbing along next to Tommy's on the hotel golf course. Didi, Cedella and Maryse all merged in the same spot, seemingly preparing for their various tours (Maryse), art classes (Didi) and evening meal service (Cedella).

All of these people were hers, and no revelations about the past could change that. She could hardly believe she was about to be face to face with her birth parents, after decades of wondering who they were. *Perhaps I should feel more nervous, excited, scared, even joyful.* But a blank confusion had descended over her mind since her outburst on the beach. *Perhaps when I actually see Beatrice and Patrick, it will hit.*

She shook out her shoulders and quickly reached up to pat her hair in place. She locked her phone and set it to silent, pocketing it, before starting back down the corridor.

She knocked.

'Come in,' a voice called from inside, and Amelia's legs turned to water.

She stepped into the modest hotel suite, her posture awkward and steps faltering. It was one of the newer suites on the site, a vision of beachy whites and natural woods with views across the golf course spilling through the oversized bay window. Amelia had barely entered the room when Beatrice was upon her, throwing her arms around her shoulders.

'Amelia, how wonderful you look. Reception called up to say you were coming to greet us – what a lovely surprise.' Beatrice pulled back, holding Amelia by the shoulders. Her eyes were already red-rimmed. 'And how grateful we are for you to have put all this together for us.'

In that second, Amelia felt strangely powerful: of the three people in the room, she was the only one who knew what came next.

She also realised that this was what she'd been waiting for: her birth mother, smiling back at her and rushing to greet her with tenderness. Amelia waited to feel that tidal wave of emotion she'd expected, half-listening as Bea began regaling her about their journey. She waited for that overwhelming sense of connection like a *coup de foudre* straight to the heart.

But as Bea pulled away, swatting Patrick back from the suitcase he was unpacking to unearth a thank-you gift, Amelia felt nothing. The cloudy confusion was lifting, but in its place was a quiet stillness she hadn't expected.

These people were the same as they'd always been: her aunt and uncle from far across the water, whose children spoke with Union Jack accents.

'Yes, we are most grateful,' Patrick said with a grin, as Bea finally produced what she'd been looking for.

'Actually, I have something to give you,' Amelia said, her voice not sounding like her own. 'Why don't you sit down?'

The two of them sat close on the edge of the bed, their wrinkled faces still beaming at her. Amelia felt a pang of sympathy in her chest at the sight of the hand-wrapped, book-shaped gift Bea clutched close as she leant against Patrick. Their hands were knotted together, their smiles expectant. Amelia almost couldn't bear it, but she'd come this far.

'I think this is yours,' she said finally. From her handbag, she retrieved the battered copy of Shakespeare's *A Midsummer Night's*

Dream & Selected Sonnets. She held it carefully, doing her best not to disturb the cover.

Patrick's face drained of colour, and Bea dropped the gift she'd been holding. 'Where did you ...?'

'I found it, among letters. And telegrams, and postcards all from you, from Bette, from my grandmother. Even some newspaper announcements about marriages, births, independence, that sort of thing.' Amelia drew her eyeline up to face them both. 'I know the truth, now. I know I am your biological daughter.'

Beatrice stood up slowly, her hands trembling. Patrick rose beside her, his hand having moved from hers to rest upon her lower back.

Amelia held up one hand. 'I think I understand how it all came about—'

'You cannot understand,' Bea began, her voice low and shaky.

'Why don't we all sit down and—'

'No, Patrick.' Bea turned to face Amelia, taking another step towards her. 'Amelia, please. I have thought of you every waking moment, and wondered where you were, who you were with, were you happy.' Pain glistened in Bea's eyes, and Amelia couldn't help but reach to take her outstretched hand. 'But times were so different, and I was in such a dark, dark place with no other way out. And how could I say no to my sister, once I'd already agreed?'

'You were their whole life, Amelia,' Patrick added, taking another step towards her. His greying hair caught the morning sunlight like spiderwebs, his gnarled hands curling around the book of Shakespeare he'd accepted from Amelia's palm only moments ago. 'The only thing that got us through it was knowing that you had made them happier than they'd ever been. And we couldn't deny them that.'

'But why didn't you ever tell me? Why didn't you explain yourself?'

'We wanted to.' Bea tightened her grip on Amelia's hand, causing tremors to ripple through her daughter's skin. 'But it didn't seem fair. We didn't want you to feel you'd been sent away.'

Patrick nodded in agreement. 'You needed to feel chosen, not abandoned.'

'Because you weren't!' Bea shot a warning look at Patrick, whose mouth fell open when he realised how his own words sounded.

'That's not what I meant!' He pulled his hands through his hair, and returned to perch on the end of the bed. 'I mean, we didn't want you to wonder if you'd done something wrong to be given away, or worry that we'd come back and steal you from the only parents you knew.'

'And when Barkley came into the family, we worried what it might do to the boy to think everyone else was connected in some way apart from him.' Bea squeezed Amelia's hand tighter, bringing her free palm to rest atop Amelia's. 'Millicent proved, with you, that working women could adopt. She got the regulations changed, managed to take on Barkley, but it was still so contentious. We didn't want to upset the apple cart while things were still fragile.' Bea blinked back tears. 'And then all of a sudden you were so grown-up, and we wanted to tell you so we'd get to know you even better, but who would that really have been for? We couldn't start being so selfish, not when you had your own daughter to think of and your parents to care for.'

Patrick nodded, his crystal eyes gleaming. 'There was never a right time.'

Amelia dropped Bea's hand and sank into the small armchair opposite the bed. Bea pulled back her hands, looking stung, and joined Patrick's side.

Countless questions simmered to the surface in Amelia's mind. She wished she had the strength to berate them, to let rip in a tirade of accusations. *Now it's far too late. My mother's gone and my father won't understand what I'm asking. Why did you wait so long? Why couldn't you all have been honest?*

A thought occurred to Amelia as she looked from Beatrice to Patrick. 'Did you plan for this to happen? To tell me here, at the reunion?'

Bea hesitated, just for a second. 'No,' she finally said. 'I just wanted to be sure we'd see you. If we suggested London, or over in Toronto with Bette, we worried you and Maryse might not make it.' A shadow crossed her face. 'It's been so long since we've properly seen you.'

Amelia nodded. Apart from their flying visit for the funeral, staying only a short time before they had to get back to London, it had been years since they'd last come for a visit. Patrick's inability to enter the church and Bea's keening cries in the front pews of the funeral made so much more sense, now that she understood what they were truly grieving.

Amelia studied Bea's expression, searching her features for any flicker that she was lying. But nothing gave her away.

'And who else knows?' Amelia managed to ask.

'Just Bette and Matthew, but no one else,' Bea replied quickly, the words stumbling over one another.

'So your children have no idea they have a sibling?'

Bea shook her head, and Patrick placed his hand on Bea's. 'They were too young to know about the pregnancy. Bea kept it hidden. And then Bea went away for so long...' He paused at this, and Bea's shoulders began to shake. 'It's all right, Bea.' He reached up and brushed her cheek with the lightest stroke of his fingers, Bea leaning into his touch. 'We were apart, and the girls were so excited when their mum came back that they didn't really question where she'd gone. The twins were babies at the time, and Nancy was only five. Rose was three, so none of them really remember.'

Amelia nodded, her stomach a knot of anxiety. She wasn't sure what she'd wanted to hear, but this felt strangely comforting: she could tell herself that if they'd known, they would have reached out.

She turned to Patrick. 'And what about you? You were happy to go along with it, in the end?'

He cast a wary look at Bea. 'I'd be lying if I said it was easy to come to terms with Bea's decision,' he began. 'But she stood by me when my father disowned us, when things got tough out in the field and she could easily have run back to Grenada. She never did, she never left me. I couldn't leave her, not after how much she'd suffered.'

'And that meant agreeing to give me up?'

'Which broke my heart. I've thought of you every day, Amelia. I've wondered what it would've been like to watch you grow, to have you as a part of our family.' His voice caught. 'But what if Bea had fallen into a darker place? What would have become of Millicent, if she hadn't been able to raise you and prove she could raise Barkley, too?'

Amelia looked up at him, unable to answer. In that moment, she realised she was sick of always having to have the answers, always having to hold it together. Caught between being a mother and a daughter, bartering with her brother for his time, picking up the pieces of so many families who needed assistance. She was glad to do it, of course, but carrying the weight of so many secrets and stories set a deep ache in her bones. 'Can we tell them – your other children?'

Bea's eyes widened. 'Is that what you want?'

Amelia nodded, slowly. 'No more secrets.' She looked from one to the other, the strained expressions on their faces made starker by the morning light flooding the room. 'Barkley knows, Maryse knows, so it's only fair to tell everyone this involves. Let's tell them together.'

'Only if you're sure,' Patrick said.

'I'm sure.' Amelia got to her feet, the room feeling stuffy. 'When they arrive, you can explain and I can show them the letters I found from you to my mother, and Bette.'

'And for you?'

Amelia paused. 'I'm not just doing this for me. I have Maryse to think of.'

Bea shook her head. 'No, I mean the letter. The one I left for you.'

'You never left me a letter.'

Bea's eyes darted towards the book in Patrick's hands. 'I left a letter, I know I did. It was in …' Her voice trailed off. Bea turned to Patrick, who looked down at the Shakespeare book in his hands.

He peeled back the front cover: nothing. He turned it upside down, opening the back cover.

There, folded and pressed over almost six decades, was a single envelope with Amelia's name.

Amelia wanted to lunge for it, to tell them to leave so she could read it in peace. She felt as though she was running over quicksand to get to it, accepting the letter from Patrick's outstretched palms.

'Thank you,' she managed to say, at the exact moment Bea exclaimed, 'You don't have to read it now. Take your time.'

Amelia nodded, clutching the letter close. She desperately needed to get out of the room, to be alone so she could read the words left for her half a century before. She made to leave, turning her back on Bea and Patrick. 'All right, then.' She gave both of them a tight smile, heading towards the door. She needed to get out of here.

'And may I ask you something?' Bea called after her.

Amelia turned, wishing she had already left. 'Yes?'

'Can we have a little time, the three of us?' Bea's voice was heavy with hope, piercing Amelia with a sharp sting of empathy. 'Maybe just dinner to begin with, and perhaps you could come and stay in London? Only once you feel up to it, of course. There's so much more to say, even after you've read that note.'

Amelia tried not to let out a sigh when she replied, 'I'll think about it.'

'That's all we ask,' Patrick added hurriedly. 'We have so much to talk about, but we can take it as slowly as you like.'

'Absolutely. Whatever you're most comfortable with.'

Amelia nodded, making eye contact with both of them. 'All right, then, let's talk soon. I'd best be going.' She paused as she reached for the door handle, unable to get the expression on Bea's face from her mind.

She turned back, to see the pinched look of heartbreak carved across her birth mother's face. The lines criss-crossing Bea's face traced decades of sorrow and love, loss and delight, and with a start, Amelia realised she really could see the shadow of her own features mirrored in the one looking right back at her.

'Thank you, Amelia,' Bea whispered, so quietly Amelia almost missed it. 'You're being more gracious than we deserve.'

Amelia shook her head, turning the door handle. 'Everyone deserves grace, Bea,' she said, before pulling the door shut behind her.

Out in the hallway, her back against the wall, she began to read.

My dearest,
How can I explain what I'm about to do?

Amelia's heart lurched. This was it.

I don't know how to begin this letter, as I don't know how old you'll be when you get to read it. I've questioned whether or not to write something, but I simply can't help it: I want you to know just how desperately I love you, and how heartbroken I am that you won't be mine.

Our time together is almost up because today is your birthday, which means I have to let you go. You came screaming into this world a few hours ago, letting us all know right away that you are here to stay. And, my darling, I wish I could express how much I want to stay with you.

Tears started to drop onto the paper, causing rivulets of ink to bleed and pool. Amelia swiped the tears away, dabbing furiously at her eyes.

I don't know what you know by now, but if you're reading this, you'll be wanting to know God's honest truth. And if I am being honest, I have to admit that I didn't know how to love you until you were already here. By then, it was too late.

I was so scared when I found out I was expecting you, and in such a place of darkness I hope you never have to experience. I was in no fit state to become someone's mother; I had such thoughts of abandoning my children and my husband, and I truly believed that another baby would push me to act in such throes of madness that my whole world would fall apart. From the start, it was clear you deserved the life I knew was ready and waiting for you with open arms.

My sister and her husband are the most deserving people, and I know you will be so loved. Loved in a way that I may not have been capable of – loved the way you deserve to be.

You see, I made a promise that the baby I was carrying could be their child, and it is not something I can take back. The way my sister lights up when she talks about you, dreams about you, reaches out to feel you kick – it's like you were always supposed to be hers. I want you to know that in my sadness, there is so much love.

Please, my darling, please don't be angry with any of us. Perhaps you'll still be young when you read this, or perhaps you'll be all grown-up. I'm sure that whatever age you are, you'll recognise that sometimes people do things they can't explain. People say 'yes' in the moment, only to realise they should've said 'never'. We're all just people trying to learn from our mistakes, and I hope that even if you can't forgive me, you can understand that I genuinely felt I was in an impossible situation. The only way out allowed me to help my sister, and who wouldn't want to help the ones they love most?

I hope the world looks different for you than it did for me, and you can grow up in a time where love knows no boundaries. I'm sure we'll get there soon.

You are so, so loved, and so wanted. I don't have to 'wish you the best' because I know you'll have it with Millicent and Julien – with your Mom and Pop. I wish you could stay mine, but a promise is a promise. Know that I will always love you.

Yours,

B x

Amelia read it through once more, poring over each line and paragraph. A lump rose in her throat. Defensiveness reared its head as she scanned over the final words. *I know I am loved, I don't need to hear it from you.*

And yet she had to admit that the words plugged a gap she'd been carrying since she was a little girl, filling it with a bittersweet taste.

The lump in her throat thickened. Despite the anger that still boiled in her blood at the thought of all the lies she'd been told, Amelia felt an echo of sympathy stir within her.

What must it have been like, to feel your only option is to give up a baby? To hand over your child to a sibling?

Thoughts of siblings made her picture Barkley. These cousins coming to visit weren't anything like him; they didn't belong to her the way he did. Amelia already had a brother, and it was one who she'd spent long summers beside, sharing ice cream, teaching him how to jump over the waves on Grande Anse, showing him the best berries to pick at the height of the harvest and how to escape bedtime by climbing the breadfruit tree. Listening as they got older and he became a gangly teenager, confiding in her that he had fallen in love with his best friend. He'd wiped her tears when she'd cried at the thought of him leaving; she'd driven him to the airport for the flight she desperately wished he wouldn't take. Over the years they'd had screaming matches, thrown tantrums, and at times it had felt as though they'd shared one mind. When his heart broke, she felt her own shatter; his joy was her success. The best day of his life – when he'd fled the island for a faraway cityscape – had been the worst of hers. This was a sibling, their salt water bond far thicker than the blood she shared with near-strangers.

Amelia scrunched up the letter in her pocket, running double time down to the lobby.

'Mel? Meli!' Barkley called, striding to meet her at the bottom of the stairs. Relief washed over her at the sight of him, his dark eyes wide with concern. 'How did it go?'

She knew she should stay calm until they were somewhere private, and started to say, *oh yes, fine, lots to think about.*

But as soon as she opened her mouth, a strangled wail was all that escaped.

'All right, let it out,' Barkley said, enveloping her into a hug.

She felt herself being walked – shuffled – out of the lobby, doors opening and closing around her. She could hear Aidan's muffled voice over Barkley's shoulder, and felt grateful to know he was there, too.

'God, sorry,' she mumbled, drawing back and sniffing.

'Amelia, you've got to stop apologising.'

She nodded, and Barkley handed her a tissue. He'd brought a pack in his pocket, and took one for himself. 'See, you're setting me off now, too,' he said, which made her laugh.

Amelia shook her head, sadness twisting through her gut.

'Come on,' Barkley said, putting his arm around her shoulders. 'Let's talk for a minute.'

He guided her out of the door and into the shade of the coconut tree, steering the two of them towards a shaded picnic bench. Luckily it stood alone, the wood weather-worn and bleached from dappled sunlight.

'So?' he asked, straddling the bench seat so he didn't quite face her. He looked out to sea, at the swimmers bobbing in and out of sight in rhythmic motion.

Amelia looked up at him, wondering how she was supposed to explain. 'I ... I don't know what to say. It's all so ...' She trailed off. 'I don't want anything to change.'

'It doesn't have to.' He shook his head, fiddling with the strap on his watch. 'Your family is still your family, you know? Nothing changes that.'

Amelia imagined the looks on her cousins' faces when she revealed the truth. Panic flashed through her. 'But what if it does?'

'Amelia, a good family isn't a birthright. It's a privilege – you of all people should know.' He exhaled. 'And you and me, Maryse, Aidan, Pop – that's the family we've made, right? These are the people we choose, every day. And the people who choose us. You think finding the people who happened to bring you into the world takes away from all that, from all those years?' He let his hands fall to his sides, a sea breeze washing over the two of them. 'I'll never stop being your brother. You might gain some new people, but you won't lose me.'

Amelia dropped her head into her hands. 'You really think that way?'

'I do.'

She wiped her eyes. 'How are you so calm about all this?'

Barkley hesitated. 'I looked into finding my birth family, too, a couple of years ago. Don't be mad,' he added hastily. 'I went through the rudimentary stuff, I got a name ... but I didn't take it any further.'

Amelia's jaw dropped open. 'Why didn't you tell me?'

'Because I didn't want you to think I was trying to replace you, or Pop, or anyone.'

'I wouldn't think that,' Amelia said, her tone defensive.

Barkley arched an eyebrow. 'Yes you would, and that would've been OK. It's a natural reaction.' He paused. 'But when it came down to it, I didn't want to find out any more. I meant what I said. I want to leave the past where it is. Let sleeping dogs lie. There's been enough drama in the years we've already lived, we don't need to go creating any more for what comes next.'

'You're so right,' Amelia admitted. 'And look, I'm sorry for how I've behaved, snapping at you to move home. And for all the not-so-subtle hints I've probably dropped over the years. It's just hard, and I really miss you and Aidan, and I—'

He covered her hand with his. 'It's fine. I know. I'm sorry, too.'

She smiled at her brother, gratitude swelling in her chest. 'I wish I could be more like you,' she said. 'And I really wish I could talk to Mom.'

'For what it's worth, mine isn't a perfect theory. I wish I could talk to Mom every day.'

They sat for a moment, both looking out to the water beyond. The horizon line had a faint glow of orange, punctuated with faraway cruise liners and sailing boats.

'I have an idea which might help,' Barkley said eventually. 'We call it Empty Chair. Yes, it's from therapy, before you bite my head off.'

'I wouldn't—'

'It's fine.' He continued, his voice soft. 'I think it could help you.

344

You talk to the person – maybe it's your parent, a friend, your inner child – and you say exactly what you're feeling without concern or judgement.'

Amelia wrinkled her nose. 'I don't know ...'

'You don't think it could help? If you're feeling like this even after confronting Beatrice and Patrick ...' He gestured towards her, handing her another tissue. 'I can go sit back in the car if that would be easier?' he offered.

'No, it's fine,' Amelia said. 'How do you do it?'

'So choose someone – maybe it's Mom or Pop, maybe it's you as a little girl – and imagine they're sitting opposite you.' He lowered his voice. 'Close your eyes, and just picture them for a minute. What would you say?'

Amelia took a second to centre herself, her mind going straight to the parents who'd raised her. Her chest felt heavy as she pictured her father on a Good Day. She dug further into her memory and imagined her father's face without lines, his hair back to black, his arms outstretched and eyes bright. Her mother beside him, her hair tied up in one of her trademark silk scarves, a book tucked under her arm.

I should have been told the truth.

Shouldn't I?

Patrick's words crept into her mind. You needed to feel chosen, not abandoned. The parents who'd raised Amelia had done everything to make her feel chosen, make her feel special. Would the truth have caused more heartache than it was worth, simply to know who she'd come from?

Amelia opened her eyes, parted her lips to speak. But no words came out.

'Pop's still here, it's not too late,' she found herself saying. She clambered to her feet, dusting the sand from her jeans. 'Can you take me home?'

They pulled up at the house shortly after, having rescued Aidan from his drawn-out conversation with Didi. She'd almost convinced him to pose for the life drawing classes running that week, and mercifully, Amelia and Barkley had arrived just in time.

'Do you want us to wait here?' Aidan asked, opening the car door for Amelia.

'You've both done more than enough, thank you,' she said, glancing meaningfully at both of them. Barkley was right: this was her family. No revelations could change the last fifty years. She took a deep breath, hoping the tears from earlier hadn't left streaks on her cheeks, and walked into the sitting room.

Her father sat at the kitchen table with his back to her, his head angled down.

'I went into your room to try and find those headphones you said I could borrow,' he said, his voice sounding so small.

Amelia's stomach dropped, and she rushed to sit beside him. Tears were forming in his eyes, making her heart almost stop.

'Pop? What have you got there?'

'I wanted to tell you, you know.' He put down the small pile of letters and postcards in his hands – the ones Amelia had removed from her handbag that morning. Amelia's pulse began to race.

She dared lock eyes with him and realised his gaze was clear, focused. This was her chance. 'Why didn't you tell me?'

His features twisted, as though in pain, and he leant closer towards her. 'I tried, a few times. But with your mother... and with Barkley... there was never a right time.'

'But didn't you think I deserved the truth?'

He hesitated, almost looking through Amelia. *No, stay with me. One more minute, please.*

'Truth is a funny thing, isn't it?' He took a couple of shallow breaths, and for a second Amelia wondered if he was going to cry. 'The truth for me is that you are my daughter. How could I tell you otherwise? You are the little girl who made me a father, who I had the privilege of raising and who became the most wonderful big sister for Barkley.' He swallowed hard, reaching towards the chipped mug on the table. 'You've always been the daughter of my heart. Isn't that enough?'

Amelia tried to swallow, her throat feeling thick and heavy. 'You still should have told me sooner.'

'I'm sorry, Meli.' He reached out and patted her upper arm.

'You deserved the truth, I can see that now. We were selfish to hide it from you, scared of what would happen if you ever found out.' He leant in a little closer, whispering in her ear. 'But can you blame your old pop for wanting to keep you for himself a little while longer?'

Amelia brought her hand up to cover his, feeling warmth spread from her fingertips. 'You wouldn't have lost me for telling the truth.'

'You can't know that. How can our small island compete with a metropolis like London?'

Amelia sighed. 'But this is home. With you and Mom ... That's always been my home.'

Julien glanced around, his eyes lingering on the front door. 'That's right, and your mother will be home soon. She can explain it much better.'

Amelia closed her eyes, wishing she could cling on to the moment with her father that had already gone by. It felt like trying to grasp water. 'Sure, let's ask Mom,' she croaked.

'There's never enough time,' he said, his gaze solemn. 'But your mother will know what to say.'

There was so much more Amelia could have asked, but the way her father looked at her, she knew that was all he could give. She nodded. 'I'll speak to Mom when she gets home. Thanks, Pop.'

She gave him a quick hug, before standing up to make them another pot of tea. A whisper of satisfaction, mingled with sympathy, rose in her chest. This man had raised her, chosen her day after day, given her the brother she'd so desperately wanted. Helped raise her own daughter, who'd taught her that real family didn't have to look like the framed wedding photos and 2.4 children in TV shows and on glossy magazine pages.

'How about another cup of ginger tea, Pop?' she asked, trying to find joy in the simple pleasure of his smile meeting hers.

'That would be lovely,' he said. 'And how about a game of dominoes? That's your favourite, right?

MONDAY

Amelia sat on the porch of her father's house, the letter Bea had written the day she was born folded open in her lap. Amelia was meeting Barkley at the house in a few hours, to do a final walk-through before the sale process officially began. She hoped they could talk, finish the conversation they'd started the day before, and she could ask him all the questions she'd kept bottled up over the years. She wanted to understand, and even more, she wanted them both to know how to be there for each other in this new phase of life. She needed more from him, and there was no doubt he had his own questions for her. If this week had taught her anything, it was that honesty shouldn't wait.

She glanced out at the view in front of her, back at the house, and began to read once again. Tomorrow she would tell her birth siblings, so she wanted to reread the letter and prepare herself. Barkley's promise was ringing in her ears – that nothing had to change if she didn't want it to. Her family were still the people who'd raised her, who'd chosen her day after day.

She knew it would feel strange and anticlimactic, however her birth siblings reacted. One minute, she hoped their reactions would be excitement and wonder; the next, she feared anger and malice. What if they got angry at Bea and Patrick? What if they redirected their anger towards Amelia?

She'd cope with it the way she coped with such outbursts in her job, and felt glad to have so much experience in trying to piece families back together. *Deep breath, count to three, acknowledge their emotions. Respect their boundaries.* She repeated this mantra to herself, willing it to stick. She knew it wouldn't: not when it was her life. Only time would tell.

As she moved up to standing, her phone started to vibrate.

Maryse's face flashed up on the caller ID, and Amelia scrabbled to answer it.

'Ma? I'm at the hospital.'

Amelia's blood ran cold. 'I can be there in—'

'What? No, I'm having my scan.' Maryse kissed her teeth. 'Look at your screen!'

Amelia yanked her phone back from her ear, and saw a radiant-looking Maryse grinning back at her. 'Remember I told you, when it says FaceTime, that means I'm calling you over video?'

Amelia nodded, her heart rate steadily returning to normal. 'And everything's OK?'

Maryse flipped the phone screen around, so Amelia could see a black-and-white sonogram video on a screen. The steady boom-boom of a strong heartbeat was unmistakable, Maryse's voice rising over the sound.

'We're having a girl, Ma. I want to call her Meli, after you.'

Amelia's heart surged, her voice wobbling. 'Well, that's lovely, Maryse. But you don't have to decide anything until you've met her.'

Maryse's laughter popped like sugar syrup bubbling on the stove. 'I've made up my mind, Tommy's on board, too. She'll be little Meli Mallalieu-Smith.'

'That's a beautiful name, child,' Amelia replied, the scene on her little phone screen so bright and animated.

'I think so.' Maryse had started crying, and Tommy's hand came into the screen, clutching a tissue. Amelia could hear him murmuring something about ice cream, making Maryse laugh again. It warmed Amelia's soul to see her little girl so loved.

'Why don't I leave you to it?' she offered, wanting to do the exact opposite and step right through the screen.

Maryse nodded, just as a doctor walked into view. 'OK, Ma. We'll be round tonight!'

'We'll bring pictures!' Tommy added from off-screen. Before Amelia could tell them she loved them, the screen went black.

Amelia sat on the porch seat, hugging the phone close to her chest. It brought a peculiar comfort that life was continuing around her, forcing her to keep putting one foot in front of the other while she reconsidered everything she once thought she knew.

Perhaps she would give Bea and Patrick the chance to explain themselves a little more, and to get to know her. And get to know Maryse, of course. The more Amelia read her birth mother's handwriting and pictured her as she was then, the more she felt the whisper of understanding put its lips to her ear. Today was still too soon for forgiveness, but it waved at her from a far horizon.

From where she sat on her father's porch, Amelia could clearly see the morning sun starting to raise its head, and she squinted in its tangerine light. White clouds floated above the bay far below the house; the soundtrack of neighbours starting their days began to play. Families with young children called for breakfast and school bags, dogs barked and seabirds squawked their response. Doves cooed to each other as market traders from far at the bottom of the hill wished one another a good morning, checked who was all right on that fine day. The storm was still at bay, but the air smelled like incoming rain.

Far out to sea the waves chopped and swirled, whitecaps hinting at what was to come. Amelia reached for her phone, dialling the hotel. 'Beatrice and Patrick Anderson, please,' she asked. As she waited for the connection to be made, she felt a flicker of gratitude. She was where she loved most in the world, with the people she refused to imagine her life without. What would have become of Amelia, if Bea and Patrick had kept her?

Epilogue

Dear Barkley and Aidan,

Greetings from London! We've enjoyed the London Eye, taken a river boat along the Thames, and eaten afternoon tea at the Ritz Carlton. Meli behaved ever so well on the flight over, and she loves her great-great-auntie and uncle. Maryse can't wait to bring her to New York.

Also, Aidan, you were right – Tommy proposed! He and Maryse went out for supper while Bea, Patrick and I babysat. They're thinking a destination wedding in the Upper West Side, so I hope you're ready to host a reunion of your own . . .

We'll call you when we get home and share all the details.

All my love,

A x

Author's note

When I was a university student, I would meet my grandparents for breakfast in Greggs every week (it was my breakfast, their mid-morning coffee and cake stop). One morning, my grandad had a present for me. 'To help with your lectures,' he said, handing over an inscribed, well-worn copy of *The Complete Works of Shakespeare*.

Have a lovely time with this! Love Nannie and Grandad. Friday 13 March 2015, the inscription reads.

About a year after my grandad passed away, I opened that copy of *The Complete Works of Shakespeare* to find *A Midsummer Night's Dream*. Shortly after, the scenes of Beatrice and Patrick's early days were born.

The characters in this novel take their inspiration from my real nannie and grandad, 'B and Irish Stew', whose names have been changed at Nannie's request. The story of their first few years together was told to me over our weekly breakfast dates, and as I discovered more and more about their shared history and the decisions they made, I kept asking myself: *Why has nobody written this down?*

I have done my best to preserve the anecdotes, feelings and memories as they were repeated to me, and I hope I have done them justice. I was even told a story about the time they ran into Ernest Hemingway near Mount Kilimanjaro – apparently 'Patrick' nearly hit him with the jeep – but sometimes fiction is more believable than fact. In this manner, I have made certain editorial decisions to keep the story as believable, yet entertaining, as I can.

While considering what to keep as fact and what to blend into fiction, my wonderful editors and agent suggested we explore the 'what if' at the heart of this story: what could have happened if 'Amelia' really had been given up?

In reality, Bea changed her mind: Amelia was kept and raised in Sierra Leone before moving to England in 1968. Amelia grew up to become an engineer, teacher, artist and women's group volunteer – she also became my mother, to whom this novel is dedicated.

This twisting of narrative fate led to fascinating conversations with my grandmother about what it meant to keep a child she'd promised to her sister; how 'family' can mean different things to different people; and overall, it caused us all to wonder at what might have been.

I hope you have enjoyed meeting these characters, both real and imagined. I mostly hope Bea and Amelia are right, and we can one day read this story in a time when love knows no boundaries and all are free to love who they choose.

Acknowledgements

I've always loved reading the acknowledgements in a novel, to see who helped bring the story I've loved to life. As with any novel, this one truly took a village.

My thanks first and foremost must go to Rowan Lawton and Eleanor Lawlor at the Soho Agency – honestly Rowan, I don't know what you were thinking when you took me on with an empty shell of a novel idea, but I cannot thank you enough for your faith in me and your belief that these characters could hold their own in a novel. I will forever be grateful to you for your support, unwavering kindness, advice and inspiration.

Thanks also to my brilliant editors Sarah Benton, Rhea Kurien and Sanah Ahmed. Your ideas breathed a whole new life into this story, and I have felt so fortunate to work with an incredible team of talented, ambitious and inspiring women. Thank you to the whole team at Orion Fiction, with special thanks to Sam Eades for setting up the Orion Academy 2024.

Finding Rowan and working with the team at Orion would not have been possible without publishing access programmes, which for me included Hachette's Future Bookshelf and Penguin's WriteNow. For anyone reading this who thinks they might like to write a book one day but doesn't know how to get into the industry, please keep going. I promise you don't have to live in London, you don't have to do a costly creative writing course, you don't have to quit your job yet still somehow find a way to pay your bills and be creative. Write in the scraps of time you can stitch together around working hours or on commutes, apply for access events, message authors you love, read all the advice blogs you can find. The world will always need more stories from new voices – please take this as a sign to share yours.

My own voice was supported by the most wonderful family and friends who are too many to mention here. Thank you to my extended family for your kindness, with special thanks to my grandmother Elizabeth 'Betty' Evans for all your support and to Margaret and Laura Meyer for the group chat encouragement, proof-reads, and title advice. Let's all be thankful we didn't go with 'Baked Beans and Beach Balls'.

Thanks to the friends who read and heard countless versions of this story, particularly Aisling Roper and Cath Davies.

Diolch o galon Charlotte Morgan and Gethin Earles, you guys have kept me sane through the most insane workplace dramas and never fail to make me smile.

Thanks also to the friends who had absolutely no idea what I was talking about throughout this process, but supported me all the same: Sarah Davies, Emily Holding, Ellie Phillips, Alice Spurr. You once asked me why your names would appear here. Quite simply, there is no me without you, and so there is no book without you. I treasure you girls.

I'm forever grateful to Katie Brown, Bahez Talabani, Phil Meyers, Rachel Brunner and Kayleigh Walker for the years of friendship, love, and questionable decisions which resulted in the best memories. You each inspire me every day.

To my in-laws, thank you for being the most welcoming, lovely family (the polar opposites of the in-laws in this book). Mary Lythgoe, Cath, Simon, Carys and Iwan Cox, I couldn't imagine joining a more wonderful bunch – shout-out the Robinsons, Holloways, Evanses and Williamses too. Thank you, Cath, for helping with proof-reads – the Micra made it!

To Ally Rodger: if it wasn't clear from the plotlines in this story, I hope you know that family can mean a lot of things to a lot of people and bloodlines have little to do with what really matters. My family is so much richer for having you in it, and I will always be grateful for your friendship and sisterhood.

To my brother Nick, I'm sorry this book wasn't the masterpiece that was *Tiny Dude* (self-published via handwritten purple note-book, circa 2006), but I hope you know it was you who sparked my love of writing all those years ago.

To my sister Sophie, I don't know how you thank someone for a lifetime of friendship and unwavering support, so I'll just say thank you for being the most inspiring, loyal and fun big sister I could ever wish for.

Sophie & Nick, my friendship with you both is my greatest achievement; your success is my joy and your sadness my heart-break. I will forever be in awe of all you achieve and all that you are. Thank you for bringing me two of my favourite people, Cait Bolt and Alex Cutts, whom we all cherish.

To Rhydian, thank you for making it possible for me to write this book and for keeping me centred and calm while making me deliriously happy. We are a dazzling love story just beginning. I'm so excited for a future as your wife.

Lastly, to my mum and dad. No words can describe my gratitude to you both: I will always consider myself the luckiest person that I got you guys as parents. Thank you for everything.

Nannie and Grandad, I hope I've done you proud.

Love, Han x

Credits

Hannah Evans and Orion Fiction would like to thank everyone at Orion who worked on the publication of *The Mapmaker's Wife* in the UK.

Editorial
Sarah Benton
Rhea Kurien
Sanah Ahmed

Copyeditor
Steve O'Gorman

Proofreader
Linda Joyce

Audio
Paul Stark
Jake Alderson

Finance
Jasdip Nandra
Sue Baker

Contracts
Anne Goddard
Humayra Ahmed
Ellie Bowker

Design
Charlotte Abrams-Simpson
Joanna Ridley
Nick May

Editorial Management
Charlie Panayiotou
Jane Hughes
Bartley Shaw
Tamara Morriss

Marketing
Ellie Nightingale

Production
Ruth Sharvell

Publicity
Aoife Datta

Operations
Jo Jacobs
Sharon Willis

Sales

Jen Wilson

Esther Waters

Victoria Laws

Rachael Hum

Anna Egelstaff

Frances Doyle

Georgina Cutler